THE DEMON PURGE

BOOK I

OF

THE LEGENDS OF SOLUNA

M.B. Scully

Lucky Bat Books

A Lucky Bat Book

The Demon Purge
Book I of the Legends of Soluna
Copyright © 2014 by M.B. Scully

10 9 8 7 6 5 4 3 2 1
ISBN: 978-1-939051-77-6

Also available in digital formats.

Published by Lucky Bat Books
LuckyBatBooks.com

To Kevin.
Wouldn't be here without you, little brother.

PROLOGUE

Year 1 of the Age of Blood

THEY WERE COMING.

A large Earth-Wolf stood atop a small hill, just in front of the thick forest he called home, and silently watched the demon army appear on the other side of the Féarua Plains. His heart grew heavy. Even now he could tell the massing enemies far outnumbered his own soldiers. They would have no chance of winning this battle—and very little of escaping with their lives. A stiff wind tore through his ragged fur, forcing him to hunch his shoulders against the cold.

How had this happened, and where did these demons come from? Oak, the last King of the Earth-Wolves, turned his eyes to the sky, as though seeking some kind of answer in the dark clouds above. He dug his claws into the dirt and growled quietly to himself. Was victory even possible? Was this some divine punishment from Moon-Wolf and Sun-Wolf?

He sighed, relaxing his paws, allowing his memories to take him back.

It seemed like it was only yesterday he was hunting with his oldest daughter and a few of his senior warriors, without any thought of war. Peace reigned over the Taladair Forest, and over the whole island of Soluna. The prey ran thick and fast. No wolf went hungry. Even when the Uiscean Marsh grew silent, Oak had thought nothing of it. The business of the Water-Wolves was not his concern.

Then one of the Colonies near the Uisceanese border sent a messenger bearing dark tidings.

The marsh was empty; her Water-Wolf inhabitants vanished without a trace.

Before Oak could send a wolf to investigate, a second messenger arrived from the Fire-Wolf Queen. The Scaineadó Desert was under attack. Demonic creatures had appeared in the realm of the Fire-Wolves, striking the desert and crushing the Fire-Wolves with their mysterious powers. Oak attempted to send aid, but only one of his fighters returned from battle. The wolf, half-crazed with terror, did little more than repeat a single word, a name, one that would soon freeze the blood of any and still their hearts in fear at its very mention.

Letorus.

"Your Majesty, we're ready."

A tired voice brought Oak back to the present, and he shook his head to clear away his dark thoughts. His second-in-command stood beside him, staring at the distant demon horde with empty silver eyes. Oak gave her a sad look, his gaze sweeping over her skeletal frame and ragged pelt as he counted every open wound. There was no life left in the once-boisterous young female; only a ghost of the former Ember remained, fighting because she barely remembered her peaceful life before the war. There were hundreds more like her, and it pained Oak to see such precious young lives wasted.

No wolf had escaped the scars of war.

Oak sighed again and nodded, before turning to face the ragged group of wolves behind him. "Thank you, Ember. I will speak with them now."

Ember nodded and limped back a few paces. Oak paused a moment, looking out over the disorganized ranks. They had once been a grand army full of hope for victory, but now only a small, hungry group of broken-spirited wolves remained.

They had been the first to resist the demons, and the Earth King feared they would be the last.

Finally, Oak broke the silence hanging over the exhausted warriors. "For the first time in centuries, wolves from each nation have united together to fight side by side. We have fought foes none have ever seen before, and now, even as I speak, those foes are marching toward us." Oak paused, swallowing hard. "I will not lie to you...this will be the final battle fought by this alliance."

A muted murmur rippled through the ranks. Few were surprised by his words. Rumors had circulated through the camp, claiming that Letorus himself was leading the army that now marched toward them. Many felt the shadow of death looming over the army, waiting to drag the soldiers into its depths.

"Nine months ago when this war started, I called the nations together to fight. Today, I am the only leader left of the original six. We all have suffered because of these monstrosities. We all have watched our families and friends die before our eyes. We are all aware of the risk of resisting Letorus and the fate that awaits us if we are captured. But not one of you has been forced into this. You are fighting because you want to protect your home, to rid our land of this menace. You stay in this army of your own will."

Oak swallowed hard, pained by the insincerity of his statements. Many, like Ember, no longer remembered any other life. Others had nowhere to go. Very few still fought to protect their homes, pups, or even out of loyalty. Almost no one had anything to return to, and for many, their leaders were already dead.

"Therefore, I am giving you a choice. We face certain death by fighting here. That…is unavoidable. But if you wish, you may escape the battle. You do not have to fight and die with us, and I will not consider you cowards for fleeing. But know this, although you will live to see another sun, Letorus will hunt you. He will do whatever it takes to capture and punish you for avoiding the demons' rule.

"To those that do choose to escape, do this for me. An old wolf's dying wish, you might call it. Continue the fight. Stand together against the demons, and rescue our friends held prisoner. No matter what, we must resist. I know many think Moon-Wolf and Sun-Wolf have forsaken us, even sent us those monsters as divine punishment, but I know for certain the gods are still watching us." Oak paused again. He himself doubted if their gods truly supported them, but he could not let his soldiers see his uncertainty. If they believed Moon-Wolf and Sun-Wolf had abandoned them, they would lose any will to fight.

"They feel our pain and will send a savior to free us one day. But until then, fight the demons with every fiber of your being, whether you are on the run or enslaved, because even when we are held captive, our minds and hearts can never be bound by chains. We will continue to fight to free our bodies so that in the future, our pups can live in a world without demons."

Oak fell silent, his head bowed. He could say nothing more. He could only hope his words would be enough to inspire his warriors to fight.

After a few moments of silence, wolves began to flee the area. Dozens backed up and ran into the forest behind them, until only a few hundred were left. Oak looked up to see his army considerably weakened. The brave soldiers who remained, however, warmed his fur with pride. Their eyes glowed with determination, refusing to give in until death stilled their limbs. His own eyes mirrored their resolve. They were offering all they had. He could not let them down.

"Thank you. Our sacrifice will not be forgotten."

He turned back to face the approaching demon army and lifted his head high. Their foes had finally drawn close enough for one final charge. They could hear the snarls and unearthly chants and see the flashing of the demons' teeth. Oak bunched his muscles and howled. It would be the last time a wolf's howl echoed across the land for more than a hundred years. The ragged army of the last King of the Earth-Wolves howled in unison and raced forward to meet the massing demons.

And so the Age of Blood began.

CHAPTER ONE
138 years later…

WITH THE CRACKLING fire casting stark shadows on her face and the raw, gaping wound crossing her snout, Sparrow looked like one of Letorus' demons herself. The four other wolves gathered around the small fire stared at the pale gray Wind-Wolf, hardly daring to breathe as they waited for her to continue with the story of Oak's Last Stand. With a fiendish grin and her bright blue eyes glowing, Sparrow remained silent long enough for the tension to build. Suddenly, she burst out in raucous laughter, startling her listeners.

"You guys are such scaredy-pups; you should see your faces." She twisted her face into a theatrical show of fear and kept giggling. "Especially you, Hawk. You have to be the biggest one of us all."

The bright orange Fire-Wolf in question bared his teeth in a nervous smile. "It's not our fault, Sparrow, you tell a good story. But I'm a little more worried about the fire… Coal specifically told us not to, and we don't want to get him angry."

Sparrow rolled her eyes and snorted. "It's easy for *him* to sit out in the cold snow. *He's* a Fire-Wolf; he doesn't *get* cold. Coal doesn't understand that not all of us have fire in our blood to keep our tails from freezing off. Besides, he's not here right now, so *I'm* in charge. You're a Fire-Wolf, so might as well make yourself useful. Besides," she grinned, her eyes glittering with mischief, "if we hear him and Granite coming back, we'll cover the fire and he'll never know."

Hawk flattened his large ears, still doubtful as Palm began trying to convince Sparrow to tell another story. He didn't want to risk Coal getting angry with him and kicking him out of the resistance group, not so soon after joining. If he was going to be on the run, he didn't want to do it alone. He scanned the clearing to ensure no one was watching him and shook his neck fur, ensuring the collar remained hidden beneath his pelt. Even if Hawk managed to stay on Coal's good side, if the group leader ever discovered the metal band encircling Hawk's neck he would personally chase Hawk to the Taladite border and leave him for the demons.

Suddenly, something collided with his head and bounced to the ground, startling him from his thoughts. Hawk yelped in pain and scrambled backward.

Sparrow snorted with amusement from across the fire. "What is it, Hawk? Bitten by your own fire?"

Eagle, a Wind-Wolf male lying next to Sparrow, laughed, making Hawk wilt a little in embarrassment.

"No, something hit me in the head." He scowled at the offending object, only to flinch away a moment later as though a viper had appeared between his paws. "It's a coal!"

Sparrow's eyes darkened and she leapt to her paws. "Are you sure it didn't come from your fire? That it came from Coal?" When Hawk nodded, Sparrow swore under her breath. Before Coal had left for sentry duty, he told them he would send back a piece of coal as a warning if something happened. "It's too cold for the feral demons to be stirring, so Coal and Granite must have spotted a patrol. Canyon, cover that fire!"

Canyon, a heavyset Earth-Wolf with dark brown fur, nodded. With a wave of his tail, he expertly lifted a large clump of dirt from the ground and tossed it on the fire. The earth smothered the flames, and nothing remained to show any sign of the campfire. Hawk watched the procedure with a jealous eye, reminded of his pitiful skills with fire magic. The most he could do was coax small flames into existence. His lack of talent was probably the result of spending his whole life in captivity, never learning how to use his power in the first place.

"Hawk, move your tail! A demon patrol is coming this way, and we need to meet up with Coal and Granite at the river." Sparrow's shout snapped Hawk out of his thought, and he scrambled to his paws to answer.

"Yes, Sparrow!" He darted after the other resistance fighters, sliding into place at the rear of the group.

The tense silence continued as they raced away from their temporary camp, fearful of the threat of the demon patrol. His heart pounding, Hawk listened for any sign of the enemy, his long, thick legs propelling him over the frozen earth. He was so intent on concentrating that he almost overshot the river and ran straight into Sparrow.

"Watch it, Hawk! What's with you today? You're as focused as an air-sick mouse!" Sparrow stumbled away from the flailing Hawk and sent him a lop-sided snarl. "If you get us caught, I swear I'll muzzle you with your own tail."

Hawk gulped, knowing she would do as she threatened, and nodded as Sparrow turned away to scan the surrounding foliage. Canyon chuckled and gave the Fire-Wolf a small nudge that almost sent him sprawling. "You're going to get grilled for that later, scaredy-pup."

Sparrow spun around, a wild look in her eye. "Canyon, shut it!"

Canyon flinched and promptly obeyed. Though he was bigger than Sparrow, Sparrow's scars made her much more intimidating. And the stories of how she got such scars made her even more so.

The small group fell quiet as they listened for their leader, Coal, and Granite to arrive. The air thrummed with tension and Hawk's heart pounded in his chest; he feared the demon patrol would track them by sound alone.

A snap sent all four whirling around with bristling fur and bared teeth.

"At ease, it's us." Coal, the dark blue Fire-Wolf, stepped out of the shadows, followed closely by Granite. He marched straight to Sparrow, appearing to tower over her despite her greater height, his red eyes flaming with anger. "And just what, exactly, were you thinking, lighting a fire so near a demon Fortress? I believe I told you, *no fire*."

Sparrow flinched away from Coal's fury, but soon regained her confidence. "We were *cold*, and the others needed cheering up. For your information, *some* of us are still mourning Meadow's death."

Coal's face emptied of any expression as he answered in an icy voice, "Meadow is *dead*; there is no reason to waste energy on a dead wolf."

Silence fell between the leader and his second-in-command, and Hawk involuntarily took a step back from the pair. Several long, anxious moments passed, everyone wondering who would make the first move. Slowly Sparrow began to waver, her eyes darting away from Coal's cold gaze before she finally flattened her ears and lowered herself to the ground in a show of submission.

"Forgive me, Coal, it will not happen again."

Hawk breathed a sigh of relief as the tension eased.

Coal gave Sparrow a slight nod before addressing the rest of the group. "A demon patrol comprised of two Ice-Fangs, three Shade-Tigers, and two Hell-Cats is on the prowl. They saw the smoke from your fire and are coming to investigate. It is too soon after the last battle to fight this patrol, and we're too close to the Tenepis Fortress for my comfort."

Hawk's heart froze at the mention of Ice-Fangs. The last thing he wanted to do was face one of them.

"How close is the patrol?" Eagle's storm-colored eyes flashed, although with fear or anger, Hawk couldn't tell.

"It will be here in about five minutes," Coal answered sharply. "We have to leave now if we want any chance of escaping their notice. We'll split up and if we're lucky, confuse them. Head toward the hideout in the Dorasca Gorge *only* if you are certain you are not being followed. Sparrow, you go with Hawk. Canyon, you're with me. Granite, Eagle, Palm, you three will go together. I hope to see *every one of you* at the gorge."

Hawk gave a small sigh of relief upon hearing he would travel with Sparrow. Despite her rough demeanor, Sparrow often went out of her way to defend Hawk from the others when their teasing became too much.

He snapped to attention when the she-wolf padded over, a tense look on her torn face. Behind her, the others were already disappearing into the trees.

"All right, scaredy-hare, let's get going. You lead the way, and I'll cover your tracks. We can't have any demons following us."

Hawk swallowed hard and shuffled his paws before muttering, "I don't know the way…"

Sparrow narrowed her eyes and bared her teeth in an irritated growl that made Hawk flinch away from her. "*You don't know the way?* Gah!" She cursed under her breath, shaking her head. "Of course, I forgot. You haven't been to the hideout yet." She swore again. "We're *bound* to get caught at this rate!"

With a nervous swallow, Hawk ventured a suggestion, "Y-you could lead, Sparrow. There's no snow around, so I won't leave a trail."

The she-wolf spun around and snapped at him, forcing Hawk to the ground to avoid her fangs. "Use your nose, idiot. Snow's coming, and it's going to be a big storm. Why this had to happen *before* we showed you where it was…" She took a deep breath, forcing herself to stay calm. Time was quickly escaping them, and she couldn't waste any more of it. "Listen, the hideout is about due north from here, but we'll be taking a few detours. So we'll head *west* toward Lough Tost and swing around Secumare Fortress before we make our way to the hideout." When Hawk continued to shuffle with uncertainty, Sparrow swore and summoned a gust of wind to blow Hawk in the right direction. "That way! Now get moving!"

Hawk scrambled to his paws and took off in the direction the wind had pointed him. Sparrow shadowed his paws, carefully erasing any trace his fire-heated pads left behind. They had to move fast and silently if they wanted to have any chance of slipping by the patrol. Hawk only hoped he wouldn't end up distracting Sparrow because he took a wrong turn. If Sparrow got distracted, they stood little chance of evading the demon patrol.

CHAPTER TWO

SPARROW RAISED HER eyes to the skeletal canopy above her, imploring Sun-Wolf to give her patience. *I can't get too mad at him; he's never been to the hideout and he's not very familiar with Talahil...*

The Fire-Wolf in question was shuffling a few paces away, staring at the ground with a very apologetic look. "I'm really sorry...I...I just got confused..."

"I *know*, you've already said that." Sparrow growled slightly. "Shut up and let me figure out where we are."

At Hawk's flinch, Sparrow felt a twinge of guilt, but she was too irritated to apologize. They had been travelling for nearly half a day and had gotten lost at least five times. Sparrow, preoccupied with covering their tracks and watching for demon patrols, had left the actual navigating to Hawk, hoping he could follow her verbal instructions.

Obviously not.

"Okay, watch for demons," Sparrow said, pushing aside her irritation with Hawk. "I'm going to try and—"

She cut herself off and raised her head, eyes raking her surroundings. Hawk froze, his own eyes wide, making him look rather like a startled deer.

I thought I heard...

The wind turned, bringing with it a faint, but sickening, scent.

Demons.

"They found us."

Hawk barely had enough time to blink before Sparrow summoned a gust of wind to turn him around and shove him a few feet in the other direction.

"The demons, *now move!*"

A yowl rose up from the trees behind them, punctuating Sparrow's command. Hawk didn't need any other reason to take off running, his legs churning up the snow in his haste. After a brief glance over her shoulder to catch a glimpse of the approaching patrol, Sparrow raced after him.

"What do we do now, Sparrow?"

Yeah, what now? Sparrow gritted her teeth. They couldn't outrun the patrol for long. Hawk didn't have much stamina at high speeds and Sparrow was still recovering from the last battle.

The patrol outnumbers us, and Hawk's not much use in a fight, anyway…
Even as her thoughts trailed off, Sparrow already knew what she had to do.
"You keep running." She slid to a stop and spun around, hackles raised.
Hawk, startled, skidded to a halt. "Wh-what?"

"Run, you idiot! I'll hold them off for as long as I can and give you time
to get away." She glanced over her shoulder and saw him still hesitating. "I'll
catch up with you later. Just head north and don't stop until you reach the
gorge. Now *go!*"

Sparrow snarled and snapped at him, causing him to yelp and jump away.
A moment later he was vanishing between the trees, until even his orange pelt
was swallowed by the whiteness.

All right then, Sparrow…let's see what your chances are… She spun back
around, fangs bared, and came face-to-face with the very patrol that had chased
them from the Tenepis Fortress.

*Seven demons…I'll be hard-pressed to last longer than three minutes, much
less escape and catch up to Hawk.*

The patrol paused upon seeing Sparrow, surprised that she was daring to
stand and fight. She didn't give them any more time to recover. With a vicious
snarl she threw herself on the nearest Shade-Tiger, backed by a stiff wind, and
bit down on its leg.

At the demon's pained yowl, the rest of the patrol sprang into action.
Sparrow blew most of the monsters back with a gust of icy wind, but a Hell-
Cat managed to slip under her attack and grab her tail. With a sharp tug it
dragged her away from the Shade-Tiger.

Sparrow twisted and raked her hind claws across the Hell-Cat's face, making
it yowl and drop her tail. Then she lunged for the demon, only to be assaulted
from behind by two Shade-Tigers. Sparrow howled and summoned a fierce
wind to spin around them, knocking the two Hell-Cats to the ground and
startling the three Shade-Tigers.

Ice shot up her legs, freezing her in place and shocking her into dropping
the wind. One of the Ice-Fangs pounced on her back and sank its fangs into
her shoulder, while the other appeared in front of her and clawed her face.
Red splattered across her vision, leaving one entire side dark.

Sparrow bit back a scream of pain and ducked under a Shade-Tiger's lunge,
raising another wind to knock the other two to the side. She could feel her

power draining away with every passing moment, and knew she didn't have much longer.

Don't you dare fail now, Sparrow snarled at herself, cracking through the ice in one huge lunge. *You've gotta find Hawk; he won't last two breaths in the forest on his own.*

Powered on by desperation, Sparrow threw herself onto the nearest Shade-Tiger. She buried her fangs into the back of its neck and threw the demon into the two Ice-Fangs. Spinning around, she met the Hell-Cats' charge with bared teeth. Both demons were knocked to the ground by an icy wind, and Sparrow immediately took advantage of their distraction. She raked her claws down one Hell-Cat's stomach, making it yowl in pain.

Hearing the other two Shade-Tigers quickly approaching her from behind, Sparrow grabbed the Hell Cat by the leg and dragged it around, knocking the Shade-Tigers into each other with her screeching club. Then she dove for the remaining Hell-Cat, which was attempting to crawl away unnoticed, closing her jaws around its neck. Sparrow gave it a hard shake, snapping its neck with a loud *crack.*

A heavy paw collided with her head, knocking Sparrow into the dead Hell-Cat. A moment later claws tore through her fur, opening bloody furrows along her back. Sparrow howled and rolled over, ignoring the sharp spikes of pain the action caused. She raised a stiff wind to blow around her, knocking the demons away and giving her a moment to scramble to her paws.

The Shade-Tiger snarled, sending a black spear of energy through the wall of wind separating the demons from Sparrow, who moved too slow to avoid it. The spear pierced her shoulder, knocking her back. She gritted her teeth, fighting to stay upright.

Pain exploded in her paw, and the world turned over as Sparrow was dragged to the ground and thrown into a nearby tree. The second Shade-Tiger had emerged from the spear itself and attacked her. The other demons fell upon her the moment her barrier fell.

I can't die here!

Sparrow howled. The wind answered a moment later, suddenly rising to storm-like strengths. It rammed into the demons, knocking them from its summoner. Sparrow surged to her paws and leapt onto the nearest demon, all conscious thought gone and replaced by a simple, primitive need to survive. The Ice-Fang screeched and attempted to scramble away, its scales torn by

Sparrow's claws. The she-wolf only bared her teeth and dove for the Ice-Fang's throat, tearing it away with a vicious snarl. Her paw throbbed with every step, but she barely felt the pain through her frenzy.

The second Ice-Fang fell a moment later, its back broken when it was slammed into a tree by Sparrow's wind. The three Shade-Tigers lunged for Sparrow, struggling to stay on their paws as the summoned storm raged around them.

Her vision blurring and her limbs slowly growing stiff, Sparrow dove under the Shade-Tigers' joint attack, sinking her fangs into the stomach of one and dragging it to the ground. The other two tripped over their companion, allowing Sparrow time to jump away and prepare for another attack.

I will not *die here!*

CHAPTER THREE

SPARROW, WHERE ARE you?

A sharp gust of wind slammed into Hawk, nearly knocking him off balance. He dug his claws into the snow, hunching his shoulders as he struggled to stay upright. The wind tore into his fur, and only the fire in his blood kept him from freezing on the spot.

After a few moments the wind died down enough for Hawk to continue. He stumbled forward, struggling to see something, anything beyond the whiteness surrounding him. Panic started to set in.

If I can barely see past my nose, does Sparrow have any chance of finding me at all?

No...I have to trust her. She promised *she'd catch up,* Hawk told himself, firmly shoving away the small voice that said Sparrow had very little chance of escaping the patrol, much less of finding him. He had to believe she would return. It was his fault the patrol from Tenepis Fortress had caught up with them in the first place, his fault Sparrow had to fight them on her own so he could escape, *his* fault she might be terribly injured, or worse, dead.

Another blast of icy wind startled Hawk from his dark thoughts, nearly knocking him off his paws. He lowered himself to the ground, trying to escape the worst of it.

I have to find shelter...

Hawk slowly raised his head, squinting into the storm. Up ahead, a large dark shape loomed out of the whiteness. Hawk crawled closer, hope rising in his chest.

It was a tree, a massive oak tree with thick, sprawling roots. Hawk could just barely see a small hollow beneath the roots, just big enough for a lost Fire-Wolf to hide. Gritting his teeth, he pushed himself to his paws and bolted for the tree. The wind howled in his ears, pulling at his fur as though to drag him away from the tree. He shook his head and dove into the hollow, slipping between the roots and landing in a heap beneath the tree.

Hawk breathed a sigh of relief. He was safe, for now. After twisting around so he could see out the hollow, he peered into the storm. A long, wet trail led straight to his shelter, left behind by his frenzied dash. Hawk hoped the snow would cover his tracks before a demon found them. If Sparrow couldn't hold off the patrol...it might be hunting him even now, quickly closing in on its unsuspecting prey...

No...don't think like that. Hawk shook his head, trying to clear away the dark thoughts. *Sparrow will find me, she* promised. *I'll just wait here for a bit; she'll catch up soon.*

But I can't stay for long...if the patrol is still hunting us, I have to keep moving, and if I wait too long, the storm might be over, and then the snow won't be falling fast enough to cover my tracks. Hawk whimpered and laid his head down on his paws. *But I can't just keep wandering around. I've never been this far into Taladair, and I don't know where Coal's hideout is. I might walk straight into a patrol.* Panic fluttered in his chest. Indecision tore at him as his situation continued to darken.

I guess...I'll just wait here...Sparrow will *come!*

CHAPTER FOUR

THE HOURS SLOWLY dragged by, each one feeling like a year to the anxious Hawk, and still there was no sign of his wayward friend. Only a slight dimming of the light kept him aware of the actual passing of time. A few times he considered leaving his shelter to go looking for her, but the fury of the wind and the cold of the snow kept him under cover.

The screech of some unknown creature almost made Hawk jump right out of his shelter, and he strained his senses to pinpoint the source of the sound. A few minutes had passed when he heard it again, closer than before. He tensed his muscles, ready to flee if discovered, his heart pounding.

That doesn't sound like any demon I know... He crawled forward, peering through the roots and searching for any sign of the approaching enemy. *It can't be a wild demon...they don't come out of hibernation until spring. Did the patrol get reinforcements? Sun-Wolf, don't let it find me.* The icy claw of fear ran down his back as the cold metal of his slave collar rubbed against his skin. *I don't want to go back to the Fortress!*

The wind suddenly increased in strength, swirling through the roots of the tree and dousing him in snow. The snow quickly melted and the chilly water clung to his thick fur, but Hawk didn't dare shake for fear of drawing the unknown creature's attention.

Seconds later the temperature dropped and the wind grew even stronger. The tree above him groaned in protest as the trunk fought the stiff wind. Hawk shivered, realizing with shock that, for only the second time in his short life, he was cold. The naturally high body temperature of his kind kept him warm even in the most extreme conditions. It was one of the advantages Fire-Wolves had over others.

Hawk's teeth chattered and he struggled to move. He found himself unable to do anything other than shiver. His red-orange eyes raked his surroundings in wild desperation, fearing a demonic attack could come at any moment.

Then his heart stopped.

A few feet in front of the terrified Fire-Wolf, the wind and snow condensed into a vague shape that constantly shifted through strange forms, both demon and wolf. A pair of eyes, one silver and one red, remained the only constant points and seemed to stare straight into Hawk's soul.

Hawk's mind went blank with terror, and the cold in his body intensified, petrifying him in place. He had no idea what demon had terrible wolf-like eyes or a form that could not be seen. The demon before him had to be incredibly powerful, and very rare. A blood-curdling screech came from the creature, the same terrifying sound from before. Hawk closed his eyes and waited for the killing blow, but the attack never came. Instead, the cold withdrew from Hawk's body, freeing his limbs, and the storm's fury slackened. He opened his eyes and the creature was gone. He was alone in the blinding whiteness.

His body became limp with relief, and his sides heaved as he struggled to regain his breath. His close brush with death left him feeling like he had just run to the Gaoibeanna Mountains and back. Every bone in his body ached, but Hawk knew he had to start moving. He didn't know what the creature was or where it had come from, but it very easily could have been a scout for a much larger party. Even if it wasn't a demon, there was a chance it was a wraith, a ghostly creature born from a tormented soul that wandered the night devouring the souls of the living. Either way, Sun-Wolf knew how long Hawk had until something found him.

Hawk dragged himself to his paws and warily stepped out from under the tree. He scanned his surroundings, his nose twitching, seeking to ensure the demon was truly gone. He breathed a sigh of relief and turned to find another place to hide from the storm. His eyes widened in shock as he jumped back to stare up in horror at his previous hiding place.

Except for the roots and what was now only a stump, the entire tree had vanished, leaving nothing but a few scraps of bark behind. Hawk's heart leapt into his throat. Very few creatures had the power to do so much damage while holding a wolf in such paralysis to keep him from noticing anything.

His exhaustion forgotten, Hawk ran for his life. His legs moved so fast they were a blur and left behind a churned trail of melted snow. He couldn't see where he was going, swerving around trees and skeletal bushes at the last moment. He could barely smell beyond the biting wind and snow, but he didn't care. His only thought was escape.

When Hawk reached his limit, unable to run any farther, he stood panting, his sides heaving and his head spinning. With the rush of adrenaline gone, waves of exhaustion crashed down on him, reminding him that the last time he had gotten a chance to actually rest was before he and Sparrow separated from the group. His stomach growled. If he wanted to keep traveling, he needed to find shelter.

He sank to the ground in an undignified heap and allowed his eyes to close as he struggled to get his breath back. He kept his ears alert, listening for the slightest sound, but the howl of the wind and the rattle of the tree branches drowned out anything that might alert him to a potential attacker. Slowly, he relaxed his guard. He felt so warm…and it was so comfy lying in the snow… maybe he could sleep for just a moment…

A twig cracked, audible during a break in the wailing wind, shocking Hawk back into full consciousness.

Sun-Wolf, how could I have been so stupid? I stand out enough as it is with my stupid orange fur, do I have to go and fall asleep in the middle of enemy territory? His red-orange eyes raked the surroundings, searching for any sign of his stalker. *Could it be the same demon from earlier?*

Hawk's ears flicked backward, detecting the slight sound of paws on snow. He had no time to register the threat before a large creature landed on him from behind, knocking him to the ground. The air rushed out of his lungs from the force of the attack. He struggled to stand, but his attacker kept him down. In desperation Hawk ignited his fur, allowing small, hot flames to dance across his pelt. The creature leapt off him in surprise, a yelp escaping its throat. Hawk whirled around to face his attacker, teeth bared and ready to fight for his life…and stopped.

The eyes glaring into his were not those of a demon, but of a wolf.

With the dark of the storm and the blowing snow, his attacker's features were barely distinguishable, but Hawk saw enough to determine his attacker was no demon. The wolf towered over Hawk, like an eagle looming before a mouse, easily six feet tall. Her thick, stocky build marked her as an Earth-Wolf, but the dark blue-gray fur and cold navy blue eyes did not belong to an Earth-Wolf. Then Hawk's eyes fell to the breed mark on her left shoulder.

It was a navy blue double wave.

"You're…you're a Water-Wolf." Relief at meeting a potential ally gave way to shock, and Hawk was unable to do more than stare and gape like a beached fish.

The she-wolf snarled, baring her curved fangs. "So what if I am? What's it to you, demon?"

"But…I th-thought that all Water-Wolves disappeared at the beginning of the war. We haven't seen them for over a hundred years!" Hawk drew back a little, his ears flattening. "And I'm not a demon; I'm a F-Fire-Wolf."

Her eyes narrowed slightly before flicking down to Hawk's left shoulder, noting the red flame-mark decorating it. Then they slid back to meet his. "No, I can see now that you're not. Other than your breed mark, you look more scared than a new-born pup. *Demons* are incapable of feeling any emotion other than *hate*." She seemed to spit out the last statement as though it was poison, and she snarled quietly to herself.

Both wolves froze when a long, eerie yowl reached their ears.

Hawk's eyes widened in fear when he recognized the cry. "I know that call; it's a Night-Lynx."

The she-wolf ignored him and listened for a moment, trying to pinpoint the demon's location. With a low growl, she was off running, leaving Hawk to stare stupidly after her. He galloped to catch up. The last thing he wanted was to be left for the demon, especially after being separated from Sparrow.

"Wait! Don't leave me for that thing!"

With a growl, the she-wolf whirled around to snap at Hawk's face, forcing him to slide to a stop to avoid her sharp fangs. "Stop whimpering, you coward!" Looking behind him, she snapped, "And turn off your fire or something, you're leaving a trail for the Lynx to follow."

A second yowl joined the first one and both wolves shot off into the swirl of snow again. Hawk struggled to keep up, his breath coming in ragged gasps. "I can't 'turn off my fire.' It's a part of my breed."

Hawk winced when the Water-Wolf swore under her breath. He held back a muttered apology, sure she would only snap at him.

"Then we'll have to fight them."

Hawk stumbled, paling under his fur at the Water-Wolf's suggestion, and shook his head vigorously. "I can't do that! I don't know how to fight."

"You're useless!"

Hawk flinched. His ears flattened, and he shrank away from the furious she-wolf.

She slid to a stop in a small clearing marked only by a small pile of boulders on the far side. "Fire-Wolf, stay here and distract the Night-Lynxes. Do whatever you need to, but don't look at their eyes!"

Hawk gulped but dared not protest. He turned to face the direction from which the demons were approaching and tried to stop his limbs from shaking. "Wh-what am I...?" he started to ask turning to look back at the she-wolf, only to find that that she had already disappeared into the snow and wind.

At the sound of vicious snarls, Hawk's head snapped around to face his attackers. Two Night-Lynxes stalked toward him, their long, thick legs narrowing the distance between them and Hawk much faster than he would have liked. The demons had thick fur patched with gray and black, which helped camouflage them at night. White claws glinted from heavily furred paws that barely made a print in the snow. Their box-like muzzles bore razor-sharp fangs that protruded from their upper lips. Hawk forced himself to focus on the white patches on their foreheads and bared his fangs in what he hoped was a menacing snarl.

The first Night-Lynx flicked its long ears in anticipation, seeing its prey petrified before it. Its hiss sent chills down Hawk's spine. He started to shake when the demon spoke in a silky voice, one Hawk knew could hypnotize the listener.

"Look at what we have here, Dens—a lost puppy. It was worth waking from our slumber to find such easy prey."

Their slumber? Hawk blinked with confusion. *They're feral demons...not attached to any Fortress or patrol...thank Sun-Wolf.*

The first Lynx's companion, Dens, bared its teeth and scanned the clearing, its white eyes sweeping past Hawk.

"But I had smelled a second one, where is she?" Those terrible white eyes swung back to Hawk and a cajoling tone entered its voice. "Can you tell us, lost puppy?"

Hawk's legs began to quiver, and he struggled to form a plan while keeping his eyes from making contact with the Night-Lynxes' hypnotizing gaze. *What was that she-wolf intending to do? Is she abandoning me so she can escape?*

When the thought crossed his mind Hawk's heart sank to his paws. The Water-Wolf only wanted to use him as a decoy, leaving him to the mercy of the two Night-Lynxes. And once they found the collar around his neck, he would be facing a fate worse than death.

Dens flicked its ear in Hawk's face as it circled him. Hawk could only shake and try to keep both Lynxes in his view. "Look at him tremble, Caligo! The puppy must be *scared*. So scared, he can't even *speak*. It's rude not to answer a direct question, you know."

Caligo laughed, its sickeningly sweet voice grating on Hawk's fraying nerves. "Yes, it is. And he won't even look at us. That's rude as well." It stopped to crouch in front of him, looking up with its wide, inviting white eyes. "Won't you look at us, lost puppy? We can help you; we'll *end* your fear."

Almost unconsciously, Hawk started to lower his eyes. He struggled to look away, already caught fast in the Night-Lynxes' spell. *Maybe their nightmares will kill me, and I won't live to face the consequences of running away. Oh Sun-Wolf, let my death be quick!*

As Hawk began to lock gazes with the demon Caligo, a large shape rocketed into the Night-Lynx, shoving it into its companion. The two demons screeched in surprise, snapping at each other in anger before turning their focus to their attacker. Hawk scrambled away from them, not wanting to get caught in the confrontation.

Baring her fangs at the Night-Lynxes, the Water-Wolf bunched her muscles for another attack. Her opponents snarled, recovering from their surprise in seconds. They charged the she-wolf, mouths open to reveal their wickedly sharp teeth. The she-wolf met their charge with tooth and claw, tearing through their fur and snapping at their throats. Hawk drew back from the violent display, his eyes wide and his heart beating fast as the Water-Wolf ripped the two Night-Lynxes to shreds. Blood flecked her blue-gray coat and coated her fangs. Even when their white eyes dulled and death stole their breath, the she-wolf continued her attack.

What is she? I've never seen a single wolf take on two demons at once and defeat them so quickly, even two sleepy ferals. Hawk swallowed hard. *Why won't she stop her attack? I've always heard of Water-Wolves being peaceful... but I guess...the demons have changed us all.*

Summoning his courage, Hawk tried to reach the enraged wolf. "P-please stop, the Night-Lynxes are already d-dead."

The Water-Wolf stopped her frenzied attack and swung her gaze up toward Hawk as though she had only now remembered his presence. The intense, blood-thirsty look in her eyes made Hawk shudder. He gulped and struggled to keep the words from sticking in his throat. "It's time to stop."

At Hawk's words, the she-wolf's eyes cleared. She seemed confused, almost as though she didn't remember what had happened. Looking down at the bloody carcasses at her paws, she snarled. Her eyes hardened, but this time her fight appeared internal.

Hawk took a careful step forward, his head lowered so he wouldn't appear threatening, and glanced at her out of the corner of his eyes. "Are you...okay?"

Whipping around without answering his question, the Water-Wolf took off into the forest. Hawk, afraid of being alone again, sped off after her. "Wait! Please don't run!"

The she-wolf didn't seem to hear Hawk, so he gave up trying to call her back and instead focused on following her, hoping no more demons would discover his trail of melted snow. *She's so fast, but does she even know where she's going?* The Water-Wolf leapt over a fallen log as though it were little more than a stick, leaving Hawk to claw his way beneath it. He barely managed to keep her in view. *Why am I even following her? After seeing her attack, there's no way she can be sane.*

They reached the southern banks of Lough Tost before the Water-Wolf finally came to a stop. *Thank Sun-Wolf, she ran out of energy. I don't know how much longer I could run on an empty stomach.* Hawk slowed his pace and stumbled to a stop beside the dark blue-gray wolf. He shook with exhaustion, panting as he tried to catch his breath.

After a few moments of silence, the Water-Wolf glared at Hawk with icy eyes and curled her lip in a snarl. "Why are you still here?"

Hawk didn't quite know the answer himself. "Well, I'm sort of...lost, and I don't want to run into any more demons, so..."

The she-wolf turned and started to walk away without waiting for the rest of what Hawk had to say. "I won't help you."

Afraid of being alone in the Taladair Forest to find his own way to Coal's hideout, Hawk jumped forward to stop the Water-Wolf. "Please, at least point me in the right direction!"

The Water-Wolf paused and glared at Hawk, who stubbornly held his ground. "Fine. I'll help you find which way to go, but then you're *going*. Got it? I *don't* want you following me."

Hawk's heart immediately lightened with her words, and his entire body sagged with relief. Now he hoped this she-wolf was traveling in the same direction as he was, so he wouldn't have to travel alone.

"But with this storm still blowing, you won't be able to travel anywhere tonight," the Water-Wolf continued. "We should find some shelter." She shoved her way past Hawk and, without waiting for him to follow, started to walk away.

Hawk trotted a few steps to catch up with her, thankful he wouldn't be alone in the cold, dark night.

CHAPTER FIVE

"THERE! I THINK this should be enough." Hawk spat out several splinters after dropping his last bundle of tinder and shook shards of ice from his pelt. "I probably won't find any more dry wood...the storm's picking up." He pushed the sticks together into a haphazard pile before crouching before the wood. Eyes narrowed in concentration, he tried to summon a flame. A spark appeared on the bark, only to splutter and die. Hawk growled in frustration and tried again but achieved the same result. A quiet chuckle broke his concentration, and he looked up to find the Water-Wolf watching his efforts with amusement.

"I've never seen a wolf have such a hard time summoning his element. Did those demons scare you so much you can't work your magic, Fire-Wolf?"

Hawk grew hot with embarrassment, and forced himself to ignore the Water-Wolf. *Come on, catch fire!* Hawk growled again, glaring at the wood until a small flame appeared. Tail wagging, he blew on the tongue of fire, causing it to roar up and light the other sticks. Soon a cheerful blaze crackled in the cold cave. But his pride over his accomplishment vanished when the she-wolf asked, "What's that ring around your neck?"

Hawk immediately jumped to his paws and backed away a few paces, terror at being discovered coursing through him.

"H-how did you..." The words died in his throat, and he blinked at the Water-Wolf with confusion. Her innocent question was not what Hawk expected. "You don't know what this is?"

The she-wolf's eyes narrowed with confusion. "Am I *supposed* to know?"

Hawk hesitated before answering, carefully watching the other wolf. "Yes... this is a slave collar."

"A slave collar? Who keeps *slaves*? It's forbidden by Moon-Wolf and Sun-Wolf."

"The demons, who else?" Bitterness flooded his voice as Hawk sat back down. "They need someone to build their fortresses for them."

Surprise flashed across the she-wolf's blue-gray eyes before they narrowed again in thought. Quietly she asked, "How long since the demons arrived?"

"It's been over one hundred years...how do you not know that?" When she didn't answer, Hawk ventured a question that had been on his mind since meeting her. "What exactly happened to the Water-Wolves?"

Leaping to her paws, the she-wolf bared her curved fangs, her eyes dark with anger. She snarled at Hawk, the flames casting twisting shadows on her face. "What does it matter to you what happened to us, Fire-Wolf? I have no reason to tell you!"

Hawk flattened his ears against his head and cowered, terrified at her sudden display of fury. "I'm sorry! I was just a little curious, but I won't ask again!"

Hawk's apology seemed to soothe the other wolf's anger, and she lay back down on her side of the fire. A few moments of silence passed before she said, "Tell me your name."

"Hawk...my name's Hawk," he answered, still a little shaken.

The Water-Wolf cocked her head. "Hawk? Sounds more like a Wind-Wolf name...are you part Wind-Wolf?"

"No...I don't know who my father was, but I don't have a dual breed mark." He shifted to show her his left shoulder, which bore only the flame-shaped mark of the Fire-Wolf. Those of dual heritage also bore a second mark, positioned below the first.

"Slaves," the she-wolf muttered, before raising her voice. "I'm River."

River fell silent after this and rested her head on her paws. Hawk realized she would offer no more conversation for the night. He sighed and lowered his head. She now knew so much about him, but he knew nothing of her but her name.

Chapter Six

HAWK WOKE TO the bright sunlight penetrating the cave and lighting the interior. He yawned and sat up to stretch. Silence met his ears. River was nowhere to be seen, and if Hawk didn't know better, he would think she had never been there in the first place.

Dread creeping into his thoughts, Hawk padded to the cave's exit and looked around for any sign of River. The sun hung high overhead in a sky marked only by a few fluffy clouds. Snow lay like a blanket, coating the skeletal branches of the trees around him. There were no tracks to show where the Water-Wolf had been, and with the snow, Hawk couldn't catch her scent.

River might have left hours ago or just as he awoke; he had no way to tell.

It's no use looking anyway, he thought bitterly. *If all the stories are true, she probably turned into mist and went on her way without leaving a trace behind.* He shuffled uncertainly under the cave's overhang, wondering what he should do.

He couldn't help but feel doubtful about her return, but just as he started to consider what he would do without her, she appeared between the trees, holding a hare's carcass in her mouth.

Hawk leapt to his paws, relieved. "River? Where did you go?"

Dropping the hare in front of Hawk, River snorted. "I don't know when you ate last, but I heard your stomach growling all night."

Hawk flattened his ears and shuffled a little sheepishly. "I don't know how to hunt…"

Rolling her eyes again and muttering something about 'idiot wolves who don't know how to hunt,' River bent down to nudge her catch toward Hawk. "Eat. I'm not going to care for a wolf passed out from hunger."

Obediently, Hawk took a grateful bite out of the carcass. River sat down and glared at him a little impatiently, no doubt eager to start the journey. "Now, where exactly are you trying to go?"

Hawk swallowed before answering. "I'm not sure…" River sighed in exasperation, and Hawk continued. "I'm supposed to meet up with my resistance group somewhere in the northern part of…the Dorasca Gorge, I think."

"The Dorasca Gorge." River paused for a moment. "What's...a resistance group?"

Hawk paused, glancing up at River out of the corner of his eye. *How does she not know? The demons invaded every nation in Soluna. Even if some Water-Wolves had managed to hole up somewhere, it doesn't explain why she knows so little.* "It's a pack formed by free wolves to fight the demons, following the wishes of King Oak at his final stand. Although...we don't do much more than hide and try to escape notice...not many packs dare to openly stand against Letorus..."

"Doesn't sound like much of a resistance. But you said you were a slave, how did you end up in one of these packs?"

Hawk gritted his teeth in slight annoyance, though he had to admit, it was a relief to talk openly to someone and not worry about being killed for it. "I *was* a slave; I was born in Ignimor Fortress, in the Scaineadó Desert. One day after my...master beat me...the slave-stone loosened. I managed to knock it off and escape."

"Slave-stone?"

"It's a stone that represses a wolf's elemental magic. Slaves can't use magic with the stone in their collars. That's how the demons can keep so many slaves under control, and it's probably why my powers are so weak, because they were repressed for so long," Hawk said in a sorrowful tone.

River narrowed her eyes. "You were scared when I pointed out the collar last night, why? Why don't you just melt it off? I'm sure even with your meager powers you might eventually manage it."

Hawk grimaced and started to explain, once again wondering why *she* got to ask all the questions. "The band is made from a similar material to the slave-stone, so it's resistant to elemental magic, which is why I can't break the collar, although I can still *use* my magic." He winced. "The...penalty...for an escaped slave is...harsh. The penalty for harboring one is even more so. If... it were known that I...am an escaped slave, I could be killed on the spot, even by other wolves." He sent River a pleading look. "So please don't tell anyone!"

River sniffed. "We're not going to be together much longer, so why should it matter whether I tell or not? Now hurry up and finish eating, we're leaving soon."

After scoffing the rest of the prey in a few bites, Hawk burned the leftovers. It took a few attempts, with River growing evermore impatient, but the remains of the hare were finally reduced to ash and scattered to the wind.

"You took too long," the she-wolf complained, standing and shaking to clear her fur of snow. "I'm sure the smell of the kill will attract every demon for miles around. Now, what to do about you..."

Her burning stare caused Hawk to shift uncomfortably, his eyes sliding away from hers. "What...about me?"

"The snow stopped falling early this morning, which means it won't be covering your tracks. If a demon finds your melted prints we'll have a horde of them on our tails before you can howl. So you either turn off your fire or find a way to not walk!"

Hawk's heart sank in despair. "I can't just 'turn off my fire.' It's in my blood! It's not something I can control."

River sniffed and started to turn away. "Well then, I guess I can't help you. I can't afford to have any followers."

She's leaving! She's going to abandon me! "Wait!" Hawk called, leaping forward to catch up. "My pack leader was a Fire-Wolf, and he created this method of covering our tracks."

The she-wolf paused but did not turn around. "I'm listening."

"He used the abilities of another wolf to shift the earth and snow around and cover our tracks. In our group, we had both Earth-Wolves and Wind-Wolves to do this, and it took a lot of practice, but you're a Water-Wolf! You can summon snow to cover my tracks!"

River still didn't turn around. "How do you know I can summon snow? I'm not the Winter-Wolf, so how can you be so confident?"

She started to pad away, and Hawk's heart sank to his paws. He had to convince River to let him travel with her, even if only for a few days. He couldn't wander the forest alone. "Because I've heard the legends! No one has seen a Water-Wolf for a century, but we haven't forgotten them!"

At his statement, River stopped again, and Hawk took his chance. "We know they control water, and snow is a form of water! Water-Wolves can swim really well and can even dive underwater! They...they were the peacemakers of the wolves, and oftentimes their opinion was asked by the rulers of the other nations." *Although...your attitude when fighting doesn't fit the description...but maybe what we know about Water-Wolves is wrong...or maybe it's just you,* Hawk almost added, but managed to bite back the words before they left his jaws.

Desperation rushed through Hawk, and he took a few more steps forward, hoping she would believe that he sincerely needed her help. "So please, *please* help me. I just need to get to the gorge."

"You're wrong," River bared her teeth. "We are *not* peacemakers."

The vehemence in River's voice startled Hawk, and he thought he caught a glimpse of pain flash through her eyes as she turned away from him. "Now get moving. I'll help point you in the right direction, but then I never want to see you again."

Relieved, Hawk nodded his thanks and scurried forward to lead the way. River said nothing as they began walking, causing Hawk to cast a quick peek over his shoulder, just to make sure she followed him. She ignored him and kept her eyes fixed on the ground, although her ears remained alert. Small flurries of snow appeared around River's paws as she stepped into his exact prints, covering the pools of melted water and erasing any trace of their passage.

Hawk turned his head back to focus on the path before him. "So are we going the right way, River?"

"Of course we are. Just keep walking straight until I say otherwise."

The hours slowly ticked by. Neither wolf spoke unless they had to, usually when River needed to tell Hawk where to go. The snowy forest around them was just as silent, the quiet only occasionally broken by the sounds of small animals scurrying about in the undergrowth. Hawk was happy he didn't have to bear the silence alone, even if he had to bear it with an irritable she-wolf as a companion.

Eventually, however, Hawk couldn't resist the urge to strike up some sort of conversation. He scrambled for something to say that would elicit a response from River, before remembering something strange she had mentioned before.

"River, you mentioned something about a 'Winter-Wolf,' what is that?"

River hesitated before answering, "I'm not sure...not much is known about it. It's not a wolf, nor is it a demon, but it first appeared a little after the war began. Legend says the Winter-Wolf is a hybrid of both." She hesitated again. "When it appears, a snowstorm appears around it. No one has seen the true form of the Winter-Wolf, and the only thing that remains the same are its bi-colored eyes, one silver and one red."

Suddenly Hawk stopped, and even his heart seemed to have frozen in fear. River pulled up short to avoid running into him and growled. "Hawk, what are you doing? We *need* to keep moving."

"A Winter-Wolf has two different colored eyes," he whispered.

"*The* Winter-Wolf, there's only one, but yes."

"One silver, the other red?"

"Yes, why are you asking me this? It doesn't concern you." River growled, irritated at their prolonged pause.

"Because…I think…I think I've seen it." Hawk closed his eyes, remembering the mysterious creature that had appeared before him, the one that destroyed the tree. It had to be the Winter-Wolf River described. No other demon had bi-colored eyes or a form that couldn't be seen. Hawk swallowed hard.

Why did it appear like that? Is it…hunting me?

A loud, angry curse from River shook Hawk from his thoughts. He turned just in time to see her whip around and take off, diving through the skeletal bushes behind her and disappearing into the thick undergrowth. Startled, Hawk stood and blinked with confusion for a moment, before launching himself after her.

"Wait! River! Where are you going?"

A ball of freezing water smacked Hawk's face, and he slid to a halt. River's detached voice echoed in the silent forest, as though coming from all directions at once, leaving Hawk clueless as to where she was.

"Stay away from me!"

Panicking at the thought of losing his guide, Hawk tipped his head back and howled, "Don't leave! What did I do?"

Silence met his cry. The blue-gray Water-Wolf had disappeared. Hawk shivered, suddenly very afraid. He was alone and lost in hostile territory, and no longer had anyone to cover his tracks.

And if there were any demon fortress nearby, or even a patrol, Hawk would soon have bigger problems to worry about. His howl probably echoed for miles around. Demons would soon be swarming to his location like crows to a kill.

"Well, I'm two days from the Tenepis Fortress, and I think I've been traveling in a western direction," Hawk said out loud, more to comfort himself than to actually make a plan. "I know I'm at Lough Tost, and if I remember what Sparrow said, I think I'm near the Secumare Fortress. It's not a strong one, but we knew it had a lot of…"

Hawk's voice trailed off when he remembered what kind of demon made up most of Secumare's ranks. Ice-Fangs. The same kind of demon that had held Hawk captive at Ignimor Fortress his whole life.

I have to get out of here. His red-orange eyes raked their surroundings. He was alone in the forest, but not for long. The Secumare Fortress was located just across the lake, but although he and River had avoided traveling along the shore for fear of being seen, his howl would have carried straight across the waters. *But where can I go? I don't even know where I am! And even if I do run, the demons can just follow my tracks!*

Hawk looked down at his paws, which were already standing in shallow pools of water. Panic rose in his chest.

I don't want to die!

Paws churning the snow, Hawk dashed off through the trees. He didn't care that he was leaving a clear trail for demons to follow. He just wanted to get away, hoping that maybe, just maybe, he could stay ahead of any demons. He stumbled over a small hill, barely managing to avoid tripping and tumbling the rest of the way down. The wind picked up, throwing snow into his face and blinding him, but he never slackened his speed. The branches above him rattled as the wind strengthened, and the trees creaked as they swayed.

A clap of thunder sent Hawk scrambling for cover, diving beneath the nearest bush with his tail between his legs. His heart almost stopped when the thunder boomed again, causing the entire forest to shake from the force of the sound. Shards of ice poured from the clouds, turned into deadly projectiles by the fierce wind. Hawk flattened his ears and shoved his face into the snow, wishing the skeletal bush still had its summer leaves to protect him.

This is an even worse storm than before, he thought, cautiously peering past the thin branches. He saw nothing but whiteness. *But it happened so suddenly…*

Hawk shook his head and slowly crawled out from under the bush. Eyes squinted against the hail, he started running as fast as he could. He had to get as far as he could before the storm stopped, and the demons could track him.

Not even the Ice-Fangs could find him in a storm this strong.

CHAPTER SEVEN

THE MOMENT THE wind began to blow, River knew she was in trouble. She swore under her breath and forced herself to run faster, until she was practically flying over the snow.

But she couldn't outrun the storm.

Soon the ice and snow were all around her, threatening to knock her to the ground with their power. River only snarled and continued running.

Suddenly the entire forest shook, and a peal of thunder boomed just over her head, so loud River's ears rang. She tripped and fell headfirst into the snow.

"You should know better than to try and run."

The Water-Wolf growled, her hackles raised, and slowly stood.

"You don't exactly hold a lot of my trust, Winter-Wolf."

River turned her head just enough to glare at the ethereal figure behind her, barely visible through the cloak of snow.

"You left the Fire-Wolf to die. Have you sunk so low that you would break your own promises?"

"Why should you care?"

The wind suddenly died around them, creating a bubble of calm within the storm. The Winter-Wolf padded forward until it stood in front of River, piercing her with its bi-colored gaze.

"You also did not heed my warning."

River growled quietly. The few times she had met the Winter-Wolf, she had attempted to question it, to find out why it was so interested in her, but to no avail.

"I will say it one more time," the Winter-Wolf said now. "*Alone you will fail.*"

"*Alone* is all I have," River snarled, drawing back her lips to bare her teeth.

"So you have said."

"Then why am I still repeating myself?"

If the Winter-Wolf was capable of emotion, River was sure it would have growled in frustration by now. Instead, all she got was an empty look.

"Why do you think I appeared to the Fire-Wolf?"

"So you could stalk me..." River muttered under her breath.

Suddenly the bubble of calm burst, and thunder boomed, rattling the trees around them. The Winter-Wolf snarled, growing twice its size and towering over River.

"I do not have time to argue with you, Wolf. You do not realize the risk I take simply by being here, speaking to you. This storm will not escape *his* notice, and he will soon send demons to investigate." The Winter-Wolf's bi-colored eyes narrowed. "Find the Fire-Wolf. Without him, you cannot succeed."

A peal of thunder sounded just above River, causing her to flinch away from the noise. When she looked up, the Winter-Wolf was gone.

River stood for several minutes as the storm slowly dissipated, and she growled quietly to herself. She didn't trust the Winter-Wolf or its cryptic words, but she couldn't get rid of the nagging thought at the back of her mind.

One that warned her that what it said was true.

CHAPTER EIGHT

HAWK STUMBLED TO a halt just in front of a wide river, his sides heaving. He had been running almost non-stop since the blizzard had started, continuing even when it had finally died down. He had long-since lost track of how long he had been running, focused only on creating as much distance between himself and Lough Tost.

I think...I'm safe...for now... Hawk raised his head slightly and cocked his ears, listening intently for any sign of life in the forest. He heard nothing other than the rustling of a few birds in the bushes and the soft gurgling of the water, and even those noises were muffled by the snow. *But now what?*

He looked around the silent forest. Hawk may have escaped the demons, but now he was well and truly alone. After the second blizzard, there was no chance of either Sparrow or River finding him, and without them, he also had no chance of finding Coal's hideout.

Just when I had managed to finally find a wolf to travel with... Hawk lowered his head with a sigh. The flight from Ignimor Fortress to Taladair had been tumultuous, as Hawk had been focused solely on getting as far from Scaineadó as he could. He avoided resistance groups, fearing recognition as an escaped slave. He had nearly died trying to travel alone, with no idea of where to go and little knowledge of the outside world. It was only thanks to Sparrow, who had saved him from the clutches of a demon patrol and convinced Coal to take him in, that Hawk survived at all.

The silence of the forest suddenly became oppressive, weighing down on Hawk's shoulders as though it wanted to crush him into the earth. The river seemed to laugh at him, mocking his plight.

Luck alone had kept him alive so far, but now Hawk feared it was running out.

No, don't think like that. Hawk shook his head sharply to clear his head of his dark thoughts. *I can't give up yet. What would Sparrow do if she were here?*

Hawk closed his eyes and imagined Sparrow was standing there beside him. She would probably tease him for his uncertainty and ask him if he had a hare for a father to make him so flighty. Then she would laugh and give him a shove, before saying that they should find some shelter.

"Hole up somewhere you won't be bothered, then start making plans," Hawk said to himself, repeating what Sparrow always said if Coal left them without instructions. He opened his eyes, feeling a small spark of hope.

"I'll find a place where demon patrols won't find me, and then I can figure out what to do next." Hawk raised his head slightly, but then looked down at his paws.

He was still faced with the problem of moving without leaving a stark trail.

Hawk swallowed, eying the river in front of him. He could avoid leaving prints if he walked in the shallow waters, but it made him uneasy. It went against his natural instincts as a Fire-Wolf to enter Water's domain.

Ignoring the sick feeling settling in the pit of his stomach, Hawk padded into the cold waters of the river. He could not risk leaving any prints behind. Chills ran down Hawk's back, caused more by his innate fear of water than the cold, but he continued walking.

He would follow the river until he found a place to hide, and then he could rest for a bit and plan.

And maybe, just maybe, he would be okay.

Chapter Nine

RIVER SWORE SILENTLY to herself, facing another dead-end of Hawk's trail. She had managed to follow his scent from where she last saw him for a few miles, but then it had faded until even River's keen senses couldn't detect it. The Winter-Wolf's blizzard had all but erased the trail.

If it wants me to find Hawk so badly, it should have left me something to track, River thought irritably. She would like nothing better than to continue on her way and forget the Fire-Wolf ever existed, if only to escape any of the Winter-Wolf's meddling, but even she had to admit it would be futile. The Winter-Wolf would be back to nag her about something else.

For now, at least, she would play along. Despite the Winter-Wolf's untrustworthiness, it had a knack for knowing things it shouldn't, things that no mortal creature, demon or otherwise, could know.

River owed her original escape to the Winter-Wolf.

The blue-gray Water-Wolf sniffed the freshly fallen snow once more before growling. Nothing.

If I were a half-wit Fire-Wolf without a scrap of directional sense and lost in a blizzard, where would I go?

The forest around her offered no answer to her unvoiced question. It almost seemed to mock her with its silence. River growled quietly again and flattened her ears. It was entirely too peaceful. Too quiet. Too…*safe.*

River's legs trembled, and she envisioned a dozen different demons hiding in the snow-covered bushes around her, watching her, stalking her. Suddenly the forest seemed oppressive. The trees leaned in toward her, seeking to trap her between their branches, to tie her to the ground and make her easy prey for her enemies…

No, stop it! River shook her head furiously, shoving aside her growing panic. There were no demons in the woods, no enemies waiting to attack. She weakened for a moment and let her fear rule her mind. *Stay focused; don't let it take over.*

The feeling of oppression slowly faded, and River turned her attention back to finding the wayward Fire-Wolf. Given what little she knew about him, she guessed that he ran blindly forward, only changing direction when something blocked his way.

There had better be something impressive about this Fire-Wolf, River thought sourly, racing lightly over the snow without leaving a trace behind. *I don't have time to waste on a fool's hunt.*

CHAPTER TEN

SPARROW WOULD BE mad if she saw me like this, Hawk thought, his head on his paws. A day had gone by since Hawk had found a shallow cave to shelter in, and he had yet to think of any sort of plan. He felt safe in the cave and didn't want to risk leaving it.

A soft growl came from his stomach, reminding him that he couldn't hide forever.

But with night quickly approaching, the forest was becoming more and more hostile. Night belonged to the demons. Without the sun's blessing, it would be suicidal for Hawk to venture out now.

The hours slowly ticked by, and the forest grew darker, until Hawk could barely see past his nose. The shadowy shapes of the trees outside the small cave twisted themselves into nightmarish forms. Hawk swallowed hard and backed away from the entrance, until he hit the cave wall.

Please don't let any demon find me. Hawk's heart started to race. The shadows seemed to grow darker and creep toward him, long claws of blackness that reached for him. The wind howled around the cave, sounding like a demon's cry, coming closer and closer...

A thump made Hawk flinch so hard he knocked his head against the ceiling.

Biting back a whimper of pain, Hawk curled up, trying to squish himself into an even smaller space at the back of the cave. The thump could have been caused by anything, a tree branch knocked to the ground by the wind, another wolf...

Voices reached Hawk's ears, and his breath caught in his throat.

"Curse that blizzard. It will take us another day to reach Secumare now."

"Lord Mars will not be pleased with our lateness."

Demons! Sheer terror surged through Hawk. *And they're...*

"We found and destroyed the wolf rebels it wanted. That should smooth its anger over."

Four shapes appeared outside the cave, leaping down from the ledge over Hawk's head. Even in the darkness, Hawk could make out their reptilian forms and glittering scaly hides.

...Ice-Fangs!

All feeling drained away from Hawk's body. Four of his most feared enemies stood just a few lengths from him. They were the demons that held him captive at Ignimor Fortress. He shook silently, too scared to even whimper. If they turned around, if they caught his scent…

"Such an annoyance." One of the Ice-Fangs yawned. "I wish they had tried running a bit longer."

A second Ice-Fang snorted. "If they had continued to run, we would be even later, brother."

Did they find Coal and the others? For a moment, Hawk forgot the danger of his own situation, worried for his companions. Then he dismissed the worry. *No, Coal's too smart to be caught by Ice-Fangs…me, on the other paw…*

Hawk silenced even his thoughts when he saw one of the Ice-Fangs turn in his direction. He stilled his breath, wanting nothing more than to disappear into the earth.

"Brothers, do you smell this?" The Ice-Fang lowered its muzzle to the ground, sniffing at the snow. Hawk didn't move. He had managed to sweep away his tracks with a branch, and hopefully it was dark enough that the demons couldn't see the obvious signs of cover, but there was nothing he could do about his scent.

"A wolf passed this way, not long ago." The Ice-Fang raised its head and sniffed the air, trying to catch a trace of where the scent led. One of its brothers did the same, sniffing the bushes clustered around the cave's entrance.

"Perhaps you can fulfill your desire for a chase, Brother Lacero," an Ice-Fang said, whipping its tail in anticipation. "The wolf is not far…his scent is still strong…"

"Yes…" Lacero slowly swung its head around, carefully sniffing the air.

Hawk tried to push himself even further into the cave, but his back was against the wall.

He was trapped.

Suddenly ice shot across the cave, slicing through Hawk's fur and barely missing his skin. Hawk yelped, surprised, and the noise echoed off the smooth walls. The Ice-Fangs yowled in triumph.

"The wolf thought he could hide from us, brothers!" Lacero snarled, diving into the cave, his teeth shining in the half-light. Hawk ducked under the Ice-Fang's lunge and tore toward the entrance, blind with terror. He ran straight into the waiting claws of the other three demons.

"Look how scared he is, brothers," one of the Ice-Fangs taunted, whipping its long tail across Hawk's face when he attempted to escape through the circle of demons.

"Don't hog him, Brother Testa!" A second Ice-Fang jumped on the first, knocking it away from Hawk. The two snapped at each other, and Hawk slid around them as they squabbled.

The third Ice-Fang suddenly appeared in front of him, its eyes glittering with malice. "There's nowhere to run, Fire-Wolf." The Ice-Fang lowered its head and growled. "We have you now…you'd only be delaying the inevitable."

"Brother Squama, let him run, let him try an escape!" Lacero came up behind Hawk, making the Fire-Wolf jump. Testa and the last Ice-Fang, their spat forgotten, completed the circle, trapping Hawk inside. "I want to see him run from us, see the hope fade from his eyes when we catch him!"

Hawk lowered himself to the ground, his ears flat against his head. His heart raced in his chest, feeling as though it was about to burst.

Please don't recognize me; just kill me now! Hawk prayed desperately they wouldn't discover his collar. Ice-Fangs were closely connected to one another. News of Hawk's escape from Ignimor Fortress, run by an Ice-Fang, had surely been spread to all the Ice-Fangs in Soluna.

A fate worse than death awaited him if he were recaptured.

"We have no time for a chase, Brother Lacero," Squama said. "Lord Mars awaits our return. If you must have a chase, you can take one of the slaves."

Lacero growled, but a glare from Squama silenced it.

"What should we do with this one?" Testa asked, sending ice to slowly creep over Hawk's limbs, holding him in place. Now Hawk had no chance of escape, even if he gathered the courage to do so.

"Kill him and leave his corpse for the ferals." Squama turned away, leaving its brothers to deliver the killing blow.

Testa and Lacero leered at Hawk, unsheathing their claws and baring their teeth. Hawk whimpered, and tried to press himself further into the earth.

"Wait, look closely…he seems familiar…" The last Ice-Fang shoved the other two out of the way and peered down at Hawk.

"Brother Sudis, who cares?" Lacero groaned. "Let us have our fun."

Suddenly Sudis dove for Hawk's neck, its teeth closing around the metal band hidden beneath his thick fur and wrenching Hawk up, straining him against the ice that held him captive.

No!

"A slave!" Testa snarled, its eyes narrowing and its scales shivering with fury. Behind it, Squama whirled around.

"What did you find?" it said, pushing its way back through Testa and Lacero.

"The slave that escaped our esteemed brother, Lapsus, Lord Mars of Ignimor," Sudis snarled around Hawk's collar. "The one who dared raise a claw against our brother, and slew many a demon before fleeing the Ignimor Fortress."

"We would earn a great reward by turning him in." Squama narrowed its eyes and stalked closer to Hawk. He had been discovered. He was dead. "Brother Lacero, summon an Ice-Spirit to carry the slave. We shall take him to Lord Mars."

As the demons yowled in triumph, Hawk's eyes widened, and he started to shake.

No, they're going to take me back to Ignimor! I can't go back! I can't… someone, please…HELP ME!

A savage snarl suddenly cut through the yowls, and Hawk was shoved back to the ground when Sudis collapsed on top of him, screeching in pain. The ice encasing Hawk's limbs shattered, and silvery blood splattered his fur. He looked up to see a large dark shape, silhouetted by the faint light of the moons, perched on top of the Ice-Fang with teeth sunk deep into the back of its neck. A pair of wild navy-blue eyes stared back.

Sudis yowled and jerked violently, attempting to rid itself of its attacker. The other three Ice-Fangs yowled as well and threw themselves on top of their enemy, only to fall on their injured brother.

Teeth closed around Hawk's scruff, dragging him out from beneath the pile of demons. He instinctively tried to resist the pull but was given a hard shake for his efforts.

"Run, you stupid wolf!"

Hawk's eyes widened in shock.

It was River.

She came back…

He was shaken from his thoughts when River shoved him toward the trees. "Run!" Behind her the Ice-Fangs were quickly recovering.

Hawk didn't hesitate a moment longer, racing through the trees as though Letorus himself chased him. River snarled again, raising the snow from the ground and causing it to whirl around herself and the Ice-Fangs. Within moments, Hawk could only hear the vicious yowls and screeches of pain. The battle itself had been hidden from view. Then even the cloud of snow disappeared as Hawk continued to run.

For a moment, Hawk's pace faltered. He didn't want to face the Ice-Fangs again, but he also didn't want to leave River to die for him. Then he remembered her battle against the Night-Lynxes and shuddered.

He almost pitied the Ice-Fangs.

Chapter Eleven

"What happened to you? Why didn't you fight back?"

Hawk jumped to his paws, surprised by River's sudden appearance. He looked up and blinked in confusion, almost convinced the wolf before him was a creation of his fevered mind. After he had judged he was far enough from the battle, he collapsed on the ground and was left alone with a mind whirling with raw emotions.

"Well? Are you going to answer me?" River snapped, looking quite irritated with Hawk's silence.

Something in Hawk snapped, and he rushed forward to bury his muzzle in her thick shoulder fur, his body continuing its uncontrollable shaking.

"Hawk?" River tensed, but Hawk paid the action no mind.

Eventually he calmed down enough to stutter an apology to River. He backed away and looked at the ground, now embarrassed with what he had done. River watched carefully, surprising Hawk with her calm.

"The demon that owned you, was it an Ice-Fang?"

He nodded a little shakily. "The Ice-Fang that ruled Ignimor Fortress where I was held captive was sent there for punishment. It had a tough time living in the desert and hated us Fire-Wolves for being at ease in the heat. The day I ran away…was the day it killed my mother. It was picking on her, because even though she was so weak and sick the heat did not affect her. It was too much for her…and she died from her wounds." He swallowed. "I saw her die in front of me…and I was so upset and angry…I attacked my master in my rage…"

River snorted, as though she had a hard time imagining Hawk angry enough to attack an Ice-Fang.

"I was punished for defying him," Hawk continued, "and somehow during the scuffles the slave stone got loosened. When my master later…confined me…I managed to get the slave-stone off and I escaped." Hawk shuddered, the terrible memories washing over him once again. "Seeing so many at once… coming for me…it was *terrifying*."

After a few moments of silence, River shook herself and turned away. "Come on, we need to get moving and find shelter. If anything noticed the battle, they'll be coming to investigate the commotion. It'd be better for us to hide until things calm down."

As she turned, she revealed a deep, long wound on her left shoulder, just below her Water-Wolf mark. The torn skin had turned blue, frozen by the icy cold of an Ice-Fang's touch, and it cut down to her bone.

"River, you're hurt." He scanned the rest of her body, but found no more wounds. *That's it? That was the only harm all four of those Ice-Fangs did?*

River glanced down at her shoulder, almost as though she hadn't noticed the wound before, but she seemed surprisingly unconcerned about it. She only sniffed and started to walk away. "Come on Hawk, there's a cave nearby."

Hawk darted ahead of River so she could cover his tracks, dozens of questions clouding his mind. He debated voicing a few but didn't want to risk making her leave again.

He didn't know if he could bear being left alone for the third time.

It soon became apparent that 'nearby' had a different definition to River than it did to Hawk: the sun was rising by the time she stopped and pointed out their shelter. "The cave's just up ahead; just slip through the crack in the rocks."

Hawk stared at the large pile of rocks sitting in front of him. If River hadn't brought his attention to the long crack splitting the biggest boulder, he would have walked right past it. "This is the cave? Are you sure we can go through the crack?"

"Just shut up and go through."

Obediently, Hawk stopped talking and stepped up to the crack. He gave it a wary look, still a little hesitant to go through. River rolled her eyes and pushed by him, disappearing through the narrow gap. Hawk's jaw dropped, and he hurried to follow the she-wolf. Once inside, Hawk's jaw dropped even further. He expected a narrow, cramped space, but what met his eyes was magnificent. Hidden in the rocks under the forest's frozen earth was a large, spacious cavern. Tall walls broke up the floor, making several different-sized rooms. A sharp incline dropped beneath Hawk's paws to the cave's floor, where River stood waiting.

"I told you this was a cave."

Hawk slipped down the slope, still staring around the cavern. "How...how is this here? How is it so big?"

"This used to be the camp for Clan Uiscuar, and they were the ones who created this place. It was safe, warm, and hidden—the perfect camp." River brushed her nose against the wall, her eyes closed, lost in memory. "They were a strong clan, and their leader was brave and wise."

Breaking off his inspection of the underground hollow, Hawk sent River a curious look. She had to be the strangest wolf he'd ever met. Her knowledge of the current war was pitiful at best, yet she spoke of the past clan as though she had once walked among its wolves.

Is that possible? No, she can't be any older than ten ...maybe she's heard stories about them? He sighed. It was unlikely she would answer any questions about the current location of the Water-Wolves. Instead, his mind turned to another question, one that had bothered him since River returned. "Um, River, can I ask you something?"

River swiveled her gaze back to Hawk, her eyes clouded with memories. She blinked a few times before answering. "Depends on the question."

"How...how did you find me?"

Her expression darkened. "I didn't. We happened to cross paths."

Hawk flattened his ears. *Then why is she here?* "Oh...then...are you going to leave again?"

"No." River turned around sharply, obviously intending for their short conversation to come to an end.

A dozen more questions sprung up in Hawk's mind, but he was too afraid to ask half of them. Finally, he settled on one.

"Wait! Then...when I said I saw the Winter–"

Suddenly River was looming over Hawk, her eyes aglow with fury. "Don't say its name!"

Hawk immediately fell to the floor, his tail sweeping between his legs. "W-when I said I s-saw the...snow demon...you g-got mad. Why d-did you?"

Backing away slightly, River lowered her head and sighed. She was silent for a few moments before finally saying, "This...certain demon is immensely powerful...but we know very little about it. What we *do* know is it can be anywhere...*go* anywhere...and can find you no matter where you are. It might even lead the hordes of Letorus right to your paws."

Hawk stiffened. Could this Winter-Wolf lead demons to him and punish him for running away from slavery? Caught up in his personal worries, Hawk nearly missed what River said next.

"I didn't want it finding *me*."

His rush of thoughts ground to a halt, and he gave River a curious look.

If it was as powerful as River said, then anyone would be afraid of the Winter-Wolf, but something in River's voice made Hawk pause. It sounded as though she had the weight of the entire world on her shoulders, and discovery by the Winter-Wolf would cause everything to come crashing down. He wondered again what happened to the Water-Wolves at the beginning of the war, and if it had anything to do with her fear now. His thoughts flitted over all the legends he had heard about the lost children of the Uiscean Marsh.

One legend came to the forefront of his mind, born from the words of King Oak at his last stand.

When the time is right, a savior will appear, sent from the water to wash away the demon filth.

Something stirred deep within Hawk, and words started falling from his jaws, almost unconsciously.

"We all knew the Water-Wolves had disappeared at the beginning of the war. Even the few half-wolves vanished. No one knew what happened…but some believed it was the Water-Wolves that had started the war, and had even…become the demons themselves."

River tensed, but she didn't say anything, so Hawk continued. "But many more believed the Water-Wolves were the only ones who knew how to defeat the demons, which was why they had disappeared. The Water-Wolves, it's said, were either captured or killed by Letorus to prevent the secret from getting out. At the beginning of the war, we believed one day the Water-Wolves would come back and release Soluna from the demons. Even now, there are…some who still believe that. Could it be…that's why you're here?"

"No!" River snarled, her hackles raised. "No, I am not doing anything like that!"

Hawk shivered inwardly at River's fearsome display, but he stood his ground and continued in a quiet voice. "I think you are…and if it's possible…I would like to help."

Startled, River took a step back. Her eyes filled with confusion, but then became wary as she studied the orange Fire-Wolf. "You…would like to help… me?"

He nodded, although he was just as surprised by his offer, but something told Hawk he needed to stay close to the Water-Wolf. "Yes, if you'll have me."

"But why? Why do you want to help me?" River's eyes narrowed and filled with suspicion. "I am a stranger; you shouldn't care what I do."

Hawk paused. He had no real reason, nothing that could be put into words. "Because…no one should have to be alone, not in times like these," Hawk said finally, suddenly struck by a sense of familiarity, as though he had spoken those same words before. It faded quickly.

Surprise clouded River's expression, and for several long moments she was speechless. Hawk shuffled uneasily, unsure of how she would react once she gathered herself.

What if she leaves again? Hawk swallowed but said nothing. River seemed to be waiting for him to take back his words or laugh it off. Pain and suspicion flashed across her eyes, seemingly at odds with each other, but almost immediately disappeared.

"Fine."

River's short answer came as a surprise, but also a relief, to Hawk. The single word carried more weight than it should have and seemed to hang over the room. Hawk swallowed again. He hoped he hadn't just bitten off more than he could swallow.

"But," the blue-gray wolf continued, "you are to respect the fact that I will not tell you about what exactly I'm going to do. All you need to know is that I know how to kill Letorus and that I *will* kill him. The less you know, the safer you'll be."

Hawk's eyes widened in surprise. He had guessed River had a way to defeat the demons, but to go so far as to say she could kill the Demon Overlord himself was almost impossible to believe. Although he very much wanted to ask what her plan was, he respected her demand and simply nodded.

River stared at Hawk for a few more moments, before nodding as well. "Go to sleep. In a few hours we'll set out."

With that, River promptly turned away and settled down to sleep.

Hawk blinked, surprised by the abrupt end of the conversation, but then he yawned and lay down as well.

Have I just traded one danger for another? He yawned again, and his eyelids grew heavy. *Well…at least I don't have to worry about her finding out I'm an escaped slave…she already knows and won't turn me in. But how does she intend to kill Letorus?*

CHAPTER TWELVE

COLD CREPT OVER *Hawk's limbs, freezing his blood and slowing his heart. Fear welled up in him, and he struggled to jump to his paws, to escape the terrible cold. His legs were frozen to the ground, and his jaw was fused together. He couldn't speak, he couldn't move, and he could hardly breathe.*

Wind roared in his ears, and snow rushed by him, tearing through his fur. He closed his eyes, begging to be released from this nightmare.

Suddenly, the wind died, and warmth rushed back into Hawk's body, making him gasp. His heart resumed its beating, and he slowly opened his eyes.

"Greetings, Fire-Wolf," a voice said, echoing in Hawk's mind, sounding like a thousand different wolves and demons, male and female, all speaking at once.

A snowy forest appeared around him, as though summoned by the words, and Hawk scrambled to his paws. "You're...you're the Winter-Wolf." Hawk swallowed hard, keeping his eyes trained on the spirit before him. Without the cloak of the storm, Hawk could clearly see its chosen form, a large white wolf. Its eyes, however, remained the same.

Red and silver.

The Winter-Wolf cocked its head slightly. "So River told you about me?"

"A...a little..." Hawk froze. What if this was the actual Winter-Wolf, and not just some fevered dream created by what River had told him? What if the Winter-Wolf was tracking him, using him to find River?

"Why are you here?" Hawk asked slowly, backing away a few steps from the spirit.

"To reawaken certain memories," the Winter-Wolf said after a pause.

Before Hawk could ask what the Winter-Wolf meant by its words, the spirit tipped its head back and howled. The cry echoed in the frosted trees, reverberating through his ears and mind. He whimpered and crouched, ears flat. He had only heard a howl a few times before, as slaves were forbidden to do so and the free wolves did not want to be discovered by demons, but the Winter-Wolf's haunting melody sounded nothing like a wolf.

Pain exploded in Hawk's head, forcing his eyes shut as some invisible force pounded on his mind. Images flashed in front of him, moving far too fast for him to tell what they were. He caught a few glimpses of unknown wolves and snippets of conversations. Beneath it all, however, was a song.

A howl echoed in his mind, drowning out the howl of the Winter-Wolf. It sounded familiar, although Hawk was certain he had never heard it before. Dozens of unknown sensations rushed through him. The song felt at once fiery and gentle, immobile and flowing. The images suddenly froze, stopping at one of three red moons covering a silver sun.

Then everything began to fade, the howl slowly dying as the images disappeared. The last thing Hawk heard was the ominous message of the Winter-Wolf

"A demon will turn twice before Sun meets Moons and the King is struck down. Then a sacrifice must be made by the earth-born flame, to banish the Dark and free the land."

Chapter Thirteen

"Hawk...Hawk! Wake up, you idiot."

Hawk groggily opened his eyes to discover River scowling down at him. He lurched to his paws, filled with a sudden sense of urgency, forcing River to stumble backward to avoid knocking heads with him.

"Watch it!" River growled, narrowing her eyes.

"I...uh..." Hawk blinked. There was something important he knew, something he had to tell River...but nothing came to mind. The sense of urgency slowly faded, leaving Hawk to wonder why he had jumped up in such a rush in the first place.

River's tail twitched with irritation. "What?"

"Nothing," he said finally.

The she-wolf gave him an unreadable look, but then snorted and turned sharply away.

"Whatever. Now let's go. We have a lot of ground to cover."

"Where are we going?" Hawk asked, quickly following after her.

"The Dorasca Gorge, to find your pack," she said as she slipped through the cavern's entrance. "You still need to meet up with them so they know you're not dead in a river somewhere, and I need more information. If you can't even find your way to the *Dorasca Gorge* I doubt you could steer us away from the fortresses."

Hawk laughed a little weakly. "I've only been in Taladair for a few months..."

"Thought as much," the she-wolf said with a sigh. As she turned away, Hawk caught a glimpse of her injured shoulder and stopped.

No wound marked her fur.

How did it heal so fast? He opened his mouth to ask her about it, but cut himself off, not wanting to irritate her more.

Chapter Fourteen

After hours of mostly silent travel, River finally called for a halt. It was a little after noon, and Hawk's paws throbbed. He sank to the ground, thankful for the chance to rest, only to be dragged back up by his companion. "Ouch! What was that for?"

River just rolled her eyes. "You should be *used* to this sort of thing, with all the work you did as a slave."

"I wasn't a work-slave...I just carried water out to them..."

The she-wolf gave him a nonplussed look. "Figures. Now do you want to eat or what?"

Immediately perking up, Hawk wagged his tail and asked, "You're going to hunt now?"

"No, *you're* going to."

Hawk's tail lowered. "But...I don't know how to hunt."

Very few slaves at Ignimor Fortress could hunt. The demons preferred to keep the slaves completely reliant on the protection and care of their masters. A slave who could hunt was a slave who could fend for himself and thus had the potential for rebellion.

The Water-Wolf showed no sympathy for his situation. "Have you even *tried* to hunt?"

When Hawk shook his head, River simply sat down and said, "Then go try. Rely on your instincts."

Then she melted into snow and vanished.

Hawk stared at the spot River had occupied just moments ago. *Now what?* With the resistance, there had always been someone to trade duties with, always someone who wanted to get out of something and who would rather be out hunting, but now River wanted him to use his instincts.

Maybe I can just wait for River to come back, and beg her to share her prey with me... The image of River giving him a scornful look floated across his mind's eye. He could almost hear her calling him *pathetic*.

Gritting his teeth, Hawk flattened his ears and growled. "I will *not* give River another excuse to call me weak! I *will* catch myself some prey, and I *won't* let her have any!"

Proud of his outburst, Hawk strode off through the trees. He only got a few paces before he was faced with several problems.

How am I supposed to look for prey? How am I supposed to chase it down and kill it? What if I get lost? How will I find River? He took a deep breath, trying to keep his thoughts from taking over and making him panic. *I won't get lost; all I have to do is follow my paw prints. And…and if I sniff around long enough, I should find something…I'll worry about how to kill it when I need to.*

Closing his eyes, Hawk inhaled deeply through his nose, sorting through the vast array of scents assaulting him. It took him several minutes to make sense of the disorienting mass of smells, and even longer until he could begin to pick them apart and label them.

The freshly fallen snow…the sharp pine needles…and the gooey sap of the trees around him. Hawk pushed past them, trying to find even a trace of prey.

A faint smell ghosted across his senses, something that smelled familiar. It smelled like the forest, but alive and moving —it smelled like the hare River had given him yesterday.

Prey!

Hawk opened his eyes and licked his lips. *Now I'll show River that I'm not weak!*

Keeping his steps light, Hawk slowly followed the scent, growing more excited as the scent grew stronger and he got closer to his prey.

Soon Hawk was able to see the hare. It was crouched at the base of a tree, its white hide rendering it nearly invisible against the snow. Hawk crept forward on silent paws, focused only on the prey before him. He crouched, ready to spring and attack the hare, when it suddenly stood up straight, nose quivering. It turned and looked right at Hawk before dashing away through the snow. Hawk growled and darted after it, but was forced to stop after a few strides when the hare disappeared into the whiteness.

Panting, Hawk stared hungrily in the direction the hare had gone. It would be pointless to track the hare again, not with his meager skills. He sniffed around for more prey but found nothing.

Hawk sighed and turned back to follow his trail through the trees. He would have to wait for River to return and ask her to share her prey.

Now how am I supposed to face River? I tried to hunt, but the stupid hare scented me. Why do hares have to be so fast? If I were a Wind-Wolf, I bet I could have caught it. Suddenly Hawk stopped, whining a little.

Sparrow...

By now Hawk had given up all hope of her being alive. She was an excellent tracker, and if she had escaped the patrol she should have found him already.

And it's my fault she's dead...how am I going to explain that to Coal? First Meadow, then Sparrow...he's lost two of his second-in-commands in a little less than a week! Worse...how am I going to explain it to Eagle? He'll kill me for getting his mate killed!

A muffled voice startled Hawk out of his thoughts, making him jump.

"What took you so long? You get lost?"

Hawk whirled around to see River standing behind him with a white rabbit in her mouth. His stomach growled at the sight of food, and he hung his head. "No...I couldn't catch anything."

To his surprise, River gave a short laugh, her eyes glittering with amusement. "I didn't think you could. I just wanted to see if you would actually *try* to hunt."

"So I went chasing after that rabbit for *nothing*?" Hawk's tail fell, and he gave River a look of exasperation.

"Not for nothing. You showed spine. If you had simply refused to hunt and instead begged me to do it for you, I would have deserted you right then and there. I now know that you are willing to *try* and you *do* actually have a scrap of bravery, which is what you're going to need if you're going to travel with me." She brushed by him, heading back to where they had stopped earlier. "Now come on."

She just wanted to see if I had any courage? Hunting doesn't take a lot of 'spine'...maybe she wanted to see if I would try to prove her wrong? He eyed the she-wolf, flattening his ears a little.

Any other thought Hawk might have had on the topic disappeared when he found a large hare waiting for him back at their temporary camp. Ignoring River's eye-roll and muttered *'airheaded wolf,'* Hawk pounced on the hare, eagerly sinking his teeth into the prey.

It probably would have tasted better if I caught it...maybe River can teach me next time. Hawk's tail thumped the ground a few times. He was simply glad to have something to eat.

"Do you know where your group's hideout is?" River asked suddenly, tearing off a piece of her hare.

Hawk winced slightly. "No, I don't. At least, not *exactly*. I *do* know that it's located somewhere in the northern part of the Dorasca Gorge, but maybe a day or so north of the Lough Tost. If we can get close, then I'm sure that we can find Coal and the others."

"Humph, well I hope you're right. I'd rather avoid any demon fortress at all costs." River paused, narrowing her eyes in thought. "Depending on where the hideout is, it'll probably take us several days to go around the gorge…"

"Oh, Coal can get across the gorge."

The she-wolf's eyes snapped up. "What?"

"Um…Coal knows how to cross the Dorasca Gorge…" Hawk looked away, the intensity of River's gaze unnerving him. "I know he's crossed the gorge before…I don't know how, but I think the Earth-Wolves in our group have something to do with it."

"How…interesting…I've never heard of a wolf being able to go straight across the Dorasca. It's a mile across at its widest." River turned her gaze away from Hawk, fixing her sight at some point between her paws.

"Well…that's just what Sparrow told me…" Hawk trailed off. He really wanted to know why she wanted to cross the Dorasca and where they would be going, but he was afraid River would get angry at his prying.

Finally, he ventured a quiet question. "Why do we need to cross?"

Instead of a sharp reply like he was expecting, River simply flicked her ears and said, "To get to Lough Domhgeal."

Lough Domhgeal? Hawk had heard all sorts of stories about Lough Domhgeal and the other three Lakes of Moon and Sun. Each nation contained a sacred lake, and in the times before the war they served as the places where the nations' leaders could communicate with Sun-Wolf and Moon-Wolf. The lakes were each guarded by ancient magic, and anyone not approved by the gods was forbidden from entry. Lough Domhgeal itself was at the center of the Crétioll, a massive underground labyrinth. Letorus lost hundreds of his demons there when he tried to invade it, right after Oak's Last Stand.

Hawk sent River a wary glance out of the corner of his eye. *What could she possibly need to do there? She couldn't be thinking of actually entering the Crétioll…could she?*

"B-but…you c-can't…only the Earth-Wolf Monarchs…" Hawk stammered, trying to come up with some reason why River could possibly want to go to Lough Domhgeal.

"I *have* to."

A dozen more questions clouded Hawk's mind, but he sensed that River wasn't going to elaborate further and kept his jaws shut.

She must have some sort of plan... He glanced at River again but could determine nothing from her expression.

"Cover your kill," River suddenly said and stood. "We still have a ways to go. It'll take us at least another day to reach the Dorasca Gorge, and Moon-Wolf knows how long it will take us to find your resistance group."

Hawk bit back a groan. His paws ached just thinking about how far River would push them until sundown, if she even decided to stop then. He wouldn't put it past her to continue until the moons were high in the sky.

Under the impatient glare of River, Hawk quickly covered the remains of his hare and set out into the forest. Silence fell over them once more, and the hours slowly ticked by. They met only a few animals, who blinked curiously at them as they passed.

As it got close to sunset, and Hawk started to think about asking River to stop for the night, the forest suddenly fell silent. Even the small noises of forest creatures and the slight rustling of the wind through the branches stopped. Hawk, not taking any notice of the eerie silence, continued walking until River lunged forward, sank her teeth into the scruff of his neck, and dragged him back.

"River, what...?" Hawk stumbled, trying to stay on his paws, but stopped when he glanced back and caught the she-wolf's glare, which seemed to say *'speak and I will rip your fur off.'* He swallowed his words.

Then a cold feeling washed over him, seeping into his bones and freezing his blood. Heart racing, Hawk tried to ask River what was happening, but his tongue felt heavy and useless in his jaws. The ground suddenly rose up to meet him, and his vision fractured.

Hawk could see the forest around him from a thousand different angles, all at once. His heart nearly stopped. He couldn't feel anything, he couldn't move, it was as though he had become nothing more than a ghost.

"Don't panic, keep calm or the spell will break and you will reform."

If he had a body to use, Hawk would have fainted at the sound of River's voice whispering in his head.

"River?! Where...what happened?" Hawk asked, surprised to find that he could communicate as well.

"I sensed a demon nearby, a very strong, very powerful demon."

Hawk paused, surprised. He had sensed no demon before becoming...like he was now, and although his other survival skills were weak at best, Hawk knew he could sense a demon almost as well as Coal. And if it was a demon strong enough to make River want to hide, then Hawk should definitely have sensed it.

He was so caught up in his thoughts he nearly missed River's next words, which made what little feeling Hawk had left in his insubstantial body drain away.

"...and it is alone."

That scared Hawk more than a patrol of demons ever would. Demons never hunted alone. Even Blood-Frenzies, who were second only to the Demon Overlord Letorus himself, traveled in a group. If this demon was alone, then either Letorus stalked the forest, or it was a demon just as powerful and evil.

"We melted into snow," River continued, seemingly oblivious to Hawk's terror. "Hopefully the demon will not sense us."

Hawk's fear turned to confusion. Melting into snow was something only Water-Wolves could do, so how did River manage to make Hawk melt with her? As a Fire-Wolf, he might be able to turn into flames if he tried long enough, but turning into water went against everything a Fire-Wolf was.

"I used my power to overcome yours and force you to melt," River added, knowing Hawk's next question.

Hawk suddenly realized how exhausted River sounded, even through her mind-voice. Channeling her power into him had to have taken a lot of effort in order to overcome the barriers between fire and water.

Just how bad is this demon to make River this...I'd almost call it scared, but River never gets scared...

Suddenly Hawk felt even colder than he had before. Fear crept into his heart and sent it racing like a desert hare. Something utterly evil and impossibly strong was coming, and all Hawk could think was to get out of there right now. Somewhere in the back of his mind he knew he was only feeling the effects of the aura of fear demons often exerted, but he couldn't keep his terror from rising.

Hawk lost all coherent thought when the demon itself came into view.

An enormous Earth-Wolf-like creature appeared in Hawk's fragmented vision. Its long, thick tail was held curled up over its back. The demon had dark red fur and a large black mask-like patch over its face, shaped so it looked like a pair of giant red eyes staring straight at Hawk. The small voice in his head assuring him it was only a trick of the patch's design was drowned out by the rest of his mind screaming in terror, certain that the demon could see him. The snow crunched under heavy paws, which looked as though they could easily crush the life of a terrified Fire-Wolf. The demon's claws glinted at Hawk, sending visions of razor-sharp talons tearing his fur through his head.

Hawk's mind went blank with terror as the demon drew closer, until the creature was only a few feet away. He had to get away; he had to escape this horror, even if it meant getting caught by another patrol. Anything would be better than facing the monster before him. In his fear, Hawk started to reform, his vision slowly solidifying as his body tried to pull itself together and run from the demon.

The demon stopped, sensing another presence. It tilted its head a little, its ears swiveling around to listen carefully. Slowly, it started to turn its head toward Hawk, and the aura of fear sent out by the demon increased until Hawk could feel it physically weighing down on his mind, crushing him beneath it. He could hardly breathe with the pressure…

"Hawk!" River's strained voice screamed his name in his mind, and he was startled to his senses. He stopped reforming, and the snow quickly settled. The demon bared its teeth in a silent snarl. Hawk knew it was angry to have lost the scent of its prey.

Hawk watched, silently struggling to stop himself from panicking again, as the demon turned and stalked away. Long minutes passed before the aura of fear the demon carried vanished; it lingered even after the creature itself was gone. Life returned to the forest, as though it was releasing a long-held breath, but River and Hawk remained in their melted state for a few more minutes.

Finally, the feeling of coldness left Hawk, and suddenly he was sprawled in the snow, the chill of the ground creeping through his fur. He panted and lurched to his paws. His legs shook and his head pounded. Although he had not exerted any kind of energy in his melted-water state, the fear caused by the demon and the water magic used to melt him had worn him down, leaving him exhausted.

River was worse off; she looked like she had run all the way to the sun and back. Water darkened her pelt, and her thick fur clung to her skin, making her look thin and frail. Her sides heaved as she struggled for breath.

"Are…are you okay?" Hawk asked.

"Of course not!" she snapped. "You think it's easy—" River cut herself off with a gasp, her head falling back on her paws. Her eyes clenched shut. "I used…too much power…melting you. I…can't…travel…like this."

Hawk's eyes darted nervously around the snowy forest. The demon was gone, but there was no telling if there were any patrols in the area. They had to find shelter.

"Need water."

"Wh-what?"

River gave a quiet growl. "I need…to recover…my magic. I need…water."

"I could…I could try melting the snow?" Hawk said, not sure what River was asking of him.

"It's not…real water, you idiot. I need…running water…like…" River trailed off, her breaths becoming shorter and more rapid. Hawk's chest tightened. He had once seen Eagle in a similar state after a particularly long battle. Eagle had nearly died because he used up most of his magic.

Running water… Realization hit Hawk. Sparrow had rushed Eagle off somewhere, but when they returned his magic had returned. She had claimed she found the Wind for him. "Like a river?"

River nodded weakly. "Source…of magic…"

She fell silent again. Hawk stood for a few moments, staring down at her and shivering slightly, still uncertain as to what to do. The sound of branches cracking startled him out of his stupor, but when he looked up it was only a small bird fluttering in the tree above.

Can't stay here. Hawk looked around again before taking a step toward River and nudging her a little. "Can you stand?"

Several moments passed before River gave any sign of hearing him. She growled and shifted. Her legs shook as she struggled to her paws. Hawk jumped forward to catch her on her shoulder when she fell.

"Where's the river?" Hawk asked. When River didn't answer, he glanced at her out of the corner of his eye. She was breathing heavily and had her eyes closed. It probably took all of her energy just to stand.

"I guess…I have to guide us…" Hawk swallowed nervously. It was up to him to get them through the forest safely. "There has to be a river nearby, right?"

His companion didn't answer.

CHAPTER FIFTEEN

HAWK STUMBLED THROUGH the quiet forest, half-dragging River after him, for hours. At first, the slow pace wasn't too much of a concern. With River's magic still flowing through him Hawk didn't leave behind any pawprints. The longer they walked, however, the hotter Hawk's body got, and soon a trail of melted snow followed them.

And they had yet to find running water, with River growing weaker with each step.

Just what was that demon, to make River do something like this? Hawk barely saw the way ahead, so focused was he on keeping his companion upright. *She had no problems fighting the other demons, but that one she wanted to avoid at all costs.*

Suddenly the ground disappeared beneath Hawk's paws, and, with a cry of surprise, both he and River fell into a crack in the earth. He slid down a steep slope, turning head over tail several times before slamming into a large stone. The impact drove the breath from his chest and caused him to see stars.

River. Trying to ignore his spinning head, Hawk rolled over and stumbled to his paws. River lay a few lengths away, having been lucky enough to miss the encounter with the stone. Hawk limped over to her, his body aching from the fall, and gave her a quick sniff. With her breathing so slight it barely moved her flanks, Hawk would have thought her dead if not for her scent.

Hawk glanced up at the slope behind him. It was almost vertical, and would be impossible to climb. *We're stuck here.*

Panic threatening to overtake his mind, Hawk turned away from the slope and looked around the narrow, dark cavern he found himself in. *There has to be another way out. There* has *to be.*

He didn't know what he would do if there was none.

A little of his panic faded when Hawk spotted a crack in the wall opposite of him. With one last glance at River, he hurried over and peered through. He thought he spotted a small spot of light on the other side. Hoping it would lead back to the ground above, Hawk squeezed through the crack. He stumbled out into another dark room, his eyes fixed on the soft green glow before him.

Please be something that can help us, Hawk said silently, carefully making his way across the room to the point of light. He had no idea what a light could possibly do for him in his situation, but he couldn't think of what else to do.

His nose brushed against the smooth surface of a gem before the green light suddenly intensified. Hawk jumped back, blinded and startled as the room was filled with light. Still blinking, his eyes struggling to adjust to the sudden brightness, Hawk spun around and ran back to the crack, only to find it had disappeared. Terror shot through him.

What did I do?

Faint voices reached his ears, and Hawk froze, eyes wide. The voices slowly grew louder, but Hawk couldn't tell where they were coming from. They seemed to be all around him.

"... awakened..."

"...her return...our vision..."

"... second coming...could only mean..."

His heart pounding, Hawk turned back and searched the blinding whiteness around him. Several silhouettes appeared, vaguely wolf-shaped, and moved closer to Hawk, who stood petrified. The shapes flitted around him, as though inspecting him. Hawk swallowed hard, his eyes darting around and searching desperately for a way to escape.

One shape stopped in front of Hawk. Its form slowly became more distinct, until Hawk could identify it as Earth-Wolf. A pair of ancient green eyes looked down at him, but seemed to stare straight through him. The rest of the figures stopped their circling. Hawk felt a dozen invisible eyes boring into his pelt.

"Wh-who are you?" he asked, his legs shaking.

"I am the first King of the Earth-Wolves," came the reply, the rumbling voice echoing in Hawk's mind. *"My name I have forgotten, but I have long awaited your arrival, my son."*

Hawk gasped. The first king lived thousands of years ago. How had his spirit survived until now? He nervously looked around at the other shapes. "Who are they?"

"Those sworn to serve me, even after death." The spirits circling Hawk stirred, muttering indistinctly. The Earth King tilted his head slightly. *"How have you come to disturb our slumber?"*

River! Hawk shot a look over his shoulder, hoping to see the crack again, but the line of spirits blocked his view. He turned back to the Earth King. "I...

River and I were traveling through the forest, going to the Dorasca Gorge, when we came across this really powerful demon. It…It scared River so badly that she had to use most of her magic so I have to find a river or something so she can recover but then we fell and–"

"Do not fear, Hawk, we are here to guide you," the Earth King interrupted with a little amusement. *"The Island fell because we failed to unite against our enemy. You must have the strength to bring every wolf together. We will help guide you on your journey."*

The room grew even brighter, until Hawk had to close his eyes to shield them from the glare. The spirits around him raised their voices in a howl, their haunting song shaking him to his core.

Howls ringing in his ears, blackness stole over Hawk's mind. He fell to the floor, his legs crumpling beneath him as he lost consciousness. The last thing he heard was the Earth King's voice saying in his mind.

"Troubled times are ahead. Have faith in yourself and you will emerge victorious. Stay close to your friend, and do not let her go."

Chapter Sixteen

HAWK'S EYES SNAPPED open. The blurred image before him slowly sharpened into a snowy forest. Confused, Hawk rolled over and lurched to his paws.

How did I get here? He looked around and could see no sign of the Earth King and his companions. River lay next to him, her sides rising in deep, even breaths. Hawk breathed a sigh of relief. *At least she's okay…but what happened?*

A streak of brown, a stark contrast against the white snow, behind River caught Hawk's eye. He cautiously padded over, noting the tangle of pawprints leading to it. One set was a clear trail of melted snow, while the other consisted of long furrows, as though something had been dragged across the ground. Hawk stopped just in front of the streak and discovered it to be a long fault in the earth, filled in with dirt and rock. He glanced over at the tracks, which ended at the edge of the fault.

This has *to be where we fell…there aren't any more tracks around the crack.*

A growl from River brought him out of his thoughts. He turned around to see her dragging herself to her paws.

"River! Are you okay?" he hurried over to his companion, his confusion temporarily overridden by his concern.

The Water-Wolf growled again and glared at him. "Where are we? What happened? My magic has returned, but I see no running water."

Quickly Hawk told her about how they fell through a crack in the earth and his encounter with the Earth King. He glanced back at the line of dirt behind him and added, "I think that's where we fell…our tracks lead right to it, but it's all filled in."

Narrowing her eyes, River stalked past him to inspect the crack. "This looks like it was filled in seasons ago. But I can sense a faint power emanating from it…there is old magic at work here."

"How…how can you tell?" Hawk tilted his head slightly. He felt nothing out of the ordinary about the crack.

"Every wolf should be able to sense magic, how else are you supposed to use your own if you can't even feel it?" River shook her head. "Doesn't matter, I doubt the demons spend much time teaching their slaves how to use magic.

Somehow your presence awakened the spirits below. But why *you*? You're not even an Earth-Wolf."

She gave Hawk an intense stare, making him shuffle a little uncomfortably. Finally she looked away and dropped the subject.

"Well, come on then. We won't make it in time to talk with Coal if we don't start moving."

The pair walked in silence for some time, each wrapped up in their own thoughts. Hawk, when he wasn't thinking about when they would stop and eat, tried to figure out the meaning behind the Earth King's words. Every so often he would sneak a quick glance back at River, wondering if she was thinking about what the Earth King had said.

River pushed them at a blistering pace with few breaks. Even when a blizzard descended upon the forest once more, the she-wolf only scowled up at the dark sky and continued on. The storm, although it made the journey difficult, served to shield them from any other travelers, demon or otherwise.

Finally, after five days of almost nonstop travel, they reached the Dorasca Gorge.

Chapter Seventeen

With the setting sun, the Dorasca Gorge itself was cast into darkness. Hawk peered nervously over the edge, wondering just how deep it was.

It looks like it could go straight to the center of the world. Legend says it was created by an Earth-Wolf during some big battle ages ago…but how could a single wolf have the power to cause something this…big?

He flattened his ears and eyed the tree line behind them. The forest stopped several dozen feet from the gorge itself, leaving them very exposed. Hawk turned his gaze back to River, who, although a little tense, gave no sign of sensing any unwanted watchers.

"Where do you think Coal will be?" River asked.

"Knowing him, he probably found a way to actually hide *in* the gorge, and he used Canyon or one of the other Earth-Wolves to make a cave in the gorge walls." Hawk paused. "I don't know how he'd get *down* there…or how we'd know where, exactly, he is…"

"Then we'll just have to try and catch their scent."

River immediately turned to walk along the edge of the Gorge, her nose to the ground as she searched for some sign that would alert them to the resistance group's presence. Hawk bounded after her. "I don't think that will work. Coal's really good at covering his tracks; he can even cover his own scent."

"Are you doubting me?" River asked, turning slightly to bare her fangs. "Do remember that snow is part of *my* element. Coal may be able to throw a demon off his scent but he won't fool a Water-Wolf's senses."

Thoroughly chastised, Hawk turned to search in the opposite direction, hoping to at least look helpful. He wasn't any good at tracking, especially in the snow, but he might be able to spot some kind of sign. If Coal and the others were still around, which was doubtful, and if Coal still thought that Hawk was alive and actually thought it important to wait for him, which was even more doubtful, then he would have left behind something to let Hawk know where to go. It was most likely going to be a dead coal, or a palm branch carved into the ground, something that would symbolize one of the pack members.

He nearly jumped off the cliff's edge when the ground in front of him rumbled. He jumped back, and a large fissure opened up in the earth. Heart racing, Hawk was about to call to River for help when Palm, a pale green Earth-Wolf male, emerged from the crack.

"Hawk?" he said curiously as the crack closed behind him. Suspicion darkened his gaze. "Is that you?"

Hawk's muzzle parted in a toothy grin. "It's me! I made it!"

Relief flooded Palm's eyes, and he wagged his tail. "I can't believe it…you found us. Coal was about to give up on you returning."

"I can't believe *you're* here…I mean, I hoped you'd wait, but I was certain Coal would have left days ago."

"Sparrow convinced him to wait until the second full moon to leave. She was certain that you would make it."

Hawk gasped, hardly daring to believe what he had heard. "Sparrow… Sparrow made it?"

Palm nodded. "Yes, she arrived just two days ago. We were surprised she managed to find the hideout at all. When we found her wandering along the edge of the Dorasca, she was in shock, completely delirious from loss of blood." The Earth-Wolf winced, and added, "Oh, and you might want to avoid Eagle. He was furious when he saw the state that Sparrow was in…and he immediately blamed you."

I kind of figured that, Hawk thought with a flinch. *He has every reason to believe it was my fault — because it* was *my fault that the patrol found us in the first place — but at least Sparrow's alive.*

"Let's get back to camp, before Coal starts thinking I was killed on patrol," Palm said, half-jokingly.

Hawk wagged his tail a little. The resistance group leader was nothing if not paranoid. He assumed the worst if a member was even a minute late from patrol. "Wait, I need to go get my friend…"

"You have a—" Palm was suddenly cut off by a large shape barreling into him, knocking him off his paws. Hawk stood motionless, stunned by the sight of River pinning down the Earth-Wolf, her eyes dark with fury and bloodlust. Palm looked equally surprised, and his shock only deepened when he saw the wave breed mark on River's left shoulder. "Water…Wolf?" he gasped.

River bared her fangs and snarled, and suddenly Hawk got the feeling that if he didn't step in now, Palm was going to die. He hesitated a moment longer, fearing that he would end up getting killed if he got between River and her target. Pushing that thought aside, he jumped forward and tried to push River off of Palm. "River! Stop! He's a friend; he's not a demon!"

River glared at Hawk, then looked more closely at Palm, who shrank away from her gaze, shivering. Finally, after what seemed like years to Hawk, River let Palm up, who quickly scrambled to his paws and jumped away from her. With a wary eye on the she-wolf, who returned his look with an icy stare, Palm muttered, "*This* is your *friend*?"

Hawk nodded and whispered back. "She needs to speak with Coal."

"I can hear you." River's stare turned to one of annoyance, and Palm flinched.

Turning quickly, Palm stepped onto a nearly invisible path on the side of the cliff. Hawk blinked. He had never seen the usually impassive wolf so rattled.

Then again, I've never seen anyone able to bring Palm down so easily. Although...I can't really blame him...I think even Coal would falter when faced with the full fury of River's anger, and Palm only felt a small fraction of it.

"This way, then." Palm glanced back at River before adding to Hawk in an undertone, "Mountains are going to crack when she meets Coal, you know."

"I heard that too," River snapped, making Palm jump. He wasted no more time in continuing down the path, but Hawk hesitated, glancing at River out of the corner of his eye. Something about her tone didn't seem right.

If Hawk didn't know better, he would have said she sounded afraid.

Hawk quickly looked away and followed after Palm. The mere thought of River being afraid of anything was akin to saying an Earth-Wolf could fly. River feared nothing and no one, that much Hawk had surmised from the short time he had known her.

As they went deeper into the Dorasca Gorge and darkness closed around them, Hawk kept looking back at River. Her eyes darted everywhere and her entire body was tense, as if she was waiting for something to jump out at her from the shadows. She looked ready to fight for her life at any moment.

Before he could stop himself, Hawk turned back to ask quietly, "River, are you okay?"

River snarled, her hackles bristling. "I'm fine!"

Despite her claim, Hawk could see the fear clear in her eyes and hear it in the forced tone of her voice. *She really is scared of something...but what? She's faced down Night-Lynxes and Ice-Fangs without a problem...so what could possibly be so bad it scares* River?

Hawk, on the other paw, felt strangely at home, even though the ledge they were walking on was so thin the slightest misstep would send him plunging into the darkness below. Palm, too, seemed to have calmed down now that he was surrounded by earth and gravel. At least, he wasn't trembling anymore from River's assault.

Finally, they reached the camp. A large hollow had been carved into the wall of the gorge, and was so cleverly hidden that Hawk didn't realize they were at the camp until he stepped into the hollow itself. Even the light of the fire was shielded from view by a thick veil of vines with only a few gaps to allow broken wisps of smoke to escape. After he and River left the path, a boulder silently slid into place, effectively sealing off the camp.

Hawk's tail wagged as he looked around and saw the familiar camp activities taking place. Coal was stoking up the fire, while Eagle and Canyon buried the remains of the group's meal. The rest appeared to be settling down for the night, and Hawk was overjoyed to see Sparrow among them. Palm padded over to Coal and whispered something in his ear. The dark blue Fire-Wolf looked up and glanced at Hawk before moving on to stare at River. His eyes fell to her shoulder, and his usually emotionless eyes lit up with surprise. He stood, directing his full attention to Hawk and River.

Almost immediately, the camp fell silent, and Hawk became uncomfortably aware of the stares they received, although River appeared not to notice. Instead, she had locked eyes with Coal, stormy navy-blue meeting cold red. The tension in the air thickened as the two continued to glare at each other. A few of the wolves shuffled nervously, and Hawk tensed, uncertain how he should step in.

"Hawk!"

The tension shattered with Sparrow's shout, causing everyone to heave silent sighs of relief. Sparrow hobbled over to Hawk, grinning lopsidedly. Horror coursed through him when he saw the cloudy gray Wind-Wolf. The cut on her snout had healed, but many worse wounds had taken its place.

Several ragged slashes ran down the right side of her face, two covering her right eye, which was swollen and crusted shut from blood, and three cutting across her cheek, which drew her lips back in a perpetual snarl. But what gave Hawk the most dismay was Sparrow's wounded paw. It looked like it had been broken in several places, and Hawk wouldn't have been surprised if the bones had been shattered. As it was, her front right paw was bent into an unnatural shape, twisted and grotesquely contorted.

He feared she would never be able to walk on that paw again.

"I know I look horrible, but they don't hurt as bad as they look," Sparrow said when she noticed Hawk staring at her wounds. "I won't be able to see out of my right eye again, and my paw's out of commission as well." Although Sparrow spoke in a carefree tone, Hawk knew that the loss of her paw hurt her the most. To a Wind-Wolf, being able to run freely was everything. There was nothing more pitiable than a lame Wind-Wolf. Hawk was surprised that Sparrow was allowed to stay in Coal's pack: Coal hated to have wolves who would pose a risk to them. Sparrow must have somehow convinced Coal that she was still able to keep up. "Quite frankly," Sparrow continued, "I don't know how I survived that battle. I was *so* sure that I was going to be killed, but I just kept thinking that I had to survive long enough to give you a chance to escape."

Hawk looked down sorrowfully, and muttered an apology. It was his fault that Sparrow ended up like this, if he had only been able to fight, he could have helped Sparrow. Guilt tightened his chest; he hated that his own weakness had forced Sparrow to sacrifice so much. Feeling an icy glare boring into him, Hawk knew that Eagle thought the same.

Sparrow shook her head. "No, no, don't worry about it. What counts is that I'm alive and kicking."

Coal butted in before Sparrow could say more. "Yes, we all can see that you're alive. What I would like to know is why you brought *her* here."

With a jolt, Hawk remembered River was still standing just behind him. He glanced out of the corner of his eye and found the Water-Wolf looking very annoyed. Swallowing a little nervously, Hawk swept his tail toward River. "This is River…and she needs your help."

River shot Hawk a murderous look for admitting that she needed 'help.' Hawk flinched and returned an apologetic glance before turning back to Coal. The dark blue Fire-Wolf studied River for a moment with impassive red eyes. "No."

Shocked, Hawk broke form and protested, "What do you mean, 'no'? All we need is to know where the demon fortresses are located. Can't you help with that?"

Coal bared his fangs and snarled. "No, I will not help that *creature* with anything. I do not trust her. How do I know she isn't on the side of the demons, if not a demon herself?"

Hawk shrank back, curling his tail between his legs.

"Very well then." All eyes snapped to River at the sound of her icy voice. Ignoring their gazes, she turned sharply and stalked back to the boulder blocking the entrance. Granite, who happened to be nearest, stepped forward to remove the rock, but a glare from River stopped him in his tracks. River threw her weight against the boulder, and it slipped from the ledge it was perched on. Granite and Canyon rushed to halt its descent as River disappeared into the gloom beyond the campfire.

"River, wait!" Hawk shouted in dismay as he raced after her without a second thought. He tore up the narrow path leading down to camp and was quickly swallowed by the darkness of the gorge.

Chapter Eighteen

Silence filled the camp as all eyes turned to Coal, who only glanced over to Granite and Canyon to say, "Replace the boulder."

The two Earth-Wolves sent each other an uncertain look before nodding. The rock slid back into place with a sort of finality. Coal said nothing more, and returned to sit silently in front of the fire.

Sparrow limped over to Coal and sat down beside him. "Don't you think that was a little hasty of you?"

"No, that she-wolf will only bring trouble. She felt like a demon."

The she-wolf only snorted, prompting a glare from her companion. He knew what she was thinking. Coal was unusually sensitive to the presence of demons, but his paranoia often led him to the wrong conclusions. It wouldn't be the first time he mistook a wolf for a demon because of his 'senses.'

"How are we to know she isn't one in disguise?" he continued, ignoring Sparrow's skepticism. "Everyone knows the Water-Wolves were killed at the beginning of the war. How could one still be alive?"

"Well, obviously they weren't. And River is no demon, I can assure you. She came with *Hawk*."

Coal gave his second-in-command a long look before growling quietly, "A Noxond would find it simple to disguise itself and fool that pup." He paused and flicked his ears at the muffled sound of a shout echoing somewhere in the gorge, but Sparrow never looked away from him.

"Then look at her eyes if nothing else will convince you," she said in exasperation. "Not even Letorus himself would be able to disguise his eyes, and River has the eyes of a Wolf."

"Still, I have no reason to trust her, nor do I have any reason to help her."

"Then don't trust her. Trust me." At Coal's narrowed eyes, she amended herself: "Trust Hawk." When the dark blue Fire-Wolf said nothing, Sparrow pushed on. "Help the Water-Wolf for Hawk. And remember what I said before, Coal. *This is supposed to happen.*"

Coal's silence continued for a few minutes as he stared impassively at the flames. Around them, the camp had returned to its normal routine, ignoring the hushed conversation occurring between its two leaders. "Fine."

Chapter Nineteen

Hawk had gone several lengths down the path before sliding to a halt, sudden realizations crashing down on him.

The sun had long since set.

The campfire's light didn't extend beyond the hollow.

It was dark.

Hawk strained his eyes, struggling to see anything past his nose. *I'm fine...I'll just summon a flame...it's no big deal. I should be worrying about River...did she make it to the top? What if she fell? She was so...on edge before...what if she panicked?*

Worry clouding his mind, Hawk quickly summoned a flame to hover just by his ear and hurried up the path. Suddenly a shape loomed out of the shadows, nearly sending Hawk right over the edge in his fright. He scrambled back a few steps, biting back his startled yelp.

River! Relief flooded his body, only to be quickly replaced by confusion. The she-wolf stood in the middle of the path, her entire body tense, and she had yet to notice Hawk. Her sides heaved, and there was a wild look reflected in her dark eyes.

"River...?" Hawk lowered his head and padded a few steps closer. River immediately whipped around, spinning on her hindpaws, and launched herself at him. Both wolves were knocked to the ground, almost rolling right off the edge. Hawk's heart leapt into his throat, and his blood burned when he saw the crazed look in River's eyes. His flame flickered, casting part of River's face into darkness, and he barely managed to keep it from going out. He didn't want to be left alone in the darkness with the raving Water-Wolf.

"River! It's just me!" The she-wolf only snarled and bared her teeth.

She's going to kill me! Panic surged through Hawk when the she-wolf tensed, and he squirmed to try and escape her hold on him.

"River!"

The echo of his shout seemed to stop River — or at least make her hesitate in her attack. Several long, tense moments passed with River's fangs poised over Hawk's throat. Hawk hardly dared to breathe for fear of breaking the tension. Finally, River blinked, and the haze of fury and fear masking her eyes slowly faded. She relaxed slightly and stepped back, confusion clouding her face. Hawk scrambled to his paws but stayed low to the ground, his ears flat and his tail between his legs. "Are…you…okay?"

River kept her eyes fixed on the ground between her paws, her legs shaking. A shadow of some unknown emotion passed across her face. When she spoke, Hawk could barely hear her voice, and he was shocked to hear the fear in her words. "Can we get out of here?"

Hawk blinked and slowly stood, but River didn't move. "S-sure…" He slid around her, carefully avoiding the edge of the path, to lead the way. River followed him, her eyes still cast downward.

The few minutes it took them to reach the end of the hidden trail felt like years to Hawk, who kept glancing back at River, unnerved by the way she was acting. He put out his hovering flame at the top, as the stars and the moons gave them enough light to see by.

A thump made him turn around. River had collapsed on the ground behind him, a few paces away from the path itself, her eyes closed in relief. The Fire-Wolf shuffled uncertainly, eyeing the Water-Wolf. In the short time he had known her, he had never seen her so scared, not even when he had mentioned the Winter-Wolf for the first time.

He didn't think he had ever really seen her scared at all.

"Um, River?" Hawk crept forward a few steps, not sure what kind of reaction his question would get, but unwilling to let his companion lie alone in fear. "Are you okay?"

Instead of a sharp reply, River merely nodded. Hawk couldn't help staring at her in shock. *What is it about the Dorasca Gorge that scares River so much?* "My brother," she said in a low voice, "was killed by…a thing like this."

What does that mean? Hawk, although dying to ask, didn't push her to elaborate. He only sat down beside her and listened as she continued.

"My mother…too…and many others of my…family. It was so dark in that place… We lived in fear…everyday… We never knew if they were…going to kill us… We were never safe."

Wherever the Water-Wolves were, it sounded as if they were being trapped by someone…or something… Hawk sent River a sidelong glance. *She might have seen her family killed right in front of her…*

Images of a red Fire-Wolf, her broken body at the paws of an Ice-Fang, flashed in Hawk's mind, making him wince. *That's something I can relate to…*

Hawk turned his gaze to the starry sky above. "Living…at a demon fortress as a slave is hard. To the demons, we're nothing more than objects, things without any feeling." Hawk paused and gave a short, harsh laugh. "Demons have no feeling anyway, so it would be hard for them even to imagine the possibility of emotions. But…if demons *have* any kind of 'emotion'…they would have anger and hate. And most of the time…" He lowered his voice, trying to keep the terrible memories at bay. "Most of the time the slaves bore the brunt of their master's anger. If a slave was killed because her master beat her too much, it didn't matter. And we could be beaten for any reason — or killed for any reason, for that matter."

Hawk swallowed, looking down at the ground, his voice barely a whisper. "Every day I lived in fear because I didn't know if I would survive to see the next sunrise. The Wolf sleeping next to me might not be there when I woke up, or the wolf who maimed his paw during work might not return. The only thing we…I …had was hope, hope that grew from legends I had heard, stories that said one day a savior would come and end the reign of demons." A few moments passed, and River said nothing. If not for the way she pricked her ears, Hawk would have doubted she was even listening. He wanted to comfort her, to reassure her that she didn't have to be alone. "I know I can't replace your family…but I *can* be your friend. No matter what happens…I'll be here." He didn't know where the words came from, but somehow he felt as though they were the right ones. *Maybe I heard them somewhere…from someone…*

River tensed slightly before slowly raising her head to meet Hawk's gaze, her own eyes unreadable. "Friends are a sort of family…" she muttered, so softly Hawk almost missed it.

Before he could ask what she meant, a voice interrupted them. "Move. I need to get by."

Hawk jumped, surprised to find Coal standing at the top of the path, and scrambled to move away and allow his former leader to pass. River didn't move, forcing the rebel to step around her.

How long has he been there? Hawk's fur burned with the thought of the other Fire-Wolf overhearing his conversation with River. His embarrassment was immediately forgotten when Coal sat down in front of them and said, "I'm sorry for making a hasty decision."

"Wha…" Hawk gaped in shock, but quickly snapped his jaws shut at a glare from Coal.

"I will tell you where to find the demon fortresses here in Taladair, but there my knowledge ends," Coal said. "You will have to seek out other resistance groups if you want the location of fortresses in the other nations."

Stretching out a claw, Coal drew a rough map of Soluna, marking down the different landmarks familiar to the wolves and outlining the Taladair Forest. He put small crosses to represent the demon fortresses of Taladair. Finally, he circled the areas frequently visited by numerous resistance groups.

After giving Coal a long, hard look, River bent over and inspected the map. She spent a few moments in silence, carefully studying what he had drawn. Then she started questioning him, asking about the frequency and known paths of demon patrols, what kinds of demons were stationed in which fortresses, and how to find other packs. Coal answered the best he could.

Hawk's head spun as he struggled to keep track of the information being exchanged. He couldn't imagine how River was going to keep it all straight in her head.

"That should be all, thank you." The she-wolf scuffed out the map and stood. "Is there a way we can cross the Dorasca Gorge?"

Coal nodded his head slightly. "There is."

When he made no move to elaborate, River gritted her teeth. "*How*?"

The rebel leader's expression emptied, his eyes becoming even colder than before. Hawk shuddered. Although Coal rarely showed any emotion, the complete lack of it was usually a worse sign. "While it *is* possible to cross the gorge, I no longer have the means to do so. If you want to reach the other side you have two choices: go south or go north. Demons do not come near the gorge; they won't even go beyond the tree line, so you can travel without worrying about staying under cover."

"What's *that* supposed to mean?" River gritted her teeth, obviously trying very hard to resist losing her temper.

Ignoring her demand, Coal turned sharply on his heels and stalked back to the hidden path. "You may stay the rest of the night here." Then he was gone.

Hawk stared at where his former leader had been standing just a moment before, shocked by Coal's actions. While the other Fire-Wolf was nothing less than blunt, to give them no reason for his inability to help them cross the gorge seemed cold.

A few of Coal's words floated across Hawk's mind. *I no longer have the means to do so...*

"That arrogant…I'm going to freeze him to the back of a swamp boa, and see if he *still* wants to be so tight-jawed." River's eyes narrowed, and she looked ready to murder Coal. Hawk hurried forward to stop her from running after the other Fire-Wolf.

"Wait! I think…what Coal meant was he *can't* get straight across the Dorasca Gorge, not anymore, anyway."

River turned her furious gaze to Hawk, making him wince. "There…used to be four Earth-Wolves in the group." Hawk's voice lowered to a whisper, uncertain if Coal was still within earshot. "But Meadow was killed a week ago during a skirmish with a demon patrol…" He paused. "I don't know how Coal gets across, but I don't think he *can* with only three Earth-Wolves."

When River said nothing, Hawk took a hesitant step back. "We…we should probably head back down. Tomorrow morning we can figure out where we're going to go."

"No." River gave the gorge behind Hawk a suspicious glare before turning around and curling up right where she stood. "You go. I'm staying up here."

She doesn't want to go back into the gorge… Hawk flattened his ears, looking from the hidden path, to River, and back again. A comforting fire and a safe place to sleep waited for him in the hideout. A grouchy she-wolf was all he could expect here.

…but I don't want to leave her on her own…

With a slight sigh, Hawk padded over and lay down as close as he dared to River, curling his thick tail around his nose. She gave no sign of noticing him. Putting any thought of warm fires out of his head, Hawk closed his eyes and quickly fell asleep.

CHAPTER TWENTY

"GET UP, HAWK, we're leaving."

Startled into wakefulness, Hawk jumped to his paws. He blinked, his mind struggling to catch up with his body. For a split second, he half-expected to hear the shouts of the demon overseers, calling the slaves to work. Instead, only an impatient River stood before him, an irritated expression on her face.

Sudden awakenings are becoming a regular thing, Hawk thought wryly, biting back a wide yawn. "Where are we going?"

"North, around the Dorasca. It'll take too long to go south." With that, River turned and padded away.

Hawk hesitated, glancing toward the gorge. There was no sign of Coal and the others.

What will they think if River and I just vanish? Hawk hesitated a moment longer, before bounding after River. *I don't think they'll care…and Sparrow's the only one I would want to say bye to…if anything, Coal will just be mad that I'm leaving behind so many tracks.* He winced at the sight of the partially melted and churned up snow. Coal would not be happy to see the mess when he emerged from the hideout.

"Um…River, shouldn't we get under cover?" Hawk asked when he finally caught up with the she-wolf, sliding in front of her so she could cover his tracks. Their path took them right along the edge of the Dorasca Gorge, which was bare of any sheltering trees or bushes. A demon patrol could easily spot them from within the shadows of the forest.

"We're fine. Coal told me the demons won't come anywhere near the gorge. Even the nearest Fortress is positioned closer to the coast."

"Why not?" Hawk watched the dark forest out of the corner of his eye, not entirely convinced.

"No idea," came the short reply. "Better for us that they stay away."

"And where do you two think you're going?"

Hawk and River spun around, the Fire-Wolf nearly falling to the ground in his haste, to find Coal standing at the top of the hidden path. The rest of the pack appeared behind him, stumbling out of the gorge with varying degrees of sleep clouding their expressions, most likely after being forcibly awakened by their leader and brusquely marched up the path.

"Why should I tell you?" River flattened her ears and growled.

Coal flicked an ear, unimpressed by River's hostility. "We're escorting you north around the Dorasca, and sneaking away in the early morning is a poor way to show your appreciation."

"*What?*" River's lips drew back even more, spitting out the word as though it had personally offended her. Hawk could only gape. He glanced over at the other rebels, who looked irritated at Coal's words. It had obviously been a split-second decision on the part of the leader, and no one was happy with it.

Even Sparrow doesn't look pleased, Hawk thought, a little hurt. The Wind-Wolf kept shooting Coal furious glances, which he completely ignored. *Maybe she's just mad because he didn't consult her about this...*

"Couldn't hear me? Clear the down from your ears."

River tensed. "Maybe I should claw the skin from *yours.*"

"You'd have to move a lot faster than you did just now to even reach my tail, *pup.*"

"Knock it off, both of you," Sparrow growled. "We won't get anywhere if you keep arguing."

"*We're* not going anywhere." River dug her claws into the ground, but Hawk took a step forward to keep her from pouncing on either Sparrow or Coal.

"Why? You don't have to escort us..." Hawk flinched a little when Coal turned his red-eyed gaze to him.

"I don't trust her." Coal looked back at River. "Nearly one hundred and forty years have passed without a single trace of the Water-Wolves. Now *you* appear out of nowhere, with demon-stink clinging to your fur. So forgive me," Coal narrowed his eyes, his tone anything but apologetic, "but I'm a little suspicious as to who you actually are and why you're here."

"Forgive *me*, but I'm not obligated to tell you *anything*," River shot back, her fur bristling. "All I needed from *you* was information about where the fortresses are located and a way across the gorge."

"You asked me for information that anyone who's managed to survive a year without capture should know already. Either the Water-Wolves have managed to hole themselves up somewhere they can hide from the hell Soluna is being forced to endure or you're spies of the Overlord himself."

River shoved past Hawk, nearly sending the smaller wolf sprawling, until she stood nose-to-nose with Coal.

"Wouldn't you like to know? If you think I'm a spy, then why give me the information I asked for?"

Coal only snorted. "The information was false. I never intended to let you wander off on your own, not until I could get the information *I* needed."

Hawk looked nervously between Coal and River. If someone didn't intervene again soon, the two were most likely going to break out into an actual fight, but he didn't dare get between them.

"Coal."

Hawk's gaze snapped to Sparrow. Her voice had suddenly deepened and had taken on a slight-gravelly edge to it. Her eye seemed to have darkened as well, until it appeared almost black.

Sparrow's interruption caught the attention of the two arguing wolves as well. Coal shared a long look with Sparrow, before growling and turning back to River, who stared at Sparrow with narrowed eyes.

"Whatever you are or wherever you came from, if you're going to keep quiet about it, fine. I don't trust you, and whether you like it or not we *will* be leading you around the Dorasca. If I decide that you're small enough of a threat, then I'll give you the actual information you need." Coal bared his teeth. "If not..."

He let the threat hang.

Hawk cocked his head slightly. *Coal's always respected Sparrow's input... but since when has she had enough authority to make him back down like that?*

River growled, her ears pinned against her head. Hawk glanced nervously at her, worried that she would refuse and fight the resistance group anyway. He didn't want to get caught up in a battle with Coal and the others.

Even River wouldn't be strong enough to get away unscathed.

"Fine."

To Hawk's surprise, River simply clicked her jaw shut and turned away from the rebel leader. Coal's eyes narrowed at the sudden acceptance, but he nodded his head.

"Good." He glanced over his shoulder at the silent wolves behind him. "Let's move out. We have a lot of ground to cover."

Without another word, Coal padded past River, the rest of the group following after him. River didn't move until Hawk nudged her. "We should follow..."

He flinched when she shot him a furious glare. The she-wolf said nothing, but turned and stalked after the pack of rebels. Hawk lowered his head slightly and whimpered.

This is going to be a long journey…

CHAPTER TWENTY-ONE

AFTER SEVERAL HOURS of silent travel along the edge of the gorge, Sparrow finally managed to trap Coal into talking. He knew she was furious with his decision to follow Hawk and River, and had spent the trip so far avoiding her and her inevitable lecture.

"Coal."

The rebel leader glanced at Sparrow out of the corners of his red eyes before turning his attention back to the path ahead. "I believe I asked you to keep an eye on the Water-Wolf."

"Eagle's playing puppysitter." Seeing that the Fire-Wolf was about to come up with something that would force Sparrow away again and delay the conversation, she tried again. "*Coal.*"

He flinched at the change in her voice, which had deepened more than a she-wolf's should. The single word seemed to reverberate in his mind. Coal shot her a vicious glare before sending a quick look back at the rest of the group. The three Earth-Wolves were talking quietly with each other, and Eagle was watching Hawk and River at the very rear. Only Hawk seemed to notice their quiet argument, but he quickly looked away when Coal caught him staring.

Coal swung his glare back to Sparrow, who met it unflinchingly.

"You *know* what I'm going to say," the she-wolf muttered, her voice returning to its normal pitch.

"And *you* know what my reply to that will be."

Sparrow narrowed her eyes. "You were only supposed to give them the information they needed and send them on their way. We...*I* cannot get involved."

"You are welcome to leave."

"*You know I can't!*" The she-wolf flattened her ears, furtively glancing back at the wolves behind them to ensure she hadn't been heard. "I told you about my...*mission* on the condition that you would go along with it."

"That was before I actually met the Water-Wolf. I don't know what she is doing here, *that's* something you *conveniently* left out of your little explanation and *refuse* to tell me, but I get a bad feeling just looking at her."

"There are bigger things at work than your *paranoia*, wolf."

Coal shot Sparrow another hard glare at the change in tone.

"We are walking a narrow trail, and if you cause more than a century of delicate maneuvering to collapse, then I will have you *removed*."

"Wouldn't that cause your *delicate maneuvering* to collapse?" Coal said easily, unruffled by the threat. "I've been told I have a part to play in all this."

"You can be replaced."

"Not so easily as you would have me believe."

The air around them hummed with tension, each suspiciously watching the other. Finally Sparrow growled and looked away.

"We're a whisker from throwing you over the cliff. Your current position, and *only* that, is keeping you alive. But the *moment* you become too much trouble…" She trailed off, letting the threat hang.

Coal only sniffed and looked away. "Relax. I have no intention of ruining your precious plan. I'm just going to keep an eye on them for a bit, and then let them go their own way."

CHAPTER TWENTY-TWO

HAWK KEPT HIS eyes fixed on the ground in front of him. He could hardly put one paw in front of the other with Eagle's eyes boring into him.

He's furious that I caused Sparrow to get hurt so badly, Hawk thought, shooting the male Wind-Wolf a nervous look out of the corner of his eye. Eagle hadn't stopped glaring at him since they started walking.

And River's doing nothing to help... Hawk turned his gaze to his companion. The she-wolf seemed determined to make the entire journey without breaking her icy glare from Coal, who was too busy quietly arguing with Sparrow to notice.

Unease filled Hawk, and he turned his eyes to the two rebel leaders at the front of the group. Their entire situation made him uncomfortable. Hawk had only known Coal for a short time, but his recent actions seemed extremely out of character.

Sparrow, too, was acting strange. She hadn't said a word to him since the start of the journey, had even ignored Eagle, and spent the entire time trying to pin down Coal.

What are they arguing about up there?

Try as he might, no matter how hard he strained his ears, Hawk couldn't hear what was being said. Whatever it was, both seemed very agitated about it. Hawk had never seen the two so angry with each other.

Between Coal and Sparrow acting weird, and River furious with everything, I just hope we can get to the other side of the Dorasca Gorge in one piece. Hawk sighed and trained his eyes on the snowy ground in front of him once more. The sooner they parted ways with Coal and his group, the better.

⌒

"WE'LL CAMP HERE TONIGHT."

Hawk breathed a sigh of relief when Coal finally gave the order to stop. After a day of near-silent travel, enduring the thick tension between Coal and Sparrow, the almost physical waves of anger coming from River, and Eagle's glares, Hawk was more than ready to fall into sleep's embrace.

"Palm, Canyon, Granite, build a shelter." Coal's eyes glinted in the near-darkness, moving to each group member as he gave out orders. "Eagle, with me. We will patrol the area, and if it's clear, we can have a small fire."

There was a collective sigh at the possibility of a fire. After the sun had set, the temperature had dropped to the point where even Hawk's ears tingled a bit. No one wanted to spend the night shivering.

"You two, stay here," Coal said, turning his sharp gaze to Hawk and River. The she-wolf only sniffed before curling up right where she stood. Hawk flinched and did the same.

Coal nodded once at Sparrow, silently handing her control of the group, and padded off into the darkness, Eagle close behind him.

Hawk watched the three Earth-Wolves raise a wall of rock to surround them, effectively shielding them from any unfriendly eyes from the forest behind them. Sparrow set to digging a small hole for a fire pit, awkwardly scraping out the dirt with her unbroken paw. He was considering going over to her, to help her and finally get a chance to talk to the cloudy gray she-wolf, when a sharp jab to the side broke through his thoughts.

"Tell me about this pack," River muttered, watching the proceedings through half-closed eyes. "Who are they?"

"Um…what do you mean?"

River gave an almost imperceptible sigh. "Who's the ragged Wind-Wolf?"

"That's…that's Sparrow…"

"Where did she get those injuries?"

Hawk flinched. "We…had to split up to avoid a patrol, because we were all pretty beaten up from a previous battle. Sparrow was supposed to lead me to the hideout, but the patrol found us. She held them off while I escaped."

"She fought off an entire patrol herself?" River opened her eyes and stared at the Wind-Wolf, who had started arguing with Canyon over the placement of the walls. The Water-Wolf looked almost impressed. "She's a powerful Wind-Wolf, then."

"Well, she doesn't have a lot of control over her wind magic. Sparrow likes…out-maneuvering her opponent and attacking with her fangs…" He flinched again. *She won't be able to do that with her paw…*

River narrowed her eyes, studying Sparrow for a few moments before asking, "And the Earth-Wolves?"

"The green one is Palm…Canyon is the brown wolf…and Granite is the dark gray one."

"What's their relationship with each other?"

Hawk glanced at River. "Why…do you ask?"

"Just curious."

I have the feeling it's more than that, Hawk thought, but answered anyway. "Palm and Canyon are brothers, and I think Granite is their uncle. I don't know much about them, because they usually stick close to each other." Hawk tilted his head a little. "Actually, I don't think I've ever heard Granite speak…"

"Are they good fighters?"

"They work really well together," Hawk said slowly. *She couldn't be planning to try and escape, could she?* "I saw them fight once. Granite kept the demons pinned with his earth magic, while Palm and Canyon dove in and tore the demons to shreds under cover of Granite's rocks."

The she-wolf nodded slightly. "Who is the other Wind-Wolf, who left with Coal?" She paused, and then added. "What exactly did you do to make him look like he wants to feed you to a Blood-Frenzy?"

"Eagle…he's Sparrow's mate…and he blames me for almost getting her killed."

"Sparrow's mate? Interesting…" Before Hawk could ask what she meant by *interesting,* River turned her cold gaze to him and said, "Tell me about Coal."

"There's nothing much to tell. I know almost nothing about him."

"What *do* you know?'

"He's been fighting demons for his entire life…and has no living family…" Hawk trailed off, trying to remember anything else about the enigmatic resistance group leader. "Oh, Sparrow once told me that he was taken to a fortress once, before I joined them, but he returned a day later with barely a ruffled pelt." His eyes glittered. It was a story the group loved hearing, although it was told in whispers behind Coal's back. The rebel leader had forbidden them from talking about his miraculous escape. "Later, we heard that the Lord Mars—"

"What's a 'Lord Mars'?" River interrupted.

"It's the title given to the demon in charge of a Fortress," Hawk said. "They're usually the strongest demon in the Fortress and I've heard that they're personally selected by the Overlord."

"And Coal did something to this 'Lord Mars'?"

Hawk nodded. "The Lord Mars was found dead in its room. Well...*parts* of it had been found."

"Parts?" River narrowed her eyes again.

"Ah, you're telling *that* story again?"

Both Hawk and River jumped at Sparrow's sudden intrusion. The three Earth-Wolves soon joined her, seating themselves behind the Wind-Wolf.

"Tell the story from the beginning," Palm said, his eyes glittering. "Quickly, before Coal gets back."

"Of course. River's obviously never heard the tale of Demonbane's mysterious escape, and what better than to tell a secret story in the dark of night?" Sparrow chuckled, drawing back her lips in a fearsome grin, the look made all the more scary by the wounds on her face.

"Demonbane?" River said, nonplussed.

"It's a silly title other wolves have given him, but that's not important. Let's see...it happened about three years ago, I think. It was me, Eagle, Meadow, and...Feather." Sparrow paused, glancing at River. "Meadow was the lieutenant before me. She was killed in a skirmish about two weeks back. And Feather... well, that's part of the story."

River nodded, but said nothing. Sparrow flicked her ears, listening to ensure Coal wasn't sneaking up on them, and continued. "We were in the Scaineadó Desert, a few dozen miles south of the Gaoibeanna border. We had two patrols on our tails, and they'd been chasing us for *days*. I've never run so long in my life, and I was *sure* that we would all die of exhaustion before the demons caught us. The only one who *didn't* look as though his paws were about to fall off was Coal. I swear that wolf is a bottomless lake of energy."

A chuckle rippled through the listeners. Hawk and the three Earth-Wolves were well-acquainted with the rebel leader's unending endurance. River looked mildly impressed.

"But he had a plan. The moment we set paw in the desert, we were in *his* territory. It only took us two days to get rid of the patrols." Sparrow stopped to laugh. "The demons ended up tracking *each other* halfway to Lough Soluna. All because of Coal. The rest of us didn't have a *clue* about what was going on, we just followed his orders. Suddenly we were safe and allowed to rest for a day, and better yet, we were all still alive and mostly in one piece."

Her expression darkened. Hawk's breath caught. He had heard the story a few times already, but this part always managed to get to him.

"Then...it fell apart."

Sparrow looked around, as though searching for any unwanted listeners, before leaning in slightly and saying in a subdued tone, "A different patrol, consisting of nothing but Darkclaws and Shade-Tigers, attacked us in the middle of the night. To this day I have no idea how many of them were in that patrol. There was just darkness everywhere, and shadows reaching up from the ground to drag us into the waiting fangs of a demon." The Wind-Wolf paused and took a deep breath. "Coal snatched me from the jaws of this enormous Shade-Tiger and threw me to safety. He ordered me to run. He ordered all of us to run. Somehow he managed to hold back the demons long enough for the rest of us to get away. At the time, I thought *he* had escaped, too. This was the invincible *Coal*, we're talking about, the one who outwitted two demon patrols at once."

"But he didn't escape," River said simply.

Sparrow shook her head. "It wasn't until we were about a mile out that I look around and realize that Meadow is crying and we're one member short. Coal had been taken. He had sacrificed himself to save us."

Hawk whined quietly. It was hard to imagine the severe Fire-Wolf caring enough to allow himself to be captured. *Sparrow's told me that he was nicer when Meadow was alive...I wish I could have seen that.*

"Of course, we weren't about to leave him to his fate. We'd been causing all sorts of trouble with the demons, and we knew they weren't going to simply kill him. But by the time we got back to the spot where we had been attacked, the patrol was gone.

"We spent all night and most of the next day trying to get some sort of scent. But the thing about night demons...trying to track them is, literally, like trying to track shadows. They *have* no scent." Sparrow's eye narrowed, and she growled. "Feather was the first one to give up. She tried to convince us to leave, to get away before more patrols came to find us and bring us Coal's fate. We were *fellow conspirators*. That's when she let it slip."

River tilted her head. "She was the one to betray you."

"Oh yes. Turns out she had been working with the demons the entire time, since she joined up with us."

"Coal never suspected her? He doesn't seem like the type to be so easily deceived."

Sparrow just shrugged at River's question. "I think he might have known at some point, but he refuses to talk about it, so I don't know. But apparently she used to be a slave and was chosen to infiltrate Coal's group. Obviously, it worked."

"What happened to Feather?"

The Wind-Wolf bared her teeth in a silent snarl. "Meadow killed her. In the time that I knew her, I only saw Meadow get seriously angry twice. We couldn't have held her back even if we wanted to." She paused and shuddered. "Meadow was very weak when it came to earth magic...but when she turned on Feather...you could feel the earth shaking clear to Ignimor Fortress."

Hawk stiffened, and River glanced at him out of the corner of her eye.

"We managed to find out from Feather that Coal had been taken to Ignimor, before she...died. And we wasted no time in getting there." Sparrow gave a short, harsh laugh. "We were crazed with grief, and weren't thinking straight. Meadow more than all of us together. I'm pretty sure our only plan was to throw ourselves at the gates and hope the demons would run from our utter insanity."

"Seeing as you're still alive, I assume you never actually attacked the Fortress itself?" River said dryly.

Sparrow just rolled her eye. "*Obviously.* No one attacks a Fortress and lives. We finally reach Ignimor, ready to tear the place apart, when who do we run into but Coal himself. Alive. *Free.* And looking as though he had just walked away from a brief battle with a patrol, *not* like he had just crawled from the depths of a demon fortress. A few deep cuts, a torn claw, a broken tail, and that was it."

"How did he survive?" Palm asked, speaking for the first time since the story started. Sparrow snorted.

"You ask me that every time. No one knows how he escaped. I don't think he even told Meadow how. There's been all sorts of theories and rumors about it, word travels fast among the rebel packs, and it didn't take long for everyone to know Coal's name, and all the various titles wolves gave him after his escape."

"What about the Lord Mars, found dead?" River interrupted.

Sparrow's eye gleamed. "Ah, *that* was something I personally found out. Had to snag quite a few demons to get all the information. I overheard a demon from Ignimor talking about it once and immediately set about to learn more.

"The day after Coal escaped, the demons of Ignimor entered the Lord Mars' room. The door had been melted shut, which was why it had taken them so long to get in. When they did, the rebel Fire-Wolf was nowhere to be seen, and their own leader was…ah, *decorating the walls*, to put it lightly. One of the demons I *'talked to'* about it nearly had a breakdown describing what he had seen."

Hawk shuddered. He remembered Coal's arrival at Ignimor. He had been the one ordered to help Coal to the Lord Mars, as the rebel had been beaten almost to the point of unconsciousness. He had been the one ordered to clean the horrific mess left behind.

Coal was so badly injured he couldn't even walk. He doesn't even remember me from the Fortress. How did he escape and appear before Sparrow and the others with hardly a scratch?

He had never told the others about meeting Coal at Ignimor.

"Okay, now you have to take the oath of secrecy," Sparrow said, immediately dispelling the somber mood that had settled over them. *"We will never speak of this within earshot of Coal lest he skin the pelts from our bones."*

River gave the other she-wolf a nonplussed look, but before she could answer a howl sounded from the forest.

"That was Eagle!" Sparrow leapt to her paws, stumbling when she landed on her injured one. "They've been attacked. Let's go!"

"Are you able to fight?" Canyon asked, eyeing her broken paw. He flinched when she glared at him.

"Of course I can. Now shut up and move. Hawk, River, come with us. If Eagle's howling for help, then they're in a major spot of trouble."

Hawk immediately scrambled to his paws, fear digging its icy claws into his heart. *What could be strong enough to make them howl?*

Sparrow took off, moving surprisingly fast despite her injuries. Granite sighed and loped after her, silencing her protests with a look when he leaned into her to help her run. Palm and Canyon quickly followed, shadowing their uncle's pawsteps. Hawk swallowed his nervousness, but before he could take off as well, River's voice stopped him.

"Wait." The Water-Wolf stood, her expression unreadable. "Leave them. We need to go."

"What…?"

"We can't have Coal following us. I'm sure he can handle whatever it is that's attacking them. Now let's go."

She started walking, away from Sparrow and the Earth-Wolves, who had already disappeared into the darkness, and from the unknown enemy threatening the resistance group. Hawk hesitated, looking between River and the forest, torn between his promise to help the Water-Wolf and his lingering loyalty to the wolves who had taken him in.

He took a deep breath. "We have to help."

River stopped.

"We only howl if the risk of being heard by other demons is less than the danger of being captured or killed. They're in trouble…and I owe them."

Before he could change his mind or River could drag him away, Hawk spun around and raced off, headed for the distant forest.

Where did they go? Hawk squinted, trying to see something in the near-darkness. Sparrow and the others couldn't have gotten far, not with Sparrow's injury. *Unless Granite tried moving them underground…*

"They're straight ahead. They've already reached the forest."

Hawk jumped, shocked by River's sudden appearance. Her eyes were fixed on the rapidly approaching tree line, and she refused to look at him.

"Thank you…" Hawk didn't know why she decided to help, but he wasn't going to question it.

The she-wolf snorted. "Don't make me regret this."

Chapter Twenty-Three

It only took them a few minutes to reach the trees. River burst through the undergrowth and immediately stopped, leaving Hawk to career into a bush in his attempt to stop as well. The she-wolf ignored his flailing and put her nose in the air, searching the air for any scent of the missing wolves. "I've lost the Earth-Wolves."

Hawk stumbled over, shaking twigs and snow from his pelt. "They probably went underground, so Sparrow wouldn't have to run as much."

"How do we *find* them, then?" River growled, glaring at the earth as though hoping the look would reach the wayward rebels.

"They can't keep it up for long, because it takes a lot of power…"

River sighed. "All right, we'll just head for Coal and Eagle." Then she tipped back her head and howled. Hawk flinched, the sound of her call grating on his ears. A moment later, Eagle's howl answered her, more desperate than before. It ended abruptly.

"Let's go." River charged forward, launching through the skeletal bushes. Hawk scrambled after her, his heart pounding.

The two wolves tore through the undergrowth, making no attempt to keep their movements silent. Their only thought was to reach Eagle and Coal as quickly as possible. Another howl echoed through the dark woods, before suddenly spiking in pitch and stopping.

Eagle's trying to keep us going in the right direction, but whatever's attacking him must be trying to keep him silent, Hawk realized.

A moment later he nearly careened straight into a tree when a deep howl sounded right beside him. Canyon burst through the bushes, the other three close behind him. Sparrow looked furious, but brightened slightly when she saw Hawk and River.

"Great, you're here. I was afraid you wouldn't be able to find us after *this idiot* dragged us underground." She sent Granite a glare, which he ignored in favor of driving her around a thick tree trunk.

"They're just up ahead; I can smell the demons' stink." River snarled, her eyes already glowing at the prospect of a battle. Hawk swallowed nervously, feeling a slight twinge of regret at getting himself into another fight he had no business being in. He could barely defend himself without another's help, much less save a powerful Fire-Wolf like Coal from some unknown demon.

"Here!"

Snow suddenly rushed by Hawk, nearly knocking him off his paws. It immediately melted into water and surged forward, crushing a path through the barren bushes and leaving a large patch of bare earth behind. River snarled again and threw herself after the wave of water, which crashed into several large, dark shapes.

"Got to hand it to her, she's got power," Sparrow panted, sliding to a halt beside Hawk. "You three, go! Keep an eye out for Coal and Eagle; drag them back here if you get the chance. Hawk, watch my back; I'm going to try and keep the battle contained here."

The three Earth-Wolves raced after River, who had already pounced on one of the demons, an unusually large Shade-Tiger. Granite raised a wall of earth and slammed it into the demon, knocking it out from beneath the Water-Wolf, who landed lightly on her paws. Canyon and Palm dove for the Shade-Tiger, sinking their fangs into the monster's pelt.

A second Shade-Tiger suddenly appeared, dripping wet and hissing with fury. Hawk scanned the trees around them and spotted a third Shade-Tiger picking itself up off the ground.

River's attack must have scattered them…but where are Coal and Eagle?

"Come on…help me out here…"

Hawk snapped his attention to Sparrow, who was growling quietly to herself. "Sorry?"

She glared at him. "Not talking to *you*."

Her eye seemed to glow for a second, and then suddenly a large wind kicked up, tearing through the icy trees. Hawk shivered when it hit him, so strong it felt as though it was blowing straight through him. Shards of ice raked through his fur, although Hawk couldn't tell if they came from the trees above or the wind itself. The blast of wind shifted, moving so it encircled the battling wolves and demons, keeping them trapped within.

"Hawk, pay attention." The sound of Sparrow's strained voice shook him from his shock. She was gritting her teeth and digging her claws into the earth, as though resisting some invisible power that threatened to tear her away. "I can't move if I'm holding this thing up…and one of the demons is bound to notice me. Keep them off my tail."

All feeling drained away from Hawk's body. "H-how?"

"I don't know, make a light! These are Shade-Tigers, so blind them with fire!"

Suddenly Hawk was knocked off his paws and sent crashing to the forest floor. Something wrapped around his legs and yanked him away from Sparrow, who could do nothing other than swear and watch him get dragged toward the battle. Hawk struggled, desperately trying to escape whatever was holding him, but found that his legs were unable to move.

Shadows! His heart stopped upon seeing the inky black vines wrapped around his limbs. A moment later Hawk was staring up into the white eyes of a Shade-Tiger. The demon snarled, baring its curved fangs at him, before sinking its teeth into his ruff and throwing him into the air. Hawk slammed into Granite with a yelp.

Taken by surprise, Granite stumbled. His wall of rock crumbled, leaving Canyon and Palm open. Another Shade-Tiger pounced on them from behind, a wave of darkness knocking them to the ground.

Granite ignored Hawk's babbled apologies and threw himself onto the Shade-Tiger. The three Earth-Wolves were trapped in a violent brawl with the Shade-Tiger, whose movements became a blur as it fended off their attacks.

I have to get back to Sparrow! Hawk tore his eyes from the skirmish before him, searching his surroundings for the Wind-Wolf. To his relief she was right where he had left her, unharmed but struggling to keep the barrier of wind. He was knocked to the ground a second time when a heavy paw collided with his shoulder. He had no time to react before the Shade-Tiger dove for his throat.

A blast of wind drove the demon away, sending the monster careening into a tree. Eagle suddenly appeared in Hawk's vision, blood dripping from a deep cut above his eye.

"This changes nothing," he growled, dragging the smaller Hawk to his paws. "Where's Sparrow?"

Hawk nervously gestured toward the other Wind-Wolf. Eagle nodded and took off, leaving Hawk alone with the quickly recovering Shade-Tiger.

Hawk bared his teeth, trying to appear at least a little intimidating. His eyes darted around the small battlefield, hoping that someone was close enough to help him. With the trees blocking the light of the moons and the waves of shadows crashing everywhere, he could barely see past his nose. He didn't know how many Shade-Tigers there were, if any had been defeated, or even where his allies were.

"We did not expect you to put up such a fight," the Shade-Tiger growled, sauntering forward with the air of one who knew its opponent was hopelessly outmatched. "Even those two wolves alone were quite the mouthful."

Hawk took a few steps back to try and keep some distance between himself and the demon, but the striped monster continued to approach.

"You're a bit out of place here, aren't you? Haven't seen much battle?" The Shade-Tiger chuckled, stopping just in front of the terrified Hawk. It towered over him, its cold white eyes boring into him. "You won't be much fun...so how about we make a deal? I'll let you go free...if you tell me what you know about the blizzard."

Hawk paused, confused. "The...blizzard?"

The demon nodded. "You know which one I'm talking about, the storm wasn't exactly hard to miss. But it definitely wasn't natural...and the Overlord is *very* curious as to where it came from. You rats wouldn't have anything to do with it...would you?"

Hawk immediately thought of the Winter-Wolf. *When it appeared...it brought a snowstorm with it...is that what the Shade-Tiger's talking about? But why would Letorus be so interested in it?*

"Ah...you *do* know something." The Shade-Tiger's eyes glinted, and it leaned in closer to Hawk until all he could see were the demon's vicious fangs. "Tell me, and I might not hunt you down later..."

"Get down!"

A dark shape sailed over Hawk's head, barreling into the demon. Hawk scrambled away from the flailing paws, not wanting to get caught between the Shade-Tiger and its attacker.

"Coal!" Hawk blinked, surprised by the rebel leader's sudden appearance.

The dark-furred Fire-Wolf snarled, sinking his fangs into the Shade-Tiger's leg and making it yowl in pain. He wrenched his head to the side, pulling the demon's paws from underneath it.

"Light a fire. We have to blind them," Coal ordered, his voice calm despite the chaos around him. The Shade-Tiger hissed and lunged for the Fire-Wolf, who ducked under the attack and dove for the demon's throat.

"I…I can't!" Hawk jumped backward as the two rolled toward him, fangs snapping at each other as they slid around the other's attack and attempted to land one of their own.

Coal spared a second to glare at him. "Do it!"

Why can't Coal? Hawk thought wildly, fear threatening to take over his mind. There was no way he could summon a flame so quickly, especially not one big enough to blind the Shade-Tiger. *He has to be better at fire magic than I am!*

Making a desperate decision, Hawk threw himself at the Shade-Tiger. He landed on the creature's back and bit down as hard as he could on the demon's ruff. The Shade-Tiger roared and jumped back, twisting around in an attempt to dislodge its unwanted passenger.

"I'll distract it! Summon a fire!" Hawk was thrown to the ground the moment he removed his fangs from the Shade-Tiger's pelt. The demon immediately turned on him with a hiss. With a strangled yelp, Hawk scrambled to his paws and dove under the Shade-Tiger, narrowly avoiding a blast of darkness, which instead splintered the trunk of the tree behind him.

Coal clamped down on the Shade-Tiger's tail, wrenching it backward. The striped demon spun around and a shadow rose up behind the rebel leader. Coal easily dodged the attack, darting over to Hawk and causing the Shade-Tiger to dive into its own shadows. "I can't," he said simply, raising his voice over the pained yowl of the Shade-Tiger.

"But I'm terrible at summoning fire!" Hawk protested, his mind whirling at Coal's strange response. "I won't be able to summon something big enough to do anything!"

"Doesn't matter. Even a little flame will help scatter the shadows." Coal grabbed Hawk by the scruff of his neck and dragged him to the side, just as a black wave surged past, ruffling Hawk's fur with its nearness.

"You can summon something bigger, something that will actually help!"

All three were forced to duck when a chunk of earth sailed over their heads. Taking advantage of the Fire-Wolves' temporary distraction, the Shade-Tiger snarled and lunged toward them, fangs bared. Coal reacted instinctively, meeting the demon with a vicious snap to the neck. Hawk yelped and jumped to the side, before diving for the Shade-Tiger's paw. He yanked the limb away, tripping the demon and allowing Coal to sink his teeth into the demon's throat.

Both wolves were forced to retreat when shadowy tendrils rose up from the forest floor and attempted to wrap around their necks.

"I *can't*," Coal said again.

Hawk sent him a shocked look. "But…you're a stronger Fire-Wolf…you could probably blind them all…" *Why hasn't he done so before now?*

The rebel leader snarled and glared at Hawk with enough force to make the younger Fire-Wolf step back. "I *can't* because I don't have any fire magic!"

Chapter Twenty-Four

"WHAT...?"

"I have no magic. Now stop whining and summon a fire!" Coal roared, charging the Shade-Tiger.

Hawk was shocked into obeying the order. He ran after Coal, turning as much of his attention as he dared to drawing a flame out of his magic. Suddenly Coal turned away, leaving Hawk alone to charge the snarling demon.

Hawk yelped, just as a tongue of fire burst into existence, arcing toward the Shade-Tiger, which yowled in pain and slid to a halt. The shadows surrounding it vanished, banished by Hawk's flames.

I did it! Hawk thought triumphantly. His euphoria drained when the Shade-Tiger melted into the shadows of the tree behind it. Coal crashed to the ground, his attempt to pounce on the distracted demon foiled by its disappearance. The rebel leader swore and jumped to his paws.

Fangs suddenly closed around Hawk's back leg. He had enough time to yelp a strangled, *"Coal!"* before he was dragged backward. His concentration lost, the flames immediately died, allowing the shadows to return in full force. Coal snarled and raced toward Hawk, but a wall of shadows rose up in front of him.

Hawk flailed his free paw, terror coursing through him, but his struggles didn't even make the Shade-Tiger flinch. The demon simply growled and jerked his head, raising Hawk from the ground and letting him dangle in the air.

"As much as slaughtering you rats would please me, the Overlord requires information," the Shade-Tiger growled around Hawk's leg. It growled again and sent a second wave of shadows at Coal, who jumped a second too slow and was caught in the attack. The Fire-Wolf was thrown into a tree hard enough to splinter the trunk's bark. A loud *crack*, and a branch fell, pinning Coal to the tree.

"Coal!" Hawk shouted, seeing the other wolf fall limp. The shadows of the Shade-Tiger were draining Coal's energy with full force. If he couldn't escape, he would be killed, and Hawk would be at the mercy of the Shade-Tiger.

The demon growled before throwing Hawk to the ground. A shadow twisted around his legs, lashing them together and destroying any chance of his escape.

The Shade-Tiger chuckled and lowered its head, baring its curved fangs. "I should have time for one kill before I must leave," the demon growled.

Coal finally stirred and opened his eyes, which immediately narrowed upon seeing the approaching enemy. He snarled and attempted to move, but his leaden limbs didn't have the strength to move the branch immobilizing them.

Hawk strained against the shadow holding him in place, but only succeeded in making his head spin. His body was becoming heavier, and his vision was growing black. Soon the shadows would render him unconscious, and the Shade-Tiger would have no trouble in stealing him away.

Help…we need help… Hawk raised his head slightly, searching for any nearby ally. *River…where is River?* "River, *help!*" he howled, hoping that his voice would carry above the noise of the battle. *Please hear me!*

"Hawk, summon a flame and get out of here!" Coal bellowed, never taking his eyes from the Shade-Tiger.

The Shade-Tiger lunged for Coal, and Hawk closed his eyes, not wanting to see his former leader torn to shreds. He opened them a moment later at the sound of a shocked yowl. The Shade-Tiger crashed to the ground, its paws slipping on the sheet of ice that had suddenly appeared beneath it.

River leapt up from the snow, barreling into the Shade-Tiger and knocking it away from the pinned Coal. She jumped back to avoid a heavy paw swathed with shadows, and splashed the demon's face with water, which froze instantly. Leaving the Shade-Tiger to wrestle with the ice holding its jaws shut, River raced back to the two Fire-Wolves.

"I turn my back for one second and you almost get yourself killed," River growled, sinking her fangs into the shadows holding Hawk in place and tearing them away. Hawk shuddered and scrambled to his paws. "Come on, the ice won't stay for long."

Hawk limped after River, blinking to try and clear the black spots from his vision. His head spun, and he felt ready to collapse at any moment.

"You…cut it close…Water-Wolf," Coal growled when River approached.

The she-wolf just rolled her eyes. "Well forgive me for trying to fight off two Shade-Tigers at once. Next time I'll be sure to finish them faster before coming to rescue you."

With Hawk's help, she shoved the branch off of Coal, who tumbled to the ground in an exhausted heap. He lurched to his paws a moment later, limbs trembling. "Get ready…it's recovering," he said, just as the Shade-Tiger behind them cracked the ice off its muzzle.

"Think you can keep up?" River asked, whirling around and tensing for an attack.

Coal only scoffed. "I should be asking *you* that, whelp." Coal glanced at Hawk. "Prepare a fire. If you can blind it for a few seconds we may be able to deliver a killing blow."

"We'll be here all night if we wait on him. *You* get something burning."

"Unfortunately the Shade-Tiger drained any power I had left," Coal lied easily. "Do it, Hawk!" He threw himself forward, meeting the striped demon's charge.

River growled and glared at Hawk. "Don't waste any time."

She growled again and lunged for the Shade-Tiger, thrown into her path by Coal's ferocious attack. Spears of ice rose from the forest floor, tearing into the demon's pelt. The striped monster hissed and snapped at River. She twisted out of the way, causing the Shade-Tiger to stumble. Coal leapt up from behind, landing on the demon's head, and buried his teeth into the back of its neck.

Hawk stood still for a precious few seconds, fear paralyzing him. A strangled bark from Coal shocked him back into reality and brought his attention back to the fight. While both Coal and River were formidable fighters, the Shade-Tiger was powerful, even when wounded, and both wolves were beginning to tire as the fight wore on.

Hawk took a deep breath and closed his eyes. He had to summon something bigger than he had the first time, something that would incapacitate the Shade-Tiger.

Concentrate…you're not a slave anymore…there's nothing stopping you from summoning fire… Hawk imagined drawing a flame from his pool of magic. At first, there was nothing. Then suddenly power surged through him, and he yelped with surprise.

Immediately a ball of fire appeared, exploding from a spot just in front of his muzzle. River, feeling the sudden heat at her back, slid beneath the Shade-Tiger and reared up, knocking the demon off balance. Hawk scrambled backward to avoid the Shade-Tiger, which fell right into fire. The shadows surrounding it vanished as the monster screamed, flames burning through its pelt.

Before the Shade-Tiger could recover, both Coal and River dove for the demon's throat. It thrashed, its scream turning into a yowl of pain and fury, but the two wolves only sank their fangs in deeper.

Slowly, the Shade-Tiger's convulsions stopped, and the striped monster fell limp. Coal and River jumped back just before the corpse melted, turning into the shadows it once controlled. A few moments later Hawk's ball of fire burned itself out, casting the three wolves into darkness.

Hawk sighed with relief. The Shade-Tiger was dead. He glanced over to where the others were fighting. Only one Shade-Tiger remained, and it was quickly getting beaten back by the combined efforts of Canyon, Palm, Granite, and Eagle.

"Coal," River said suddenly, her voice eerily blank. Hawk sent her a sharp look. She had a calculating look in her eye as she approached the rebel leader. "I think it's time Hawk and I left and continued on our own."

Coal turned his full attention to the Water-Wolf and narrowed his eyes. "Really, now?"

"Unless you want your little followers finding out about your *weakness*, then yes, really."

The she-wolf stopped just in front of Coal, towering over the smaller wolf, and looked down at his paws. Hawk's blood ran cold when he followed her gaze.

Solid snow lay beneath the Fire-Wolf's paws.

"I thought it was a little strange that you were leaving *Hawk* to try and summon fire. It would have been better for you, a more experienced wolf, to do it," River continued, looking back up to meet Coal's unreadable eyes. "Then I noticed something even stranger. Traveling with *him* taught me that Fire-Wolves have an annoying habit of leaving trails…so why are your prints solid?"

Hawk tensed when Coal said nothing.

River had a triumphant look in her eyes, and she seemed perfectly willing to wait while Coal struggled to come up with some kind of retort or explanation.

"If you keep your jaws shut, I will let you go on alone," the rebel leader said finally.

"No following us. If I even get a *whiff* of being followed…"

Coal nodded when River trailed off. Her eyes glinted, and she bared her teeth in a satisfied look. "Glad we could finally agree."

The Fire-Wolf ignored her in favor of padding toward the others, who had managed to finish off the last Shade-Tiger. Around them, the wind barrier slowly fell, the heavy gusts fading away into soft forest breezes.

"Report!" Coal said as he approached. "Anyone dead?"

"I am!" Palm called, wagging his tail cheerfully despite the fact he was being held up by both Canyon and Granite. Three nasty wounds marked his back, which was a matted mess of blood and fur.

"Well, that saves us from possibly fighting our way out," River said, padding over to sit by Hawk. She had nothing more than a shallow cut on her leg to show for the battle, and while Hawk managed to avoid any serious injuries, his entire body ached.

He swallowed nervously, watching as Coal went around to each resistance fighter, taking note of all wounds.

"Are you...are you sure that was okay to do? He keeps his powerlessness a secret for a reason..." Hawk ventured. He had only ever heard of a wolf being without magic in some of the old legends, and it was usually the result of a curse or terrible accident. Very rarely did the magic-less wolf survive long after the loss.

River only snorted. "It was either that or we get followed all the way to the Crétioll. I don't care why he has no fire magic, or how he lost it, but if it lets us leave without a fight, then I'm going to use the information to my advantage."

"River, Hawk."

Both wolves looked up at Coal's call. The rebel leader had padded back over to them, backed by Sparrow. "Since you two are determined to go off on your own, I suppose I have to give you information concerning the demon fortresses." Coal paused and quickly cleared away some snow with his tail. Then he drew a rough map of Taladair. "Here are where the fortresses are located. Patrols are usually sent out four times a day: two at dawn, one at noon, two at dusk, and one at midnight. Sometimes extra patrols will be sent out at random times. Got it?"

River nodded, her eyes on the dirt map.

"Once you get to the end of the gorge, look for these symbols," Coal continued, drawing two strange marks below the map. Hawk shuffled a little closer to get a better look. The first symbol was an upright cross over a circle, while other one was a triangle on top of cross.

"Walk *straight* over them. They'll lead you to a bridge, which will get you across the Dorasca." Coal scuffed out the map and the symbols with his paw and looked up at River. "Any questions?"

The she-wolf stood and shook her head. "No."

"Good. Now get out of here."

River gave him a sharp nod before suddenly spinning around and stalking away. Coal left a moment later, ignoring the confused questions from the others, leaving Hawk to stare after him, shocked that their final departure would be so easy.

"I…I guess I better follow her," Hawk said, glancing nervously at Sparrow, who had yet to move.

The she-wolf tilted her head slightly. "Before you go racing off, I've got a message for you."

Hawk flattened his ears slightly. "A…message?"

"You've got a long, hard road ahead of you, but don't lose hope. You're going to have a big part to play in what's coming, and you'll have a difficult decision to make. No matter how bleak things seem, trust in yourself. You're stronger than you think." Sparrow paused, and her one good eye seemed to lighten, so that it almost looked silver. "Seek out the ancient one, and listen to his story. And when all is lost, look to the Star Twins, and use their power to bring light to darkness."

What does that mean? Hawk's ears flattened against his head. Before he could ask her about it, River gave a sharp call, saying that if he didn't hurry up she was going to drag him by his tail. With a quick nod to Sparrow, Hawk darted after River, who was waiting impatiently several feet away.

"Sorry…just saying bye," Hawk muttered.

River snorted. "Whatever, let's go."

As they padded off into the forest, Hawk looked back over his shoulder. Coal was growling orders to the others and seemed to take no notice of their departure, but Sparrow was sitting where Hawk had left her, silently watching.

He stumbled, shocked, before hurrying after River.

Sparrow's wounded eye had opened, and unless Hawk was mistaken, and he fervently hoped he was, then both eyes had changed color.

One was silver, and the other was red.

Chapter Twenty-Five

Sparrow waited until Hawk and his Water-Wolf companion disappeared between the dark trees before letting out a heavy sigh. She closed her eyes.

This is what you wanted, right, Winter-Wolf?

Almost immediately, a second voice answered. **Yes…I would have preferred that we kept to the original plan.**

Coal has a way of doing that.

The ghostly being in her mind seemed to sigh. **No matter…you have one more task before you can go to your rest. Do not fail me…no matter what Coal says or does.**

As if. I could never live with the shame if I failed something as simple as that. Coal just took me by surprise this time around. Sparrow shot back, growling softly to herself. *Still, it is a little scary knowing that the next time I see Hawk… is when I die.*

We all must die, Sparrow. Nothing lasts forever. Be thankful you were given extra time.

Sparrow gave the Winter-Wolf a mental eye roll.

"I suppose you're happy now."

The she-wolf opened her eye to see Coal approaching her. She said nothing in favor of standing and stretching, dimly noting the fact that her limbs she was sure should be sore caused her no pain. The silence continued as the group gathered together and started limping back toward the gorge.

"We could have avoided a lot of trouble if you had let them go in the first place," Sparrow finally said, keeping her voice low enough so the wolves behind them wouldn't overhear their conversation.

Coal just snorted. "You said nothing about there being a *Water-Wolf* accompanying Hawk. I don't trust your…*source of information*, so I acted accordingly."

"I shouldn't have told you *anything*, but because, for some reason, *it* considers you an exception, I was allowed to reveal certain things."

The Fire-Wolf growled under his breath, no doubt cursing Sparrow's cryptic words. Sparrow rolled her eye. "Don't get your claws twisted over it. Things have been put into motion now, and there's nothing you can do about it. Time's running out for the demons, and *they* have something to do with it."

Coal gave Sparrow a careful look out of the corner of his eye, and then glanced quickly back at the others. Eagle quickly looked away when he saw his leader watching, no doubt curious about what Coal and Sparrow were whispering about, and Granite and Canyon were too busy carrying Palm to take any notice of the hushed conversation at the front.

"Then *your* time is running out as well."

The she-wolf hesitated for a second, fear making her heart skip a beat. Coal's eyes narrowed, but to Sparrow's relief he said nothing about noticing.

"I know, but I'm already a dead wolf walking. A few extra days make no difference." Her voice grew quiet. "I…was supposed to die back there…but I *chose* to stay. This is my choice."

Coal grunted, but thankfully dropped the topic. He turned away to round up the others, informing them that they would not be following after Hawk and River. She closed her eyes and took a deep breath.

Not much time left… she thought, remembering several days before, simply struggling to drag herself across the ground…

⌒

SPARROW STRUGGLED TO DRAG HERSELF across the ground. Blood poured from numerous wounds all over her body. Behind her were the remains of the patrol, a token to the long, harsh battle that nearly claimed her life. But Sparrow's mind was not on her victory, but on getting under cover and out of the blizzard.

Finally, after an agonizing crawl across the snowy forest floor, Sparrow dragged herself beneath a low bush. Its skeletal branches pulled at her ragged fur, causing her to hiss in pain. She collapsed, sprawled under the bush, and closed the one eye that could still see.

I hope Hawk got away…and that he reaches the Dorasca Gorge okay. *Sparrow chuckled weakly, although even that simple action pained her.* Sorry scaredy-pup, but it looks like I won't be meeting up with you. Don't let the others push you around…

Sparrow opened her eye once more to look out at the snow-covered forest before closing it for good. She caught a glimpse of the shadowy form of a demon appearing before her, but her strength had already left. Even the roar of the wind died away as blackness enveloped her, leaving her alone in the silence and the dark.

Goodbye, Eagle…

Her breathing slowed, before finally stopping completely.

"Awaken…Sparrow…"

Sparrow's eyes suddenly shot open and were blinded by sheer whiteness. The voice boomed in her ears and echoed in her mind at the same time, sounding both demon and Wolf, male and female, like a thousand creatures speaking at once. Before her stood a giant white wolf, ice frosting its fur, with silver and red eyes. A storm raged around the wolf, almost drowning out the words, and prevented Sparrow from seeing anything else.

"I have a task for you." *The voice echoed again, although the wolf's jaws didn't move.* **"It is too early for you to die."**

"What do you mean?" Sparrow croaked, finding it hard to speak. Her body was trapped in the fangs of Death, and it was slowly tightening its grip.

"There are certain things that must come to pass, and for that I need you. But your body has already yielded itself to Death, and your soul will soon follow. Let me show you what was, and what is to come…"

Tipping its head back, the wolf howled, the sound rising above even the roar of the storm. Suddenly images flashed through Sparrow's mind, like memories given life. She saw the beginning of the war, the arrival of the demons, and the disappearance of the Water-Wolves. She saw King Oak's final stand, and the 138 years of war against the demons. She saw Hawk meeting the Water-Wolf, River, and their journey to the Dorasca Gorge. More images poured into her mind, flashing by at an impossible speed, yet Sparrow was able to clearly see every single one. As the white wolf showed Sparrow the images of the future, Sparrow also saw what must happen, what could happen, and what could be done to decide what would happen.

Finally the stream of images ended. The Winter-Wolf, as Sparrow knew it to be now, looked back at her, fixing her with its all-knowing gaze.

"What…do you want…me to do?" Sparrow took a deep breath and tried to steady her shaking limbs. Her vision was fading, and she knew she wouldn't last much longer.

"I can tie your spirit to this world for a short time, but in return you must do exactly what I ask of you," *the Winter-Wolf replied.* **"I will have to occupy your mind, but you cannot speak of it."**

Sparrow hesitated. "Does this mean…I'll die…anyway when you're…done with me?"

"**Yes.**" *The Winter-Wolf paused, and Sparrow thought she saw a hint of sorrow flash across its stoic face.* "**I cannot guarantee that your soul will survive. Containing god-like power may destroy it.**"

She fell silent for a moment. "So, it's either…I die…now, and go on to the next life, or I…die later, with the chance of dying forever?"

The Winter-Wolf nodded.

Sparrow sighed and chuckled softly. "Coal would…roast my tail…if he knew…I gave up a chance…to help Soluna." *She took a deep breath, trying to ignore the darkness appearing at the edge of her vision.* "He's…a father to me… gotta make him…proud somehow…right?"

Sparrow looked up, locking eyes with the Winter-Wolf.

"I accept."

Sadness flashed through the Winter-Wolf's expression again, but it was tempered with a bit of pride. "**Thank you, Sparrow. Your sacrifice will not be forgotten.**"

Just as the last strings tying Sparrow's soul to the mortal world snapped, the Winter-Wolf howled. Wind, ice, and snow swirled around it, erasing its form before funneling into Sparrow. She stiffened as the brutally cold wind tore through her ghostly body, freezing her spirit in place. The Winter-Wolf's presence grew in her mind as the feeling of death lessened, and strength returned to her limbs.

"**Go, Sparrow. Here is what you must do…**"

Sparrow suddenly lurched to her paws, life flooding back into her body. The action startled a Hell-Cat, the lone survivor of the patrol that had returned upon the end of the battle. She shook the snow from her fur, never even noticing the terrified demon fleeing. She felt stiff, as though her limbs were made of ice. Even the inside of her head felt cold.

This wouldn't happen to be a side-effect of sharing my head with you, would it? *Sparrow thought irritably. A chuckle was all she got in return, but the presence of the Winter-Wolf lessened slightly. The feeling of complete cold faded slightly, until Sparrow felt she could move again.*

"Sparrow, are you alright?"

Eagle's voice shook Sparrow out of her thoughts. He watched her with concerned eyes, obviously worried that the battle with the Shade-Tigers had injured her further. Sparrow brushed her muzzle against his to reassure him.

"Yeah, I'm alright. Let's get going before Coal leaves us behind."

CHAPTER TWENTY-SIX

HAWK FELT AS though he had just fallen asleep when River scared him into wakefulness, claiming that the sun had long since risen and they had to move quickly to make up for lost time. He silently wondered if she were just trying to create more distance between them and Coal.

The next several days fell into a similar pattern. River pushed them as far as Hawk could last, often traveling well into the night, and continuing after a few hours of rest. At River's relentless pace, they reached the end of the Dorasca Gorge within a week.

At the sight of the ocean, however, Hawk immediately forgot how tired he was.

He had never seen so much water at one time. It seemed endless, stretching all the way to the edge of the sky. The sea shone and reflected the brilliant reds and oranges of the setting sun. Just below, at the base of the impossibly high cliff, waves pounded the rocky shore, destroying themselves on the spires that pierced the surface of the water.

"Amazing," Hawk said, standing at the very edge of the cliff, trying to see everything at once. He was torn by uneasiness at being so close to such an immense body of water and the awe at the sea's majesty.

River stood a few paces away, seemingly unimpressed by the sight before them. "You've never been to the sea?"

Hawk shook his head. "Ignimor…isn't near the coastline"

"Hm." After a slight pause, River padded a few steps closer. "It's called the Sea of Soluna."

"I've heard a few wolves talk about it, but I never thought it would be so… *big*."

"The Sea surrounds the entire island and reaches the end of the world; of *course* it's going to be big."

Hawk shot the Water-Wolf a startled look and squeaked, "*The end of the world?*"

She sighed and gestured toward the horizon. "See where the sun is disappearing? That's the end of the world. There's nothing beyond that, just an endless sky holding the ocean in place."

"*Nothing?*" Hawk turned to ask how it was possible for the world to just stop, but River had already padded away, no doubt looking for Coal's strange symbols. He looked back at the distant horizon. It seemed kind of strange that nothing would exist beyond what they could see.

If that's true...then where did the demons come from? Maybe...there's something beyond the horizon...something that we just can't see...

"Hawk, get over here."

River's shout shook Hawk from his thoughts, and he bounded over to see what she wanted. He was unsurprised to see that most of the snow had already been cleared away from the cliff's edge in her search. She pointed a claw at the ground in front of her, where a series of scratches marked the hard stone. Upon a closer look, Hawk found that some of the scratches were connected together to form two shapes.

"Coal's symbols!" Hawk looked up, remembering the rebel's instructions to walk right over them, but he saw nothing but empty space between them and the opposite cliff. "How are they supposed to help us cross?"

River sniffed at the symbols. "They've been imbued with magic somehow," she muttered, before turning her attention to inspecting the gorge. "How could a magic-less Coal come up with something like this?"

"Maybe he had help?"

Hawk received a noncommittal grunt in reply. Then River sighed. Before Hawk could stop her, she stepped over the symbols and jumped right off the cliff.

Hawk's panicked yelp died in his chest when he saw that River was not falling, but instead standing in midair. Her paws were splayed and her legs trembled slightly, as though whatever invisible platform she stood on was weak and it took all her strength to keep her balance. After a few moments, River slowly straightened and looked back at Hawk.

"Well? Come on."

He blinked. "Wh-what?"

"We don't have much time before the sun completely sets and we can't see the other side. So we cross now."

When Hawk continued to stare at the empty space beneath River's paws, the she-wolf just sniffed and turned back around to continue padding along the invisible bridge. "Fine. You can wait out the night on your own."

Hawk whined, hesitating for a few more moments before his fear of being left alone pushed him to walk over the scratched symbols and onto the open air.

To his surprise, his paws found solid footing. He stepped completely onto the invisible platform, amazed. It felt like he stood on a very smooth stone, and if Hawk didn't have the terrifying stretch of darkness below him, he could almost trick himself into believing that he had not yet left the cliff.

"Don't look down. You'll freeze up."

Despite River's warning, Hawk's eyes start to drift downward. With a muffled whine, he dragged his gaze upward, instead focusing on the back of River's head. It became harder to stay focused as the sun continued to set. Soon the darkness of the gorge was all around them, and only the shine of River's fur kept Hawk on track. He sped up his steps to get closer to the she-wolf, lest he risk losing her in the blackness.

At least now I won't have to worry about looking down; down looks the same as everywhere else... Hawk swallowed nervously, trying to convince himself that the bridge wasn't shrinking and he wasn't about to walk right off the edge. *I hope River knows where she's going.*

"Um, River...?"

She jumped before suddenly whirling around and pouncing on Hawk, her fangs bared in a feral snarl. He yelped, shocked, as he was sent crashing into the invisible bridge. To his horror, his head met with no resistance as it flew back, although the rest of his body slammed into the solid platform.

With River silhouetted against the moons, Hawk saw nothing but a large dark shape towering over him. The only detail he could make out was how tense she looked, her entire body trembling. Suddenly he remembered how she had acted back at the hidden camp, and her fear of whatever it was that held the Water-Wolves captive.

"River...it's m-me," Hawk said, struggling to keep his voice calm, cursing the slight tremble that slipped through anyway.

A moment later the weight keeping Hawk pinned to the invisible bridge disappeared. He caught a glimpse of River's face as she backed away. Her expression betrayed nothing, but her body remained tense. Without another word, River turned and continued walking, her tail stuck straight out behind her in an effort to keep from curling in fear.

Hawk scrambled to his paws, moving away from the edge. He took a deep breath to steady himself.

I hadn't meant to scare her...I guess I should have known better...it's exactly how she reacted that first time. And now, she can't get away from it...not until we get to the other side...

Ignoring his pounding heart, Hawk hurried after River. He carefully pulled up beside her, walking close enough for their pelts to brush against each other, but said nothing. He knew what it was like to be trapped in a dark fear, and he wasn't about to let her suffer alone.

If River appreciated the gesture, she gave no sign of it.

CHAPTER TWENTY-SEVEN

HAWK WAS EXTREMELY grateful to reach the other side of the Dorasca, and even River sighed with obvious relief when her paws were met with solid, visible ground. Hawk's display of relief was much more enthusiastic as he leapt off the bridge with an excited bark, and promptly rolled.

"I'm *never* walking across something I can't see *again*," he said, not caring how ridiculous he looked. It had been a long time since he could be so carefree, even for a moment. Not only had they finally made it to the other side of the Dorasca Gorge, but the recent snowstorms hadn't managed to cross the gap, which meant the snow was firmer and harder to melt. Hawk's trail wouldn't be nearly as noticeable.

"Get up," River growled, but her voice contained a wistfulness that surprised Hawk. "You look like an idiot rolling around like that."

After a few more good rolls, Hawk jumped to his paws and shook the snow from his fur. "Are we going to keep going tonight?"

"We'll stop for the night and continue in the morning," River said, before adding under her breath, "away from the gorge. I don't want to stay here any longer than we have to."

Hawk shot the she-wolf a look as she brushed past. She was still a little tense, although she no longer looked as though she would tear the throat out of any wolf who made a sudden movement. She was probably eager to get away from the dark canyon and any associations it held with her fear.

Seeing that River was quickly drawing away, Hawk shook himself again and bounded after her. His initial excitement was starting to wear down, and waves of exhaustion were washing over him. He was glad they were going to stop for the night, although judging from the height of the moons he doubted they would be resting for long.

The forest was much closer to the gorge on this side of the canyon. The trees here loomed out of the darkness, their thick boughs of needles blotting out the light of the moons. Hawk swallowed nervously and padded closer to River. Both were silent as they disappeared into the undergrowth and were swallowed up by the snowy woods.

TRUE TO HAWK'S suspicions, River had them set out the moment the sun rose and it was light enough to see. She did, however, track down a small hare for them to eat and didn't make him hunt for his own meal, which made the early wake-up call a little easier to bear.

It didn't take long for Hawk to feel utterly exhausted. As there was no longer a need for River to cover Hawk's tracks, she could travel even faster than before. Soon Hawk was having a hard time keeping up.

"Hey, River, why do we have to go this fast?" Hawk asked a little breathlessly as he struggled to run beside River. The last thing he wanted was to be left behind.

"To make up for lost time. If we can keep up this pace, then we will reach the Crétioll by morning."

Hawk flattened his ears slightly at that. *What could River possibly need at the site of the Lough Domhgeal?* Hawk hoped that River didn't actually need to enter the caves of Crétioll. Stories of what happened to those who dared to enter without permission came to the forefront of his mind.

The she-wolf said nothing more about her intentions, leaving Hawk to his dark thoughts. Almost the entire day passed without either a word or a pause in their travel, but Hawk barely noticed the miles passing. He was too busy worrying about what River had planned, and if there was any way he could possibly talk her out of doing something that would result in them getting killed.

Suddenly River stopped. Hawk stumbled over his paws trying to avoid running into her, but River didn't seem to notice his floundering. Her ears twitched, prompting Hawk to listen as well.

The forest was silent. Not an oppressive silence like Hawk had felt when the black-and-red demon had passed…but enough to make Hawk nervous. He sidled a little closer to River and whispered, "River, what is it?"

River sniffed the air, and then swore under her breath. "A patrol. Five demons. Four Hell-Cats, and one Fire-Fang. I thought we were far enough from the Fortress to avoid the dusk patrol."

Although Hawk was impressed that she could tell what demons made up the patrol just by smell, it wasn't enough to quench the fear rising up in him.

"We'll try to avoid the patrol, but if we can't outrun them, then we'll have to stand and fight," River whispered, voicing exactly what Hawk expected her to say. Without another word she took off, leaving Hawk to scramble to catch up.

Several minutes passed as the two dashed through the undergrowth, running as fast as they could without making too much noise. Hawk kept his senses alert, searching for any sign of detection, but the forest remained silent. He relaxed slightly.

A chilling yowl broke through Hawk's thoughts, sending his heart plummeting to his paws, only to leap straight into his throat when River spun around and started running in the other direction.

We're going to fight them! Despite his rising fear, Hawk kept pace with the she-wolf.

"We can't let them call for help," River said between breaths. "I will deal with the Fire-Fang, but *you* have to keep the four Hell-Cats distracted. They aren't that smart, so it shouldn't be too hard. Just keep them from helping the Fire-Fang, and keep them off my back. Don't let a *single* one escape; it would be disastrous if the Fortress near the Crétioll noticed us."

Hawk swallowed and nodded. He wasn't sure how he could keep four Hell-Cats distracted, but he knew he had to try. *I knew I would have to face danger when I agreed to travel with River. I can't back down now!*

All too soon, the patrol appeared. The Hell-Cats, wide-shouldered beasts with reddish-brown fur and a bright red stripe down their back, charged ahead of the Fire-Fang with teeth bared. The patrol faltered for a moment, not expecting their quarry to face them head-on. River put on an extra burst of speed and leapt over the Hell-Cats' heads, landing on the Fire-Fang behind them. A wave of freezing water followed her flight, crashing down on the lean demon. The water sizzled on the Fire-Fang's hot scales, and it hissed in anger. River sank her fangs into its neck, making it yowl in pain.

The Hell-Cats slid to a stop, their beady eyes confused. Two glanced hungrily at Hawk, and then looked back at their leader. They seemed torn between the need to save their leader and the need to kill Hawk. The Fire-Wolf didn't give the Hell-Cats, or himself, any more time to think. Throwing caution to the winds, Hawk snarled and leapt at the nearest Hell-Cat, snapping at its neck. Immediately all four demons forgot about the Fire-Fang and turned their full attention to Hawk. For a moment, he froze at the sight of four Hell-Cats staring at him with murderous hunger, but he forced his fear back down.

He had to hold on, at least until River had defeated the Fire-Fang.

Hawk summoned flames to dance across his pelt, was surprised when they instantly appeared, and barreled into the nearest Hell-Cat, which screeched when its dark pelt was set alight. The smell of burning fur reached Hawk's nose, and he nearly retched from the stench. Swallowing his nausea, Hawk attacked the next Hell-Cat. It yowled and clawed Hawk's shoulder, its wicked talons raking through his skin and leaving long, bloody furrows in his fur. Hawk bit back a scream of pain, and instead bit the Hell-Cat's throat, taking the demon by surprise with his instantaneous reaction.

The burning Hell-Cat barreled into them, moving so fast Hawk didn't have time to detach his fangs from the first Hell-Cat. Its yowl of fury and pain was suddenly cut off when its neck snapped, bent at an unnatural angle by the force of its ally slamming into it. Hawk immediately opened his jaws and jumped back, shocked, and barely noticed the other Hell-Cat dashing off into the forest.

He had no time to let the fact that he had just killed the demon sink in. The other two Hell-Cats were still alive, and River had yet to join him, meaning she was still fighting the Fire-Fang. Hawk hoped she would defeat it soon. His shoulder burned even through the numbing haze of adrenaline, and even the shallow cuts dealt by the now-dead Hell-Cat dripped with blood. He didn't know how much longer he could last on his own. Only the combination of the Hell-Cats' innate stupidity and Hawk's luck had kept him alive so far.

River, hurry!

Suddenly, the two remaining demons took Hawk by surprise. Any instinct he had been relying on before was forgotten at the sight of the demons bearing down on him.

If I don't move they'll kill me! Hawk scrambled backward, tripping over his own paws in his desperate attempt to escape. Moments before they could pounce, a wave of icy water crashed into them, sweeping the demons off their paws. Hawk stumbled, his limbs weak with relief.

River!

The she-wolf appeared immediately after her magical attack and threw herself on the two Hell-Cats. Hawk jumped away from the fray, not wanting to get caught in the melee. He glanced over his shoulder to where River had battled the Fire-Fang. A faintly glowing pile of ash marked the demon's grave.

"I'm impressed. You lasted longer than I thought you would."

Hawk turned back at the sound of River's voice. She had made quick work of the Hell-Cats, coming away no more injured than she had been from her fight with the Fire-Fang. He was unsurprised to find that she had no wounds at all from the skirmish.

"I thought you said you couldn't fight."

Hawk shot River a look, uncertain if she was teasing him or not and unable to read her expression. Finally Hawk gave up and instead just stared at the ground. "I didn't know what I was doing half the time, and I was just waiting for you to finish your fight so you could help me. All I did was attack blindly."

"But you managed to hold off all four of them, and even kill one," River responded, almost sounding impressed. Then her expression darkened. "You *did* let that one escape. It won't be long until it reaches its Fortress, and soon the whole area will be alerted to our presence."

Hawk flinched, a little uncomfortable with the knowledge that he actually killed something that wasn't prey. He hadn't thought he was capable of such a thing.

"Hell-Cats can't talk, can they?" he ventured. "They aren't smart enough, so it's not like they can tell the other demons that they saw us. Besides…the one that escaped is the one that I set on fire, so it might not even make it back to the Fortress."

River gave Hawk an incredulous look, and suddenly burst out laughing, startling him. Her laughter filled the empty woods while Hawk stared at her with wide eyes.

Is something wrong? She couldn't be laughing…that's just so…not-River. Hawk took a nervous step back.

Finally, River got a hold of herself. She was still snickering when she looked up at Hawk. "Oh, don't give me that look. It's just, the thought of you lighting a demon on fire and sending it packing was just too funny. I didn't know you could be capable of something like that."

The way she puts it makes it sound like I can't scare off anything bigger than a mouse, Hawk thought with a slight scowl. Still, her unexpected outburst made him wary, so he just nodded.

Suddenly River became serious. "There are ways to search a creature's memory, if words fail to convey a message. If that Hell-Cat makes it to the Fortress, its memory will be searched for the reason of its wounds. My… our presence here won't be kept secret for long, and I want to make it to the

Crétioll without any more mishaps." She paused and eyed the wounds marking Hawk's orange pelt. "We can't have you bleeding all over the snow. Do you know how to cast a Cneasaithe?"

"A...a *what*?"

"A *Cneas*...look, just do what I say and no complaining. Light a fire."

Although he very much wanted to ask, Hawk only nodded and obeyed, summoning a small flame after several attempts.

"Say '*sana me.*'"

"What's that mean?"

"I don't know and I don't care, it's just the spell. Now say it."

"S-sana me." Hawk yelped and nearly lost his flame when it suddenly changed from orange to red. River rolled her eyes.

"Good, now burn your wounds."

"*What?*"

"Do it or I'll use *my* magic on you."

Not wanting to suffer the effects of River's water magic again, Hawk swallowed and placed the flame on the cut on his shoulder. Immediately pain seared across the torn flesh, and River closed her jaws around Hawk's muzzle to keep him from yelping. The flame spread to cover the entire wound, even after he had released control over it, and burned for several seconds before fading.

To Hawk's rather pained surprise, his cut had closed.

"That healed nicely." River nosed his shoulder, making him wince. The new skin was rather tender. "It's a little weak, and might tear...but it'll keep you from leaving a trail of blood."

"Wh-what...*was* that?" Hawk blinked, black spots appearing in his vision. His head throbbed, and he felt much weaker than before.

"A Cneasaithe, a healing spell. You lose some of your blood and energy, but it's an effective way of quickly healing wounds. Works better the worse you're wounded, but then you might die from losing the rest of your blood or your power."

"Oh..."

"Now, let's go, before you pass out. The other wounds aren't bleeding enough for a healing. You can rest later."

Biting back a groan, Hawk stumbled after River, focusing simply on staying conscious.

This is going to be a long journey...

Chapter Twenty-Eight

"**Are we going** to have to cross *that*?"

Water surged past Hawk's paws, the sound of its roar pounding in his ears. The river was a dozen feet wide and probably several feet deep. Numerous rocks split the wildly flowing water, churning it into a chaotic mess of rapids. After a week of near-constant travel, River had allowed barely any stops for fear of discovery by the demons searching for the Fire-Fang's killers, Hawk had thought things couldn't get worse.

He regretted such thoughts.

River paused and glared over her shoulder. "Of course! What's the…oh." Realization flashed across her face and she sighed. "Look, a little water won't kill you."

"B-but it's going so *fast*…" As a Fire-Wolf, Hawk had an innate fear of water born from his magic's weakness to it. All wolves feared their polar opposites.

Hawk eyed the water and flattened his ears against his head. He had more reason than most Fire-Wolves to be afraid. Memories of the last time he had found himself before such a large river crept to the front of his mind. Water rising up over his head and rushing down his throat, getting thrown against rocks by the current…

He closed his eyes and shuddered.

"What's wrong?"

Hawk's eyes shot open, and he gave River a surprised look, startled by her sudden concern.

"Just…after I escaped…" he began slowly, unable to read her expression, "I came to a river…I was delirious and slipped when I tried to get close enough to drink. I was too weak to swim, and I got carried away by the current…"

"How did you escape?"

"I…I don't really remember…the water suddenly turned cold, and something grabbed me by my scruff…" Hawk trailed off, remembering the intense panic he had felt when the water almost froze around him. "When I woke up later, I was on the riverbank. There were no paw prints or any scent…if it weren't for the cut on my head or how soaked my fur was, I would have thought I dreamed about my fall or something…" He fell silent, nervously eying the rapids before them.

Now he was faced with rushing water again, with no way around it.

River sank her teeth into his scruff and dragged him toward the water.

"No, River, stop!" Hawk flailed, struggling to free himself. River simply ignored him. He would have had as much luck forcing his way through a stone wall.

Cold water touched his paws, making him yelp. He immediately gagged when it splashed into his mouth, and he was forced to snap his jaws shut or risk swallowing even more as River pulled him all the way into the water.

"'top m'ving or I'll dro' you," the she-wolf growled. Hawk froze and squeezed his eyes shut, his stomach churning as the river surged around him, pulling at his fur and his paws. He whimpered every time a wave splashed against his muzzle.

After what seemed like years to Hawk, his paws brushed solid ground. River dragged him onto the bank and dropped him, spitting out a few tufts of orange fur. "There, now that wasn't so bad, was it?"

Hawk stared at her with as much shock as he would have if she had said that Letorus had decided to give up being Overlord and was going to spend his days frolicking with marsh hares. The very wet and very scared Hawk almost wished he could be facing an Ice-Fang rather than swim through a river like that again.

"Let's go. We can travel a little further before stopping to rest, and then we can slow our pace a little. The patrols shouldn't look this far, so we should be safe for now."

River padded away, leaving Hawk to struggle to his paws and stumble after her. His entire body ached, and his wounds from their last battle throbbed. River had smeared a poultice on it a few days ago, but it had washed away. Hawk felt ready to collapse and let the next demon take him, but he forced himself to keep walking.

One of these days River is going to get me killed.

CHAPTER TWENTY-NINE

SEVERAL DAYS LATER, Hawk stood at the enormous entrance to the Crétioll, staring up in disbelief with wide eyes.

River had said this was where she was going…but I still can't believe we're actually here, Hawk thought, feeling both awed and nervous, wondering what River intended to do now. He swallowed. *Does she mean for us to enter the Crétioll themselves?*

Hawk thought of the stories surrounding the Crétioll and the other Elemental Guardians of Soluna. Each nation had one like it; there was the Fáinéitin surrounding Lough Tighrian, the Ardgao holding Lough Gaoghrian, the Archeo covering Lough Uisceal, and of course the labyrinthine Crétioll guarding Lough Domhgeal.

Each Elemental Guardian protected those sacred lakes, and only the leaders of the nation could enter and leave alive.

Neither of us is a Monarch…much less Earth-Wolf…so what could River possibly want here? Hawk glanced at River, noting the calculating look on her face.

To his horror, River took a step forward, almost into the entrance itself.

"I am River, daughter of Rain and Mist. I seek to use the power that slumbers within this sacred place to defeat the Demon Overlord. Therefore, I beseech you, Mother Moon-Wolf, to grant me safe passage through the Crétioll." The last echoes of her voice faded away, but River made no move to enter the cavern.

Hawk waited, frozen, his eyes flicking between the she-wolf and the cave. *What does she mean by that? Is she waiting for an answer?*

Seconds ticked by, and finally River took a hesitant step forward into the cave. The moment her paw passed the threshold, the earth shook and bits of the cave's ceiling fell to the ground. Hawk tripped over his own paws trying to scramble away from the entrance, but River merely stepped back again, her cool unshaken even when the earth itself shook. Hawk wanted to ask her what she would do now, now that the Crétioll had so obviously rejected her entrance, but he was unsure if he should.

Finally, he gathered enough courage to ask, "What now?"

Her head snapped around at Hawk's voice, and suddenly Hawk was under the full force of an intense stare. He swallowed nervously, not liking the way the calculating look was turned to him. "Wh-what's the matter?"

In answer, River stepped forward to grab Hawk by the scruff of his neck and drag him to stand where she had been just moments before. Hawk looked at his companion in confusion, a question already on his lips, but River interrupted in a low voice, instructing, "You woke the spirits of the ancient Earth-Wolf Monarchs…maybe you can do the same thing here. Say exactly what I said, maybe the caves will accept you."

Hawk stared at River, bewildered. The she-wolf just glared at him as she backed away several paces and motioned for him to start.

Swallowing his fear, Hawk tried to keep his voice from shaking too much. "I…I am Hawk, son of Phoenix and…well…someone else. I seek to use the p-power that s-slumbers…within this s-sacred place to defeat the D-Demon Overlord. Therefore…I beseech you, M-mother Moon-Wolf, to grant me… safe p-passage through the Crétioll."

The ground shook again, but with less force. Hawk looked back at River to see what he should do now and was surprised to see the shock on her face. *Did I do something wrong?*

Movement out of the corner of his eye brought Hawk's attention back to the cave. He tensed, scanning the darkness for the source, ready to flee at a moment's notice. Then something stepped out of the shadows, making Hawk freeze entirely.

It was a wolf made of dirt and rock.

Two glittering silver stones served for eyes, and despite their lifeless-ness they held a piercing gaze that seemed to look straight through Hawk. Stopping in front of him, the creature bowed its head before turning around and walking back into the cave. It paused and motioned with its tail for him to follow.

Hawk looked back at River, but she hadn't moved. She seemed to be trying to tell him something with her eyes, not daring to speak out loud and draw the attention of the strange creature. He flattened his ears, not understanding what River was trying to say.

Do I have to go in…alone? But I don't even know what I'm here for!

"Wait!" Hawk called out to the stone wolf, which paused again just before it would disappear into the shadows. "I…I w-want River to c-come with me."

The wolf turned its head sharply, and glared at Hawk. It shook its head.

Hawk swallowed nervously and tried again. "Please, sh-she has more right than I d-do to enter. I am n-not a child of Moon-Wolf, and she is."

"No, Hawk, you have more right than you realize, even more than she."

Both River and Hawk tensed when they heard the cool female voice. It seemed to be coming from the wolf of dirt, although it had no jaw that Hawk could see.

"...but she may enter with you."

Hawk breathed a sigh of relief as River walked forward to join him before the cave. The stone wolf turned back and led the two into the darkness. A few moments later, the wolf began to glow softly. The numerous gems and rough jewels packed into its dirt pelt shone with an inner light, reflecting rainbow glimmers onto the walls.

Walking in the dark, Hawk lost all sense of direction. He soon also lost track of how long they had been walking. There was a chill in the air, and it was just as dark, and yet Hawk felt secure.

It didn't take long for Hawk to learn why only those accepted by the Crétioll could pass through safely. Even if trespassers didn't get lost and starve to death, the magic of the caves would finish them off. Several times River, Hawk, and their silent guide passed collapsed tunnels, blocked by immovable piles of rock and dirt. Once Hawk saw a bit of a skeletal paw jutting out from the wreckage.

Hawk didn't know how long they walked before he saw a soft glow up ahead. His heart started to race with excitement.

Are we finally there? Will Lough Domhgeal be just as beautiful as the legends say it is? He took a deep breath, his tail wagging a little. *I'm going to be the only Fire-Wolf to ever see the sacred Earth-Wolf Lough, and the first wolf at all in over a century!* He cast a side-long glance at River. She, too, seemed excited. *Is she eager to see it...or is she more excited to reach the 'slumbering power' she mentioned when begging Moon-Wolf for entrance?*

Stepping into the light being emitted from the Lough, the jewel-encrusted wolf fell to pieces. Hawk, however, hardly noticed. He and River stood on a rise above the Lough, looking down upon its splendor. Just as the stories said, it was shaped like a crescent moon. A silvery liquid, shimmering with light from an unknown source, filled the pool. The lake itself glowed, and the waters rippled with gentle waves. The surrounding cave was bathed in the lake's gentle, silver light, and the walls seemed to reflect the brilliance. Even River seemed stunned by its beauty. Hawk felt as if he were intruding on something, and that it was a sin for someone as unworthy as he to be here.

After a few moments of standing in silence and absorbing the awe-inspiring view, River motioned for Hawk to lead the way down the narrow path.

Chapter Thirty

Lough Domhgeal was even more striking up close. Hawk felt humbled standing by its sacred waters, which looked thicker than normal water. *It's almost like it's mud…but much cleaner and purer…maybe the water is affected by the earth magic of the Crétioll…*

"Hawk, I am going to need you to speak for me again." River's voice was low, as though she were afraid of breaking the sacred silence that hung over the Lough. "You will need to stand on the banks of the crescent's inner curve, over on that flat stone," she gestured toward a large, flat gray stone that lay several feet away, "and say these words. Don't worry about the meaning. That will be *my* concern."

Quietly, she instructed Hawk in what to say, making him repeat it several times before she was satisfied that he had it memorized. Nervously, he walked up to the flat stone and placed a paw on its smooth surface. He immediately pulled his paw back when the stone glowed softly with a silver light. The faint print left behind slowly faded. After a glance at River, he stepped back onto the stone. He stood, frozen, for a few more minutes, gathering the courage to speak. When he did, he surprised himself with the strength of his voice. "I, Hawk, son of Phoenix, stand before you, Mother Moon-Wolf, to beg for your help. The land and your children are enslaved by a monster, and I seek to free them. Only with your help will I be able to do so. If you so will it, grant me the power I need by the Night of Moon-Sun. I swear that I will not use your power for evil deeds, and if I should break my word, my life may be taken as punishment."

Hawk hoped that he wouldn't accidentally 'misuse' this power; he didn't want to die for making some stupid mistake. River had reassured him that he wouldn't need to worry about it, and that she would take care of it when the time came.

As the last echoes of his short speech died down, the waters churned. The light grew stronger, until Hawk had to close his eyes or risk being blinded. When the light dimmed, Hawk opened his eyes. The cave was dark, and even the glow from the silvery waters was subdued.

Looking back at River, Hawk saw her motion for him to come away from the waters. Gladly, he did. The loss of the lake's light made him uneasy, and it seemed like a strong presence had left the cave. Silently, River led the way back up to the entrance, where the dirt wolf had reformed once more and was waiting for them. When they reached it, it turned and started leading the way through the tunnels, its soft glow much dimmer than before.

Finally, Hawk and River stepped back out into the forest. Most of the day had already passed, and the sun's dying rays were just barely penetrating the cloudy sky overhead.

Their guide fell apart, and the two wolves were left alone in front of the imposing entrance to the Crétioll. River stood silently in the shadow of the caves, lost in thought, for several minutes. When the silence continued, Hawk cast a glance back at her. The she-wolf was giving him an intense stare again.

Quickly Hawk turned back around. "What do we do now?"

"Now...I think it is time I told you everything, Hawk."

The Fire-Wolf turned sharply and stared at River, shocked. "What? Tell me about what?" he asked warily. *I have to pry answers from her for even simple questions...and now she suddenly wants to reveal everything?*

"There is more to you than meets the eye," River replied cryptically, her eyes narrow. "After all that...I think you'll be more helpful to me than I realized at first. But if you *are* to help me, then you need to know more."

Silently, River padded past Hawk and disappeared into the forest. Hawk hurried after her, his heart pounding in excitement.

After several minutes of walking, River managed to find another abandoned clan camp beneath an enormous oak tree. After pausing to collect some sticks for a fire, the she-wolf led them into the camp, which was much bigger than any camp they had stayed in before. Hawk wondered for a brief moment if perhaps this was the clan that housed the Earth-Wolf Monarchs, but he soon turned his attention to starting a campfire. As he coaxed the flames into life, his stomach grumbled, but he was too curious about what River had to say to even think about attempting to hunt.

River remained silent for a long time, staring into the flames. She seemed apprehensive about speaking. Hawk waited, equally silent, until River finally looked up, her expression neutral.

"Do know that if you hear this story, you will be in much more danger than before. Letorus would hunt you down mercilessly if he knew there was another who knew this. Are you sure you want to help me? Now is your last chance to back out."

Hawk tilted his head slightly. He was already constantly in danger due to his status as an escaped slave, but he knew River was trying to warn him away from something even worse. His stomach turned at the thought of getting into more situations like the battle with the Shade-Tigers or the flight from the wraith, but the words of the Earth King and his own promise to River kept echoing in his head. "I know it's going to be dangerous, but I won't leave," he said firmly.

River held Hawk's gaze for a few seconds, as though trying to see if he was truly sincere. Finally she nodded. "Very well then. First I will tell you what… what happened to the Water-Wolves."

Chapter Thirty-One

Hawk held his breath, trying to keep from looking too excited as River began her story.

"About four months before the demons came, Clan Archeo found…something strange outside the Archeo. It just hung in the air, like some gaping wound. A Rift. My…they were astonished; they had never seen anything like it before. Nothing could get closer than a few feet to it; birds flying overhead simply swerved to avoid it." River paused, her expression darkening and her voice hardening into a snarl.

"It emanated a strange power and feeling of evil. So what do the Water-Wolves do? They try to get close to it." The she-wolf scraped her claws across the ground, as though trying to physically hold herself back from flying into a rage. "Any *sane* wolf would have avoided such a thing, but the Queen, the leader of the Uiscean Marsh at the time, was anything *but* sane. She only saw the Rift as a source of *power*. They studied the Rift and tried for months to get close to it, and many Water-Wolves died in the process. Many began to think they should leave the Rift alone, but no one dared to go against the Queen — her word was law.

"Finally, something…broke, and the Water-Wolves were able to get close to the Rift. The Queen was searching for a way to harness the power the Rift produced. She got it into her head that they should try to *enter* the Rift and snatch the power from the inside. Did she know if it was even possible to go into the Rift or if the wolf who entered would survive upon entering? No, but she didn't care. She was too consumed by her greed to think of others." River stopped, baring her teeth.

Hawk shuffled a little as her silence stretched on, uncertain if she was going to continue. Just as he was gathering up the courage to ask what happened next, River began speaking again. "By that point, the whole clan knew of her insanity, but she was still the strongest, and no one dared to oppose her. It took time, but finally they were able to find a way to open the Rift a little and allow a wolf to pass through. The first one…my…my brother…never came back. The second one…came back alive, but completely deranged. He raved about demons and hell and tried to convince the other members of the clan to forget about the Rift. The Queen imprisoned him for that. The third wolf who entered came back alive and sane — or so they thought. *This* wolf said he had found a way to open the rift even more, and he told the Queen that by opening it she would be able to control its power."

River's voice grew so quiet Hawk had to strain to hear. "But the wolf was *lying*. He had been possessed by a demon, and tricked the clan into opening the Rift to allow…a greater evil to escape."

Hawk's stomach churned, and he swallowed. He could guess what that 'greater evil' was.

"When the Queen…entered the Rift…her entry opened it enough to allow Letorus to escape. He killed her and cast the rest of the clan in, allowing some of the demons to escape. But Letorus didn't stop there. He feared that the other Water-Wolves knew what we knew, so he imprisoned every last Water-Wolf in Uiscean Marsh inside the Rift and freed most of his army in the process. That…was when he invaded the rest of Soluna."

The she-wolf fell silent, her eyes fixed on the flames between them.

"We're…still there, trapped in the Rift. I…I can't tell you what it's like."

Hawk perked his ears when River started speaking again, barely able to hear her whispered voice. She sounded more vulnerable than Hawk had ever heard her.

"If…if I could forget it all, I would." She paused and took a deep breath before continuing a little louder. "We knew that we were the only chance of saving Soluna, and we spent many years trying to find a way to kill Letorus, and return the demons to the Rift. Finally…we did. We found a way to fix our…*my* mistake…and even close up the Rift. It was a risky plan. We weren't even sure it would work…but it was our only hope."

River fell quiet again, leaving Hawk's mind whirling with the surge of information.

Wait …her mistake? Hawk tilted his head slightly in confusion. *River said her brother was the first to die…it was* her *mistake…but that all happened over a century ago. How could she have a brother then and still be alive today?*

But if she had been trapped in the rift all these years, it would explain so much. The mysterious and complete disappearance of the Water-Wolves, how the demons were able to take the Island by surprise…even River's fear of the Dorasca Gorge. *I can't even imagine what being in there would be like…the home of the demons. The Water-Wolves must live in terror every day…* Hawk glanced at River, who had yet to look up from the flames. *And the rumors that claim the Water-Wolves brought the demons here are true. They're the ones who…started this war. But…I can't really be angry with them…it's not like they* intended *to cause all this.*

But Letorus is so powerful…how can he possibly be killed?

River spoke again. "We could only send one of us through the Rift safely, and everyone else would be needed to…help them through. Many were apprehensive about leaving, knowing that once they did Letorus would hunt them mercilessly. So I…volunteered, and I managed to escape while Letorus was summoning demons. Unfortunately, he saw me escaping…and probably suspects that I know how to defeat him. I fled the marsh, and have been on the run since."

Doesn't that sound familiar? Hawk winced slightly. He himself hadn't stayed in a single area for more than a few weeks ever since his escape from Ignimor Fortress. Constantly living in fear and always wary of capture would wear anyone down, even the strongest spirit. *Considering just where she came from, I'm surprised River's not totally insane.*

"In six months, there will be a total Eclipse of the Sun. If, by that point, I have gathered the elemental energy that resides in each of the sacred Loughs of each nation, and I can trap Letorus near the original opening of the Rift, then I can re-open it." A strange gleam appeared in River's eyes. "When I do *that*, I can kill Letorus, banish the demons back to the Rift, and pull out every wolf who's trapped there."

"How…"

"The way the Rift works," River interrupted, "is that if something leaves it, something else must enter it. By releasing the wolves trapped inside, I can draw in a large amount of demons. The few that escape banishment can be easily killed."

Mind spinning, Hawk tried to digest this new flow of information. *A total Eclipse, when all three Moons cover the Sun? According to the legends, it's only happened once or twice before, but can something like that really do all that River said it would?* "I don't understand. What will the Eclipse do? How does it work? What do the Loughs have to do with it?"

"The Eclipse is nothing more than a vessel for power. What you did at Lough Domhgeal was release the ancient earth magic, which is a diluted form of moon magic, and the closest thing we can get to *pure* moon magic without breaking into Lough Soluna." The she-wolf paused and grimaced. "We're not desperate enough to do *that*, yet. When I channel the power of the Loughs through the light of the Eclipse, it will be purified and return to what it was originally: pure energy of Moon-Wolf and Sun-Wolf."

River intends to use the pure power of the gods? A mixture of shock and horror rushed through Hawk. *That would be suicide! To try and wield so much power would burn up any wolf...not to mention the fact that River wouldn't be compatible with sun magic. She's a Water-Wolf; her power comes from Moon-Wolf.* "But sun magic will kill you; a Water-Wolf can't bear Sun-Wolf's power," he protested. "I'm a Fire-Wolf; let me help you use the power of the Eclipse!"

River shook her head. "No, that won't be possible. The Eclipse's energy will be a mix of both sun magic and moon magic, you can't separate the two. Only one wolf will be able to channel it. I am prepared to die if it means I can save Soluna."

The steeliness in River's voice told Hawk that she wasn't going to allow anymore arguments, so Hawk dropped the topic for now. Instead, he asked, "River...how old are you?"

"Eleven." The blue-gray Water-Wolf narrowed her eyes in suspicion. "Why do you ask?"

"You...you said you had...lost your brother to the Rift...that he was the first to enter. That was over a century ago...so how is that possible?"

"Time doesn't pass at the same rate inside the Rift. I thought it had only been a few decades since we were first sealed into the Rift...but I know now much more time has passed." River paused for a moment. "My people have been trapped in there for more than one hundred years, but not one of us is a day older than we were when we entered the Rift. I was eleven when I was trapped with my people all those years ago, and I am still eleven now."

Hawk's eyes widened. *The Water-Wolves have been stuck in that timelessness...for the entire war.* That's *why River knew nothing about the fortresses or the resistance groups or slavery...none of that existed when the war started.* Then another thought hit him. *If the Water-Wolves didn't know that they were frozen in time...then what if that makes the date of the Eclipse...wrong?*

When Hawk said as much, River growled. "For all I know, we could be wrong, because we only had the words of a Seer to rely on. But you were able to release the energy from Lough Domhgeal, so we must be right." And with that, River turned away from Hawk and the fire, signifying the end of any conversation for the night. Hawk put his head down on his paws, but his mind was whirling with so many thoughts that he couldn't settle down to sleep. There was so much he still didn't understand, so much he didn't know.

Only months ago I was a slave…now suddenly I'm wrapped up in a plot to free the Island! I don't even know what to think anymore… But knowing there was a chance, however slight, that Letorus could be killed and Soluna saved gave Hawk hope and encouraged him to trust River. He could find answers to everything later.

Eventually, Hawk managed to quiet his mind and fall into a dreamless sleep.

Chapter Thirty-Two

THE NEXT MORNING River woke Hawk early.

Very early.

He was fighting back huge yawns when he emerged into the cold, early winter morning sunlight. It felt as if he had been asleep only a few minutes.

"Why do we…" A wide yawn interrupted him. "…have to get up so early?"

River snorted. "Because we need to hunt, and knowing you, it will take most of the morning to track something down, and that's not including the time it will take you to actually *kill* your prey."

Growing hot with embarrassment, Hawk shuffled his paws and muttered an apology.

"Just get going, and try not to take too long," River said as she padded off into the trees. "And please try to catch something; I would rather not hunt *for* you."

A little disheartened, Hawk turned and walked off in the other direction. He wished that River would at least stay with him to help, because he would rather not be alone in the quiet forest. He was a little comforted by the fact that if the wind was blowing in the right direction, and he tried hard enough, he could smell her.

Determined to prove himself to River, Hawk put his nose in the air and breathed in deeply, sorting out all the forest scents. He could smell several birds, but they were too far up in the trees for him to get. There was a large animal of some sort that Hawk didn't recognize nearby, but Hawk didn't think he would be able to hunt it on his own. He wasn't even sure if the animal was dangerous or not.

I should probably just give it some space…

Skirting around the unknown animal, Hawk kept searching for attainable prey. Finally, he found a scent. He didn't know what it was, but it smelled tasty — and small enough to be easy to take down.

Please don't be a rabbit…or be one with a broken leg…I can't run fast enough to catch something like that…

Pain suddenly exploded behind Hawk's ears, but he was given no chance to cry out before darkness swam across his vision and he fell unconscious.

Chapter Thirty-Three

"Hawk!" River tried to keep her voice down, not wanting to shout too loudly for fear of alerting others, demons or otherwise. A few hours had passed, and she had yet to find any trace of her wayward companion. It was as if he had simply vanished. The snow that had started thirty minutes earlier wasn't helping her search. Normally, such things wouldn't bother her, but her senses were still a little blocked with the scent of blood after hunting, and Hawk's usual trail of melted snow was nowhere to be seen.

At first, River thought Hawk had simply gotten lost. He was the kind of wolf who would lose his own tail if it wasn't attached to him. Now, however, she was getting a little worried.

River snorted irritably. For a moment River entertained the idea of simply continuing on without him. If Hawk had gotten captured by a patrol, that was his problem. She had no time to waste on heroics.

Then she remembered how Hawk had been able to enter the Crétioll when *she* had been refused entry. *I don't actually need him to* use *the power, he just released it so it'll be free to answer my summons at the Eclipse…but I might need him for the Guardians of the Sun Elements. If the Crétioll wouldn't let me in, I doubt the Ardgao or the Fáinéitin will.*

I could always threaten another wolf into doing that for me. River hesitated, wavering on whether or not to go after Hawk or leave him. Then she remembered the sheer terror in Hawk's eyes when he was attacked by the patrol of Ice-Fangs and how much he shook when any other demon appeared. She also remembered how scared Hawk had been when she first saw his slave collar. How he had promised to help her and be her friend, although she had given him more than enough reason to leave, and how he kept to that promise even when she had warned him that Letorus himself would hunt them.

River sighed. She was getting soft. There was no way she could live with herself if she turned away now and abandoned Hawk. A few days ago, she wouldn't have given him a second thought.

Now, things were different.

Besides, I already told him everything. I don't want that information falling into the wrong paws. Despite what she told herself, River knew at the back of her mind that such a reason didn't mean as much as she pretended.

Her ears swiveled, detecting the faint sound of leaves crunching under paws. She spun around, teeth bared in a vicious snarl, ready to kill any demon who dared attack her.

Instead, staring at her with wide, frightened eyes was a young Earth-Wolf with dark red fur and stormy gray eyes. It took a moment or two before River was able to flatten her hackles and assume a slightly saner expression. "Who are you?" she asked, barely able to keep the growl out of her voice.

"My...my name is Bracken," the other she-wolf stammered. Then her eyes fell to the breed mark on River's shoulder, and they widened. "Are you a Water-Wolf?"

"No, I'm a purple-feathered squirrel. Of course I'm a Water-Wolf!" River snapped, feeling her anger rise again. *Stay calm; it would* not *help matters if you killed her, it would only attract unwanted attention...*

Bracken flinched at River's harsh tone. "I'm sorry, it's just...unbelievable. I thought all Water-Wolves were...gone."

"Well, guess what? Here I am." Now she was starting to get irritated. She had already decided to go hunting after Hawk, and she was anxious to get moving. The Fire-Wolf's trail was getting colder the more time she wasted, and River needed to find it before it disappeared completely. It was obvious that this Earth-Wolf was nothing but an empty-headed idiot incapable of anything but staring.

Abruptly, River turned and walked away, intent on finding Hawk's trail before it became impossible to follow. She hoped that the other she-wolf would take the hint and leave.

Unfortunately, that was not the case.

"What are you doing?"

Much to River's displeasure, the younger Earth-Wolf had sped up to pad alongside her. River growled and quickened her pace. "Looking," she said bluntly.

"For what?"

Moon-Wolf, give me patience, or I will end up doing something I will regret, River thought, struggling to keep her anger in check. "For someone."

"Who?"

This is getting ridiculous. I thought Earth-Wolves weren't supposed to be this bubble-headed.

"A wolf," River answered shortly. *Maybe it'll be okay to bite her...just a little...*

"Another Water-Wolf?"

Make that a big bite. Maybe if I chomp down on her rump she'll finally be sent packing, River growled to herself, seriously considering acting on her thoughts.

"He's a Fire-Wolf."

"He? Is he your mate?"

"No! Now shut up and leave me be!" River stopped suddenly, spinning to face Bracken and snarling viciously. Her eyes were darkening with anger as she struggled to maintain control.

It would be a bad thing to kill her, a very bad thing. Bad, bad ba–

River's thoughts were suddenly cut off as a large shape slammed into her. Caught by surprise, River's breath rushed from her lungs as she was thrown to the earth.

"Mother!" Bracken jumped away, equally startled by the sudden appearance.

Caught up in the battle, and happy that she could finally dig her claws into something, River lost connection with her surroundings. She surged to her paws, breaking the Earth-Wolf's pin and knocking her opponent off balance. Even though the other she-wolf was large for her breed, River had her beat by at least a foot. The difference in size didn't surprise River in the least. Water-Wolves were always taller than Earth-Wolves, something River had discovered seemed to have been forgotten in the time the Water-Wolves had been gone.

Teeth bared, River bunched her muscles as she prepared to jump, only to be thrown back to the ground when the earth suddenly shifted beneath her paws. Before she could recover, the other Earth-Wolf leapt on River, her teeth clamping down on River's scruff. River immediately melted into snow, causing her opponent's jaws to snap shut on empty air.

"Stop, Mother!" Bracken raced over, throwing herself in front of the older Earth-Wolf, trying to prevent her mother from burying all the snow within view under a thick layer of stone. "She's not a demon; she's a wolf, a Water-Wolf!"

The Earth-Wolf stopped at her daughter's words, surprised. She had been so busy attacking her daughter's would-be attacker that she hadn't even stopped to register the wave breed mark on the Water-Wolf's left shoulder.

River, on the other paw, wasn't so easily deterred. The moment her opponent was distracted, she reformed and struck. Taking both Earth-Wolves by surprise, River had the older wolf pinned and was at her throat before either of them could react. Her opponent stared up at her with frightened eyes, and dimly River could hear Bracken shouting something. She sounded oddly like…Hawk.

Hawk?

"…*stop…my mother…Earth-Wolf*…"

Slowly, the red mist obscuring River's vision faded, and the Water-Wolf saw how close she had come to murdering Bracken's mother. The older Earth-Wolf's dark brown eyes flooded with relief when she saw the other she-wolf relax and her eyes lighten.

She had narrowly escaped death at the Water-Wolf's jaws.

Still slightly numb with the realization of the atrocity she had nearly committed, River slowly stepped back to let Bracken's mother stand. Bracken immediately ran over and began licking her mother's face with relief. The Earth-Wolf returned her daughter's enthusiastic licks, a little shaken by what had just happened. River backed away several more paces, trying to clear her head.

Warily, Bracken and her mother padded over to River.

"I'm sorry for acting without thinking," Bracken's mother bowed her head slightly, but without moving her eyes away from River. "From my point of view, it looked like you were about to attack my daughter, but you were probably just telling her to get out of your fur. I know how…friendly she can be with strangers. I'm Pine."

Actually, River *had* been just about to tear Bracken's throat out, but she wisely neglected to correct Pine. Looking up at the older Earth-Wolf, River got a good look at her former opponent for the first time. Her pelt was colored a rare pale yellow, and her eyes, now that they weren't clouded with fear, were warm and welcoming.

"Mother, the Water-Wolf said she was looking for someone."

Pine cocked her head. "Are you? You wouldn't happen to be connected to that poor Fire-Wolf male we saw taken by the demons, would you?"

Immediately, River's entire demeanor changed. She leapt to her paws, practically shoving her muzzle in Pine's face. "You saw Hawk? Where? When? What did the Fire-Wolf look like?"

Bracken's ears dropped in confusion. "Hawk? Isn't that a Wind-Wolf name? I thought you were looking for a Fire-Wolf…"

River waved her tail dismissively. "Hawk's a Fire-Wolf. Now answer my questions!"

"He was rather large for a Fire-Wolf," Pine said, interrupting anything else Bracken tried to say, "and he had bright orange fur. I'm surprised he hasn't been caught before now, a pelt like that could be seen for miles around."

"Where did you see him? And when?"

"About a mile or so north of here, and two hours ago. He was captured by a patrol of four Hell-Cats, one Ice-Fang, and three Night-Lynxes."

River groaned at the sound of the Ice-Fang. Hawk was probably scared out of his wits right now, and that was only if they hadn't caught sight of his slave collar. *If they find out about that…* She didn't finish the thought.

"I need to go." River abruptly turned to the direction Pine had gestured. Before she had gotten two paces, however, the two Earth-Wolves stopped her.

"You can't possibly be thinking of taking on that whole demon patrol on your own!" Bracken protested. "There are too many for a single wolf to fight."

Growling, River tried to push her way past Pine and her daughter. She had as much success as if she had tried to walk through a stone wall. "Let me through. I can handle a patrol of that size."

Pine shook her head. "No, you can't; you won't be doing your friend any good if you rush in there without a plan and get yourself captured." River opened her mouth to speak, but Pine cut her off. "Let us help you. We have our own scores to settle with that particular patrol anyway."

The yellow Earth-Wolf's voice grew hard, and River gave her a long, scrutinizing look.

"Is it just you two?"

Bracken shook her head. "No, there are four more with us: two Earth-Wolves and two Wind-Wolves."

River, realizing that time was ticking away the more she argued, relented. "Fine. Get the rest of your group."

Both Earth-Wolves nodded, obviously relieved, and turned to lead their new companion back through the trees.

"You never told us your name, Water-Wolf," Pine said over her shoulder as she carefully navigated across a partially frozen creek, her heavy paws making the ice groan.

"River."

"Well, River, nice to meet you. Pity we couldn't have met under better circumstances."

By the time they finally made it to Pine's camp, River was feeling very antsy. The other four members of the group were lounging around, seemingly waiting for something. One of them, a wild-eyed Wind-Wolf with gray fur and several long scars along his side, jumped up when they appeared.

"Pine! Bracken! Finally! We were about to send out a search party for you two."

"We're fine, Crag," Pine answered. "Although I worry for the safety of the camp if *this* is how it is when I'm gone. Did none of you think to set up a watch? What if some demons had found you? They could have taken you by surprise."

Crag shrugged. "We hadn't scented anymore patrols nearby, so I figured we were safe."

Pine nipped his muzzle. "Never assume anything. Always expect the worst, that way the only surprises are good ones."

The Wind-Wolf just rolled his sky-blue eyes. "Yeah, whatever. Did you figure out where the patrol that took Oak is headed?" Then he noticed River, who stood slightly behind the Earth-Wolf females, watching the rest of the group a little apprehensively.

"Who is that?" His eyes widened. "Is she a Water-Wolf?"

Bracken nodded excitedly. "Yes, her name is River."

River glared at each member of the group, not liking the sudden attention they gave her. It kept them at a respectful distance but didn't stop their mixed looks of shock and curiosity.

"All right, everyone, listen up!" Pine stepped forward, interrupting the group's inspection and drawing their full attention.

"This is River. She's the companion of the orange Fire-Wolf we saw captured by the same patrol that took Oak. She'll be coming with us."

There were a few murmurs, but they quieted when Pine continued. "I also found out where the patrol is headed. They'll be meeting up with another patrol sometime tomorrow morning, but their final destination is the Obsolium Fortress, on the other side of the Bann River."

The Water-Wolf growled quietly. More demons meant a higher chance of Hawk's secret being discovered. She had to hurry, or there might not be much of Hawk left for her to find. River paused, a little surprised by how much she was worried for her companion. "So let's leave now." River turned and immediately started walking out of camp, not caring if the others followed or not.

A wall of earth rose up in front of her, stopping her in her tracks. "Hold on, River." Pine took a few steps forward to meet her. "We can't just go rushing in without a plan. Shortly, we won't have just one, but *two* patrols to deal with."

River spun around, snarling. "The longer we take to track them down, the colder the trail gets!"

Although the others of her group shrank back a bit in face of the River's fury, Pine kept her cool. "I understand that, but we know where the patrol is headed, so there is no need for us to track them."

That still doesn't make a difference! "You don't understand. Hawk…is an escaped slave. The more time we waste here the more likely it is that that'll be discovered!"

A flicker of surprise crossed Pine's face, but her demeanor did not change. "I understand your worry. My mate, Oak, was taken by the patrol, and he is also an escaped slave. As am I."

With a jolt, River suddenly noticed the slave collar encircling the Earth-Wolf's neck. It was mostly covered by Pine's thick yellow neck fur, and the metal itself was tarnished with age. It was also covered in some kind of yellowish paint. If Pine hadn't pointed it out, River may have never noticed it.

Looking around at the others in the group, River saw that they were all in fact escaped slaves, even Bracken. Taking a deep breath, River forced herself to lower her hackles and speak in a calmer voice. "Fine. What is your plan?"

Pine gave River a grateful nod, and then gestured for her companions to gather as she outlined her plan. "We know that the patrol that took Oak and Hawk are going to meet up with another one soon. We don't know what that second patrol will consist of, but it's best to assume that it'll be just as strong as, if not stronger than, the first one." She drew a rough map into the dirt, marking where the patrol's end destination was located. "The last we saw of the patrol was here," Pine made another mark not too far from their current location, "and it will probably take the patrol thirteen days to reach the Fortress. Here," she circled a spot a few days from the Fortress, "is where we'll stop them. There's an abandoned clan camp there, and we'll use that to trap the demons."

River narrowed her eyes, not entirely sold on the plan. "How do you know the patrol will be there? They could take any route."

"The patrol is escorting captured wolves; they're not going to waste time wandering around and waiting to be attacked. The most direct route will lead them past the clan camp by a few hundred feet, but once they get close enough, we'll lure them into the right spot. We'll get the demons over the caves, and make the earth collapse." Pine bared her teeth, her eyes glittering. "The demons will be trapped."

Bracken, Crag, and the others nodded to show their understanding. River, however, spotted a hole in the plan. "Doing that would bury Hawk and Oak as well."

Pine snorted. "You're forgetting something. My mate is an Earth-Wolf. It would be pretty pathetic if he was to allow himself to get buried, and I'm sure he would be watching out for Hawk and any other captured wolves as well."

Grudgingly, River had to admit to the brilliance in Pine's plan. It played exactly to the strengths of the group.

The yellow Earth-Wolf swiped a heavy paw over the map to erase it. "All right, let's move out."

Finally. Relief filled River as they raced out of the camp. *I'm on my way, Hawk.*

CHAPTER THIRTY-FOUR

HAWK WAS TERRIFIED. Waking up in the clutches of demons was never a good thing, but waking up to find himself surrounded by demons nearly made Hawk fall back into unconsciousness.

"Easy, lad," a voice near Hawk's ear whispered. "It's best to pretend you're still out."

Despite the advice, Hawk nearly jumped right out of his fur. He quickly obeyed, however, when he noticed the Ice-Fang lying a few lengths away. The demon appeared to be sleeping, but Hawk didn't want to do anything to attract notice from the other demons gathered in the small clearing. The lack of a campfire helped obscure the slight movements of the two captives, shrouded as they were in the dark of the forest.

"Sorry, I didn't mean to scare you."

Without moving or giving any sign of being awake, Hawk glanced out of the corner of his eye. A light green Earth-Wolf lay beside him, also feigning sleep.

"My name's Oak, by the way," the Earth-Wolf muttered, his voice barely audible. "If they think we're asleep or unconscious, they'll leave us alone. It'll give us a chance to talk. What's your name, son?"

"Hawk."

"Nice to meet you, Hawk. How did they get you?"

The two wolves fell silent when another demon, a Night-Lynx, passed by and said something to the Ice-Fang. When the Night-Lynx had continued on and the Ice-Fang settled back down to sleep, Hawk answered in a low voice, "I was hunting, and something attacked me. I don't really know what happened. What about you?"

"The Night-Lynxes got me. I'm ashamed to say I didn't put up much of a fight. One of the blighters caught my eye, and I was out like a light. You're very lucky they didn't see your slave collar, though, with the way they were handling you when they first brought you in."

Hawk's blood immediately ran cold. "Y-you saw?"

The Earth-Wolf only chuckled softly. "Don't worry, lad, I won't tell. I was a slave as well."

Breathing a sigh of relief, Hawk flicked his eyes to the other wolf's neck and could just barely pick out the slave collar there. The Earth-Wolf's naturally thick coat covered most of the collar, and what could be seen was colored with green paint.

"I think it was mostly because your fur, which is the thickest I've ever seen on a Fire-Wolf, covered it. But just to be safe, I'll help you hide it better. Here's a trick I learned a while back."

Keeping one eye on the Ice-Fang, Oak quietly summoned up some reddish earth, flicked it onto Hawk, and quickly rubbed it into the metal. The collar's silver soon dulled, tarnishing until it appeared more orange than gray, and was almost invisible against Hawk's fur.

"There we go, now it's even more unnoticeable."

They fell silent again when two Hell-Cats passed by. Hawk was almost certain that his heart was beating loud enough for everyone in the camp to hear. But the demons walked on past, only pausing to sniff curiously at the two prisoners.

"Now just sit tight, lad," Oak whispered when the Hell-Cats were gone. "My pack is close by, and they'll find a way to free us."

Hawk felt a glimmer of hope rise in his chest. *Help is coming!* Then another thought hit him. *What about River? Was she captured as well?* He immediately dismissed the notion, highly doubting the possibility of such a thing. If River did run across some demons, it was either kill or be killed. 'Capture' was not an option. It was even more unlikely that River *had* been killed.

I wonder if she noticed I was missing. I don't know how long I was out, or how far I am from where I was captured. Will she come looking for me? For a moment, Hawk wondered if River would simply leave him, but he firmly pushed the thought away. *No, I have to have faith in River.*

What if River meets up with Oak's resistance group? Hawk clenched his teeth a little in worry. *She doesn't exactly...do well with strangers. What if she gets into a fight with them?*

"Get the prisoners up; we're moving out!"

The harsh command of one of the Night-Lynxes startled Hawk out of his thoughts, and he hurried to stand, far too familiar with what happened when a wolf was too slow to obey. His shoulder groaned in protest at the sudden movement, stiff after being pressed to the ground for so long. He winced and crumpled.

The Ice-Fang, upon seeing Hawk's struggle to get up, growled. It marched over and shoved Oak, who tried to help Hawk to his paws before the demon could reach them.

No! Hawk's heart leapt into his throat, but he could do nothing as the demon sank its fangs into his scruff, only to pull back a moment later with a hiss of pain when its teeth scraped across the metal collar instead of soft skin. All feeling drained away when a cruel glint appeared in the Ice-Fang's eyes, and it dove for Hawk's neck. Teeth closed around his collar and hauled him to his paws.

The Ice-Fang had found his slave collar.

Chapter Thirty-Five

Four days into the journey, they lost sight of the demon patrol.

Pine appeared unconcerned, claiming that the patrol had simply strayed from their projected path in order to meet up with the other patrol. She kept them to their path, which ran parallel to where they thought the demons were, and picked up the pace so they could reach the Bann River first and set up their trap. They were now five days from the Obsolium Fortress, but had yet to find any sign of the patrol, something that made River a little nervous.

We should have gone after the patrol the moment we lost them, picked up their trail, and made sure they were going the way we need them. What if they took a different route? They could be approaching the Fortress while we waste our time here cleaning our pelts!

"Hey River, I'm going hunting, want to come?"

River struggled to hold back a groan of frustration when the bubbly Bracken appeared. The empty-headed she-wolf had yet to leave River alone, despite attempts to make Bracken get a clue and stop bothering her. The friendly, open Earth-Wolf just kept bouncing back.

"No. I'm not hungry." River would have liked nothing more than to go find something to eat, as she had had nothing since the small thrush she had caught the day Hawk was captured, but she refused to spend any more time than she had to in the company of the irritating Earth-Wolf. A loud growl from her stomach made Bracken wag her tail. River huffed and turned away. "I hunt alone."

That didn't dissuade Bracken, however, because she still tagged along, bouncing after River. Soon the rest of the group had joined them. River was steaming with frustration. Aside from Hawk, her brother had been the only wolf who could put up with her temper.

Shoving aside the pang of grief at the thought of her brother, River gritted her teeth and turned her focus to the struggle to avoid murdering everyone for being so annoying. "Does *everyone* have to come?"

An Earth-Wolf female with dark green fur, named Leaf, gave River a toothy grin. "Of course! It's easier if we hunt as a group — and more fun."

River mumbled under her breath and attempted to slip away from the group unnoticed. The two Wind-Wolves, Crag, and a smoky gray she-wolf named Breeze, saw her sneaking off and stopped her, sandwiching her between them.

"Come on, River, don't be a spoil-sport," Breeze said, giving River a companionable shove.

"Yeah, you've been nothing but a grump for the past two days, loosen up a bit!" Crag added.

"I don't need to 'loosen up,'" River snapped, struggling to escape her captors. "Now let me go!"

"Quiet in the ranks!" Pine called back. "We've scented a deer!"

Immediately the three fell silent, although neither Wind-Wolf lessened the pressure they were keeping on either side of River, offering her no chance to escape.

River gritted her teeth, resigning herself to her fate. *I might as well humor them.*

Pine looked to Mud, a dark red Earth-Wolf male, who nodded. He gestured with his muzzle, pointing in the direction he had scented the deer. Now that River was focusing, she could smell the deer in question, although it was still too far away to spot between the trees. Silently, Pine motioned for the others to gather around. Crag and Breeze immediately left River, who followed after a moment's hesitation, to obey.

"River, you and I will strike from the front and surprise the deer," Pine whispered. "The rest of you are to surround the deer and block off his escape. Don't show yourself until the deer runs your way. And be careful, the stag smells a little weak, but he won't hesitate to run you through. We cannot afford any injuries."

Everyone nodded before separating and slinking away through the undergrowth. Within seconds, the wolves of the resistance group had disappeared. Pine and River crept forward toward the deer, keeping downwind of their prey. Soon they were rewarded with the sight of a large buck with a broken antler. Blood caked one of his legs, remnants of a partially healed gash on his shoulder.

Picked a fight with the wrong enemy, River thought with a little amusement, eyeing the remaining whole antler. *He shouldn't put up much of a struggle, but we'll have to be wary of that antler. He could still do some damage.*

Pine and River separated a bit, and slowly crawled forward, keeping to the shadows of the trees to stay hidden. Just as the stag raised his head in alarm, River and Pine pounced, teeth bared. The stag immediately leapt back, only to run into Mud. As his other escape paths were blocked, the buck became increasingly more panicked. The wolves darted in and harried the deer, nipping at his sides and dodging blows from his antler.

Finally, the great beast fell, tripping when Leaf lunged for his injured leg. Breeze immediately leapt in and sank her teeth into the buck's throat, ending his life. Both Earth-Wolves jumped back to avoid the falling body as it crashed to the ground.

"Well done," Pine said with a wag of her tail. "Now, let's eat!"

The wolves eagerly fell to their prey. Bracken gave River a toothy grin, somehow appearing next to her, much to River's displeasure. "See? Isn't this much better than hunting on your own?"

River merely grunted and didn't bother to reply.

The wolves ate quickly and buried the remains before setting out once again. Bracken was pulled away from River by Breeze, giving River a precious few minutes to lose herself in her thoughts.

If we don't find the patrol soon I might ditch these wolves and go on my own. I can take a patrol or two, or at least, I can hold them off long enough for Hawk to escape. I hope he's still in a condition to run. If they found his slave collar, he might not be...

A large shape suddenly barreled into her, shocking her so much she jumped straight into the air. Bracken stumbled over her paws when River jumped away, losing her balance. River growled and shoved the younger wolf aside, furious that she had been taken by surprise. "Watch it!"

"Sorry!"

Breeze bounded up and gave Bracken a companionable shove that knocked her into River again. "Dork, you weren't supposed to go that far. I didn't push you *that* hard."

The red Bracken grinned and wagged her tail before pouncing on the gray Breeze. The two young she-wolves were soon tackling and chasing each other around the group. Pine simply rolled her eyes and ignored their antics, and the other wolves followed her example.

River was hard-pressed to stop herself from giving both Breeze and Bracken a bite they wouldn't forget easily. It irritated her that they could be so carefree.

How can anyone be so...so happy? We're chasing down a couple of demon patrols before they can reach the Fortress and Hawk is lost. They shouldn't be so...perky. She sighed as Bracken brushed past her.

This was going to be a *long* journey.

CHAPTER THIRTY-SIX

HAWK BIT BACK a whimper of pain when he stumbled, wincing when the Hell-Cat padding beside him snarled and bared its fangs threateningly. He struggled to maintain his balance and keep walking, although every movement jostled his sprained paw. They had been walking almost non-stop for ten days now, and Hawk was hungry and exhausted. Oak, limping along behind him, didn't fare much better.

After the Ice-Fang had discovered Hawk's slave collar, they had searched Oak for his. Both wolves were forced to endure torment from all demons present. By the time they had met up with another demon patrol that had two resistance fighters in their possession, four days later, Oak and Hawk could barely walk. Each of them had more than their fair share of cuts, scrapes, and bruises. The only thing that kept Hawk walking was the fear of the Ice-Fang, and the hope that River would save him.

A hope that diminished with each passing day.

The demons of the patrol were in much better condition. Their pelts shone with health, and their eyes glittered menacingly. The Ice-Fang, realizing the fear it struck into Hawk, took advantage of that fact. Every so often it would leer at Hawk, causing him to nearly faint with terror. The Fire-Fang, running a little behind Hawk with the two Wind-Wolves, took great pleasure in spitting tongues of fire at its prisoners and taunting them for their helplessness. The seven Hell-Cats, not the smartest creatures, also took part in the torment. They could only bare their fangs at the captives and snarl viciously, unable to actually speak and help with the verbal abuse. Only the Darkclaw, considering itself superior to the other demons, remained silent and aloof.

It was well past sundown when the Darkclaw finally called the patrol to a halt. Hawk sank to the ground with relief but immediately forced himself to his paws when the Ice-Fang snarled, "Get up, we didn't tell you it was time to rest."

Only after the demons had set up camp — a process that involved little more than scraping out hollows to sleep in — and had restrained the four prisoners were the wolves allowed to sleep.

Oak was out like a light within moments, but Hawk took a little longer to fall asleep. It was very hard to calm himself down enough with an Ice-Fang sitting just a few paces away, watching him. Plus, his mind was buzzing. *Did River ever notice that I'm gone? Did she abandon me or is she looking for me? Did she get captured? How far are we from the Fortress? Will River make it in time before we get there?*

Hawk dreaded to think of what would happen if he walked through those gates before River could rescue him. It was nothing good, and despite how things were now, he was actually better off in the claws of the patrol than within the walls of a Fortress.

The punishment an escaped slave faced was worse than death.

Chapter Thirty-Seven

"I THOUGHT YOU said finding the patrol wouldn't be a problem once we got here!" River glared at Pine with an intensity that would have caused most wolves to back down immediately.

The resistance group had reached the abandoned clan camp Pine had intended to use for the trap early in the morning. The entire journey had taken roughly twelve days, and that was only because River had forced the others to increase their speed. They had spent the rest of the day searching for any sign of the demon patrol. River had become increasingly more irritable as time passed and they found nothing.

A flicker of frustration crossed Pine's face. She should have known River would be furious, but she had hoped the other she-wolf could see reason. "I know that's what I said, but there's nothing I can do if the patrol took a different route. And we *are* here ahead of schedule, so the patrol might not even be here yet. We can adjust the plan as need be."

The rest of the group watched as the argument continued.

"How can you act so calm?" River demanded. "Your own mate is in the demons' clutches! And an escaped slave! If they find his collar, who knows what they'll do to him!"

"Don't you think I already know that?" Pine's eyes darkened dangerously. *How dare she bring Oak into this. I'm doing the best I can.* "I'm only calm because I have to be! If we were all hot-tempered idiots like you, then we'd be dead!"

"Oh, so trying to act on a situation makes me a hot-tempered idiot? If we had just gone after the patrol in the first place, then we wouldn't have lost it!"

"Are you questioning my authority?" Pine growled, her hackles raised.

"I'm not asking you out for a hunt!"

Before either enraged she-wolf could attack, Mud slipped in between them. Turning to Pine, he said quietly, "*We* respect your authority, Pine, so there is no need to anger yourself over the dissatisfaction of an outsider."

River growled a bit at that, but fell silent when Mud turned to her. "You are very worried about your friend, but that is no reason to take it out on Pine. She is doing everything she can."

Speaking to both she-wolves now, Mud continued. He never raised his voice, but he was heard clearly by every wolf present. "There's still time for the demons to get here. Give it until the end of the day before you go running off. If we haven't found the patrol by then, we'll have to come up with another plan."

Pine tightened her jaw, knowing the truth in Mud's words. She was furious with herself for letting her emotions get away with her. She couldn't lose herself like that, not with the entire group relying on her.

"Fine," River spat before turning sharply and marching away from the group.

"Leave her," Pine said when Leaf and Bracken moved to follow her. "We need to scout the area and find out where the patrol is headed. I'll talk to her later."

The two she-wolves shared a look, but nodded.

﹏

AT SUNSET, Pine went to go look for River. They had seen neither hide nor tail of the irritable Water-Wolf since Mud had convinced her to back down, and Pine was worried that River had gone off on her own. After a few minutes, she found the blue-gray she-wolf sitting on the banks of the Bann River. The trees around her had been stripped of their bark, and most of the mud washed into the river itself. It was obvious the Bann had taken the brunt of River's anger.

She must have been furious... Pine carefully approached the Water-Wolf, wary of her anger.

"It's sundown," River said before the Pine could speak, "and you've seen nothing."

Pine neglected to point out that River had no way of knowing whether or not the patrol had been found, because it was true. She had sent the others searching all over the area, and there had been no sign of the demons that had taken their friends. The only demons they found were from a patrol originating from the Obsolium Fortress itself, half a day's journey upriver.

"I know, and I'm–"

The Water-Wolf stood and brushed by Pine, cutting her off without a word. With a sigh, Pine turned to follow her.

The others of the rebel pack were waiting anxiously when they arrived, obviously both relieved and surprised when the two she-wolves returned unscathed.

"Well, we couldn't find anything," Pine said, cautiously watching River for any sign of the explosive outburst that was sure to come. To her surprise, the Water-Wolf didn't even appear to be paying attention to her, and instead was furtively glancing at something off to the side. Pushing aside her slight worry, Pine continued, "There is a chance that the patrol got delayed somehow, so I'll be leaving—"

"No." A dangerous glint came into River's eyes and her attention snapped back to Pine. "We tried *your* way, and it failed. Now we're going to do it *my* way."

And then she put her head back and howled.

CHAPTER THIRTY-EIGHT

THE ICE-Fang growled and dug its claws into the snow-covered ground. The Darkclaw had been right; the resistance group that they had picked up the Earth-Wolf from was trying to set up a trap for the patrol. The Ice-Fang didn't know what exactly the group intended to do, but they clearly thought that they had a chance.

The Ice-Fang seethed with anger when it remembered how the Darkclaw had snuck off earlier that afternoon, going Letorus knows where, and came back to announce that the wolves were lying in wait for them. The Ice-Fang did not like the Darkclaw. It thought that the Darkclaw acted too self-important, just because it was higher up on the demon hierarchy, just below Noxonds, Blood-Frenzies, and Letorus himself.

There was nothing lower than an Ice-Fang or a Fire-Fang, who shared the same rank, other than a stupid Hell-Cat.

So while the Fire-Fang was charged with keeping an eye on the prisoners and the Hell-Cats that guarded them, the Ice-Fang was sent to observe the group and report back to the Darkclaw. Not wanting to actually do the dirty work itself, the Ice-Fang had summoned an Ice-Spirit to go investigate, while the Ice-Fang itself sat hidden several hundred yards away in safety. The Ice-Fang also didn't want to risk getting into a fight with the rebels if it was discovered.

It was quite boring, really, just sitting there and watching the wolves through the Ice-Spirit's eyes. The summoned creature didn't have any ears, so the Ice-Fang couldn't hear what was being said. Several times it had to wake itself up after drifting into a light sleep. The only really interesting part was when the one blue-gray wolf nearly came to blows with the yellow one. The Ice-Fang was very disappointed when the dark-colored Earth-Wolf stopped them; it had been looking forward to some bloodshed. Unfortunately, the group split up after that, leaving the Ice-Fang to watch an empty clearing for hours until the wolves finally returned.

Ha, these rats have no idea what they're doing. They pose no threat to us.

Just as the Ice-Fang was about call the Ice-Spirit back and return to camp, it froze, an unfamiliar sensation of fear gripping its body.

The blue-gray wolf was staring right at it, locking eyes with the Ice-Spirit.

No...that's impossible. The Spirit has no scent, makes no sound, and it's completely hidden from view. So how can that wolf know it's there?

The Ice-Fang shuddered, its terror quickly growing with the feeling that the blue-gray wolf was staring through the ice-spirit and at the Ice-Fang itself.

Stop acting like a half-witted Hell-Cat. You're safe here, where none of the wolves can find you. The wolf isn't really looking at you; you're just scaring yourself.

A long, drawn-out howl jolted the Ice-Fang into action. It knew what that howl meant, although it had never heard a wolf give it.

A demon was on the prowl.

Chapter Thirty-Nine

River's howl made everyone jump. Fear shot through Pine as the sound echoed through the snowy woods. Although they had found no signs of the patrol nearby, there was no way they would miss the sound of River's challenge.

If I didn't know better, I would have thought it was a demon's hunting call, Pine thought nervously, River's voice sending chills down her spine.

Before Pine could order River to silence her howl, the Water-Wolf snapped her jaws shut and took off running.

"After her!" Pine shouted, charging after the other she-wolf. *She's making too much noise; the Obsolium Fortress will notice us!* "River! You're insane!"

River just flashed Pine a toothy grin, her eyes glittering madly, and kept running. Pine growled and pushed herself to run faster, struggling to keep up with River, who didn't seem to care if the rebel fighters were following.

"What should we do?" Crag asked, coming up beside his leader and easily keeping pace with the racing she-wolves.

Pine shook her head. "Just follow her and make sure she doesn't get herself killed!"

Her mind spun. She had to come up with something fast, before the patrol found them. The forest would soon be crawling with demons searching for the source of the howl, and the patrol that had taken Oak and Hawk would no doubt inform Obsolium of their existence. *Think, Pine!*

But the moment the Ice-Fang appeared ahead of them, Pine forgot everything else. She recognized that Ice-Fang. It was the same one that had taken her mate. Rage blinded her as she pulled ahead of River and launched herself on the demon, taking it by surprise. The Ice-Fang shrieked when Pine sank her fangs into its shoulder.

River swerved around the battling pair and kept running, but the rest of the group slid to a stop, unsure of what to do. Pine roused herself from her battle long enough to shout, "Follow River!"

She dimly heard Crag order Mud to stay and keep an eye on her, but her attention was taken by the Ice-Fang. It pleased her to see the abject fear in its eyes, and she let all the emotions she had been keeping locked away bubble to the surface.

"No one lays a claw on *my* family," she snarled.

Chapter Forty

Hawk looked all around him for River, hoping that she would suddenly appear out of the trees. He wondered if she would be able to track him. Even with two creatures, Hawk and the Fire-Fang, leaving behind clear trails of melted snow, the Darkclaw managed to cover their prints. It did it by summoning some strange black substance to cover the water. When the black stuff disappeared, so did the water, leaving no trace behind.

But no vengeful River appeared, even as the night wore on and they continued to run.

The Darkclaw drove its patrol and the prisoners mercilessly. They raced over the frozen earth, although the two Wind-Wolves did everything they could to slow the demons down. They knew the patrol was being chased and that the Darkclaw didn't want to risk losing the prisoners. Hawk was contemplating helping them when the Darkclaw did something that made Oak, Hawk, and the other Wind-Wolf forget about doing anything other than run. It spun around and snarled, forcing the entire patrol to come to a stop. Cold stole over Hawk's heart, slowing his movements. The others stumbled around him, startled by the sudden halt.

The other demons had hungry looks in their eyes.

Then the Darkclaw lunged, its fangs closing around the first Wind-Wolf's throat and killing him before he could even cry out. A moment later black energy surged from the demon's shadow and into the dead wolf. The body dropped to the ground in front of his friend, who could only stare in horror.

"Rise," the Darkclaw growled.

The corpse lurched to its paws, its eyes black and devoid of any life, forcing his former friend to scramble back several paces.

Hawk trembled, his eyes wide with shock. Terror filled him, more than just from the aura of fear the Darkclaw still exerted. He had never seen a Darkclaw use its ability before but had heard plenty about how they could animate the bodies of dead wolves and control them for a time.

"Disobey me further, and I will not hesitate to do the same to you." The Darkclaw's white eyes slid to each of them in turn, ensuring that its remaining prisoners got the message. "Now run."

The three wolves wasted no time in obeying, and Hawk desperately hoped River would appear shortly and save them all. Behind him, he could hear the Wind-Wolf crying as he watched his friend run with the demons, snarling at his former friends.

It was sickening.

The patrol burst out of the trees, landing in a large clearing. Looming up ahead of them was the forbidding bulk of the Obsolium Fortress, which sat on the rushing banks of the Bann. The three moons shone down on the stone structure, giving it an ethereal glow that seemed much too peaceful for such a house of evil.

Hawk's heart dropped to his paws. River was too late.

Suddenly her hunting howl sounded again, tearing through the air with as much force as a gust of wind. Sneaking a peek over his shoulder, Hawk caught a glimpse of River charging out of the woods, with several unfamiliar wolves a ways behind her. They were shouting at her to stop, but she completely ignored them.

The Darkclaw snarled at one of the Night-Lynxes, which immediately dropped back to face River. She leaped on it with her fangs bared, snarling like a demon herself.

Oak barreled into one of the Hell-Cats, attempting to slow the patrol enough to give the other wolves a chance to catch up. The demon stumbled, taken by surprise, but the hole created by its slip was quickly filled by the dead Wind-Wolf. The animated corpse snarled at Oak and shoved him back, forcing him to keep running.

"*River!*" Hawk howled, fear constricting his throat as he was swept through the gates of the demon Fortress. "*Help!*"

Chapter Forty-One

Her vision covered in the red mist of bloodlust, River was focused on only one thing: kill whatever dared to face her. When the Night-Lynx charged her, she leaped on it with pleasure, her eyes gleaming. It was dead within seconds.

"River!"

At Hawk's terrified cry, River looked up in time to see him dragged through the gates of the Obsolium Fortress. Demons poured out and ran across the clearing, intent on capturing or killing the wolves who dared to rise against them. River snarled and bunched her muscles to charge forward. Crag rushed forward to block her.

"Don't, River," he said in a voice that was sad, terrified, and angry all at the same time. "They're gone, you can't save them now."

"Get out of my way," River growled, her eyes flashing dangerously.

"Don't sacrifice yourself needlessly! Would Hawk really want that?" Breeze asked, slipping up to stand beside Crag.

The demons were coming closer, and Bracken, who had stopped beside River, looked nervously over her shoulder. Fear was reflected in all their eyes. River sneered at their cowardice. "Look at you," she spat, "you're like puppies, whimpering at shadows on the cave wall. What happened to the proud nations I used to know?"

Crag narrowed his eyes. "The demons came."

"Yeah? *So?* You're stronger than they are! The Earth-Wolves have the power to move the earth itself, and the Wind-Wolves can control the very winds of storms! Before the war, not a single wolf would have even considered fleeing this battle."

Breeze shifted from paw to paw, her eyes constantly flicking toward the oncoming demons. "But the demons are too powerful, we can't beat that many."

"The only thing the demons hold over you is fear," River returned. "Fear of capture, fear of death, fear of the unknown. Remember that, because they are *nothing*."

The rebel wolves fell silent, and River pushed her way past Breeze and Crag.

"I'm fighting them, whether you're with me or not."

"I'm with you."

All five wolves turned sharply when they heard Pine's familiar voice come from behind them. The large yellow Earth-Wolf padded up to stand beside River, Mud right behind her.

"I'm not going to give up Oak without a fight," Pine said firmly. "Even if I have to tear this Fortress apart, stone by stone."

After a few more seconds of wavering, the others found their resolve.

"We'll stand with you, Mother, and you, River." Bracken raised her head high with pride, speaking for them all.

The demons attacked.

CHAPTER FORTY-TWO

THE BATTLE WOULD become legend.

There were at least a dozen demons, Hell-Cats mostly, and the wolves fought hard. Emboldened by River and Pine's courage, they fought with the strength of the wolves from before the war, before the fear drained them of the will to fight.

Pine and her daughter fought side-by-side, facing off several Hell-Cats. The stupid creatures couldn't stay upright once the two Earth-Wolves started shifting the ground. The two she-wolves made quick work of their opponents.

Leaf, a usually soft-spoken, very gentle wolf, fought like a crazed beast, surrounded by two Hell-Cats and three Fire-Fangs. The demons panicked and broke ranks under the onslaught of attacks Leaf sent at them. She drove large cracks in the earth and launched chunks of stone at her opponents. They didn't stand a chance.

Breeze and Crag were literally a whirlwind, summoning up huge gusts of air to send their opponents flying before falling upon them with teeth bared. Those demons that tried to escape found their way blocked by walls of wind.

Mud fought tooth and claw with a vicious-looking Night-Lynx. The two were evenly matched. Every time Mud tried to move the earth and unbalance his opponent, the Night-Lynx distracted him with an aura of fear and turning to try and catch Mud's eyes in its petrifying gaze. Mud would respond by jumping back and raising a mound of earth to block the Night-Lynx's vision.

River swept demon after demon away with cascades of boiling water, raising waves of it from the snow around her. Their screams echoed across the clearing; many tried to escape her fury. They were unable to make it far before River appeared before them.

Blood ran freely across the snowy earth.

When the last demon on the plains had been killed, River put her head back and howled a challenge to the Fortress before them. Pine and the others raised their voices as well to join her. River led the rebels forward, sending the Earth-Wolves out in front, and charged the fortress gates. Leaf, Bracken, Pine, and Mud drove huge cracks in the earth, shaking the very foundations of the Fortress itself. More demons poured out of the gates, which quickly shut behind them to block entry. River, Breeze, and Crag met the enemies to protect the Earth-Wolves while they continued the assault on the Fortress.

More cracks appeared in the earth, racing toward the thick walls of the Fortress. The stone walls started to shake, and the demons defending it yowled with fury. Chunks of rock and dirt tumbled from the walls, knocking off several demons in the process.

Finally, the gates themselves cracked and split open, and River quickly drowned her final opponents in a last cascade of icy water. Then she raced into the gates, the pack of rebels close on her heels.

Inside was utter chaos.

The slaves, hearing the commotion outside, had started an uprising. Even with their elemental powers cut off by the slave-stones they wore, they fought their masters with tooth and claw. Oak and the other Wind-Wolf from the patrol that had captured Hawk were leading the slaves in the revolt. The demons, assaulted on all sides and heavily outnumbered by the wolves, were getting pushed back and cornered.

River took a deep breath, inhaling the invigorating smells of the battle. *This is what I was waiting for!* Her head pounded, and darkness colored the edge of her vision, but she paid it no mind. The red mist of bloodlust clouded her eyes, urging her to let everything loose and throw herself into the battle. A small voice at the back of her mind warned her to stay in control, reminding her she had a purpose in invading Obsolium, but it was quickly shoved aside in the search for her next opponent.

River howled, launching herself onto a Hell-Cat and burying her fangs into the back of its neck. She relished the open battle and the fact that she didn't have to worry about finishing a fight quickly and escaping before more demons came. *All the demons are here in one place, so there's no need to hold back!*

"River!"

Hawk's terrified cry snapped River out of her trance. Startled, she looked up from the dying demon at her paws.

Hawk! The sight of Hawk cornered by several Ice-Fangs made the breath catch in River's throat. The Fire-Wolf cowered at the top of a set of stairs leading to the ramparts above, his red-orange eyes seeking River's navy-blue ones in the fray.

Terror and fury surged through River, and she snarled. Plowing through wolves and demons alike, River raced to help her companion, who was trying to fend off the demons with fire, but was too cold and too scared to be successful. The Ice-Fangs only laughed at Hawk's pathetic attempts to defend himself. They took turns lunging at him, snapping at his paws and forcing him back against the wall. Hawk whimpered, struggling to avoid the lazy attacks.

River suddenly loomed over the Ice-Fangs, her furious snarl startling them away from their torment of the former slave. She quickly summoned all the snow from the ground behind her and heated it to boiling, dumping it on the Ice-Fangs before they had time to recover. The demons screamed with pain as the outer coating of their icy skin melted. Hawk surprised both himself and River by summoning a huge wall of fire to engulf the Ice-Fangs, melting them further. Soon the demons were nothing more than a puddle of water on the ground.

"You…you came…" Hawk gave a weak wag of his tail, relief shining in his eye. Open and bleeding wounds covered his body and one eye was so swollen he couldn't open it. He favored one paw, and even the simple action of breathing seemed to hurt. The sight of him in so much pain cleared River's head of any lingering bloodlust, and she flattened her ears, an unfamiliar feeling of guilt pulling at her heart. *I should have gotten here faster…I should have stayed focused…he wouldn't have been hurt as much if I had paid less attention to the battle and more to my actual goal.*

"Thank you, River…for saving me."

River shuffled a little, her eyes sliding away from Hawk's. *Probably shouldn't mention that most of the reason I ended up attacking the fortress was because I nearly lost control…*

"I…I never thought I would see the day that the demons would be beaten in their own fortress."

River looked as well and was surprised to see just how badly the demons were being defeated. Already the ground was littered with the bodies of Hell-Cats, Night-Lynxes, and wolves alike. Puddles of liquid were scattered about the area, remnants of Ice-Fangs. Piles of ashes marked where Fire-Fangs had fallen. There was nothing to show where the sole Shade-Tiger in the Obsolium Fortress was killed.

All that was left was the Darkclaw.

Even when outnumbered by hundreds of wolves, the Darkclaw refused to surrender. It was covered in deep wounds that would have killed a lesser creature, but no one had managed to get close enough to deliver the final blow. Its eyes glowed with hate as it fended off attacks from all angles. The area around it was clear of corpses, as the Darkclaw had summoned dark spirits to claim the dead bodies strewn around it. Many fighters found themselves not battling a demon but the cold, empty corpses of their friends. Whenever another wolf was killed, the Darkclaw was quick to possess the body before the other wolves could save it.

If the Darkclaw wasn't stopped soon, it could wipe out every wolf in the fortress simply by trapping them with their own dead allies.

"It's making them fight their friends," Hawk whispered, horrified. "No one can fight against their friends, even if they know it's just a corpse possessed by a dark spirit."

River growled, and bunched her muscles. Before Hawk could stop her, she took off, charging along the rampart until she was just above the demon. Then she dropped from the ledge and landed right on top of the Darkclaw.

It quickly recovered from its surprise and returned River's attacks with equal ferocity, but it soon became apparent that it was no match for River, who was uninjured.

"This is for taking him," River snarled before closing her jaws around the black-furred demon's throat. The Darkclaw wailed and attempted to wrench itself away, but River twisted her head, snapping the demons' neck. Immediately, the corpses it controlled dropped back to the ground, dead, and the Darkclaw itself disappeared into a cloud of darkness.

Silence reigned in the defeated fortress. No demons remained. The wolves sent each other confused and shocked looks, uncertain as to what to do.

Such a victory against the demons had not been known since the beginning of the war.

"We did it," Hawk laughed and winced and laughed again. "We did it!"

His words were quickly repeated by others, growing louder the more it was said.

"We did it!"

"We destroyed the Fortress!"

"We have victory!" Pine called, leaping onto a bit of fallen stone to stand above the gathered wolves and quickly catch their attention. Hawk limped down from the stairs to stand beside River as they all listened to Pine's words.

"Today is a great day!" Many wolves howled their agreement. "We have lost companions, but we have brought this mighty demon fortress to its knees! For over one hundred years, we have been living in constant fear, oppressed by the demons that taint our land. We all know the stories. In the beginning of this Age of Blood, we were shocked by the arrival of the demons. We feared the power that could have caused an entire nation to vanish overnight, without alerting the rest of the island! Even when King Oak united Soluna, we were lost, torn apart by our unwillingness to work with others not of our breed."

The listening wolves fell silent, remembering the sad stories of how an alliance with the potential of defeating Letorus failed because of the selfishness of the fighters. The army was separated into factions, which were easily defeated by Letorus' hordes.

"When King Oak made his final stand against the demons, a stand that ended in his death, we feared that we would never be able to rid our beloved island of these monsters," Pine continued in a growl. "Most of us were enslaved, and those lucky enough to remain free or escape hid in the shadows. For an entire century we waited, praying to Moon-Wolf and Sun-Wolf for a savior, praying that they would listen and free their children of their plight. Today, *that savior has come!*"

Several wolves standing nearby immediately turned to look at River and Hawk. River tensed and sent them a vicious glare.

"The one who convinced me that we still have the strength to fight the demons and there is no reason to live in fear any longer was none other than a Water-Wolf, straight out of the legends of our past!" Pine exclaimed, causing the attention of the entire fortress to turn to River. "River's very presence tells us that our gods have not abandoned us, and they have heard our prayers! This is our chance to rise up against the demons, which have grown lax in their century of control. When other wolves, both captive and free, hear of our victory here, they, too, will be inspired."

"Won't this just end in the same way it did before?" one wolf called out. "If our rulers couldn't fight the demons, what better chance do *we* have, when we've been weakened by years of war?"

Pine bared her teeth, a cunning glint appearing in her eyes. "We have something our ancestors didn't," she said. "*Knowledge.* After one hundred years, we know the demons almost as well as they know themselves. No longer do the demons have the advantage of mystery. Unlike before, we know how to fight the demons. Unlike before, we are not separated by boundaries of nations. We have been scattered all across Soluna by the demons. Slavery, the very thing that keeps us under the claws of the demons, will be what brings us together! Finally, after more than one hundred years, we will be free, because unlike before, *we are united and guided by the paws of the gods!"*

"How did she know? *How did she know what I'm doing?"* River snarled to Hawk as all the other wolves in the fortress raised their voices in a victorious howl.

"She doesn't really know, River. Remember I told you about the legends of the Water-Wolves' disappearance? She's just taking from those when she says that."

Nobody can know what I'm doing, River thought, fighting the urge to turn back and hide away from the eyes of the gathered wolves. She bared her teeth in a silent snarl when several bold wolves approached them with questions and shows of gratitude. *I cannot risk* him *learning of me.*

Breathing a sigh of relief, River was inwardly grateful when Pine managed to turn their attention to the task of collecting the dead and injured. For now, at least, she could avoid prying eyes. *I have to be more careful in the future. Uprisings like this are good to create a little confusion, to keep the demons' attention away from anything I'm doing, but if I make too much noise then the Overlord will become suspicious.*

If that stupid Winter-Wolf hasn't betrayed me and told him everything.

CHAPTER FORTY-THREE

THE LITTLE THAT remained of the demons was dumped unceremoniously into a large hole dug out by Earth-Wolves. The bodies of the wolves were laid out carefully so their friends could say their final good-byes. Former slaves worked to break the slave-stones from their collars. And after a prompting from Pine, Hawk and River visited the injured fighters. Pine claimed the wounded wolves would benefit from seeing the Water-Wolf who freed them. Although Hawk very much preferred finding a place to curl up and go to sleep, he agreed. River, obviously still uncomfortable with the looks they received, stayed silent as they walked among the fighters, leaving Hawk to do most of the talking. He didn't say much to the wolves, as he was so tired after two weeks of nearly non-stop travel, but what he did manage to say seemed to bolster the spirits of the fighters

When River came to a sudden stop, Hawk stumbled into her, blinking in confusion. He hadn't even realized that they had left the lines of the injured and now stood among the fallen.

He slowly regained his balance and looked up at River, a little surprised by the sad look on her face.

"River?"

When she didn't answer, he wondered if she had even heard him. She padded forward several steps before stopping in front of three wolves, laid out side-by-side. If it weren't for the stench of death that pervaded the air around them, they could have been mistaken for sleeping. Hawk limped after River, staring at the bodies of the wolves, two Earth-Wolves and one Wind-Wolf, with a muted curiosity.

"Bracken, Mud, Breeze," River whispered finally, so low Hawk had to strain to hear. "They were part of the resistance group that helped me find you. Bracken was a bubble-headed idiot, but kind. You hardly ever noticed Mud, but he was strong. Breeze was stubborn and much too curious for her own good, but caring." She paused before looking up to where Pine was working with Leaf and several other Earth-Wolves to bury the remains of the demons. "I wonder if they know."

Hawk followed her gaze. Pine's tail wagged, and Leaf laughed at something her leader said.

"Pine doesn't know. None of them do." A haunted voice from beside Hawk caused both him and River to jump. Oak ignored their surprise and padded past them to bury his muzzle in his daughter's cold fur.

"Bracken was one of the first to fall prey to the Darkclaw," he said quietly. "Mud tried to save her…but she was taken over by the Darkclaw's spirits and forced to attack him and Breeze. They couldn't bear to fight Bracken, even knowing she was gone, and were killed by her fangs."

His voice broke. He was silent for a moment before continuing. "I will tell Pine later, when she is away from the others and can howl her grief privately. Now," he said looking up at his mate, who was now directing several wolves to prepare graves for their fallen, "she has too much to worry about."

Hawk could sympathize with the haggard Earth-Wolf. River, however, had other ideas. She brushed past the two males and padded over to Pine. Realizing what River was going to do, Hawk hurried to stop her, but was almost instantly left behind. In his current state, he was no match for a nearly-fresh River.

"Pine," River said, and motioned the yellow Earth-Wolf female away from the other wolves. Hawk and Oak were too far away to hear what the Water-Wolf said to Pine, but they both knew what River was telling Oak's mate. Pine went very still for a few moments before looking over at Oak, as if for confirmation. Her mate nodded sadly. The yellow Earth-Wolf bowed her head. River turned away and walked back toward Hawk and Oak.

"You should have more faith in your mate's strength," River said as she passed. "It was better to be told now, than to be shocked with the discovery when she went to go visit the dead."

Hawk muttered his condolences to a silent Oak and hurried to catch up with River. He panted from just that little bit of exertion but said nothing, not wanting to appear weak or make her worry, although the former was more likely. River didn't seem to notice; she was too preoccupied with helping the rest of the injured wolves, something she threw herself into with a surprising amount of zeal.

Chapter Forty-Four

That night, as snow began to fall once more from a cloudy sky, the wolves prepared to bury their dead. They were all gathered on the edge of the clearing that held the fortress. There were nearly a hundred wolves total, and only a few dozen had been killed. Even so, there was much sadness at their loss. Pine stood before a stone pyre with Hawk, River, and Crag behind her and faced the gathered fighters. She waited while some of the wolves said their final farewells before beginning the ancient rite of passing that ensured a safe journey on the Path of Stars to the next world.

"We are gathered here to send the spirits of our pack mates on their final journey," Pine said, her voice strong even with the grief weighing down on her. "Today they gave their lives courageously to free themselves and their fellows. They helped us to win a great victory, the first of a great many victories we will continue to win."

A few wolves murmured to each other, excited by Pine's words.

"Tonight they leave us to join Moon-Wolf and Sun-Wolf, where they are truly free. They will walk among the stars on their way to their reward, leaving prints of life-light behind for us to see and remember. As their spirits pass into the next world, they leave behind families and friends, memories and emotions for us to remember them by. They will be watching us as we continue the struggle that began so long ago by King Oak and the other rulers when they created the alliance. They will be with us as we fight, supporting us in their own way."

Pine paused a moment, preparing herself to send her only daughter on her final journey. Then she lifted her head and sang, "Fallen Earth-Wolves, may the earth forever sing your names and the trees grow with your wisdom. May your strength be passed to our children, and even when those who knew you are gone, may your memory remain with us for all times."

She fell silent, bowing her head. The stars seemed to glow with a faint silver light for a second, so quickly it was almost imperceptible. Pine smelled the scent of her daughter for the last time and looked up to the stars. She could almost see the outline of Bracken, padding away to join Mud in the sky.

Good bye, Bracken. Pine took a deep breath and stepped back, allowing Crag to take her place.

The Wind-Wolf gave Breeze's cold body a long look, and then turned his eyes up to the stars and sang in a hollow voice, "Fallen Wind-Wolves, may the wind forever howl with your voices and the mountains echo with your names. May your speed be passed to our children, and even when those who knew you are gone, may your memory remain with us for all times."

Pine's heart ached for Crag, and she wondered if he had caught a glimpse of Breeze as she passed on. The two Wind-Wolves had been very close.

As when the Earth-Wolves passed, the stars seemed to glow brighter than usual, but with an orange light. Crag stepped back, and Hawk padded forward to say the final rite of passing for the Fire-Wolves. "F-fallen Fire-Wolves…" His howl was shaky, but slowly gained strength as he continued. "M-may the fires f-forever burn with your spirit and the sands whisper with your names. May y-your will be passed to our children, and even when those who knew you are gone, may your memory remain with us for all times."

The stars glowed faintly with orange light. Pine watched the battered Fire-Wolf as he took a deep breath and padded toward the pyre in which the bodies had been laid in a bed of sticks. He blew on the sticks covering the bodies. Instantly the wood caught fire, and the flames quickly spread to fill the pyre. He backed up a few paces before turning away from the fire.

"Thank you," Pine whispered as he padded past. Hawk nodded silently before rejoining River, who sat a few feet away from the blaze. Pine kept her eyes on the flickering flames before her, watching as they devoured the remains of her puppy. Her only wish had been for her daughter to live in a world free of demons. *With River's appearance, that wish may be realized. If only you could see it, Bracken.*

"I always used to tell my brother that the stars are the paw prints of the spirits of wolves as they walk up the sky to the heavens," Pine heard River say quietly. "They are created as the life energy the wolf has leaves the spirit, making prints in the sky. Those stars carry everything the wolf had during life — memories, emotions, hopes, and fears. Sometimes, you can even feel what each star carries."

River fell silent, and Pine heard Hawk shuffle a little. Pine pricked her ears slightly. She had always been told that the stars were only the steps leading up to Land of the Blest, where the souls dwelled with the gods, but she liked

River's tale much better. It was comforting to think that maybe there was still a piece of Bracken that remained.

"I'm sure that your brother is up there, too, River," Hawk whispered, catching Pine's attention. "And that he's proud of you."

"No. He's not."

Pine turned back, shocked at the anger and sorrow in River's voice. The Water-Wolf stood abruptly and quickly padded away into the trees behind them.

The shock soon turned to understanding, and she turned back to the burning pyre as Oak appeared to join her.

How can our loved ones be proud of us if we did nothing to stop their deaths?

Chapter Forty-Five

PINE AND OAK stayed up all night apart from the rest of the wolves, silently mourning their lost daughter. As she was seen as a leader of the gathering, Pine knew she couldn't afford to let herself be chained down by grief. She had to be an example to the others.

They emerged from the forest just in time to see River and Hawk quietly making their way around the sleeping bodies of the former slaves. River obviously was anxious to get away but was forced to slow her pace to accommodate for Hawk's injuries.

"Shouldn't we stop them?" Oak asked his mate in a tired voice.

Pine shook her head. "No. We would only hinder them. There are other ways we can help."

Oak gave Pine a questioning look. She didn't return it, only kept her eyes on the retreating forms of Hawk and River as they ran through the trees, quickly disappearing in the predawn darkness.

"We'll spread their story, telling every wolf we meet. When the time comes, they will have the support of every wolf in Soluna."

"What do you mean?"

"You know as well as I that times have been growing darker," Pine said. "Those actively resisting the demons are becoming fewer in number. Is it really a coincidence that a Water-Wolf appears now? The Water-Wolves disappeared for a reason, and if they have returned, then it can only mean the end of the war draws near." She turned to her mate, her eyes glowing with a renewed hope. "Our time is coming, Oak, and we must be ready, if only for Bracken's sake."

She turned her gaze to the lightening sky. *I may have failed you as a mother, but I will not fail you as a wolf of Soluna. Then, perhaps, you can forgive me for not being there to protect you.*

Chapter Forty-Six

Two weeks later, Hawk found himself staring up the Gaoibeanna Mountains. He had passed through the mountains before, during his flight from Ignimor, but remembered little from the journey. He had forgotten just how big the ancient giants could be.

"Hawk, close your mouth before you swallow a bug."

Startled, Hawk clamped his jaw shut, although he couldn't draw his eyes away from the mountains, slowly tracing the stone sides all the way up to the peaks hidden in the clouds above.

"Never seen the mountains before?"

"No...I have...I don't remember much from the last time I was here..."

"Unless the landscape has changed in the past century, then doesn't the Scaineadó Desert have volcanoes? You should have seen those quite a bit."

Hawk winced slightly. "I haven't even seen those. The Fortress I was... enslaved at wasn't near any volcanoes..."

"Oh."

And with that, River padded across the border between the Taladair Forest and the Gaoibeanna Mountains. Hawk hesitated a moment, casting a look over his shoulder at the tall trees behind him. It was easy to tell where the forest ended and the mountains began. Where the trees abruptly ended, the mountains suddenly rose up from the earth. On the forested side, Hawk smelled dirt and moss, and growing things. The rocky side carried the scent of wind, cold, and clouds.

"Hawk! Hurry up!"

Hawk jumped and hurried after River, who was already disappearing down a mountain path. The path inclined sharply up the mountain and quickly rose to a dizzying height above the ground. Hawk tried not to look down. *At least I can see where my paws go.* Memories of the harrowing walk across the Dorasca Gorge flitted across his mind. *But I couldn't imagine living here... always one step from a long fall.* "River, do you know where we're going?" he asked when he had finally caught up, wincing slightly at the twinge of pain from his still-healing wounds.

Although the location of each land's Elemental Guardians wasn't a secret, it wasn't something wolves liked to talk about to outsiders. It would make sense for River to know where the Crétioll was, because both Earth and Water were Moon elements and historical allies. But Wind was a Sun element, and an opposite element to Water and Earth. It would be strange for River to know where the Wind's Elemental Guardian, the Ardgao, was.

Of course, Hawk himself didn't know the location of the Ardgao. He didn't even know where the Scaineadó Desert's Fáinéitin was. All he knew were the legends surrounding them.

"I know the general location," River replied. "But it shouldn't be that hard to find."

Hawk wasn't so sure. There was a reason the Elemental Guardians were protected and not discussed with outsiders.

"But what about the fortresses? Do you know where any of them are?"

River hesitated a second before snapping, "No, but I'll find out. Now, quiet, so I can concentrate."

Obediently, Hawk fell silent. They walked along the path without speaking for a few hours, Hawk carefully watching River out of the corner of his eye. *I wonder if River really does know where she's going...*

Hawk was forced to the ground when a large body landed on top of him. His breath rushed from his lungs, and pain lanced through his body at the sudden impact with the rocky path. River reacted instantly to her companion's yelp. She whirled around and leapt on the creature attacking. The weight holding him down was shoved aside when the she-wolf barreled into it.

Leaping to his paws, Hawk pulled his lips back in a snarl, although his legs shook with fear. River and whatever it was that had attacked him fought so ferociously and so quickly that he couldn't get a good look at River's opponent.

Suddenly, for the second time, something fell on Hawk from above and he was forced to the ground. He was flipped over onto his back, and his attacker, a Wind-Wolf, bared his fangs and snarled, "Stop fighting if you want your friend to live."

Hawk froze, desperately hoping that River would hear those words through the haze of battle and obey. To his relief, and surprise, River immediately leapt back, releasing her opponent.

"Who are you?" River growled, her eyes flicking from one attacker to another. Now that she wasn't trying to rip their throats out, she could actually see who it was that attacked them.

They were Wind-Wolves, one male and one female. The male was the one pinning Hawk to the ground, his sharp fangs poised over Hawk's throat. He had ragged black fur; his lean body was covered in scars, and his blue-gray eyes glittered cruelly. He would not hesitate to kill Hawk if River made a move. The female was a grayish-yellow in color, with black eyes and a black swirl mark on her left shoulder. She favored her right front paw, which bled heavily due to a vicious bite from River.

"I don't have to tell you anything," the female Wind-Wolf snarled. "You've got a lot of guts to show your cowardly face here, Water-Wolf."

River snarled, her eyes darkening with anger, and crouched to leap on her opponent again, but she stopped when the Wind-Wolf male threatened to sink his fangs into Hawk's neck. The terrified Hawk looked up with pleading eyes, silently begging River to not attack.

With a great effort, River forced her hackles to lay flat. "I don't know what you mean. I'm no coward."

The Wind-Wolf female snorted, "Oh yeah? Water-Wolf. All cowards. Where have your kind been for the past century? Where were you when the demons came? Have there been *any* Water-Wolves helping us fight the demons? No!"

Before anyone could react, the gray-yellow she-wolf threw herself on River, shoving the other wolf scarily close to the edge of the path. River immediately reacted by snapping at the Wind-Wolf's face. The black Wind-Wolf pinning Hawk to the ground immediately jumped away, swearing under his breath as he raced over to break up the fight. Hawk scrambled to his paws and tried to help. Just as the two males reached the fighting she-wolves, River's hind paws slipped.

For a brief moment, shock flitted across her face, and she locked eyes with Hawk. Time seemed to hold still as all four wolves realized what had happened.

"River!" Hawk screamed as time sped up again, racing to the cliff's edge. With a strangled yelp, the two she-wolves tumbled off the cliff. The Wind-Wolf male rushed forward, shoving Hawk back from the cliff and preventing him from throwing himself after them.

"Stop! There's nothing we can do." The black wolf took a step back once he knew Hawk wouldn't try to follow the two she-wolves, his eyes trained on the thick gray clouds that had swallowed any sign of their companions. Hawk stared in horror at the clouds below, his entire body numb.

"River...*River!*" His breath caught in his chest as his pain-filled howl echoed through the mountains.

Chapter Forty-Seven

HAWK STARED INTO the bright fire in front of him, his red-orange eyes empty. He didn't even look up when Jay, the black Wind-Wolf male, dropped a large mountain hare in front of him. They may have been enemies only that morning, but when night had fallen and the two males took shelter from the harsh winds in a small cave, they were made companions by their shared grief.

"Starving yourself won't bring her back," Jay said, and nudged the hare closer to Hawk, although the Wind-Wolf himself made no move to eat.

"I just…I just can't believe she's gone." Hawk closed his eyes. He couldn't even believe he was saying those words. Everything seemed surreal, like he was simply playing a part, and that River would soon stalk into the cave and yell at him for moping around. *After everything that had just happened…now she's the one who's lost.* "River always seemed…invincible. She never got hurt, no matter how strong the opponent was, and she always knew what to do."

Jay was silent for a few moments before answering. "Scrub was my sister. I know you only saw her as an enemy, but she was a very kind wolf. She usually doesn't like fighting."

"Why was she angry that River was a Water-Wolf?"

Sighing, Jay looked out into the dark night, as if he were waiting for Scrub to appear, too. "I'm sure you've heard all kinds of stories about why the Water-Wolves disappeared at the beginning of the war." When Hawk nodded, Jay continued, "Before the war…the Uiscean Marsh and the Gaoibeanna Mountains had a sort of alliance. We…didn't take kindly to the Water-Wolves' disappearance. It's their fault Soluna fell to the demons."

Hawk tried not to flinch. That was partially true. If it weren't for the Queen of Uiscean Marsh, then the demons never would have come through the Rift and into Soluna.

"My sister…especially believed that the Water-Wolves brought the demons here and that they then ran away in fear. Where? She didn't know — or care."

The two wolves fell silent again, each lost in his own thoughts. After several minutes passed by, Jay asked, "What will you do now?"

Hawk flattened his ears. He didn't know what he was going to do. Before he met River, his only goal was to survive to see another day. Then he became part of a plan to free Soluna, and even that had become complicated when it became apparent that Hawk was needed for more than support. He was the one who gained entry to the Crétioll, probably the first to do so for a century, and he was the one who had released the power that slumbered within the Earth's Elemental Guardian.

For the first time in his life, Hawk had actually been important.

Now, River was gone, and he had no idea how to continue. Hawk was sure that she would want him to complete the mission, but he didn't know how. Although the Water-Wolf had revealed her plan, there was still much she hadn't explained.

"Well, you could always come with me."

Hawk dragged his gaze up from the floor to give Jay a curious look.

"Scrub and I are part of a resistance group, and we were supposed to be scouting out demon patrols today. I'm going to head back to camp tomorrow, and we'd always welcome another fighter…even if that fighter was previously travelling with a Water-Wolf."

Hawk bristled a little at Jay's clearly derogatory remark about River, but he let it go. It wasn't worth the effort. It wouldn't bring River back. "I'll think about it."

Chapter Forty-Eight

THE TWO WOLVES rose before the sun and immediately set out, Jay leading Hawk down a series of mountain paths, past incredible waterfalls that plummeted into empty air and curious mountain goats that bounded away as soon as the wolves came close. Hawk, however, was still too caught up in his grief to wonder at the beauty around him. He only wondered if it was possible to give River a final rite of passing in spite of Hawk not being a Water-Wolf. He didn't even know how to give a Water-Wolf a rite of passing, much less one with no body present.

"Jay!"

Hawk looked up, startled, to see a slim Wind-Wolf male barrel into Jay. Hawk had to jump back to avoid getting tackled as well.

"Jay!" the dark grey Wind-Wolf exclaimed again. "You're back late, did you spot a patrol? Ooooh, who's that?" he added when he saw Hawk looking on with confusion. "Where'd he come from? Hey, where's Sissy? I saw this humongous eagle, and I even found its nest. She likes eagle feathers, so I want to show her…"

The wolf's voice trailed off when he noticed the weary and saddened expressions on both Hawk's and Jay's faces. His excitement drained away and his tail stilled.

"She's not coming, Falcon," Jay said quietly, his voice barely a whisper.

Falcon drew back, horror flashing across his dark blue eyes. His gaze flicked over to Hawk, who looked away, unable to meet it.

"Come on," Falcon said finally in an empty voice. "We need to tell Mom and the others."

Hawk took a deep breath and followed the two Wind-Wolves, not looking forward to sharing the story of Scrub's and River's deaths.

The brothers led Hawk to a tall fault in the mountainside, cleverly masked by a clump of scraggly bushes. After a tight squeeze, Hawk found himself standing in a wide cavern with a small pool of water at the center. A small cloud of steam hovered over the water. The air itself was several degrees warmer than outside, and several Wind-Wolves and a Fire-Wolf lounged around the pool, enjoying the heat.

The arrival of the three wolves quickly caught the attention of the others in the cavern. Hawk found himself subject to suspicious stares when they realized Scrub was missing.

"What's happened?" one of the other Wind-Wolves asked, quickly rising to his feet and padding toward them. He had white fur and black eyes that narrowed upon seeing Hawk standing beside Jay. Hawk swallowed hard and tried to ignore the calculating gaze. Finally, the white wolf turned his hard eyes to Jay. "Where's Scrub?"

Jay didn't say anything until he stood in front of an elderly Wind-Wolf female. Her brown fur was heavily streaked with gray, and her blue eyes were milky with age and blindness. The swirl mark on her left shoulder was a pale blue.

"Scrub fell from a cliff, Mother," he said quietly, and yet his voice echoed in the silent cavern. "She and the Water-Wolf companion of this Fire-Wolf. There was nothing we could do to save her."

Hawk heard a few snarls at the mention of River, and saw several heads turn to give him a harsh glare. He flinched but didn't say anything to defend himself or River. *What good would it do? River's...*

"They're not dead."

Everyone in the cavern looked up sharply at the old wolf's voice, cracked with age. Hawk shivered and almost immediately looked away, unnerved by the strange way she stared at him, as though she could actually see.

Jay only sighed, his blue-gray eyes sad. "Okay, Mom."

The she-wolf swung her gaze to her son. "I know you don't believe me, Jay. None of you do. But I am right in saying that neither River nor Scrub is dead. You'll see."

The black Wind-Wolf shook his head and padded away. The other wolves gathered around him to hear of how Scrub met her death. Hawk remained where he was, staring at the blind elder a little nervously.

How could she know River's name, if all Jay had said was 'Water-Wolf'?

After a moment of hesitation, he padded around the pool and approached the elderly brown Wind-Wolf.

"You have something you wish to ask me, young Hawk?"

Hawk froze. "How did you know my name? And River's?"

The elder laughed. "I may not be able to see, but I have other ways of knowing. I have been watching your approach for many moons now."

Hawk carefully lay beside the Wind-Wolf elder. "How?"

"Dreams are messages from Sun-Wolf himself."

Hawk wasn't sure what to make of that answer, so he asked a different question. "Elder, do you really mean it when you said River isn't dead?"

"Hawk, dear, you may call me Fall. That is my name. But yes, River is still alive."

River is still alive.

It was a naive hope, relying only on the words of an old Wind-Wolf who claimed to have dreams from the gods, but Hawk was desperate. He didn't want to believe that River was dead; it seemed impossible for it to happen. If there were even a slight chance that River was alive, Hawk would jump on it.

But how could she survive such a fall? Hawk's ears flattened. No matter how hard he hoped and prayed for it to be different, there was no way a wolf could live after falling from a cliff like that.

"Come now, Hawk, do not get so down. While we wait for our wayward sisters to return, shall I entertain you with a story?"

Hawk perked up a little, eager for something to distract him from his dark thoughts. He loved hearing stories; they were often the only thing to keep up a slave's hope during the long days and nights in Ignimor Fortress.

"Yes, please, Elder Fall."

Fall settled herself more comfortably, chuckling a little at Hawk's puppy-like eagerness. "Ah, I know a good one. My father told this story to me when I was a young pup. Tell me, Hawk, do you often look at the stars?"

Hawk nodded. He always liked to imagine he could see his mother up there, looking down on him. Just as he realized that nodding was useless to a blind wolf, Fall continued.

"Have you ever noticed the strange formation of a certain group of stars?"

"No." Hawk cocked his head. He never noticed any shapes in the stars; he simply enjoyed the fact he could see them unframed by fortress walls.

"I am not surprised; it takes a bit of looking to find this constellation, but here is how it came to be.

"It was nearing the end of the Age of Stone, when the son of Rock held nearly all of Soluna under his cruel claws. Stone and his officials, known as the Stoneteeth, controlled the Uiscean Marsh, the Taladair Forest, and the Scaineadó Desert. Only the Wind-Wolves of the Gaoibeanna Mountains remained free, and we did all we could to try and help the other lands.

"It was during this time that Spark, a great Fire-Wolf Seer, gave a strange prophecy." Fall paused, her brow furrowed. "Ah, I should be able to remember it all…" She paused. *"A savior is born to free a land bound by stone chains, coming from the heights, born as one yet living as two. She will lose herself with victory, wait for herself among the stars, and be reunited with herself when it is done."*

Jay and Falcon padded over to listen, although they sat a few lengths away from their mother. Fall made no sign that she noticed their presence. Slowly, they were joined by the other wolves, all eager for a distraction from their grief.

"No one knew what Spark's prophecy meant. Many wolves even dared to declare the Seer *mad*. But four years after the prophecy was given, something very unusual happened. Twins were born here in the Gaoibeanna Mountains."

"Twins?" The sudden whispery voice next to him nearly startled Hawk out of his skin. A silvery Wind-Wolf with pale eyes had settled herself next to him to listen. He shuffled away a little, unnerved by the vacant expression on her face. It was as though her mind was leagues away.

"It is different than what you are thinking, Cloud," Fall replied. "Twins are different from litters of two pups. Twins are born when a single soul is split into two bodies, creating a single entity in two forms. They are very rare, and stories say that twins often have very unusual powers."

"What kind of powers?" The dark yellow Wind-Wolf appeared on Cloud's other side with the paler yellow Fire-Wolf. The Wind-Wolf shot Hawk a glare before turning back to Fall, her eyes glittering at the mention of unusual powers.

"It is said they could hear one another's thoughts and even communicate across long distances," Fall said. "Some have even claimed that twins possess a strong enough elemental magic that they could even call upon the powers of Sun and Moon."

"I heard a tale of how the Twins once sang the clouds out of the sky," the white Wind-Wolf said from right behind Hawk, making him jump again. Hawk discretely glanced up at the other wolf, only to find the dark-eyed wolf staring down at him. He quickly turned back to Fall.

"I have heard that tale as well, Sky," she said, before continuing her story. "These Twins were named Fae and Thar, and even their names signify their unusual circumstances. The Twins' mother created their names by splitting the name 'Feather' between them. Fae and Thar lived deep within Gaoibeanna, never knowing the full horrors of war until their mother was killed trying to save an Earth-Wolf family from the Stoneteeth. The sisters tried to hide from the darkness that plagued their land, and it wasn't until a strange spirit appeared before the Twins that they realized their destiny."

"What spirit?" Jay interrupted.

Fall cocked her head slightly. "No one knows who, or what, revealed to the Twins their destiny, or even exactly what that spirit said. All we have is what was heard from the Twins themselves

"The Twins travelled all over the Gaoibeanna Mountains, gaining support from their fellow Wind-Wolves and the refugees hiding from Stone. They launched an attack on the Scaineadó Desert. Slowly but surely, the armies of Fae and Thar pushed back the enemy, freeing the wild Fire-Wolves of the desert. Next they invaded the Uiscean Marsh. This time Fae and Thar were aided by the many revolts the Water-Wolves started, disrupting the Stoneteeth army. Stone's officials fled before the army of the Twins, who seemed unstoppable.

"It seemed as if Fae and Thar would push Stone and his ragged army straight to the Sea of Soluna, and that the island would finally be free from their tyrannical dictator…when the unthinkable happened. In the Battle at Crétioll, Fae was killed by Stone."

The dark yellow Wind-Wolf and Falcon, who had slowly crawled closer to his mother, both gasped. Hawk was certain they had heard the story before, as had he, but were just as enthralled by it as he was.

This story is different from the other versions I've heard…some never mentioned Fae's and Thar's names…one version even made them appear as one wolf. None had said they were Twins.

"Thar nearly gave up everything, even to the point of almost taking her own life so she could be with her sister. And how can we blame her? She had lost her Twin, a part of herself, even, and she could not find the strength to continue. But on the night after her death, Fae visited her sister. She had anchored herself in the stars instead of walking down the path in the sky to join Sun-Wolf and Moon-Wolf. Fae promised her sister that she would remain in the stars, watching Thar, until it came Thar's time to join her.

"With new strength, Thar led her army to corner Stone and his remaining officials on the mountain that now bears his name: Stone-Trap Mountain. She killed the tyrannical ruler and thus brought the Age of Stone to an end. All of Soluna rejoiced, but their victory was tempered with sadness. For immediately after the battle Thar, mortally wounded even as she dealt Stone his death blow, threw herself from the peak of the mountain to join her sister." Fall paused a moment, her milky eyes sad. "So that Soluna would never forget the sacrifice of the Twins, Sun-Wolf and Moon-Wolf burned the image of Fae and Thar into the sky. Even now, if the stars are shining bright, you can see them, the Star Twins, where they watch over us for all time."

Hawk's eyes widened, and his breath caught. Something Sparrow had said to him before he had left came back, echoing in his mind. *Seek out the ancient one, and listen to his story. And when all is lost, look to the Star Twins, and use their power to bring light to darkness.*

That constellation must be what Sparrow was talking about...but it still doesn't make any sense. Fall is old...but she's not a 'he', so she can't be the 'ancient one.' I'm kind of lost now...but it's not all 'dark,' not if Fall's right and River is somehow still alive...

"Do you think they were watching over Scrub?" Falcon asked, his dark blue eyes wistful.

"Falcon, I've already told you, neither Scrub nor the Water-Wolf is dead."

Jay snarled and jumped to his paws, making Hawk jump, but the other wolves just looked away in pity. Hawk's eyes flitted between Jay and his mother, worried by the younger Wind-Wolf's sudden anger.

"Scrub is dead, Mom! How many times do I have to say that? You said the same thing about Da, but no matter how long we waited he *never came back.*"

"Storm is not dead either."

"Yes, he is! I...*saw* it." Jay's voice cracked. "His throat was bitten by a Shade-Tiger, and he was thrown over the waterfall. No matter what you may claim, *you can't see things in your dreams!*"

Without waiting for his mother to reply, Jay whirled around and raced out of the cave. His brother, Falcon, ran after him, shouting for him to come back. They left a tense silence behind. The other wolves quickly rose from their places and moved away from Fall and Hawk, occasionally shooting them both venomous glances. Hawk couldn't help but wonder if most of those were for him.

They probably blame me and River for Scrub's death...

"I suppose you're wondering what's going on here," Fall said with a sigh, looking out in the direction her sons had fled. Hawk found it eerie that she could tell exactly where everything was in spite of having no sight.

"I...I wasn't going to ask—" Hawk started to say, although he was burning with curiosity, but Fall interrupted him.

"No, you're much too polite for that," Fall laughed softly, and Hawk reddened under his fur. "But I'll tell you anyway. I fear that I am one of the few in this pack that believes anything from the old days. The rest, even my children, have all been hardened by war and live for nothing other than killing the next demon. See Cloud? How pale she looks, almost ghostly?"

Hawk wondered how Fall could know that, being blind, but Fall gave him no chance to ask.

"We found her, at the foot of a tall cliff, an inch away from death. Scrub and I nursed her back to health, and when she finally woke up we found that she had no memory left. She didn't even know her name. 'Cloud' is what Scrub called her. I learned from my dreams that a horrible accident involving a demon's magic bleached her fur of any color. All she knows now is how to kill demons, and she's frightfully good at it.

"Sand," she continued, waving her tail in the direction of the yellow Fire-Wolf, "used to be a slave like you, Hawk, although she was not as fortunate to be captive in her own land."

Hawk froze. *How did she know I was a slave?*

"Remember, Hawk, dreams tell me much, despite what Jay may think," Fall's voice cut into Hawk's thoughts, and he returned his attention to the elder.

"What do you mean by 'not fortunate enough to be captive in her own land'?" Hawk asked, trying not to be worried or surprised about the extent of Fall's knowledge.

"You've travelled quite a bit, Hawk, so you should know. For a Fire-Wolf, nothing is better than feeling the hot desert sun warm your fur and the sand slide beneath your feet. You can't be truly comfortable in another element's homeland; your body yearns for your native element. Nothing is worse, however, than being in your polar opposite element's land, although you can eventually get used to it."

Hawk remembered how sick Eagle and Sparrow had felt the first time they had entered the Taladair Forest. It had taken *days* for them to get back to normal. Even Coal had been a little off for a few days. Hawk himself had never felt anything like it, so he couldn't imagine what they were going through.

"Anyway, Sand had her tongue cut out by her demon masters. She can no longer speak, and has a hard time eating. The only thing she lives for is killing demons. Nothing else matters, not even her own life. Lichen saw her family murdered before her eyes by a Noxond," Fall said, motioning to the dark yellow Wind-Wolf sitting next to Sand. She had been the one to ask Fall about the legendary powers of twins. "She still bears the scars of that fight, and it's a miracle she survived at all. Her only goal is to find that Noxond and take her revenge.

"I don't know much about Sky, even my dreams do not give me any information about him." Fall motioned to the white Wind-Wolf who still watched Hawk with a suspicious gaze. "He is plagued by some ghost from his past, something that drives him to fight demons with an anger that rivals their own ferocity."

The elder paused and sighed, turning her milky gaze to her paws. "My children used to be more open-minded, but ever since my mate Storm was attacked they have withdrawn from me. They believe he was killed, but I know better. He is still out there, struggling to return. But there's one thing that all of them believe. They believe that the Water-Wolves are the cause of this war, and that they ran away to escape punishment."

Hawk couldn't think of anything to say. This war, which the Water-Wolves had indeed started, even if by accident, had embittered everyone. *These wolves have no hope,* Hawk thought, *they are surrounded by death, and death is all they know.*

"Oh, dear," Fall said suddenly, turning to look toward the entrance.

Hawk looked up curiously, wondering what Fall had seen, or rather heard or whatever she did to keep track of her surroundings, and was shocked to see Falcon come racing back into the cavern. He had several long cuts down his side and a deep gash on his right shoulder just barely missed his light blue breed mark.

"Falcon, what happened?" Lichen, who was closest to the entrance, leapt to her paws. The other wolves immediately tensed, hackles raised as though they faced a horde of demons. Hawk shuddered. *They all act like Coal...but at least Coal has wolves like Sparrow to make him relax sometimes.*

"It's Jay," Falcon panted, his dark blue eyes wide. "He's been taken by a patrol."

Chapter Forty-Nine

"**How many demons**? What kind?" Sky asked, his dark eyes gleaming. Hawk was suddenly very glad he was not an enemy.

"Five, all Darkclaws."

There was a collective gasp. Darkclaws were one of the most powerful species of demon, and Hawk shuddered when he remembered seeing their power during the battle at the Obsolium Fortress. They usually worked alone at the head of a patrol or a fortress; to have five Darkclaws together meant trouble.

"What should we do?" Cloud asked in her strangely blank voice. "We're down three fighters."

"I can still fight," Falcon protested, although it was clear that he was struggling to stay conscious.

Cloud ignored him and turned her pale gaze to Hawk. "Can you fight?"

Hawk hesitated before answering. Despite participating in numerous battles since his escape from Ignimor, he had limited experience in actually fighting. *Luck and River saving me is really the only thing that's kept me alive...* "Not really...I'm not very good in a fight."

"And why is that?" Lichen growled. "How have you survived this long if you're *not very good in a fight*?"

"I...I tried to avoid fighting," Hawk said quickly. He couldn't tell them his meager fighting skill came from spending most of his life in a demon fortress.

"It's your fault we lost a fighter to begin with, and you can't even make up for our loss?"

"We don't need him," Sky cut in. "With me, you, Sand, and Cloud we'll be strong enough."

Lichen just shook her head. "It will be pointless if we just get ourselves killed."

"Then we'll just take as many demons down with us as we can," Sky returned, and Cloud nodded her agreement. Sand's eyes glittered with bloodlust, and she made a strange guttural sound deep in her throat.

"I am *not* going to throw myself into a doomed battle," Lichen snarled back. "You can go and throw your lives away, but I actually have a reason to live!"

"Like revenge is a good reason." Falcon's eyes narrowed, and he lowered his head, teeth slightly bared. "You would just leave my brother to die!"

Lichen snorted and gave Falcon a pitying look. "Well, I would think you would have gotten used to losing family by now."

With a vicious snarl, Falcon threw himself onto Lichen, but the she-wolf was ready for him and met him with teeth bared. The two turned over and over, snapping at each other and digging their claws into each other's fur. It soon became obvious who had the advantage, as Falcon winced every time he moved his injured shoulder.

The other wolves made no move to stop the fight.

Hawk stared with horror. *Don't they have any loyalty to each other? Lichen will kill Falcon if this continues! I...I have to do something!*

"Stop this nonsense!" Fall limped past Hawk before he could even attempt to move and marched right up to the fighting wolves. "You're acting like a bunch of pups! There is no reason to fight amongst yourselves."

Sky whirled on the elderly Wind-Wolf and knocked her to the ground with a snarl. "I'm sick of your prattling nonsense, you old goat! You're nothing but a hindrance!"

The white Wind-Wolf bared his fangs and bent to attack the elder. Still, the other wolves did nothing. Their eyes gleamed, and it appeared they shared Sky's feelings.

"No!" Hawk threw himself into Sky, ramming into the Wind-Wolf and knocking him away from Fall. The elder immediately rolled over and crawled away from the other wolves, her sides heaving. Her milky eyes were wide with fear.

"What are you doing?" Sky growled, head lowered into an aggressive position.

Hawk jumped back to stand in front of Fall, baring his fangs in a vicious snarl, any fear forgotten in the need to protect the old she-wolf. The other wolves gathered around Sky, and even Lichen had been distracted from her battle. Falcon lay unmoving by the cavern entrance, his blood pooling on the cold stone floor. Hawk didn't know if he was still alive or not, but he didn't dare move from his position lest the other wolves try attacking Fall.

None of them want her here, probably because she slows them down. Hawk looked to each wolf, carefully watching for any sign of attack. *Her children were the only ones keeping her in the pack.*

"You are not a part of our group," Sky continued, slowly padding forward, a haughty look on his face, one that said he knew Hawk didn't stand a chance against their combined effort. "You have no right to interfere."

"We need to get rid of that dead weight," Lichen snarled, baring blood-stained teeth. She had already left Falcon behind and had her eyes set on her new target. "With her around, we can't leave this cave. She holds us back in the hunt."

"You're outnumbered; we will kill you if you don't step aside," Cloud added, her eyes glowing with bloodlust. She seemed focused, and any feeling of her distance from the physical world was gone with her gaze boring into Hawk's pelt. Even Sand, although she could not speak, looked at Hawk as she would a demon, making a strange hissing sound.

Hawk trembled, but he didn't move. Inside, his instincts screamed at him to run as fast as he could and escape.

"Run while you can, Hawk," Fall said weakly. "Don't sacrifice yourself for my sake."

The other wolves crept closer, bunching their muscles to attack. Hawk didn't know what to do; there was no way he could take on all four wolves at once. Even one of them could easily kill him. "STOP!" he roared. The earth seemed to shake at his voice, prompting him to spare a glance at the ceiling, hoping he hadn't somehow started a rockslide.

The other wolves froze, startled by the earth's shake and the strength in Hawk's voice. He took advantage of their momentary distraction before he lost his courage. "Look at yourselves; have you really sunk this low? I…I may have been raised as a slave, captive my whole life, so I don't know much about the world, but I know that the Wind-Wolves were once a proud race!"

Sand looked shocked to hear of another slave, while the others had a mixture of suspicion and surprise on their faces.

"Fleet of foot and sharp of mind," Hawk continued. *Sun-Wolf help me find the right things to say!* "The Wind-Wolves used to be looked up to as the freest of the wolves. What land remained free even when the rest of Soluna was ruled by Rock and Stone? What land held out the longest against the demons when they came? The Gaoibeanna Mountains! I know this war has killed many friends and family and taken away our freedom, but that's no reason to lose hope. And as for you, Sand," Hawk said, giving the female Fire-Wolf a hard look. "I'm ashamed to be of the same breed. I know we've all had hard pasts and terrible experiences that have scarred us, but we can't reduce ourselves to the level of the demons! Look at what you're about to do, you were going to murder a defenseless elder!"

Sand and Lichen both looked away, ashamed of their actions. Cloud looked a little confused, but Sky kept his dark eyes locked with Hawk's red-orange ones. The white Wind-Wolf wasn't going to be easily moved.

"Before the war, elders were looked up to as wolves full of wisdom and insight. We cared for our elderly when they could no longer care for themselves. In present times, having an elder with you may hinder you, but could you really leave that elder to die, or even kill the elder with your own fangs? Isn't that behavior closer to that of the demons you claim to hate? Have you really become like our enemies?" Hawk paused, wondering if what he had just said was enough to convince the other wolves to stop their attack. Sand looked conflicted while Lichen seemed horrified at the idea she had become like the very creatures she hated. She kept looking over her shoulder at Falcon's deathly still body. Cloud still wavered, her pale eyes uncertain, but Sky's expression remained steely.

If I can convince him, the others will follow. Hawk turned his attention to the white Wind-Wolf and took a deep breath.

"Sky, I don't know what happened to make you hate demons so much. But just think for a moment. Remember the pride your people once had. Don't reduce yourself to a killer."

Shock flashed across Sky's dark eyes, but he held Hawk's gaze for a long time.

"You remind me of my brother." The white wolf finally turned away, speaking so quietly Hawk had to strain to hear. "He was always spouting nonsense about our proud history, always living in the past. It's my fault he was killed."

"I'm sure that he loves you and forgives you, no matter what, but you can still make it up to him," Hawk answered softly. "Spare Fall, and help me rescue Jay."

The Wind-Wolf paused, before slowly raising his gaze to search Hawk's eyes, to see just how serious the Fire-Wolf was. Hawk himself was surprised by his words, but he was determined to go through with it. Without looking away from Sky, Hawk raised his voice so everyone could hear. "Alone, we're weak. The demons keep us apart by making us live in fear. They separating families and friends through their horrible deeds. If we band together, then the demons can't harm us. The patrol that took Jay is strong, but if we work together and fight alongside each other, then we can *win*."

For several minutes, the cave remained silent. Hawk sensed the others were on the brink of changing their minds and all it would take was something that would prove what he had said was true.

"Not too long ago, I was recaptured and taken to a fortress, the Obsolium Fortress in Taladair Forest. River and several other wolves came to save me. They *attacked* the Fortress itself and roused the slaves into a rebellion." Hawk paused for a moment, seeing Sand's eyes widen at his words. "The demons weren't expecting us to rise up like that; they had grown lax after a century of rule. And isn't my presence here enough to tell you what happened? *We won.* We destroyed the Obsolium Fortress. Isn't that enough to tell you that the demons aren't all powerful, that they *can* be defeated?"

Hawk kept his eyes fixed on Sky, meeting the other's unwavering dark gaze.

Finally, the other lowered his tail and looked away. "What do you want us to do?" The white Wind-Wolf bowed his head to Hawk, effectively passing control of the group to him.

Hawk swallowed, a little unnerved by the elevated position he now held, and tried to keep his voice from shaking. "Lichen, help Falcon. See if he's still alive."

Lichen flinched but nodded before nervously padding over to the fallen wolf.

"Sky, Cloud, go track down the patrol that took Jay. Report back when you've found it, but do *not* let the demons catch you. Do *not* fight."

"Falcon's alive, but barely," Lichen called, looking a little uncomfortable. Falcon's blood stained her fur. Hawk wondered if he should have sent Lichen out to find the patrol instead, and kept either Sky or Cloud in the cave, but he shook the thought aside.

Hawk turned to Sand as the two Wind-Wolves raced out of the cavern. "Do you know any plants we can use for Falcon's wounds?" When the yellow she-wolf nodded, Hawk continued. "Go find what you can, quickly."

Sand nodded silently and padded out of the entrance.

"What are we going to do?" Lichen asked when Hawk padded over.

Hawk hesitated before answering. Falcon was so badly wounded that only a Cneasaithe could help him, but Hawk wasn't sure if it was safe to use fire magic on him.

Lichen would have to do it.

"I need you to do exactly as I say," Hawk replied, and then hesitated again. "And…I'm sorry for this."

The Wind-Wolf's look of confusion quickly turned into one of surprise and anger when he turned and sank his teeth into her shoulder.

"What was that for?" Lichen jumped away from Hawk, her brown eyes flashing.

Although he wanted to whimper in fear when Lichen bared her blood-stained teeth, Hawk forced himself to stand firm. *I hope I remember everything River told me…I wasn't paying too close attention when she explained how Cneasaithe worked in other elements…* "In order to use a Cneasaithe on someone else, you need to sacrifice some of your own blood."

Lichen looked at her bleeding shoulder and back at Hawk. "What?"

"Just listen. Summon a small breeze and collect some of your blood with it."

The dark yellow she-wolf hesitated a moment longer before obeying. Hawk shifted impatiently as Lichen called a bit of wind and swirled it around her wound. Falcon drew closer and closer to death the longer they took.

"Good," Hawk said when the wind turned red with Lichen's blood. "Now spread the wind over his neck wound, and say '*Curábo eum.*'"

"Curábo…eum." Lichen gave a strangled yelp when the spell took effect, surprised by the sudden drain of power. Hawk ignored her in favor of watching Falcon, praying silently that the spell would save the injured Wind-Wolf.

To his relief, the wound slowly closed as new skin stretched across the bloodied gap.

Thank Sun-Wolf. Hawk let out a sigh. Although it would take time for Falcon to replenish his lost blood and for the torn muscles to mend, he would live to see another day.

"Good job," Hawk said to Lichen when she healed the last of Falcon's major wounds, a process that took nearly an hour as the she-wolf herself grew weaker. Lichen only nodded before sinking to the ground beside the now-slumbering Falcon.

The spell took a lot out of her…she might not be strong enough to fight. Will the rest of us be enough? Hawk flattened his ears. *I wish River were here…we could really use her strength.*

"Hawk, come here a second."

Hawk looked up, startled. *Fall! I totally forgot about her…with everything that happened…*

"Fall, are you all right?" Hawk asked worriedly, hurrying over to the elder. "Sky didn't hurt you, did he?"

"No, Hawk, I'm quite all right," Fall replied, although her voice was still a little weak. "I haven't been knocked around like that for many years, and now I remember why I don't run around like you youngsters. Too hard on the body."

Hawk breathed a sigh of relief.

"But I didn't call you over to discuss my aging body. It was a very brave thing to stand up to Sky and the others, and I thank you for protecting me."

"I couldn't just let them kill you." Hawk lowered his head, embarrassed by the praise. He had only acted instinctively.

Fall waved her tail dismissively. "I was also very impressed with how you managed to change their minds. Although we call ourselves a resistance group, we never actually behave like one. The only reason this group has stayed together is because it gives them a greater chance of winning battles than any would have on their own. We aren't friends with each other. And yet you were able to not only talk them into working together but give them something even more important: *hope*."

"I only said what I was thinking…"

"And that is exactly why you won them over. You said exactly what you meant, and meant exactly what you said. You're a strong wolf, Hawk; you have a good heart." The elder paused and cocked her head. "Now, I am intrigued as to how you know how to cast a Cneasaithe, a spell art that was lost at the beginning of this war, and a *Wind* Cneasaithe at that."

"River taught me," Hawk replied.

"And how did the Water-Wolf know?

Hawk blinked. "You don't know?"

"No, my dreams only reveal certain things," Fall said with a shake of her head. "Sun-Wolf chooses what to show me, and what to keep hidden. But I *am* curious."

River wouldn't want me saying anything…she would be furious if she were here right now… Hawk hesitated, nervously looking away from the elder as he wondered how to answer.

Noticing Hawk's silence, Fall chuckled. "If you can't tell me, that's all right. Now I think you had better get back to work, alpha, your pack is returning."

Hawk didn't have any time to protest and say that he was not in any way an alpha before Sand ran into the cavern, jaws full of various leaves. She slid to a stop by Falcon and Lichen and stood patiently as Hawk bounded over.

"He's alive," Hawk said in answer to the other's questioning look. "The worst of his wounds have been closed, but I don't know how well they'll hold. Can you make a poultice for his other wounds?"

Sand nodded and dropped the leaves to the floor. The sound of more wolves entering the cave caused Hawk to look up, just in time to see Cloud and Sky slide in through the crack.

"What did you find?" Hawk asked, padding over to the two Wind-Wolves.

"We've found the patrol. They're sheltering near a waterfall about twenty minutes from here," Sky reported, respectfully dipping his head to Hawk. "Jay is alive and still mostly in one piece, but we need to hurry. Night's falling, and the Darkclaws will only get stronger with more shadows to work with."

Jay is alive...

"Good. Did any more demons join the patrol?"

"No. One Darkclaw had an unfortunate…accident and toppled over a cliff. It walked too close to the edge, and it really wasn't much of a surprise when the rocks happened to collapse."

Cloud bared her teeth in a blood-thirsty grin. Hawk knew very well that the Darkclaw had had no 'accident', but he let it slide. "Did the Darkclaws see you? Did they suspect that they were being followed?"

"Not that I could tell."

I hope they're not suspecting anything. If we're lucky, they'll think Falcon was the only other wolf in the area, and that he won't try anything against a patrol of five Darkclaws. Hawk took a deep breath, a plan forming in his mind.

Sand poked Lichen into wakefulness when Hawk began speaking.

"Okay…Lichen, I need you to stay here and keep an eye on Falcon and Fall."

The she-wolf immediately stood up to protest, swaying a bit on her paws. "I can fight! You're just leaving me behind because you don't think I'm strong enough!"

"No, but we can't leave Falcon and Fall on their own. If a demon were to discover the cavern they could easily kill them."

The dark yellow she-wolf narrowed her eyes, but her next protest was interrupted by Fall. "Don't worry about me or Falcon, Hawk," the elderly Wind-Wolf said. "There's only one way in and out of this cavern, and the entrance is very well hidden. If a demon does discover us, I can still manage to summon enough Wind to block the entrance. You will need every available wolf if you're going to attack a patrol of Darkclaws."

Seeing the determined glint in Lichen's eyes, Hawk relented. "If you're sure, Fall…"

When the elder nodded, Hawk turned to the others. "All right, we need to ambush the patrol before it moves on. If we attack now we can catch them."

"I would suggest waiting to attack, Hawk."

Hawk snapped his jaws shut and sent Fall a questioning look. "What do you mean? The longer we wait the more darkness the Darkclaws can use against us." Memories of the last time he saw a Darkclaw fight returned, and he had to hold back a shudder.

"That is exactly why you *should* wait. Take it from an old wolf who's been in a few battles." Fall chuckled. "Even if you leave now, you will be fighting in near darkness. The Darkclaws thrive in darkness; they'll be in their element. Wait, rest, and plan until dawn. Then, the Darkclaws will be at their weakest."

Hawk slowly nodded, seeing the wisdom in her words. *I'm getting ahead of myself, letting the nerves get to me.* "Okay, then we'll wait until morning. Sky, Cloud, describe to me exactly what the demons' camp looked like, and where they were keeping Jay."

Tonight we'll rest, and then tomorrow morning we'll save Jay. The tip of Hawk's tail twitched as the other wolves gathered around him, listening silently as he outlined their plan. *If only River could see me now.*

CHAPTER FIFTY

WHY THE HELL can't I find my way out of here?

River snarled at the sky as though it were personally the cause of her current troubles. For the second time in only a month she found herself separated from Hawk.

Only now, she was completely and utterly lost and didn't even know if Hawk was okay. The last memory she had of him was the sight of his terrified face as she disappeared into the clouds.

At least I had an idea of where I was in Taladair. River hunched her shoulders and growled again. *I've been to the forest plenty of times as a pup, but I've only been to the Gaoibeanna Mountains once, and I barely remember that visit.* Although River had claimed to know where she was going when Hawk had asked, truthfully she was just as clueless as he. Her pride had kept her from admitting it and she'd hoped Hawk, being part of a Sun element like Wind, would be able to sense the Ardgao if they got close.

But then she had to go and get herself thrown from a cliff with some insane Wind-Wolf who hated Water-Wolves.

To top it all off, that stupid she-wolf knocked herself unconscious, so she's no help in getting us out of here. River paused, remembering how her opponent had tried to push her away, only to knock herself into the side of a cliff. River had panicked for a precious few seconds, realizing that they were falling to what was sure to be a painful death at the bottom of the canyon.

Then she'd sensed a large river beneath them, and she'd summoned a large blast of water to slow their descent. The two she-wolves had splashed into the rapids relatively unharmed. From there it was a simple act of swimming to the bank. River had toyed with the idea of simply letting the Wind-Wolf get pulled along down the river but had reluctantly decided that it was probably a bad thing to let the other she-wolf get battered to death.

After pulling the other wolf to the shore, River had promptly collapsed into a heap and slept for several hours. When she woke, the other wolf was still unconscious, but as she was still alive and unharmed except for a large lump on her head, River left her alone to find a way out of the canyon.

It didn't take long for River to get lost. If it weren't for the river she had left the Wind-Wolf by, she probably wouldn't be able to find her way back.

As it was, she had no idea where she was, where Hawk was, or how to find him, at least not until the Wind-Wolf woke up, which didn't make her any happier. River did not like the idea of asking a former enemy for help.

To make things worse, River was starting to feel a little sick from being in a Sun element's territory.

Stick me in a marsh and tell me to find a dormouse, and I can track it, blindfolded, through mud and water, but leave me in the middle of the mountains and I couldn't even find my own nose if it weren't attached, River thought grumpily. *There's too much wind here. I can't even hear myself think!*

A scent reached River's nose, breaking through her dark thoughts and making her stop to sniff the air in disbelief. There was one smell that she could track no matter where she was.

Demon.

River bared her teeth, her dark eyes glinting, and took off after the scent.

Perfect.

CHAPTER FIFTY-ONE

WITH A ROAR that surprised him with its ferocity, Hawk charged into the demons' camp, Sky and Sand flanking him, and took the sleepy sentry by surprise. Sand breathed out a stream of fire that exploded when Sky added wind to it. Their combined inferno engulfed the Darkclaw.

By this time the other Darkclaws had been alerted to the danger and quickly recovered from their surprise. Jay, kept between two Darkclaws, sent his guards plummeting to the ground with a well-aimed gust of wind.

Hawk took advantage of the sentry's moment of surprise by leaping into the ball of fire and crashing into the demon. He wasn't nearly as successful in summoning flames as Sand was, but he was determined to win this battle. The yellow she-wolf leapt in after him, pouncing on the Darkclaw from behind. The two Fire-Wolves then took turns darting in to snap at the demon's throat before jumping back out of reach.

Keep the Darkclaw distracted, and it won't be able to use its abilities, Hawk thought, repeating what Fall had told them. *They can't keep track of fast objects, so move as quickly as you can. The moment they can exert their aura of fear over you is the moment you lose the battle.*

Sky flew past Hawk and Sand, slamming into the two Darkclaws fighting Jay with a large stream of wind, howling as he went. Before the last Darkclaw could help its allies, Lichen and Cloud leapt down from the rocks. Cloud landed on top of it, while Lichen ran over to join Jay and Sky.

A yelp from one of the others caused Hawk a precious moment of distraction. The Darkclaw, sensing an advantage, dropped to the ground just as Hawk pounced. He landed awkwardly on the demon and was roughly brushed aside as the Darkclaw rolled over and dug its hind claws into Hawk's stomach. The demon kicked him away and leapt to its paws with a roar.

Suddenly the air dropped several degrees, and Hawk shrank away, his heart pounding in his chest. Sand stopped in the middle of a pounce and fell to the ground with a strangled whimper. The Darkclaw snarled, its eyes glittering. "You *dare* face us in battle. You would have done better to continue hiding like the rats you are."

Hawk and Sand could only tremble as the full force of the Darkclaw's fear aura pressed down on them as though the weight of the mountains sat on their shoulders. Memories of torment suffered at the claws of the Ice-Fang, the pain of his mother's death, and the exhausting flight from Ignimor flashed through Hawk's mind. He whined, struggling to clear his head, but he couldn't stop the flood. More recent memories appeared, memories of seeing the Winter-Wolf for the first time, being captured by the Ice-Fangs in the Taladair Forest, just after meeting River...

River.

Hawk sprang to his paws, the aura melting away, and pounced on the Darkclaw. He snarled viciously and knocked the Darkclaw to the ground, completely breaking its spell and freeing Sand from its effects. The Darkclaw retaliated by summoning a swath of shadows and whipping it across Hawk's face. Undeterred, Hawk snarled again and bit down harder on the Darkclaw's shoulder. He was unaware of anything other than his Darkclaw opponent. He and the demon rolled over and over, each trying to gain the upper paw. Hawk, powered by newly found inner strength, was an even match for the already wounded, but more experienced demon.

A rush of water hit them, engulfing both Hawk and his opponent. Hawk was knocked out of his battle haze, leaving him to blink stupidly for a few seconds, wondering what was happening. The Darkclaw took advantage of the momentary lapse in concentration to escape. Powered by fear, the demon was over the ridge and disappearing into the pale dawn light before anyone could stop it.

Hawk was more concerned with not getting swept up in the flood than with fleeing demons. With water welling up all around him, panic froze his limbs and cleared his mind of any thought. But just as suddenly as the waters appeared, they vanished. Hawk sank to the stony ground, panting. Sand lay a few feet away, her sides heaving.

"I go running through five rapids and three mountains, fight my way past a mountain lion, getting turned around Moon-Wolf knows *how* many times, just so I can get here and sink my fangs into demon flesh, only to find that they're all dead!" River stood in the middle of five very sodden wolves, looking both angry and disappointed at the same time.

Hawk's heart leapt when he saw his friend alive and well, his tail giving a weak twitch. "Well, there might have been a Darkclaw or two left if you hadn't swept them all away."

"Oh, were they Darkclaws? I hadn't noticed. Now I'm even angrier at missing out on the battle. Where the hell have you been?" River growled the last part, stalking up to Hawk and ignoring all the other wolves. "Do you know how long I've been looking for you? Stupid mountains all look the same…"

Hawk's tail wagged harder, and he couldn't help but chuckle. *Fall was right; River survived! And here she is, grumpy as ever.*

"Where's Scrub?" Jay demanded, standing rather shakily. "Is she alive? How did you survive?"

River simply ignored the black Wind-Wolf and dragged Hawk to his paws. "Well?"

Hawk gasped at the rough treatment, wincing when the movement irritated his injuries. "I went back with Jay to his resistance group…and kind of led an attack to free him from the Darkclaws…what happened after you fell?"

River shrugged. "There was a river below us. I would have to kill myself for the shame if I were to die by water."

Before Hawk could question her further, Jay shouldered him aside, marching straight up to River and snarling in her face.

"Where's our sister? What have you done to her?"

"I haven't *done* anything," River snapped, raising her own hackles. "The stupid wolf's still alive, though she was dumb enough to get herself knocked unconscious and was *no* help whatsoever while *I* had to find a way out of that stupid canyon!"

Hawk hastily slid between the two wolves before they could attack each other. "Your sister is fine; River wouldn't have done anything to her," he said soothingly to Jay. "We'll go find Scrub in a bit. First, take Sky and clear the area. Make sure the Darkclaws are really gone. And have Sand check on Lichen. Despite what she might say, she's not at full strength, and I don't want to have two badly injured wolves on my paws."

Jay shot River a suspicious glance, but nodded and backed away to carry out Hawk's orders. The Water-Wolf's eyes widened in surprise when the resistance fighters obeyed Hawk without question.

"What did you do to get them to listen to you, howl the very moons from the sky?" she asked suspiciously.

"To tell the truth, I'm not really sure," Hawk admitted. "Jay, the black Wind-Wolf, was captured by this patrol, and everyone started fighting each other. Falcon, Jay's brother, was nearly killed by Lichen, the dark yellow she-wolf, and they were going to attack Fall, a Wind-Wolf elder. But I stopped them… and somehow convinced them to stop fighting and go after Jay."

River gave him a strange look that was a combination of amazement, pride, and utter disbelief. "Who would have known that the cowardly Fire-Wolf could talk a bunch of battle-hardened resistance fighters into behaving?"

Hawk wagged his tail, pleased that he had impressed her. "We're actually living up to our name. We're acting like real resistance fighters. Not just here, but in Taladair, too. We're starting to fight back."

"We wolves can't stay down forever," River said with a slight chuckle, before sighing.. "We'd better go get that stupid Wind-Wolf before some mountain cat does."

"Ah…right." Hawk turned back to the rebels behind him, quickly looking them over and taking stock of their injuries. They were mostly just very wet and shocked from River's sudden attack. Even Lichen managed to avoid getting too hurt, although she swayed on her paws.

She needs to rest before she passes out. Hawk glanced at Sand, who was helping the dark yellow Wind-Wolf to stand. *Sand, too. She's already shivering from her wet fur…*

Hawk was okay for now, as his unusually thick coat managed to retain some heat.

"Sand, I want you, Cloud, and Lichen to go back to the camp and check on Fall and Falcon," he said. "Jay, Sky, and I are going to find Scrub. We'll be back shortly."

The other Fire-Wolf nodded and slowly limped away with Lichen, picking up the pace when Cloud joined them. The other two Wind-Wolves padded over to Hawk and River, the latter waiting much more impatiently than the former.

"Make sure you keep up, because I'm not going to wait on you if you fall behind." River glared at Jay and Sky, growling slightly under her breath.

Sky looked nonplussed. "You'll *have* to wait for us if you want to get Scrub and find your way back without getting lost, Water-Wolf."

River shot a look full of venom at Sky, but didn't give him a reply. Instead, she turned sharply and ran down a slope leading away from the waterfall.

Hawk started to follow, but was stopped by Jay, who was sniffing the air. "Oi, Water-Wolf, you're going the wrong way."

Pausing halfway to the river, River growled, her tone dangerously cold, "What was that, Wind-Wolf?"

Jay only smirked. "I *said*, you're going the wrong way. Your scent trail leads *that* way." He waved his tail upriver.

Sky snickered and Hawk tensed, watching River nervously, hoping she wasn't about to attack either Wind-Wolf. This close to the rushing water, River would be at an advantage, and Hawk would be hard-pressed to stop her.

River gave the two Wind-Wolves withering looks and snapped, "Well, if *you're* so good at tracking, then *you* find her!"

Shrugging unconcernedly, Jay strutted up along the top of the slope, heading toward the waterfall. "Of course. Your scent trail is so clear, even a pup could follow it."

Hawk practically threw himself onto River to prevent her from tearing Jay's throat out. Sky laughed and padded after the black Wind-Wolf.

"Just let me get one bite out of him," River snarled, trying to push Hawk away. "Just enough to teach him."

"No, River, you can't do that! They…" Hawk paused, mind racing to come up with a reason as to *why* she had to let them live. "They can show us the way to the Ardgao."

At that, River stopped, although she kept shooting venomous glares at Jay. "Fine. But the next time I *will* kill him, even if that means we have to scour the entire mountain range to find the Ardgao ourselves."

River stalked away, muttering under her breath about mountains being too windy and having too much sun, and Hawk suddenly realized that River might be feeling the effects of being in a territory belonging to her opposite element.

If she's like this just by being in a sun territory…what will she be like in the land of her polar opposite, the Scaineadó Desert?

"Hawk!"

His head snapped up upon hearing his name, and he hurried to catch up to Jay.

"Since you're a Fire-Wolf," Jay said when Hawk appeared beside him, "and a Sun element like us Wind-Wolves, you shouldn't have too hard of a time tracking your friend's scent."

"Unlike a certain she-wolf I could name," Sky whispered, just loud enough for River to hear, who made a point of ignoring them all. Hawk shot him a warning glance, because he didn't think he could reach River before she attacked Sky if she were provoked. Even having two opponents against her, the odds were good for River. Both Wind-Wolves were exhausted from their fight, Jay even more so after a night of captivity. River had all the water beside them at her command, and she was fresh even after her fall from the cliff and rushed journey from the canyon.

Turning his attention back to the task at hand, Hawk inhaled deeply and sorted through the scents of the land around him. The smell of the water, a scent that was very similar to the scent of River herself, was the most apparent, overridden only by the scent of the ever-present wind blowing through the peaks of the Gaoibeanna Mountains. That scent was also tinged with sun and clung to the pelts of the two Wind-Wolves padding along with him.

Pushing aside those smells, Hawk focused on River's scent, and was surprised to find just how clear it was. He could even smell the frustration and lust for battle that River had felt when she had passed by earlier.

How can River miss something like this? Usually her senses are so sharp... Hawk shrugged inwardly. *Maybe the sun magic of the land is confusing her.* "Let's go."

Chapter Fifty-Two

RIVER HAD LEFT an erratic trail. She had crisscrossed the river several times, climbed over many ledges, and often turned back on herself. There were a few points where Hawk smelled where the she-wolf had engaged in battle with some creature. Hawk and Jay followed the trail River had left behind, often making shortcuts when it was obvious that River had simply zigzagged across the path. It wasn't long until they were overlooking a wide canyon, carved out by eons of water flowing in the river below.

And laying beside the river, unmoving, was Scrub.

"Scrub!" Jay shouted, leaping down from the ledge and tearing down the slope. Hawk and Sky followed at a slower pace, keeping an eye out for enemies, demons or otherwise. River gave an exasperated snort and padded after them.

The black Wind-Wolf quickly reached his sister's side and wasted no time in trying to wake her. After a few minutes of vigorous licking from her brother, Scrub blinked blearily and lifted her head. Immediately, pain flashed through her dark eyes, and she put her head back down.

"Jay? Falcon? Are you there?" she asked weakly.

"Scrub! It's me…Jay, I'm here." He brushed his muzzle alongside his sister's, relief flooding his eyes. "Are you okay? What happened?"

River growled and muttered darkly, "*I* told them what happened, and they still feel the need to ask *her*, who wasn't even conscious for most of it."

Sky rolled his eyes. "You didn't tell us anything, Water-Wolf."

Without deigning to reply, River clenched her jaw and stared down at the happy reunion with an air of hurt dignity, muttering something about empty-headed Wind-Wolves. Sky snickered and padded past her.

If they keep pushing her like this, at some point she's going to snap. Hawk closed his eyes and sighed, already feeling the beginnings of a headache.

"Just a little closer…" River muttered, prompting Hawk to open his eyes again. He was almost unsurprised to find her trying to move the turbulent water of the rapids out of its banks to sweep away the Wind-Wolves standing near the water's edge.

"River!"

Hawk's cry broke her concentration and the water, which had already risen a few inches above the waterline, fell back into its regular course.

"What?" The she-wolf sent him a glare.

"You can't do that!"

"I was going to fish them out eventually."

Hawk simply held her gaze until she snorted and looked away.

"Fine. I'll be waiting up there, in *peace*."

River stalked back up the slope, and Hawk turned to join the Wind-Wolves. Scrub was telling Jay and Sky what she remembered from her fall, which didn't amount to much.

"…and then that devil of a she-wolf pushed me into a rock before I could try to slow our fall, and everything went black. Next thing I knew, you were slobbering all over me." Scrub's eyes flashed. "Where is that she-wolf? I can smell her scent everywhere."

"River was the one who found us and is the reason we were able to find you," Hawk said, stepping forward. Scrub shot him a confused look, which turned into a glare as recognition flashed across her face. "I remember you; you were travelling with that Water-Wolf!"

Jay quickly bent down and whispered something in his sister's ear. She growled a bit, but seemed to accept whatever it was he had told her. "I want to hear the whole story when we get back to camp. How long was I out?"

"A day or two," Sky answered. "Can you walk?"

Scrub replied with a glare that would have sent a Hell-Cat running. She stumbled to her paws. Jay wasn't spared the look when he immediately leapt to her side, fluttering about her like a worried mother bird.

"I can walk on my own," Scrub snarled. "And anyone who tries to help me will feel my fangs!"

Sky and Jay wisely chose to allow Scrub to make her own way up the slope, but they didn't stray far from the injured Wind-Wolf. Hawk winced every time he saw the blood-encrusted lump behind Scrub's ear.

"Finally," River growled when they approached. "I was about to simply leave you idiots here and go on ahead on my own."

Sky snorted at her claim. "We'd just end up having to rescue your sorry lost pelt, Water-Wolf."

"Finally awake, I see," River said to Scrub, choosing to ignore him. "A lot of help *you* were trying to get out of here."

The gray-yellow Wind-Wolf snarled at River as she stumbled past. "If it weren't for *you* I could have easily stopped my fall."

"Oh really, then why didn't you? You had plenty of time to save yourself before you fell onto the rock."

"I would have done that if I didn't have some blood-crazed demon distracting me!"

River tensed, ready to pounce on the injured Wind-Wolf, and Hawk quickly stepped forward to stop a fight from breaking out.

"Don't," Hawk said quietly. "She's hurt…not everyone is as invincible as you."

River gave Hawk a long look, before tightly nodding. She stalked up to Scrub and shoved her shoulder into her, forcing Scrub to lean on her. Jay rushed forward, but froze at a glare from his sister.

"What are you doing? I don't need help from *you*," Scrub said.

"Yeah, well, shut up. I don't want to have you slowing our pace. You should be grateful I'm helping you, *again*."

"I won't 'slow our pace,' and I'm not grateful!"

Sky, Jay, and Hawk watched with slight amusement as the bickering she-wolves padded away. Scrub, for all her arguments, wasn't making much of effort to get away from River, which spoke volumes of the gray-yellow she-wolf's exhaustion.

At least now they shouldn't come to blows, Hawk thought, sniffing the air to pick up their trail back to camp.

"Um, River? You're going the wrong way."

Chapter Fifty-Three

"Scrub!"

Both Fall and Falcon, anxiously awaiting the return of their wayward relative outside the camp's entrance, were overjoyed at the sight of the yellowish she-wolf. Although Fall herself knew both Scrub and River had survived, the elderly Wind-Wolf couldn't help worrying for the safety of her daughter.

"Mom, Falcon!" Peeling away from River, who immediately shook as if trying to shake mud from her pelt, Scrub stumbled over to her mother and brother. The three were immediately joined by Jay, who demanded to know why Falcon was in such a state. Falcon ignored Jay in favor of showering his sister with jubilant licks.

Sky rolled his eyes and slid around the excited family, ushering Lichen, Sand, and Cloud back into the cave. "Before I start barfing, I'm going to get out of the open air where any demon walking by could see me."

River, grudgingly agreeing with the white Wind-Wolf, stalked after him, but Hawk hesitated before entering the cave, watching Fall and her children a little sadly.

It must be nice to have a family... Memories of Oak, Pine, and Bracken, and of Granite, Canyon, and Palm flashed through his mind. Even within the pack, they had a special connection, something binding them together.

They were never alone when they had each other.

I only had Mom, and she's gone now...and even though Sparrow kind of acted like a sister, I'm probably not going to see her for a while. Hawk turned away just in time to see River paused at the cave's entrance, staring at the celebrating Wind-Wolves with a look full of longing.

I don't know if River had any family other than her brother...but if they're still alive, they're trapped in the Rift. She must miss them.

River shook herself, her customary mask sliding back into place.

"Get inside, you down-for-brains," she growled, marching back over to the four Wind-Wolves. "At least three of you are ready to pass out, and I am *not* dragging your sorry hides around anymore."

Hawk sighed and shook his head as River shoved, ordered, threatened, or used all three options to get the rest of the rebel wolves back into the camp.

The three siblings glared at her but didn't fight her too much after a stern look from their mother.

Inside, the camp was just as Hawk had left it early that morning. Sand and Lichen had returned to sharing a mountain hare beside the pool of hot water, not even pausing to look up when they entered. Cloud had already fallen asleep in one corner of the cave, her thick tail covering her snout. Sky sat a few paces away, casting a Cneasaithe to close a particularly nasty bite on his right shoulder.

Lichen must have showed them how to do it, Hawk thought, before turning back to Fall and her children.

"Scrub, Jay, we need to do something about your wounds," Hawk said. "Falcon, I want you to go and rest some more. Your wounds are closed, but you lost a lot of blood, and I don't want to risk casting Cneasaithe on you…I don't think it would be smart to heal you too many times in such a short amount of time."

"Oh, no, please do continue healing him," River said with a snort. "The spell will probably just consume the rest of his life force, that's all."

Scrub bristled, but Hawk slid between them before she could come up with a sharp retort. "River, can you go with Sand and Lichen to bring back some more food? We're all going to need to eat if we're going to regain our strength." He hoped that by pairing River with the two wolves who were least likely to irritate her for the fun of it, she would find a better use for her energy than bickering.

River glared at Hawk for a few moments, before turning away with a shrug and stalking out of the cavern, barking for Sand and Lichen to follow her. Hawk nodded when the she-wolves glanced over at him, and they silently padded after River.

They should be okay…now I can get the others settled. He turned his attention back to the remaining wolves.

"All right, let's get you guys healed."

CHAPTER FIFTY-FOUR

LICHEN COULDN'T HELP but watch River out of the corner of her brown eyes. It was as if the Water-Wolf had jumped right out of the old legends, although the Wind-Wolf herself had never put much stock into them. The only thing that mattered to her was getting revenge on the Noxond that slaughtered her family.

But River is nothing like the Water-Wolves from the stories…she looks like an Earth-Wolf but has the temperament of a demon. She only has one breed mark, so she has to be a full-blooded Water-Wolf… Lichen watched silently as the blue-gray she-wolf blundered across the rocks, trying to pick up a scent. If it weren't for her temper, Lichen would have laughed at the sight. Sand had already given up trying to work with River and had vanished to go hunt alone.

Her amusement slowly faded, leaving Lichen with her thoughts again. "River…"

The blue-gray Water-Wolf jumped, startled. The sound of skittering paws reached their ears as a fat mouse fled into a small crevice.

"I almost had that!" River spun around to face the Wind-Wolf with a growl.

Lichen was nonplussed. "At the angle you were crouching, it would have smelled you long before you made a move. Remember, hunting in the mountains is very different than hunting in a forest…or a marsh."

The other she-wolf growled again, but Lichen continued. "I just wanted to ask…where did the Water-Wolves go at the beginning of the war?"

River's navy blue eyes darkened dangerously, and she bared her teeth. Lichen immediately drew back, startled by the reaction. She flattened her ears against her head and shuffled a few steps away in case the Water-Wolf decided to snap when River stopped. Emotion crossed her dark eyes, and she took a deep breath. "We…we were taken."

That was all River said, and the tone of her voice warned Lichen against asking anything more. She nodded and backed away. A moment later Sand appeared over the rise, a young goat clamped firmly in her jaws. She sent Lichen a confused look as she padded over, flicking her gaze over to River a couple of times. Lichen knew she was trying to ask why the atmosphere seemed so tense between them. Months of traveling with the mute Fire-Wolf had taught Lichen how to read Sand.

But in answer to Sand's silent question, Lichen only shook her head. She had recognized the hurt and fury in River's voice. Whatever had happened to the Water-Wolves, it cut River deeply. Much like how the loss of Lichen's family cut in to her heart every day.

The rest of the hunt was conducted in silence.

CHAPTER FIFTY-FIVE

HAWK WAS VERY glad to see River and the other she-wolves return with several hares and a goat. He was exhausted by everything that had happened and very hungry. From the way the other wolves immediately perked up when the hunters appeared at the entrance, he knew he wasn't the only one.

He ushered the hunters into the cave and distributed the prey, making sure Fall, as an elder, and Scrub and Falcon, bearing the worst injuries, were given food first. Hawk himself was the last to eat, grabbing a hare and carrying it over to River, who was crouching by the hot springs pool and glaring at the water.

"Want to share?" He dropped the mountain rabbit beside her. She eyed the offering almost suspiciously, but gave a slight nod.

"Have you asked them to show us to the Ardgao?"

Hawk hesitated. "No. They're going to want to know *why* we need to know... and they will most likely refuse to tell us outright."

"They *have* to tell us." River's navy-blue eyes flashed as she tore into the rabbit.

Hawk shuffled uncomfortably. *I don't even know how to ask about the Ardgao...the Elemental Guardians are really the only things from the old days that are truly free from Letorus' claws. Any Wind-Wolf would be wary of sharing any information about the Ardgao with outsiders...*

"I'll talk to Fall," Hawk said finally, and received a grunt in return. The two finished their hare in silence.

After making sure that everyone was resting and had eaten their fill, Hawk decided to approach the elder. *If anyone will tell us about the Ardgao, it'll be her...but how am I going to ask? I know she'll be curious...but River doesn't want me saying anything...*

"I must thank you again for saving my children, Hawk," Fall said when he padded over to where she was lying with her children, her milky eyes shining with happiness. "If it weren't for you, I could have lost them."

Hawk bowed his head to the Wind-Wolf elder, his tail wagging. "It was the right thing to do."

"And tell…River…thank you," Scrub added, looking as if she'd rather go rub her face in goat dung than actually thank her savior, but the hard look her mother was giving her was difficult to ignore.

"Now, did you need something, Hawk?" Fall asked, turning her head to face him once more.

Hawk shuffled his paws a little nervously. "Um, yes…I need to talk to you about something…"

His voice trailed off and he snuck a glance at the three Wind-Wolf siblings, who watched him curiously. He wasn't sure how he could ask them to leave without offending them. Fall, however, seemed to sense Hawk's intention, and quickly shooed her pups away.

"Now, tell me," Fall said once the others were out of earshot, "what do you need?"

"Well…I need to know where the Ardgao is."

A look of both curiosity and apprehension crossed the elder's face. "Despite your name, you are not Wind-Wolf. Why do you need to know?"

"I…I can't tell you that," Hawk replied glancing quickly at River, who was glaring at him out of the corner of her eyes.

Hawk shuffled again, trying not to look away from Fall's gaze. *It's almost as if she can actually see me…or even right through me…*

"Very well. I will tell you."

"Why don't we just show him?" Sky appeared right next to Hawk, nearly sending him clear to the ceiling in his shock.

How did he hear my question? And how did he get so close without me noticing? Hawk took a deep breath, trying to steady his racing heart. "What do you mean?"

"I'm not going to ask why you need to get to the Ardgao, and I'm not happy that you need to find it. However, you helped us, and we owe you. We'll repay our debt by taking you there."

By this time, the other wolves had gathered around. Falcon and Jay looked horrified that an outsider was trying to find their Wind Elemental Guardian, but the others simply looked curious. River remained on the outside of the little gathering, watching with interest as the rebels agreed to help Hawk.

Hawk's tail wagged, and he bowed his head to the Sky. "Thank you, very much."

Sky shrugged. "You saved us…in more ways than one. Besides, I don't like owing others."

"Who will go?" Cloud asked, her hollow voice a little thoughtful. "Neither Falcon nor Scrub will be up for a long journey, nor can we leave Fall behind on her own."

Immediately Falcon and Scrub protested, arguing that they felt quite fine and did not want anyone's pity. Hawk took charge of the situation before they started fighting. "Scrub, Falcon, Jay, and Sand will stay behind to guard Fall and the camp," he said firmly, shooting the wolves a look that brooked no argument. "Sky, Cloud, and Lichen will come with us to the Ardgao. Sky, How long of a journey is it?"

"Eight days, at the most, but we can probably make it in seven if we don't run into any demons."

"Are there any fortresses nearby?"

"Two, the Nocte Fortress and the Algidus Fortress. We'll have to pass right in between their territories to get to the Ardgao."

Inwardly, Hawk quailed at the thought of having to go near not one, but two demon fortresses, but he quickly pushed aside the fear.

"What are the strengths of these fortresses?"

"The Nocte Fortress is led by a Shade-Tiger, and is comprised mostly of Night-Lynxes and Hell-Cats," Lichen put in. "It sends out patrols during the night."

Hawk nodded and Sky continued from there. "The Algidus Fortress is led by a Fire-Fang. I think there are a few Darkclaws, but otherwise the demons from that are mostly Hell-Cats, Ice-Fangs, and Fire-Fangs. They run normal day patrols."

Ice-fangs… Hawk couldn't hold back a shiver at the mention of the demons.

"Both fortresses collaborate with each other to patrol a large territory day and night." Sky paused, his black eyes narrowing in thought. "We could probably go around them both, it would just take several more days."

"That will take too much time," Hawk said with a shake of his head. "We'll have to sneak between them."

Although Sky gave him a suspicious look, he nodded. "Very well, we'll guide you through them."

Hawk nodded as well. "Thank you, Sky. We'll leave in the morning."

And with that, the wolves dispersed to find places to sleep, although the three wolf siblings argued with Hawk a while longer before their mother cut in and thoroughly chastised them for arguing. After a little more grumbling, they finally accepted his orders.

Yawning, Hawk padded back over to River, who had watched the entire conversation with interest.

"It's about time they did something *useful*," River said, before curling up right where she sat. Hawk wagged his tail slightly before joining her, settling down a few paces away. It didn't take long for him to drift off to sleep, exhausted as he was by the day's ordeals.

Chapter Fifty-Six

THE NEXT MORNING, River was the first one to wake. Everyone else woke soon after, courtesy of the blue-gray Water-Wolf herself. "Get up, you lump of fur!" River gave Lichen a hard poke to the side. "We're wasting daylight."

The she-wolf only growled and rolled out of the Water-Wolf's reach. "You do realize it's *dawn,* right?"

"Yes, and every second you spend sleeping in is a second we could have used traveling!"

"River, do us a favor and *shut up.*"

Spinning around, the Water-Wolf snarled at Sky, who was making himself more comfortable and already falling back asleep. "I won't have you tell me what to do. We need to get moving, now!"

Hawk quickly jumped up and groggily ran over to stop the fight. Barely awake, instinct was the only thing driving him. "River, we're still tired from yesterday's battle," he said sleepily, struggling to wake himself fully. "Not everyone is like you …just give us a little bit longer to rest."

River glared at Hawk a little longer before huffing and sitting back down. "Fine. But we'll make up for lost time during the journey."

Hawk breathed a sigh of relief as River padded over to sit by the cavern's entrance. She seemed determined to wait in discomfort until everyone was ready. Hawk sighed again, but from exasperation this time. He was completely awake now, with no hope of returning to sleep. Instead, he padded over to join the irritable she-wolf.

They sat in silence for a minute or two, until Hawk ventured a question. "Have you visited the Gaoibeanna Mountains before, River?"

"Once…when I was a pup." River paused and scowled. "As the eldest daughter of the Queen, it was important for me to be acquainted with the other elements. I didn't go far into the mountains, my…mother and I met up with the Wind-Wolf monarchs close to the border of the Taladair Forest."

Hawk nodded; the implications of her words hitting him a little belatedly. "Wait…you're the daughter of the Queen?" *Then that means…* Hawk's eyes widened as memories of what River had told him before, returned.

'*Any sane wolf would have avoided such a thing, but the Queen, the leader of the Uiscean Marsh, at the time was anything but sane…She only saw the Rift as a source of power…It took time, but finally they were able to find a way to open the Rift a little and allow a wolf to pass through. The first one…my brother…never came back.*'

River's mother, the last Queen of the Uiscean Marsh, was the very wolf who sent her son to his death, and the one who opened the Rift and brought the demons to Soluna.

"You didn't already make that connection?" She snorted. "I already told you she sent my brother through the Rift first. Who else could *possibly* have that honor but one of her blood? She would have even sacrificed her two daughters if it meant *more power*."

River had a sister? Hawk thought, bewildered. *Is she trapped in the Rift with the others? What about River's father?*

"Is your sister…still alive?"

Grief flashed across River's face. "No."

"What about your father, is he still alive?" *Does she have anyone left, or is she alone…like me?*

River snarled and hunched her shoulders, her eyes dark with anger. "I don't have a father."

What does she mean by that? Hawk tilted his head slightly, seeing the sorrow that racked her mind and body. Her defenses were down, like they had been when she first told Hawk what had happened to her people. He lowered his ears. The pain of losing family was one he could understand.

Watching to make sure River wouldn't suddenly jump up and attack him; Hawk gave her a reassuring lick behind the ears. "I'm still here…" he said quietly.

River didn't reply, and the two sat in silence once more.

CHAPTER FIFTY-SEVEN

THERE WAS A bit of confusion as the wolves being left behind tried once more to convince Hawk to let them come, saying that he had a better chance of defeating patrols if there were more wolves. Hawk calmly replied that the fewer wolves that went, the better their chances of remaining unnoticed.

"Hawk, come here a second," Fall said, waving her tail to get his attention from where she lay.

He quickly padded over to the elderly brown Wind-Wolf, sitting a few paces from her. "Yes, Fall?"

"I know you have your reasons for needing to go to the Ardgao, but would you consider staying here and leading the group?"

Hawk froze. *Wh...what?*

"The other wolves respect you, and they would benefit greatly from having a strong leader to keep them in check."

Hawk blinked, shocked. He was being offered an amazing opportunity, one he never would have dreamed of having. When he managed to recover, he shook his head. "I'm sorry, Fall, but I can't."

He knew that if he were to accept, he would most likely be safer than he would be travelling with River. He would never be alone, not with the resistance at his side.

But it would mean leaving River. It would mean forgetting everything that they'd gone through. It would mean breaking his promise.

There's no way I can abandon a friend like that.

Fall nodded, and sighed a little. "I thought so. Hopefully the others have learned from you, and we will work together a little better."

Hawk warmed under his fur at the elder's praise, but quickly came back to earth at River's harsh call. He bowed his head, excusing himself from the brown Wind-Wolf, and padded to the entrance of the cave, passing three very annoyed Wind-Wolf siblings along the way.

"Good luck, Hawk," Fall called after him. "And may Sun-Wolf light your path."

Hawk raised his tail in farewell as he stepped out into the bright morning sun. Waiting a few paces away were River, Sky, Cloud, and Lichen. Sky and

River looked ready to tear each other's throats out. Lichen stood between them, trying to keep a fight from breaking out. Cloud stood a little apart and paid no attention to any of them, her attention fixed on the peaks above. In the early morning mist, she looked more like a ghost than ever.

"I am *not* going to take orders from some half-wit Wind-Wolf!" River growled, glaring at Sky.

Sky just rolled his eyes. "Well, then it's perfectly fine with me if you wander off some cliff!"

Lichen sighed as Hawk padded up to the little group. "They've been arguing about this for the past few minutes. I don't think they even remember *how* they started fighting in the first place."

"River, Sky, please stop," Hawk said, trying to get their attention. Neither wolf gave any sign of hearing him. He groaned and padded closer, hoping the rest of the journey wasn't going to be like this.

Finally, Cloud growled and sent a harsh wind crashing into all four wolves. She glared down at them and said, "You're being too loud."

Hawk quickly took advantage of Sky's and River's moment of confusion and lurched to his paws. "If everyone is ready to leave, then we'll go. Sky, please lead the way."

Picking himself up off the ground, Sky shot River a glare before nodding. With a wave of his tail, the white Wind-Wolf motioned for the others to follow him.

"We'll have to head south for a few days, until we reach the Red River. Then we'll head upriver, toward the Nocte Fortress, because there's an area downriver I want to avoid. It's being heavily guarded by the demons. We saw them moving slaves into the area, so we think they might be building something there."

Hawk shuddered at the thought. He had no idea what the demons could possibly be building right in between two fortresses, but he definitely didn't envy the slaves being forced to build it.

River muttered something about what she would do to the demons controlling the slaves, earning herself a few mildly surprised looks from the other three at her language.

"It'd be you versus a whole fortress full of demons," Sky said in answer to River's curses. "Whatever luck you had before with the last fortress, you'd just be *asking* for death attacking one on your own, because I'm certainly not going to help you."

River gave him a nonplussed look. "Did Hawk tell you about that? Then you should know it had very little to do with *luck*."

Sky ignored her. "In order to avoid the guards surrounding that area, we'll have to pass very close to the Nocte Fortress."

"How close?" Lichen asked.

"Too close. We'll be within barking distance of the walls. But we should be fine if we keep quiet and pass the fortress at noon. The demons of Nocte are mostly nocturnal and should be all asleep then. It'll be simple enough as long as we keep course and don't get *lost* along the way."

The last part was obviously directed at River, who snarled but said nothing at a look from Hawk.

"Sky, stop taunting River," Hawk said firmly, giving the white Wind-Wolf a hard look as well. "We need to travel quickly and silently if we're going to reach the Ardgao without too much trouble, okay?"

To his relief, Sky nodded and turned his attention back to the path in front of him. They walked on for several minutes, with River and Hawk occasionally stumbling over the uneven ground, the former muttering darkly every time her paws slipped. Sky led the group, with Cloud and Lichen right behind him. After a while Lichen dropped back to walk beside Hawk.

"Where were you kept?" She eyed his collar, barely visible beneath his neck fur.

"In a fortress called Ignimor, in the Scaineadó Desert. I…was born there."

"Do you have any family still there?"

Hawk shrugged. "I only ever knew my mother, but she died. If I have any other family, they're probably dead, too."

The she-wolf turned her eyes to the ground. "My family was killed by a Noxond. It just…appeared one night, and trapped us in a canyon. It murdered my mother, my father, and my two sisters and left me for dead. I don't know how I survived that, but I thank Sun-Wolf I did." Her voice grew hard, and her lips rose in a slight snarl. "It means I'll live to take revenge."

For the first time, Hawk noticed a long, ugly scar, mostly covered by dark yellow fur, running down Lichen's side and curving under her stomach.

A Noxond…I think I've heard of it before…

"What's a Noxond?"

Lichen's ears flattened against her head. "Horrible beasts, even more powerful than Darkclaws. They look like Earth-Wolves at a distance, with dark red fur and black patches over their faces that look like giant eyes. Noxond can control lesser demons like the Overlord can, and I've heard that they can also regenerate any wound instantly." Her voice dropped to a whisper. "I've even heard that Noxond have the abilities of all demons below them, and their skin is so tough that it cannot be marked by normal attacks. The only weak spots it has are its eyes and its stomach."

Memories of a mysterious demon stalking through a snowy forest flashed through Hawk's mind, and he stumbled.

That…that's exactly what that one demon looked like, the one River and I hid from in the snow. Fear made his blood run cold. *We were incredibly lucky to have avoided notice…* Hawk shuddered. *I hope we never see another Noxond.*

Lichen sped up again to lope beside Cloud, leaving Hawk to drop back and rejoin River, who was glaring daggers at Sky, the cliff they were running along, and just about anything that caught her eye.

"River…do you remember that demon we hid from that one time? Did you know it was a Noxond?"

River hesitated before answering. "Yes, I did. I've…met a Noxond before."

Although Hawk was dying to ask about how she had met a Noxond, the tone of her voice warned him against it. *She seems like she's in a worse mood than usual…she probably won't appreciate me asking a bunch of questions.* Hawk bit his lip and turned his focus back to keeping up with the Wind-Wolves.

Maybe I can ask her about it later…

Chapter Fifty-Eight

THE SUN WAS setting on the fifth day when they finally reached the Red River, but Hawk knew the last three days would be the hardest.

Tomorrow we head toward the Nocte Fortress. Hawk eyed the turbulent waters below their camp a little nervously. *At least the fortress is on this side of the river...I wouldn't want to cross it.*

He tried not to think about the fact he would have to cross it later anyway, and instead tried to settle down for sleep, joining River beneath a small overhang. The other Wind-Wolves, aside from Lichen keeping the first watch, lay across from them.

Fortunately, Hawk was so exhausted from their journey he was asleep within moments. Travelling in the Gaoibeanna Mountains was different than travelling through the Taladair Forest. The ground was very uneven, mostly uphill, and the air was much thinner. More than once Hawk had found it hard to breathe, although the three Wind-Wolves had appeared fine.

Then again, they were made to live in the mountains.

It seemed only a few minutes had passed when Sky woke Hawk to replace him in keeping watch. Hawk blearily padded out of the camp and hid himself a few paces away from his sleeping companions. Most of his energy was then spent simply trying to stay awake, and he counted himself lucky no demons appeared.

Toward the end of his watch, and just as the sun was starting to peek over the mountains, a strange sound reached the edges of his hearing. Curious, Hawk stood and crept toward the noise, his half-asleep mind ignorant of the danger of wandering off alone.

It took Hawk several minutes to get close enough to see the source of the sound, and the sight was enough to shock him into complete wakefulness. He crouched behind a pile of rocks and stared in horror at the scene below.

At least a hundred wolves, mostly Wind-Wolves, dug away at the hard, mountainous earth, carving into the sides of the cliffs themselves. Several groups had to work out of deep, dark pits. The slaves carried some sort of dark rock from the pits and deposited it at the bottoms of various piles on the other end of the excavated plateau.

Everything was carefully watched by Hell-Cats and a few of the Fang demons, while the real masters, a Darkclaw and two Night-Lynxes sat away from the pile, devouring the carcass of some mountain creature.

They're mining something, Hawk realized with a jolt. *It looks like some sort of metal...* He stared hard at the piles of rock, and his stomach turned. *There's only one metal thing I can think of that the demons use and is that color.* He swallowed hard. *The slave collars. No wonder it's so heavily guarded, the demons don't want any outside interference.*

Suddenly Hawk realized just how dangerous a position he was in. Not only did he risk getting himself captured, but he also risked exposing the others. As quietly as he could, he crept away and snuck back to camp, sickened by what he had seen.

I never knew that the metal in our slave collars was mined right here in the mountains, Hawk thought as he headed back to camp. *I guess I had assumed that it was just something that the demons themselves created, because why would our land host something so evil? I should let Sky know what the demons are doing there.*

He wasn't prepared for the four very angry wolves who met him at the camp. River was the first to attack him with questions.

"Where were you? Why did you leave the camp? Do you realize how long we've been looking for you? Why, for Moon-Wolf's sake, would you wander off on your own? If you had gotten your sorry hide captured *again*, I would not have come to save you!"

"Seriously, Hawk, what were you thinking?" Lichen asked, shoving River aside. "You left us totally unguarded while we slept, and why would you run off on your own anyway? With your pelt, a demon could spot you from a mountain away!"

"I...uh...I..." was all the Fire-Wolf could say, quite flustered from all the attention. He hadn't realized that they were so concerned about him.

Finally, Sky stepped in. "All right, let's not overwhelm him. Hawk, where did you go?"

Happy to answer a sane question without having someone shove their muzzle into his face, Hawk said, "I heard something, and went to go see what it was. I'm sorry I abandoned my post."

The white Wind-Wolf nodded, accepting Hawk's apology. "So what did you find?"

Nervously looking between Sky and River, Hawk explained what he had seen.

"It's a mine," he finished. "They're mining the metal to make the slave collars."

Silence met his words. Each wolf was horrified that such an evil substance came from the very land they called home. Finally, Lichen spoke. "I had always thought the demons created that metal."

Hawk nodded in agreement. "But what else could they be doing?"

"There have always been spots in Soluna where our elemental powers didn't work as they usually did," River said slowly, her face thoughtful. "Places where, even if a wolf was in her own territory, the elements were harder to call upon. Some spots you couldn't use any magic at all. I had heard that most of these 'dead zones' were in Gaoibeanna…"

"Those spots must have come from deposits of that metal, but they were buried too deep to really have any effect." Sky narrowed his eyes. "Hawk, how deep were those pits?"

Hawk paused, trying to remember. "I think some were about four Earth-Wolf-lengths deep. I couldn't see the bottoms of a few of them, it was still kind of dark…" He looked up to see a strange glint in Sky's black eyes, and suddenly he felt a little nervous. Cloud and Lichen seemed to pick up on Sky's thoughts, and both of them were looking very eager.

"How many demons?" Sky asked. "What kinds?"

"Uh, a few dozen Hell-Cats, several Ice- and Fire-Fangs, two Night-Lynxes, and one Darkclaw that I could see. I don't know if there are any more demons," Hawk answered, torn between desperately hoping that Sky wasn't planning what Hawk thought he was planning, and hoping that it was possible.

"If we do it right…"

"No." River bared her teeth slightly.

"But they'd never expect it," Lichen protested. "We'd have the element of surprise, and we could throw the Hell-Cats into confusion. That's most of their fighting force out already, and once the slaves see the demons losing control, they'll fight back too."

"No, we'd just attract unwanted notice," River replied, sounding oddly unlike herself.

"If we plan it correctly, we could destroy the mine before the demons have a chance to retaliate. Especially if there are Earth-Wolves among the slaves,"

Cloud said, speaking for the first time since starting the journey. Her pale eyes glowed, and she seemed to be awakening from her usual air of detachment.

As much as Hawk wanted to free the slaves and destroy the horrible mine that generated the metal to make the slave collars, he didn't see how it was possible to do so without getting the attention of both the Nocte and Algidus Fortresses.

"You three stay here," Sky ordered, starting to walk away. "Hawk, come with me. We're going to go scout out the mines."

Hawk hurried to follow the other wolf. "Are you sure this is a good idea? Even if we *could* free the slaves, how could we get them away before the Nocte and Algidus Fortresses sent reinforcements?"

"Simple, we break the slave-stones off so the slaves can use their elemental powers, and then the Wind-Wolf slaves can help the others disappear," Sky replied. "Do remember that here in the mountains, we Wind-Wolves are in our element and have an advantage over the demons."

"But you'll still be affected by the metal," Hawk protested. "It'll weaken your powers."

"A little, maybe, but all we really need is to confuse the demons long enough to rouse the slaves."

"I still think it's a stupid idea."

Both Sky and Hawk jumped at the sound of River's voice right behind them, although the Wind-Wolf quickly covered his surprise with a snarl. "I thought I told you to stay back at camp!"

"And I believe I've already told *you* I'm not going to take orders from a half-wit Wind-Wolf!"

Surprisingly, Sky only snorted. "Whatever, just stay quiet."

Several minutes later, the three wolves arrived at the mines. They quickly hid in a spot not far from where Hawk himself had been earlier that morning.

Sky gave a low growl. "You said there were a few dozen Hell-Cats…there have to be at least a hundred."

The grunts of the demon populace were everywhere, guarding various parts of the mines or running errands for the higher-ranked demons. A few Ice-Fangs watched the slaves closely, ensuring no one slacked off. Several Fire-Fangs were gathered at the other end of the pit, melting chunks of metal into thick silver bricks. There were two more Night-Lynxes than the two Hawk had already seen, and all four appeared to be dozing under a large overhang. The Darkclaw was nowhere to be found.

As for the slaves themselves, even from where Hawk crouched, he could count the ribs in every wolf's side. He shuddered, remembering the horrifying days of his own captivity.

"What's that pile of rubble?" River asked quietly. Both Hawk and Sky turned to follow River's gaze to see a smaller pile of dark-colored stones.

Hawk gasped in recognition. "Those are slave-stones!"

"Shut it!" River slapped water into his face and glared at him for speaking so loudly. He shook his head and muttered an apology as Sky asked, "So what's the difference between the metal and the stones?"

"I…I don't know, exactly." Hawk flattened his ears. "The collar itself doesn't dampen magic, although it *is* resistant to elemental attacks. The stone is what stops a slave from using his power. I always thought they were two different things…but it looks like they might be the same material…"

"The demons might be doing something different to the stones, to enhance their powers," River suggested.

Sky snorted. "Why not do that to the collar as well? Not that I'd want the demons to have a better way to keep the slaves under control, but it seems like a more efficient way."

"Stones are more receptive to spells than solid metal," River replied.

"Well, whatever they're doing to make the slave collars, we should find out. Then we might be able to cancel the effects of the metal and stone," Sky said. "But first we need to plan our ambush."

"Weren't you the one to tell me that it was suicide to attack this place?" River glared at the white wolf. "Why are you so determined now?"

"I only said it was suicide if you tried attacking on your own. *I* wanted to avoid causing any trouble here because I wanted to avoid notice. It'd be much easier to get you to the Ardgao without hordes of demons on our tail. But…" Sky paused, glancing over at Hawk. "You said you took on a fortress, and *won.* Why can't we do the same here?"

Hawk bit his lip, still a little uncertain. "If we can pull it off…we can free the slaves and destroy the mine. It might stop the demons from making more slaves…or at least, slow them down…"

"Exactly, and think of the psychological effect a victory like that will have on them," Sky said. "It'll cause confusion. After *two* successful attacks on their holdings, the demons will worry about just how much control they have over us. And the other rebels will see it as a beacon of hope, a sign that times are changing."

"But what happens after?" River asked. "Do you really think a fight here will go unnoticed by the Nocte and Algidus Fortresses?"

Sky narrowed his eyes and was silent for a moment. He looked back down at the mine.

"How many slaves do you think are down there?" he said finally. "A few hundred, maybe. The Nocte and Algidus each only have about half of a full fortress. Several months back we noticed that a large portion of their garrisons had disappeared; I guess this is where they went." He paused, turning back to Hawk and River. "Think about it. We defeat the demons here; that's like one fortress taken down. We'll just have one fortress left, and it's split in two. We'll ambush one, and by the time the other comes to help, it'll be too late."

Hawk wasn't so sure it would be as easy as Sky made it out to be. If they made a mistake, they could easily be cornered by two entire fortresses. He glanced over at River, wondering what she was thinking, but her expression betrayed nothing.

She said once before that avoiding notice was vital to her plan...defeating the Obsolium Fortress in Taladair could be attributed to a slave uprising, but something like this is a full-out attack against the demons.

"With you two leading us, we have a better chance at winning than if we were on our own," Sky continued. "With a *Water-Wolf* leading, what's that going to say? To both wolves and demons?"

River narrowed her eyes. "I thought you believed the Water-Wolves were the *cause* of the war."

"I still do. Why else did you disappear?" Sky ignored River's quiet growl. "But whether or not you actually *did* start the war, many believe the Water-Wolves will one day return to end it. I assume that *is* why you're showing up after over a hundred years. Why miss a chance like this?"

"I think we should do it," Hawk said, causing River to give him a look of surprise. "Sky's right. This is the perfect chance to continue what we started in Taladair. You're...you're the first sign of actual hope we've had in over a hundred years, River. The Obsolium Fortress was the first real victory we've had since Oak's Last Stand. I...I think this all means it's time for us to rise up again."

River looked between Sky and Hawk, her expression unreadable. Hawk held his breath, waiting to hear what she would say. Sky would probably want to go through with his plan with or without River, but Hawk knew they would need her help to succeed.

I know she wants to get to the Ardgao quickly, but we can't miss this chance! Finally, she nodded.

"We'll do it, but you'll have to do *exactly* as I say. Understand?"

"You have a plan already?" Sky asked.

River bared her teeth in a feral grin. "Oh yes I do."

CHAPTER FIFTY-NINE

THE THREE RUSHED back to camp, River refusing to say a word about her supposed plan until they joined the others.

"Do any of you know what an Amhríochta is?"

Blank expressions met River's words, and she sighed in irritation.

"I had expected as much. Listen up; I don't want to repeat myself. Amhríochta is a summoning spell, a Song, technically. By howling, instead of simple winds you could call up an entire hurricane."

The three Wind-Wolves immediately brightened, but Hawk narrowed his eyes a bit worriedly.

The demons will hear us howling and stop us long before we can cast the spell...

"There is a downside to it. Amhríochta takes a lot more energy than doing a simple elemental manipulation, which is why it's usually done in groups. Plus, the wolves casting Amhríochta have to be howling exactly in sync or it will fail. And if it does..." River winced slightly. "...the results are disastrous. But if we're to overcome the effects of the slave metal, it's what we'll need to do."

She paused, studying the other three for a moment.

"I don't know how the Wind-Wolves, or Fire-Wolves, for that matter, cast Amhríochta...it's done differently for every element, so you'll have to figure that out on your own. The basics stay the same. You know how to howl, so just howl something that will call up some wind and fire, put your power into it, and make sure you stay in sync."

"It sounds like it's just going to be us doing it." Sky shot the Water-Wolf an accusatory glare.

She returned it with a nonplussed look. "Fire and Wind are complimentary elements; they work well with each other. My Water will clash and knock the spell out of rhythm. What *you* will be doing is summoning a windstorm, big enough to knock the demons around a bit and disorient them. Hawk will add some fire to it and increase the damage."

"But while we're howling, won't that leave us vulnerable?" Lichen asked, cutting across Sky's next protest.

"Yes, it will. And you can't stop until you've finished…or messed up. But I'll keep the demons distracted and free slaves where I can, and you'll be hidden while you're howling."

"What about the other slaves?" Hawk asked.

"You'll have to aim the spell as best you can. Some slaves might get caught up in it, but let *me* worry about that," River said. "All you need to do is make sure you don't mess up the spell, or we'll have much bigger problems to worry about."

Lichen and Cloud seemed to accept River's plan, although Sky still looked skeptical. Before he could continue arguing, however, Lichen gave him a shove. "Oh, don't start, Sky. You're disagreeing just to disagree. Shut up and help us figure out what to howl."

That made Sky shut his jaw, and he reluctantly agreed. The three Wind-Wolves walked off a bit to go plan their Amhríochta, while River gave Hawk some last minute instructions.

"There's no set song when you howl Amhríochta," she said. "Not for something small like this. Let those three get started, and then join it. You'll have to howl what they're howling, but you'll also have to add in a bit of your own song as well. You need to add Fire to their Wind."

"How?" Hawk asked, overwhelmed by what River was asking him to do.

"Just put your power, your fire, into your howl and the rest will follow." She paused. "I can't help you with this. Fire and Water don't mix well. But… you'll figure it out. I have faith in you."

And then she marched away, leaving Hawk standing in a shocked silence.

Chapter Sixty

A FEW HOURS later, Hawk was hiding among several small boulders, his heart pounding in his chest as he waited for the signal to begin. He smelled River crouching a few paces away, waiting to rush down into the mines and distract the demons while he and the three Wind-Wolves summoned the windstorm.

Any moment now…I hope I remember the right notes… Hawk tensed, taking a deep breath to calm himself.

A howl rang across the mine, causing everyone down below to pause, even the Hell-Cats. Two more howls quickly joined the first one. Hawk jumped to his paws and peered around the boulders, just in time to see River race down the slope, howling her own challenge. She bowled over several Hell-Cats and a Fire-Fang before the demons had even registered her presence.

So this is an Amhríochta, Hawk thought, turning his attention to the Wind-Wolves' song. The three howled in near-perfect harmony, only a few notes off of each other as they struggled to stay in sync. The air thrummed with power. *I can* hear *the Wind in their Song.*

Slowly, as though waking from a long sleep, the wind picked up and gained strength. Gusts of it raced toward the mine, sweeping past Hawk and nearly knocking him off his paws. He watched in amazement as the very clouds above them swirled and spiraled, growing thicker as they spun.

Hawk dragged his attention back to the Song itself when he heard a slight pause, as though the Song was waiting for something. Realizing it was his cue to join in, he tipped his head back and howled.

Power surged through him, almost startling him out of howling. His heart raced and his blood burned, as though fire blazed in his veins. Hawk pushed aside the feeling, forcing himself to focus solely on the song. He had to stay in sync with the three Wind-Wolves, but howl his own part to summon the fire, and he couldn't afford to be distracted.

As Hawk's voice joined with the other three, the wind began to change. It twisted and began to glow. Hawk felt it quickly growing hot as flames appeared on the edges of his vision. Fire tore into the mine, carried by the wind, roaring as it grew into a blazing inferno that crashed into a mass of demons.

Down below, River had managed to free several slaves, who immediately turned on their former masters. The Water-Wolf herself was surrounded by several demons, a crazed look in her eyes and blood on her fangs. A few Fire-Wolves and Wind-Wolves who had rid themselves of their slave-stones helped by directing small currents of fire-windstorm away from the other wolves and turning it on the demons.

The storm raged in the mine, quickly moving beyond the control of the four singers. Hawk, Sky, Lichen, and Cloud slowly lowered their voices, letting the Amhríochta take over and run its course. Hawk stumbled, the sudden release from the Song leaving him shaky and weak. But he quickly recovered, exhilarated by its success. He barely felt his exhaustion. He jumped out of the pile of boulders, lurching around the rocks so he could get a clear view of the mines.

The very air above him blazed with flames that were twisted and turned by a roaring wind. The Hell-Cats, stupid beasts at best, ran in circles, terrified by the storm. The other demons struggled to regain control, but as more and more slaves rose up to fight, the situation continued to spiral into total chaos. Several Ice- and Fire-Fangs had already met their fates, puddles of water and piles of ash marking where they once stood.

Where's River? Hawk slid down the slope, for once eager to join the battle. He spotted her a moment later, facing a Night-Lynx and a Darkclaw at once with little trouble.

A high-pitched yelp tore his attention away, and Hawk slid to a halt. Just a few feet away, a Fire-Fang had a small Wind-Wolf cornered, with nothing but a long fall into one of the pits behind her. The tiny creature, her bright blue eyes wide with terror, looked as if she wasn't even out of puppyhood.

Almost instinctively, Hawk launched himself into the air, landing on the demon and knocking it away. He scrambled back to his paws and stood in front of the young wolf, his teeth bared and his red-orange eyes flashing.

The Fire-Fang quickly recovered and settled into a crouch, its red eyes boring into Hawk's and its long tail whipping in irritation. "You will pay for this, rat. Nocte and Algidus will reclaim this land."

Inflated with the success of the Amhríochta, Hawk threw his head back and snarled. "Soluna belongs to *us*! We will never give up until every last demon is gone!"

Hawk tackled the Fire-Fang, and sank his fangs into its throat, taking the demon by surprise. With a strangled cry, the scaly monster disintegrated into ash.

Hawk jumped back and spat the still-hot ash out of his mouth. He shook his head and turned to the small Wind-Wolf pup. "Are you okay?"

The little light blue pup's body shook from the force of her wagging tail, and she threw herself at Hawk, nearly knocking him from his paws. "I was so scared. Thank you for saving me!"

"Ah…you're welcome," Hawk said, eyeing the drop behind him a little nervously. He nudged the small Wind-Wolf, gently pushing her away. "Go and hide until the fight is over. I don't want you getting hurt."

He waited until the puppy had scampered up the slope and disappeared over the ridge before turning his attention back to the battle. The fire-storm summoned by the Amhríochta was slowly dissipating, and most of the demons had been killed by the uprising slaves. Hawk scanned the plateau, searching for River, breathing a slight sigh of relief when he spotted her. She was battling a Shade-Tiger, but seemed to be having a hard time keeping up with the demon's movements. To Hawk's horror he saw several deep cuts down her side.

It was the first time he had seen her so wounded.

And the ground around her is dry…she hasn't summoned any water to fight with. Hawk eyed the untouched drifts of snow behind River, who fought the Shade-Tiger tooth and claw. Even from where he stood, Hawk felt the cold chill of the demons' aura, although the she-wolf herself didn't seem affected. *I have to help her!*

Chapter Sixty-One

River always lost any sense of the world around her when she battled. She threw herself completely into the fight, giving in to her bloodlust, although she never even noticed the transition. Her battles usually didn't last long, as her opponent was usually quickly overwhelmed by her sheer ferocity.

Fighting the Shade-Tiger, however, was different. The demon was wily and fast, and even River was hard-pressed to keep up with it. As the fight dragged on, she found herself weakening against it. She couldn't summon water, as it would clash with the Amhríochta's sun magic and cause it to backfire.

I…cannot…lose! River snarled and threw herself onto the demon's striped back. But the Shade-Tiger foresaw her attack. It flipped around and dug its claws into her stomach. She howled as pain flooded her senses and she crumpled to the ground.

Fight! River roared in her mind, willing herself to *move* and destroy the Shade-Tiger.

Something snapped in her mind, and everything faded into blackness.

CHAPTER SIXTY-TWO

139 years ago...

"**RIVER! RIVER**, wait up!"

The blue-gray she-wolf stopped and glanced over her shoulder. "Pebble, if you don't hurry I'm going to leave you behind!" The laughter in her navy-blue eyes betrayed the firm tone in her voice.

Pebble, a young silver-eyed Water-Wolf with a rare dark green pelt, was panting by the time he had caught up with his sister. "It's...not my...fault you move...too...fast."

"Aren't the young supposed to outdo the old?"

"But I'm only younger than you by two years!" The smaller Water-Wolf flattened his ears in a mock pout.

"And still a puppy full of energy. Now come on, or we'll be late for the clan meeting."

Nodding, Pebble padded after his older sister, only to be stopped by a sudden attack of vicious coughs. River immediately leapt back to her brother's side, eyes full of concern. "Pebble? Are you okay?"

The green Water-Wolf tried to answer, but coughs cut off his words. River narrowed her eyes.

"They've been getting worse, haven't they?"

Pebble shook his head furiously. "No, I'm fine." He took a deep breath. "Let's just get to the meeting. You know what Mom's like when we're late to these things."

Irritation flashed across the older wolf's face, but she was careful to hide it from her brother.

"All right. But the *moment* you start coughing again, I am going to personally see you back to the dens, no matter *what* Mom says."

"Whatever," Pebble said with a roll of his eyes. "Hurry up now, or *you're* going to be the one who's left behind!"

⤿

BY THE TIME River and Pebble had reached the meeting place, most of the clan had already assembled. The two siblings tried to sneak into their spots before anyone noticed, but their effort was in vain.

"You're late!"

River rolled her eyes and turned to give her younger litter-mate, Creek, an annoyed glare. The elder she-wolf fought back a growl when she saw her sister's infatuated admirer, Fish.

He needs to get a life and stop inflating her ego, River thought irritably. *It's annoying enough simply with* her, *much less her little minion.* Although Creek barely noticed Fish's existence, the male adored her and hung on to her every word.

"We're not late, we arrived just when we wanted to," River replied smoothly.

Her sister snorted. "Any later and the moons would have risen."

"The Queen and King are here!"

The gathered wolves immediately fell silent and organized themselves around the edges of the meeting place, clearing a path for their two monarchs, alphas of Clan Archeo and rulers of Uiscean Marsh. Pebble scrambled to his place beneath a ledge. His sisters followed a little more slowly, still glaring at each other.

River fought back a growl as her mother passed, although she dipped her head in respect like everyone else. The silver-furred wolf barely glanced at her eldest daughter, still furious that she refused to live up to the responsibilities given to her. To River, her mother focused too much on making her daughter the perfect successor and on pursuing her own personal goals, rather than doing what was best for the marsh.

She's looking more insane by the day. River narrowed her eyes, noting the strange gleam in her mother's own black orbs. *But she's too clever to let the clan see her losing her grip, so I can't even say anything without looking like some down-for-brains pup.*

River immediately brightened when her father, Mist, padded by. The black Water-Wolf was King in name only, but he was well-liked by all in the clan. His stocky build would have marked him an Earth-Wolf, if not for the double wave mark on his shoulder.

"I haven't seen you, or your brother, come to think of it, all day," Mist remarked quietly as he sat beside his daughter, his mate continuing to the ledge above them.

"I was showing Pebble how to track mice." In truth, she and her mother had argued again that morning, and River felt the need to escape. Pebble had asked her to teach him some things, and she had readily agreed.

"Wolves of Clan Archeo, turn to your Queen!"

Each wolf in the clearing immediately perked up, eyes glittering with excitement. The air hummed with tension, as everyone had an idea about what Rain was to announce.

"As you all know," Rain began, her clear, strong voice hiding the instability within, "several days ago we discovered a strange disturbance near the Archeo. A great, long rip in the very air, floating above the ground."

Quiet mutters broke out at her words. River narrowed her eyes and scanned the gathered wolves. The clan was split on the subject of this 'rip,' or 'Rift,' as some had come to call it. Many were curious and wanted to learn more about it, but just as many were cautious and claimed that they should leave the Rift alone.

Rain was among those who wanted to investigate it.

"After much investigation," the Queen continued when the clan had quieted itself. "I have made an important discovery."

Silence fell, as the wolves gave their leader their full attention. Even River perked her ears, albeit a little suspiciously.

She never said anything to me…when did she make this 'discovery'?

The silver Water-Wolf raised her head, baring her teeth in an excited grin. "Within the Rift is a source of power."

Several moments passed before one wolf spoke out. "What do you mean, Queen Rain?"

Rain's dark eyes gleamed, her insanity shining through for a few seconds before being pushed away by the Queen's customary mask.

"River…what's wrong with Mom?" Pebble whispered, his own eyes wide. River simply shook her head, intent on listening to her mother's answer.

"Power! A great power awaits within that Rift," Rain said excitedly. "Stronger than a waterfall, or rapids, or even the waves of the ocean itself! If we could harness that power, there would be no end to what we could do."

"But how?" It was the same wolf who had asked the first question. "*How* could we do that, if we can't even get close to it? Birds fly right by it, and if we try to approach it, it's like we run into an invisible wall."

River could see a few other wolves nodding and whispering amongst themselves. Several looked excited, while others looked apprehensive.

"With enough investigation, we will find out how to get close and how to harness that power," Rain replied smoothly. "Wolves of the Water, this is something that will raise us above the other wolves and make us the most powerful nation in Soluna!" Raising her voice, the Queen led her clan in a triumphant howl.

River stayed quiet, her eyes narrow.

This is insane…where did she even get this idea? She growled to herself. *She's sunk to a level where she has no reason, but she's still the Queen.*

I can say nothing against her.

⌒⌒

DAYS LATER, River could no longer keep silent.

"You have to stop this! It's insane!" River snarled, not caring who heard.

"How *dare* you speak to me like that!" Rain spat, her hackles raised. "I am your mother, your alpha, your *Queen*; it is your *duty* to obey me!"

"How can I obey an alpha who has become so *blind* with power that she can't even see that her plan is *killing* her clan! *Five* wolves have already died trying to get that stupid rift open. The entire clan is against you and your stupid, desperate plot to gain power, but none of them are brave enough to speak out against you!"

Rain narrowed her black eyes and gave her daughter a look full of hate and rage. Her voice lowered until it was little more than a hiss and grew so cold River almost shuddered.

"My decision is final. We *will* open that Rift, and nothing *you* or anyone else can think or say will change that."

For a moment, the two she-wolves stood and glared at each other, fangs bared. The few wolves who happened to be witness to the fight quickly made themselves scarce, not wanting to be around if it came to bloodshed.

But River knew she still couldn't raise a claw against her mother, and she silently cursed herself for her weakness.

Instead, she turned sharply, without properly dismissing herself from her leader's presence, and stalked away. As she passed her father, who had been summoned by a concerned clanmate, she spat, "If you're her mate, talk some sense into her!"

Mist nodded and padded up to the silver she-wolf, who then broke down in sobs, slowly swaying on her paws. "Why? Why can she not understand?" Rain wailed, her cries echoing across the dens where the clan lived. By now, every wolf was aware of the alpha's insanity, but her descent into madness had not weakened her, and she defeated any challenger brave or dumb enough to fight her.

"Easy, my love, it will work out in the end," Mist muttered, brushing his muzzle against hers. "River will come to understand."

～

Three days had passed, and still River had yet to return to the clan. She knew if she returned, she would only clash with her mother again.

"Let the old hag waste away trying to open that thing," River snarled to herself, splashing noisily through a stream. "I don't give a damn anymore."

"River!"

Startled, she turned to see Creek racing toward her.

Where's Fish? River blinked, confused for a moment, before baring her teeth in a silent snarl. *No…he was one of the first to die. The stupid wolf was so desperate for Creek's attention that he* volunteered *to help force the Rift open. At least she finally noticed him when he burst into a ball of light.*

"If you're coming to convince me to come back, you're wasting your time." She growled and turned away.

"The Rift is open, and Mom's sending Pebble through!"

"What?" River roared, immediately spinning back around. "Why? *Why is no one stopping her?*"

Creek shook her head. "No one in the clan can stand up to her. You know that. I tried to stop her…but I couldn't."

"*Wha—?*" River cut herself off, her eyes falling to the long, ugly wound running down her sister's side. It bled profusely.

How did she even make it this far? I'm miles from the camp.

"*She attacked you?* What about Dad, has he done anything? Did *she* attack him too?"

"He's gone. He disappeared two days ago, and no one has seen him since."

Swearing, River launched into a gallop, barely pausing to shout over her shoulder, *"Come on!"*

She never noticed her sister collapse, so focused was she on reaching the Rift in time. The weak strength that had allowed Creek to run all the way to River was gone.

"I'm sorry, River…I can't…I'm going to meet Fish…" The she-wolf whispered as her eyes dimmed and her breathing slowly stopped.

⌣

RIVER'S HEAD SPUN and her legs shook by the time she reached the Rift. Most of the clan had gathered to witness the first entry. She paused on the small hill above the gathering, her navy-blue eyes searching the crowd desperately for her brother, spotting instead the thin, ragged figure of her mother standing several lengths away from the Rift itself.

The rest of the clan gave her a wide berth, staying as far away as they dared. *She's pushed the clan away entirely now…their sense of duty is the only thing keeping them…*

"Creek, we have to…"

River cut herself off, realizing that her sister had never followed her. She snarled, but froze a moment later when her gaze zeroed in on her brother.

Little Pebble, always sick and coughing, but a bright young wolf who loved to follow his older sister River around, stood shaking in front of the Rift. Even from her position, River saw the terror in his silver eyes.

"No!" River howled and tore down the slope. Rain spun around at the sound and screeched at her clan to stop her daughter. Bound to obey, several rushed forward to block her path.

"Pebble! Stop!" River screamed, struggling to get through the mob of wolves.

If Pebble heard her, he made no reply. Haltingly, as though some force pulled him forward in spite of his best efforts to resist, Pebble walked toward the wide tear in the very fabric of space. An evil and cold aura emanated from the rip, nearly a physical thing with its intensity.

"PEBBLE!" River burst through the wall of wolves, just as her brother took the last step into the Rift. Light flashed from the opening, an explosion of brightness that forced everyone standing nearby to look away.

But River could not close her ears to her brother's terrified screams.

The light slowly faded, and with it, Pebble's voice. Silence fell over the gathered wolves, who stared with shock and horror at the terrible Rift that had devoured Pebble. A few moments passed before rage filled River and she charged forward to leap on her mother. "How could you? How could you send your own son to his death?" Rain simply howled incoherently and bit down on River's paw.

With a roar of pain, River jumped back, but was immediately knocked to the ground by her mother's tackle.

"It's your fault! Your fault! *Your fault!*" Rain screeched, her ears twitching and her body trembling. River stared in shock, realizing that now her mother was truly insane. "Mist went to look for you, and he never returned! You killed him! *You killed Mist!*"

"I never saw Dad!" Rage quickly replaced the shock, and River rolled to her paws, shoving her mother away. Not a wolf stirred to stop the fight between the two. "Your *madness* drove him away!"

Rain continued as though her daughter had never spoken, moaning and swaying from side to side. "And now Creek is gone! *Gone!* You made me attack her, and now she is...*dead!*"

"*You* attacked Creek! *You* killed her!"

"Take her! Take her away!" Rain howled to her clan. After a moment's hesitation, they obeyed. In spite of River's struggles, she was eventually dragged away.

The Queen was left to howl emptily to the sky.

⌒

River stood silently, staring at the ground, her eyes clouded with grief. In the span of only a day she had lost three members of her family. Many wolves surrounded her, guards to make sure she didn't try to escape.

It didn't matter; River had lost any will to live. Another wolf stood with her, muttering unintelligibly to himself, staring up at the sky with blind eyes. Rain had ordered his imprisonment when the wolf, upon his miraculous return from the Rift, had started screaming things about blood and demons, and attacked anyone who went near it.

Another wolf had returned after him, but she claimed to have felt the power of the Rift. Rain's mind, already weakened by the hunger for that power, was consumed by it. She immediately announced her intent to enter the Rift herself and claim it.

The few wolves who dared to speak immediately fell silent when their Queen appeared. They were gathered at the Rift again, and this time the entire clan was present. Puppies, elders, mothers, every Water-Wolf of Clan Archeo had been ordered to come.

Rain swayed as she padded through the crowd. Her black eyes gleamed with a strange light and her pelt was ragged with dirt and mud. River could count every rib in her mother's side as she passed, but could no longer bring herself to care.

What does it matter what she does now? She watched with a blank expression as her mother padded to the front of the gathering. *Pebble, Dad, and Creek are all gone. Hopefully* she *will starve herself to death or something and end this madness.*

"Today is the day the power of the Rift is unleashed!" Rain called hoarsely, her voice echoing in the deathly silent clearing. "I will harness the power… and use it to punish those who have stood against me!"

Several wolves took a few steps back, worried that they would be the ones to feel the Queen's wrath. Rain, however, had eyes for only one wolf, in particular.

"River! You, who murdered my mate, my son, and my daughter, are no longer a child of mine!" Rain screeched triumphantly, but River didn't even twitch. "I will first use the power of the Rift to kill you and take my revenge for the murder of my family!"

When several moments passed and still River gave no response, Rain snarled and spun around. She raised her head and walked confidently toward the Rift. The clan watched with bated breath, wondering if Rain would return filled with power…or if the Rift would claim her life.

Some wished for the latter.

Rain stepped into the Rift and disappeared. The clan froze.

Seconds ticked by.

A scream tore through the clearing, echoing out from the Rift. Nearly every wolf present flinched at the pure pain and terror in Rain's voice. The wolf imprisoned with River backed up so fast he knocked over his guards. His blind eyes were wide with horror, and his jaws were parted in a silent howl.

Rain's scream suddenly stopped but was replaced with the cold voice of some unknown creature. River looked up, her heart frozen in her chest. All feeling drained away at the sight of a pair of cruel, dark eyes staring out at them.

"*Sum Mors...Sum Aeterna...Sum...Letorus!*"

CHAPTER SIXTY-THREE

"RIVER!"

A terrified scream dragged her back to the present, with a very familiar face of a smaller wolf looming out of the bloodlust misted over her eyes.

...Pebble?

River blinked, uncertain if her nightmares had somehow crossed over into the waking world. Her vision slowly cleared.

Hawk stared up at her, terror clouding his red-orange eyes. Her fangs hovered a whisker from his throat, and her claws dug into his thick coat.

I almost killed him.

Horrified, River backed away. She barely noticed the Fire-Wolf scramble away.

What just happened? River's legs shook slightly, and she struggled to get a hold of herself. *Why did I attack Hawk like that? I...I don't remember what happened.*

"Hawk?" She thought she heard a chuckle at the back of her mind, accompanied by a sense of hunger, but she immediately shoved the feeling away and closed down any thought about it.

It couldn't be...I locked it away.

River looked back up at Hawk, and saw traces of fear in his eyes, although he obviously tried to hide it. She snarled silently at herself. *I* will not *let this hurt him.*

"Where's that Shade-Tiger? I'm not through with it yet," she snarled instead. When Hawk did nothing other than stare, she narrowed her eyes. *What exactly did I do?* "...what?"

"Uh, I killed it. The Shade-Tiger, I mean," Hawk answered quickly. "It was trying to run away from you...so I attacked it."

River said nothing for a few moments. She was sure Hawk was lying. There was something he wasn't saying.

But River was afraid to find out what.

She gave him a stiff nod, accepting his lie. "Good. Have the rest of the demons been killed?"

Howls answered her questions, the newly freed slaves too overjoyed with their victory to care about being heard. The last of the flames from the Amhríochta disappeared, brightening the celebration.

Hawk's tail wagged as the last traces of his fear faded away, and he gave River a toothy grin.

"We won!"

His excitement was contagious, and even River couldn't help but wag her tail a little. Whatever she had done, however close she came to hurting Hawk, it seemed he was content to put it to the side.

"Can you believe it? We've taken down a fortress and a mine, in just a few weeks," Hawk said, his eyes lighting up. "We've freed hundreds of slaves, even. Maybe…maybe we really *can* save the Island."

He tipped his head back and howled, joining the other wolves in celebrating their victory. River paused for a moment, watching him. Although she was determined to see her plan through and come out successful, no matter the cost, she couldn't help but agree with Hawk.

There is still hope left for us.

Then she lifted her muzzle and howled.

Chapter Sixty-Four

Despite the joy of freedom, Hawk quickly remembered the precarious position they were in. Although they had been careful to prevent any demon from escaping, at some point the Nocte and Algidus Fortresses were bound to realize something was wrong.

"All right, Hawk, you're up," Sky said after sending Cloud and Lichen to go gather the freed slaves. "We have to work quickly so we can get out of here before the patrols come."

Hawk swallowed a little nervously. "What?"

"You've got to rouse the slaves. We've won this battle, but we still have the fortresses to take care of. You need to explain to them what our plan is and convince them to follow us."

"Wh-why me?"

"Because you were able to convince me to follow you."

Hawk blinked in surprise. Sky held his gaze, utterly serious.

"You're stronger than you give yourself credit for. I believe you can do it."

Lichen came up behind them, her eyes glowing with excitement. "They're ready."

Sky nodded. "Thank you, Lichen. We'll take it from here."

The she-wolf scurried back to join Cloud at the front of the gathering. Hawk could hear the freed slaves murmuring, watching him with curious eyes. Sky took a few steps back and nodded to a slight ledge above them.

"Tell them what you told me. It's time to stop hiding."

"He's right, you know."

Hawk jumped when River, who had been standing by silently until now, spoke. He had almost forgotten she was there.

"You're strong," she continued. "You're an escaped slave; you can understand their situation. You've seen what hope, or lack thereof, can do. I know you can do this."

Hawk's eyes widened, shocked by her words. Then warmth spread through him and he wagged his tail slightly. "Thanks, River."

He jumped up to the ledge and turned to face the crowd of freed slaves below. The murmuring quickly stopped and silence fell over the mass of wolves.

For a split second, fear fused Hawk's jaw shut and erased any thought from his mind. He glanced down to see River, Sky, Lichen, and Cloud all watching him. River gave a slight nod.

I can do this. Hawk took a deep breath, remembering how Pine spoke after the victory of Obsolium.

"Today is a great day," Hawk shouted. "We stand free under the sun once more! We lost a few of our companions, but the mine that worked to enslave more of our family and friends is now destroyed. We did the impossible."

Several wolves howled their agreement, but Hawk raised his tail to silence them. He knew he didn't have much time.

"But why stop here? Two fortresses, each with only half a garrison, are just waiting for us to destroy them. They sit content with the assumption that they are in control. Let us show them that they are wrong!"

Hawk paused for a moment, glancing down at River again. "More than a century ago, King Oak said that a savior would come to end the war. That savior is here, *now*. A Water-Wolf, from a nation we thought lost. Just a few weeks ago she led us to victory at the Obsolium Fortress in Taladair, a fortress that now lies in ruins. The time has come for us to rise up against the demons, and take back our island! That starts *here*, with us taking a stand for the first time in a hundred years. The time has come for us to show the demons that we will not take their torment anymore!"

His heart soared when the wolves gathered below howled their agreement, stoked by his words. Even River howled with them.

"First we attack the Nocte Fortress, while it sleeps," Hawk shouted, before jumping down from the ledge and rejoining his companions. He turned to Lichen. "I need you to take the ones who cannot fight and lead them somewhere safe. It doesn't matter where, just somewhere patrols won't find them. Before you go, have them help you burn the bodies of our fallen. We don't want a patrol coming by and finding them."

Although she looked a bit put-out that she would be missing the battle, Lichen nodded. "I can do that."

"You'll have to move quickly," Sky warned. "This area will soon be crawling with demons. The Overlord will not be happy when he learns of what happened here."

Lichen nodded again before darting into the crowd of wolves, quickly vanishing into the throng. Hawk took a deep breath and turned to River, Sky, and Cloud.

"We have a battle to win."

Chapter Sixty-Five

THE NIGHT-Lynx fought back a yawn, trying to at least look alert. Its superior had already come by twice to give it a vicious prod. It hated standing watch. It didn't know why they even bothered with watches. Only one demon was ever assigned to the day watches, and no wolf would be stupid enough to attack a fortress. Going on patrols or tormenting the few slaves they still had in the Nocte was much more entertaining than standing around for hours staring at the dark mountains.

A yawn split its jaws. *Just wait a little longer. Once the dusk patrol gets back, I'll be done with my watch.*

Several minutes passed before the Night-Lynx saw the dark shapes of the patrol appear on the path leading to the fortress. It blinked, trying to get a good look at them.

Stupid dusk light, making it hard to see, the Night-Lynx growled to itself. Then it sighed and began making its way down the stairs. The others weren't awake yet, leaving the Night-Lynx with the responsibility of opening the gate for the patrol. The Night-Lynx muttered curses under its breath the entire way to the gate, hating the fact that it had had to take the afternoon watch. It meant the Night-Lynx wouldn't get to sleep until dawn, after only a half a day's sleep before going on watch.

Maybe the patrol caught something while they were out, and I can convince them to give part of it to me, the Night-Lynx thought, pulling the gate open to let the patrol through. *I think the ones on this patrol are of a low enough rank that I can bully...*

A large shape burst through the gates, knocking the startled demon to the ground. An Earth-Wolf snarled and sank its fangs into the Night-Lynx's neck before it could cry out an alarm.

Chapter Sixty-Six

"WE'RE IN," Hawk said as he saw the gates open fully.

One of the wolves sent to open the gates lifted her tail to signal it was clear to go.

"Let's go," River growled, digging her claws into the stone beneath her paws. "The demons inside will be waking soon, we need to strike while they're still disoriented."

He nodded and took a deep breath. Everyone was waiting for his signal, for his command.

"Attack!" he shouted, jumping down from the rocks and racing toward the open fortress. The makeshift army of freed slaves immediately followed, pouring onto the path. River, Sky, and Cloud were close on his heels. They swept past the wolves who had opened the gate and into the open courtyard beyond.

"Sky, take some wolves and go find the slaves," Hawk ordered. "Cloud, take a group and go to the ramparts. We'll break in through the keep."

Both Wind-Wolves nodded before whirling around and diving into the horde of wolves behind them.

"Earth-Wolves, break the doors down!" River snarled, her eyes flashing. Several Earth-Wolves jumped forward to obey.

Hawk turned to the rest. "Get ready," he said as the Earth-Wolves broke two large chunks from the ground and launched them at the doors to the keep. The wood cracked, but held firm.

River narrowed her eyes. "Again!"

Growling, the Earth-Wolves raised the slabs of stone and threw them at the doors once more. With a loud *crack* the wood splintered inward, but remained shut. Then one of the Wind-Wolves ran forward and howled.

A great gust of wind blew into the courtyard, nearly knocking several wolves off their paws, and crashed into the doors. They creaked and groaned, straining against the wind. The Earth-Wolves quickly regained their balance and threw the rocks against the door, taking advantage of the wind's strength.

Finally, the doors flew open, knocked back by the combination of attacks. River howled, a cry that was taken up by the army standing behind her, and charged. Hawk raced after her, his heart beating so fast it hummed.

They burst into a large room directly across from the entrance to the keep, where a small group of demons had gathered. The demons looked up, shocked to see the mass of wolves. The freed slaves gave them no more time to recover and fell upon their former masters.

"Wh-what…?"

Hawk and River spun around to see a Night-Lynx standing in the doorway behind them. Its white eyes widened at the sight of the chaos before it spun around and ran.

"After it," River growled, and took off after the fleeing demon. Hawk called a few wolves to him before following, racing back out into the hallway.

"Attack, we're under attack!" The Night-Lynx yowled, its cry echoing off the walls. It glanced over its shoulder and saw the pack of wolves chasing it. It screeched and put on an extra burst of speed.

A second Night-Lynx burst out of side hall and crashed into Hawk, knocking him to the ground. Hawk struggled to escape the demon's claws as they rolled over. They collided with the wall on the other side, knocking the breath from Hawk's lungs. The Night-Lynx curled its claws around Hawk's collar and lifted him from the ground, its white eyes narrow with fury. Hawk rolled his eyes back, desperate to avoid being caught in the Night-Lynx's spell.

"Just what do you think you are doing, *slave*?" The demon bared its needle-like teeth and leaned in closer to Hawk. "Death awaits you and your fellows now."

Hawk glanced out of the corner of his eye, hoping someone would come to help him soon, but saw the others were engaged in battles of their own. River was nowhere to be seen.

No, I can do this. I don't have to rely on her all the time. Hawk growled and bared his teeth at the monster holding him captive. "The time of demons is ending. Death awaits *you*."

He sank his fangs into the Night-Lynx's leg, making the demon yowl in pain and fury. Hawk shook his head and dug his claws into the demon's stomach. It pulled away as fast as it could, but Hawk kept his jaws closed around the Night-Lynx's limb. He wrenched his head to the side, pulling the Night-Lynx to the ground. Hawk released the demon's leg and jumped to his paws. He lunged for his opponent before it could have time to recover.

"More demons approaching!"

Hawk looked up from the dying Night-Lynx. At least a dozen demons were racing down the hall toward them, fangs bared. He glanced behind him. The rest of the slave army were pouring out of the first room and splitting down both sides of the hallway.

"This way, charge!" Hawk howled, calling the former slaves to him. The wolves immediately turned and began racing toward him.

The two sides clashed with howls and snarls. Hawk threw himself into the battle, swept up in its fury. He ducked under a Hell-Cat's lunge and dove for the monster's hind legs.

Where's River? Hawk jumped back from the demon and spat a plume of fire at it when it attempted to pounce on him. The burning Hell-Cat recoiled with a wail, knocking into a few of its allies. Hawk risked a few seconds to scan the hall, looking for any sign of his friend.

Howls echoed from the floor above, making a few demons pause. Hawk pounced on one who hesitated, biting down on the back of the Night-Lynx's neck. The demon fell to the ground and attempted to wriggle out from beneath him, but a Wind-Wolf jumped in and sank her fangs into the Night-Lynx's throat.

"Thanks," Hawk said breathlessly. The she-wolf nodded before throwing herself into another battle. Hawk glanced up at the ceiling for a brief moment. *That must be Cloud and the rest of the army. Where is Sky? Did he find any slaves?*

A large shape suddenly sailed over his head and landed on a Shade-Tiger, knocking it mid-pounce to the ground. Hawk jumped, startled.

"Keep your eyes on the battle, Hawk," River snarled without looking away from the striped demon.

"River!"

The Shade-Tiger lashed out with its hind paws, but River jumped to the side and avoided the attack. She bit down on the demon's shoulder, dragging it back down to the ground when it attempted to stand. Hawk grabbed the demon's tail and pulled it away just as it was about to sink its fangs into River's leg. The Shade-Tiger snarled and spun around, spitting orbs of shadow in Hawk's face. Hawk yelped and dropped to the ground, narrowly avoiding the attack.

"We need light!" Memories of the battle with Shade-Tigers, back by the Dorasca Gorge, flashed through his mind. He risked a quick look out a narrow window. The sky was quickly growing darker. "Fire-Wolves, we need light!"

Howls rose up, summoning flames into existence. Several demons yowled, blinded by the sudden brightness as fires burst into existence up and down the hall. Other wolves began to howl as well, taking advantage of the demons' confusion.

River lunged for a Hell-Cat attempting to make its escape and threw it into a ball of flames. Hawk dove into the fire and closed his jaws around the screaming demon's paw, dragging it out and throwing it to the ground. River bared her fangs and bit the Hell-Cat's throat, immediately silencing it.

"How many demons do you think are left?" Hawk panted, looking around the hall a little nervously. The battle was slowly thinning out as both demon and wolf fell. *We might not be able to attack the Algidus Fortress, not if we're losing so many here. Maybe we should have planned our attack a little better...I didn't want to see so many die.* He swallowed hard. *It's my fault they're dying here...we could have escaped into the mountains...*

"Don't know. That Night-Lynx from before claimed there were over a hundred demons here, but I doubt that. It was only trying to scare us off." She paused and snarled. Hawk whirled around just as she charged by him, crashing into a Night-Lynx that had attempted to sneak up on them. The demon screeched and attempted to turn and run, but River got to it first. "Just keep fighting."

CHAPTER SIXTY-SEVEN

THE DARKCLAW HEAVED itself out of the pit, snarling every time its claws slipped. It stood for a few moments on the edge, panting, looking out over the battlefield. The bodies of the Hell-Cats lay strewn across the destroyed mine, several of them buried beneath piles of slave stones. The Darkclaw growled. It would take weeks to gather the slaves needed to repair the mine, and much more time to put it back into operation.

But the mine was the least of the Darkclaw's concerns. There were plenty of slaves to use, and there were enough materials stored in various fortresses that the demons could continue to make new slaves. Even if they ran out, the demons had no problems killing off the surplus.

What worried the Darkclaw was what it had seen during the battle. *A Water-Wolf has returned, one with unknown power. The Overlord will not be pleased with this news.*

The Darkclaw shook the last bit of dirt from its fur before turning and racing towards the Algidus Fortress. It had to get there before the rebel army reached it. Normally, it would have no doubts concerning the fortress's strength, but with a Water-Wolf leading the slaves, it couldn't be sure what they were capable of doing.

We must capture the Water-Wolf and bring her to the Overlord. That Fire-Wolf, too. He is too dangerous to be allowed free.

Chapter Sixty-Eight

"Hawk!"

Startled by the sudden shout, Hawk dropped to the ground to avoid a Shade-Tiger's heavy paw. River jumped over his head and knocked the demon to the side, allowing him to scramble away from the fight.

Sky appeared in front of him, shoving his way through the crowd of fighters.

"We have to get out of here," the Wind-Wolf said breathlessly. "I was fighting upstairs with Cloud when we saw. The Algidus Fortress realized the Nocte was under attack, and now a horde of demons are headed toward us."

"Can't we barricade ourselves in here?"

Sky shook his head. "Not unless we can kill the rest of Nocte's demons in the next few minutes. If even one demon is left, it'll create a hole in our defenses and let in the demons from Algidus. We have to escape now while we have time."

"But how? If we go out the front gate we'll be trapped." Hawk flattened his ears against his head. He did not want to get trapped between two enemy forces.

"We'll escape using the Red River. It runs through the middle of the Nocte Fortress. With our Water-Wolf ally we should be able to pull it off."

Hawk nodded. *I hope it works.*

"Cloud's group is coming down," Sky said. "There weren't as many demons upstairs. She's going to clear out a path to the river. We just need to meet her there." The Wind-Wolf howled and barreled his way through several demons.

"River!" Hawk bounded over to her just as she was finishing off the Shade-Tiger. "We have to go."

"What?"

She's not going to like running from a battle like this. "Algidus is sending reinforcements for Nocte. We have to escape before they get here. Sky says we can get out through the Red River, but we'll need your help…"

"Let's go, then." River grabbed a nearby Hell-Cat and threw it into two Night-Lynxes. "To the river!"

Hawk stood for a moment, surprised by her lack of argument. Then he bounded after her, howling to call the other slaves. "To the river!"

It took the demons a few minutes before they realized the wolves were retreating. Encouraged by the sudden turn of events, the demons fought back with renewed vigor. Hawk ducked under a Shade-Tiger and chased after Sky and River, jumping around the twisting shadows that sought to entangle his limbs. Some of the slaves summoned gusts of wind and balls of fire to keep the demons at bay.

But after two long battles, the slaves were tiring and could barely keep the winds and fires going.

We just have to make it to the Red River, Hawk thought, his paws pounding the floor as he ran. *If we make it there we can escape into the mountains and disappear.*

Sky took them around several turns before suddenly charging down a narrow staircase. River didn't hesitate as she followed him, but Hawk cast a quick look over his shoulder, not liking the chance of them getting trapped on the stairs.

We can't have the demons follow us. Hawk swallowed before stumbling to a stop. He managed to meet River's eyes for a few seconds and saw the realization flash across her face as he spun around and scrambled back up the stairs.

"Hawk!"

He ignored her shout and his rising fear, squeezing between the fleeing wolves as he struggled to reach the top. He could already hear the jeers and taunts of the demons, but he refused to allow himself to turn back around.

I led the others here. I led some of them to their deaths. I have to get them out.

Hawk burst out onto the floor with his fangs bared. He threw himself on the nearest demon, knocking it to the ground with a surprised yelp. One of the slaves stumbled, uncertain whether to continue running when his commander was standing to fight.

"Go, get out of here!" Hawk shouted before sinking his fangs into a Hell-Cat's neck. He jumped back to avoid getting buried under two more Hell-Cats and dove for the Night-Lynx behind them.

Teeth suddenly grabbed him by the scruff of his neck and wrenched him back. Hawk instinctively twisted to try and snap at his attacker, but his jaws closed on empty air as he was thrown back to the staircase.

He scrambled to his paws, ready to jump back into the battle, but stopped. A dark green Earth-Wolf stood before the oncoming horde of demons, tail raised high.

"Go, Hawk. The others need you," the Earth-Wolf said, turning for a brief moment to lock his dark brown eyes with Hawk. Hawk hesitated for a moment, confused by the sudden sense of familiarity.

A wall of stone rose up from the ground, effectively sealing off the staircase and casting Hawk into darkness. He placed a paw against the wall but knew he would never get through in time.

"How did he know my name?" Hawk hesitated a moment longer. He had never told the slaves his name, and although the Earth-Wolf had seemed familiar for some reason, Hawk was certain he had never met him before.

"Hawk!"

River suddenly appeared behind him, the worry in her eyes tempering the fury in her voice. "What did you think you were doing?"

Hawk shook his head. "Let's go."

He turned and raced down the stairs, trying to ignore the yowls coming from the other side of the wall.

Thank you.

CHAPTER SIXTY-NINE

ELK TURNED BACK to the waiting demons. They knew he had no chance of escaping. It would be a simple matter of killing him and breaking through his wall. Then they would be free to corner the slaves on the banks of the Red River.

"By the time you get down there, they'll be gone," he said. "You'll never catch them."

Several demons chuckled, dismissing his claim. Elk just bared his teeth in a vicious snarl.

"You have no idea what's coming for you, do you? Did you really think we'd be slaves forever? But by the time you realize that the earth is shifting, you'll be too late for that, too."

Then he howled and threw himself into the pack of demons.

Chapter Seventy

Sky looked incredibly relieved when Hawk and River appeared at the bottom of the staircase, although he glared at the Fire-Wolf as they approached.

"You're still alive, thank Sun-Wolf. What were you thinking?"

"I had to stop the demons from following us, to give you some time to escape," Hawk said, staring down at his paws. "But an Earth-Wolf threw me back. He blocked the stairs…and he's still up there fighting."

"We will have to honor his sacrifice later," Sky said. "Right now we can't let it go to waste. River, can you get us through?"

River narrowed her eyes. "How far is it 'til the river exits the fortress?"

"A few dozen lengths, it looks like."

"How many are here?"

Sky paused. "About forty. Can you do it?"

"Of course I can!" River growled, obviously offended at the thought. "I'll slow the flow as much as I can, but I won't be able to hold it for long."

Hawk swallowed nervously. He did not look forward to another submersion in a river. Getting dragged through one the last time was enough to satisfy him for the rest of his life. *But it's either this or I go fight my way through the demons up top,* he thought grimly.

"Hawk, you'll stay here," River said, breaking him out of his thoughts. "Warn me if the demons start to break through upstairs."

He took a deep breath and nodded. *I can't lose my nerve now. I have to see this through, if only for all those who died today…and for the Earth-Wolf who sacrificed himself to buy us some time.*

River turned to the white Wind-Wolf. "Sky, get ready. The moment I say, you need to get everyone down the river as fast as you can."

He nodded and fixed both Hawk and River with a hard stare. "I had better see you two on the other side."

"As if we'll die this easily," River said smoothly. "Now get them ready."

Sky turned to gather the other wolves. River glanced over at Hawk before turning away and jumping into the coursing waters. She growled quietly. The Red River began to glow softly, casting a faint whitish light on River's fur. The current slowed just slightly, prompting another growl from River.

The water began to rise around the blue-gray wolf, spilling out onto the banks, but further downstream it quickly got shallower. The water closer to the exit became still, while the current raged against River's control. Small waves crashed onto the banks, splattering Hawk's fur.

"Go, Sky!" River growled around gritted teeth.

"Move it, down the river!" Sky shouted, ushering the former slaves into the water. "Run!"

They wasted no time in jumping into the water and racing for the exit. Hawk hesitated for a few seconds more, looking between the fleeing wolves and the struggling River, before darting back over to the stairs.

I hope that wall holds, he thought, hearing *bangs* echo down the staircase. He winced. *It doesn't sound like we have much time.*

A loud *crack* suddenly split the air, and Hawk froze. Light streamed down the staircase, and he looked up to see the leering face of a Shade-Tiger peeking through the opening. The demon snarled.

Hawk turned and raced back to River.

"They're breaking through!" He glanced over to where the Red River flowed out of the fortress. The last few wolves were still trying to squeeze through.

"Throw some fire at them; keep them busy."

"I can't...I don't have enough energy left." Hawk looked back at the stairs as another loud *crack* sounded. *The only reason I'm standing at all is because I have to...that Amhríochta took a lot out of me.*

River swore under her breath. "How many still have to get out?"

"Three more...no, just two."

"All right, run!" River jumped away from the rolling water and ran for the exit. Hawk darted after her, not wanting to get caught in the flood.

The water's glow slowly faded, until it burst free from River's control and raced toward them with a roar. Water coursed through Hawk's legs, but he didn't dare look back for fear of loosing his footing. He could hear the Red River crashing behind them.

River slid to a stop at the small opening that allowed the water to flow through the Nocte. She grabbed Hawk by the scruff of his neck and threw him into it before sliding after him. Hawk burst out on the other side, slipping on the smooth rocks. Several wolves jumped forward to drag him and River out of the water just as the current reached them.

"Glad you two could join us," Sky said with a little amusement as the Red River thundered behind them. "Cut it a little close."

"Just get moving," River growled, dragging herself to her paws and shaking the water from her fur. "We don't have much time before the demons figure out how we got out of there."

Chapter Seventy-One

SKY LED THE ragged army as far as he could away from the Algidus and Nocte Fortresses, while Cloud trailed behind to erase any trace of their passing. They didn't stop until they reached a shallow gulley, one that afforded them enough cover to remain hidden from any passing demons.

"Well…that didn't go as I had hoped," Sky said, glancing back at the large group of former slaves, who were getting some much-needed rest after their battle. "We lost far too many."

"It's a risk we took when we decided to attack," River said with a sniff. "You knew it was likely we would lose many wolves."

"I was hoping to *at least* get away with two victories. We should have stopped after the mine, but we let ourselves get carried away."

"We *did* destroy the mine and put a hole in Algidus' and Nocte's defenses," Hawk put in. "I think we did okay."

"*They* might not see it that way," Sky said. "After everything we said, we lost the battle at Nocte."

"If Algidus had not been warned, we would have won," Cloud said suddenly. "A demon must have escaped our claws."

River shook her head. "There's nothing we can do about it now. We're not always going to have victory. War doesn't work like that. We did the best we could in our situation and took advantage of a chance to destroy a demon fortress. So it didn't work out, *so what?* Learn from the loss and move on." Her ears flicked back to the resting army. "What we need to do *now* is reassure them that today was an overall victory and that the sacrifices of their fellows won't go to waste. *Then* we plan what happens next."

All three turned to look at Hawk.

"You spoke to them first," Sky said. "You have to encourage them now. They'll be looking to you for guidance."

"I…I—" Hawk cut off his own protest. *I owe it to them.*

He shakily stood, taking a deep breath to steel himself. He padded over to the other wolves. Several looked up as he approached, most of them curious, but Hawk saw a few had a hint of anger in their eyes.

"I...I know we lost many of our friends at Nocte," he began, "but that doesn't mean our battle was a complete defeat. We destroyed an important mine, and defeated more than a Fortress's worth of demons. We didn't manage to destroy the Nocte Fortress, but we left both the Nocte and the Algidus Fortresses greatly weakened."

"Why does that matter," one Fire-Wolf demanded, leaping to his paws, "when so many of us are *dead*? We should have just left the fortresses alone, and taken our victory at the mine. That should have been enough."

Several other wolves muttered their agreement, but Hawk didn't look away from the other Fire-Wolf. *I have to convince them that what we did today was important enough to warrant those sacrifices.* "If we had stopped after destroying the mines, what would have happened?" Hawk asked. "We would have had two fortresses chasing us down. Many more would have died, and the rest of us would be made into slaves. Our fight at the mine would have been pointless." He paused and glanced over at River, who gave a slight nod, letting him know he was on the right track. "We went on to fight at Nocte so we could send a message to the demons, to tell them that they can't torment us anymore. Whether or not we won there, we sent that message. What do you think the demons are doing now? Do you think they are hunting us?"

Hawk swept his gaze over the entire gathering, but no one spoke. The Fire-Wolf sat back down without another word.

"No, they're not going to rush out to hunt us down, not immediately. They haven't had an attack on their fortresses for decades. They haven't had an outpost like the mine destroyed since the war began. We've surprised them, and that's going to make them wary. And when they hear about the destruction of the Obsolium Fortress, they'll be even more wary. They no longer know what we're capable of. And *that's* why our battle at the Nocte Fortress is counted as a victory, even though we were forced to run. *That's* why the sacrifices made today are so important."

A faint memory of something Sparrow had said to him long ago floated to the front of his mind. It was after a fight with a passing patrol, one that nearly cost Hawk his life. For a brief moment he wondered if he would have been better off back in Ignimor, where at least he had food and shelter, and the only risk of him dying came from disobedience or too much work. He had asked Sparrow why she fought to stay free. Her words hadn't made sense at the time, but now, with the ghosts of their fallen weighing on his mind, he could understand. "Someone once told me that it's better to die free, in a battle of your choosing, where you can feel the wind blowing from all corners of the land, than to die at a demon's whim between cold stone walls. Our friends who died today died for our freedom. And tomorrow, more may die. There will be more battles. Today is only the beginning. But the time of demons is ending." He paused again. "If we want to honor the sacrifices made, then we have to keep fighting for what our friends died for." Hawk fell silent, trying not to look too nervous. He had said everything he could think of, but didn't know what to do next.

The Fire-Wolf who had spoken before stood up again, but the anger in his eyes had died and was replaced with a steely determination. "We'll continue the fight. We won't let the death of our friends and family be in vain."

Another Fire-Wolf stood up, nodding her agreement. "It's time we seriously took a stand against the demons."

"Well, if the Water-Wolves are returning," an Earth-Wolf said, slowly rising to his paws, "then it must mean the gods want us to fight back."

Wolves continued to stand, until the entire gathering was on its paws and pledging to fight. Hawk blinked, his jaws parted slightly. Sky appeared beside him and gave him a nudge. "Good job, Hawk. You've even got me fired up again."

Hawk wagged his tail slightly. "I just said what I felt…"

"That's what makes your words effective," Sky said. "Like when you convinced me and the others to go after Jay. You spoke the truth." He turned to the gathered wolves, who were beginning to sit back down again. "All right, time to get some rest. We have a ways to go tomorrow."

Hawk tilted his head slightly as Sky padded back to River and Cloud. "What…?"

"We can't stay her for long," Sky said. "We're going to need a better place to recoup. So we're going to meet with Lichen…"

"We can't," River interrupted. "We have to get to the Ardgao."

"I *know*, you told me *several times* on the way from Nocte," Sky said with a bit of irritation. "But we *do* have to get these slaves to safety. *So*…" He paused long enough to glare at River when she tried to interrupt again. "Cloud is going to lead them to the Gathering. I'll lead you two to the Ardgao."

"Gathering?" River narrowed her eyes.

"Ah, Sparrow told me about them," Hawk said. "Gatherings are where resistance groups can meet to trade information, or hide their puppies and elderly. There aren't many of them, because it's so risky to have so many wolves in one place."

Sky nodded. "There's one south of the Ardgao. That's where Lichen is leading her group from the mine. It's the best place we can hide a group this large." He paused. "I don't know where you two intend to go next, but I suggest you go to the Gathering after the Ardgao."

Hawk looked over at River, but she only bent her head and said, "We'll think about it."

CHAPTER SEVENTY-TWO

EARLY THE NEXT morning, just as the sun rose, Hawk addressed the former slaves once more.

"Cloud is going to lead you to a Gathering, where the ones we left at the mines are waiting."

"What about you? Aren't you coming with us?" a Wind-Wolf near the front asked. Others nodded.

Hawk glanced at River out of the corner of his eye, knowing she wouldn't want him revealing their mission. "River and I…have something we must do. Cloud and Sky will lead you."

Several wolves surprised Hawk by looking disappointed at his words, but they didn't protest. Cloud silently padded to the front of the group, giving Hawk a respectful nod as she passed.

"Move quickly," Sky said. "Lichen will already be there by the time you arrive, and she'll let the Gathering know you're coming. I'll join you two after I get these two where they need to be." Then he turned to Hawk and River. "All right, let's go."

"Good luck, Hawk and River!" a Fire-Wolf said, wagging her tail.

Several more bid them farewell as they padded away. Hawk kept looking back over his shoulder until the group of former slaves disappeared around a bend in the path.

"They'll be waiting for you two to return, you know," Sky said, falling back to walk beside him. "They'll be expecting you to lead them." He paused and glanced back at River, several paces behind them. "Like I said last night, I don't know what you and River have planned or why you need to go to the Ardgao. I won't ask, because you two have made it clear you don't want to say, but I would like you to consider going to the Gathering and helping us raise an army."

Hawk remained silent, unsure what to say.

"You two have started something big. More slaves are going to rise up, and if we have you two leading, wolves will flock to our cause. You two are going to become a symbol of hope. I'm sure that the wolves who fought at Obsolium with you feel the same."

"I...I don't think we'll be able to lead any army," Hawk said slowly. "River and I...there's something we have to do first. If we don't...there won't be any point to leading an army." Noting the slight disappointment in Sky's eyes, he continued, "But that doesn't mean *you* can't lead them. You're right; we *have* started something. We can't let them go back into hiding; we have to continue the fight. River and I might join you later...but for now you'll have to lead for us."

Sky gave a noncommittal grunt. "I'm not the hero who saved them."

"Neither of us are!"

"Yes, you are. You two might not be the *only* ones who brought freedom to the slaves at the Obsolium Fortress, or at the mine, or at Nocte, but *you* are the one who put the wind at their backs and led them into battle, and *River* is the long-awaited savior. I can lead the army, sure, but it won't be the same." When Hawk said nothing, Sky turned away and said, "Just think about it."

CHAPTER SEVENTY-THREE

"WE'RE HERE."

Hawk stumbled to a halt, eyes wide with awe. A vertical cliff rose up before him; the pale gray stone sides smooth as metal. Low-lying clouds obscured the peak, but the sound of roaring winds echoed down through the cover.

How did I not notice it before now? He looked around in confusion. The cliff stood in the middle of a wide, flat plain. It should have been immediately noticeable the moment they stepped off the path, but Hawk distinctly remembered seeing nothing until Sky had spoken.

"Why didn't we see it before?" he asked.

"The Ardgao is protected by ancient spells. If you don't know what you're looking for you'll never even see it," Sky said. "Wind-Wolves aren't affected as much, because this is part of our home."

He turned around to face Hawk and River. "Where do you plan to go next?"

"None of your business," River said. Sky ignored her rude comment and glanced over at Hawk, who shook his head.

"We have a mission," he said.

Sky sighed and nodded. "Very well. I wish you both luck. Try not to get lost, Water-Wolf."

River rolled her eyes, but to Hawk's surprise, dipped her head and said, "Thank you, Sky, for leading us here."

The white Wind-Wolf dipped his head in return and brushed by them. Hawk wavered for a moment, before spinning around and saying, "Wait, Sky!" He bounded over to the other wolf. "In Taladair…the one who fought with us at the Obsolium Fortress. Her name is Pine. She's probably still leading the wolves we freed from the fortress, and I think she'd be open to joining forces with you."

Sky nodded slightly. "I have to stop by our camp and get Sand and the others. I think I'll send them on to meet Lichen and Cloud, and go meet this Pine." He paused. "Thank you, Hawk. You would have liked my brother. I'm sure he's grateful for you reminding me what he had fought and died for. I hope we meet again." He turned around and continued down the path.

Hawk watched until Sky disappeared between the rocks.

River growled, grabbing Hawk's attention. "Come on, then, let's get moving."

He gave her a questioning look — one that she pointedly ignored.

She sounds like she did when we first entered the Gaoibeanna Mountains... but she should have gotten used to the land's magic by now. He padded after the irritable she-wolf, who led them several paces away from the base of the tall cliff. *Maybe being so near the Ardgao, a source of sun magic, is making it worse...*

River stopped and spun around, shoving Hawk back toward the cliff. "Say what you said at the Crétioll, but address Sun-Wolf."

"O-okay..." *I wonder why she's not trying it first...maybe because I'm a sun element?* He took a deep breath, feeling a little more confident than he had the first time he had sought entrance to an Elemental Guardian. "I am Hawk, son of Phoenix. I seek to use the power that slumbers within this sacred place...to defeat the...Demon Overlord. Therefore...I beseech you...ah... Father Sun-Wolf to grant me safe...entrance to the Ardgao." The last echoes of Hawk's words faded away into silence, and even the wind around them seemed to grow quiet.

Did I get something wrong...?

Suddenly a powerful gust blew around them, nearly knocking the two wolves to the ground. The wind spun in a single spot in front of them, lightening into white streams of air as it twisted into the shape of a wolf. Two red glowing spots appeared, marking its eyes, but the rest of its body continued to shift and change with the movements of the winds holding it together.

"You may enter," a deep male voice said, the glowing eyes staring right at Hawk.

He glanced back at River, before turning back to the spirit. "Can River come with me?"

"No."

"Please, I need her help," he begged. He didn't want to enter the Ardgao on his own, not without River to help him.

The spirit's eyes flared for a moment. *"She has been touched by demons, and is impure. She cannot enter."*

River growled deep in her throat, but said nothing.

She is impure? What does that mean? Hawk glanced back at River again in confusion, before realization hit him. *She spent so much time in the Rift, with all the demons, now she probably* feels *like a demon. Coal thought she was a demon at first, too.*

"That's not her fault," Hawk argued, not even thinking about what would happen if he made the spirit angry by ignoring its words. "It's not her fault she was trapped in the Rift. She *has* to come, because this is *her* mission…and without her we would have lost all hope."

Focused on the wolf of wind, he never saw River flinch and look away.

The spirit locked eyes with Hawk, who stood unwavering. Finally, it nodded slightly. *"She may accompany you."*

The spirit growled, the sound echoing across the plain, and the clouds above them began to descend. Their guide immediately disappeared, but the growl continued. The thick clouds circled the two wolves, moving faster and faster until the wind howled in their ears.

Hawk's heart raced, but he forced himself to stand his ground. Then suddenly the earth vanished beneath his paws, and his stomach dropped as they were lifted up into the air by the wind. He panicked, flailing as he searched desperately for something to stand on, his fear increasing when River faded into the grayness.

"Do not fight it. Allow the wind to take you." At the wind spirit's words, Hawk's limbs fell limp, and a strange calm settled over his mind.

The winds swirled and carried the two wolves up the mountainside. Higher and higher they rose, until finally their paws touched down on solid ground once more. The wind blew away, pushing the clouds to the edges of the plateau, granting Hawk his first true glimpse of the Ardgao.

A wide expanse of smooth reddish stone stretched before him, just as large as the cave that held the Lough Domhgeal. Thick clouds floated along the edge, masking the view of the mountains around the plateau. Above them, however, the blue sky shone through a hole in the cover.

But what held Hawk's attention was the Lough Gaoghrian at the center of the plateau. Four triangular ponds lined the right side of a much larger circle, creating a sun-shaped image altogether. The red water glowed, casting strange coppery reflections on the surrounding rocks and clouds and twisted and turned much like actual wind.

"Hawk, are you going to stand and gape all day, or are you actually going to do something?" River snapped, making him jump, surprised by her angry tone.

The sun magic must be affecting her even more here, Hawk thought, noting how tense she seemed and the way her eyes kept darting all over the plateau, as though expecting something to jump out at her. He sent her one last worried look before padding closer to the lake, stopping in between two of the triangular sections of water. He took a deep breath. *I hope I get this right...*

"I, Hawk, son of Phoenix, stand before you, Father Sun-Wolf, to beg for your help. The land and your children are enslaved by a monster, and I seek to free them. Only with your help will I be able to do so. If you so will it, grant me the power I need by the night of Moon-Sun. I swear that I will not use your power for evil deeds, and if I should break my word, my life may be taken as punishment."

The words make a lot more sense now I know why I have to say them...

As the last echoes of Hawk's words faded, the water began to glow, until he had to close his eyes against the brightness. A whisper floated past his ears, like a sigh, and the powerful presence of the lake's magic weakened. When Hawk opened his eyes again, the water had dimmed and its movements slowed. Silently, he backed away several lengths before turning and running back to River.

"I did it!" he exclaimed with a wag of his tail.

"Wonderful," River growled. "Now let's go."

Hurt by her sharp tone, Hawk stepped back and lowered his head slightly.

The she-wolf looked at him again and took a breath. "I'm sorry. I shouldn't have snapped. It's...it's this place..."

Before Hawk could answer, the wind spirit appeared again. Its form was much less distinct and its eyes were little more than spots of red. Without a word to them, the wolf summoned the clouds again to carry them back down the mountain.

Hawk was grateful to reach the ground again. River looked as if she were too.

Hawk, in his excitement, tried to jump from the clouds. He was sent sprawling when his paws slipped, unable to gain any purchase against the fog, and tumbled to the hard stone below. River stepped down much more gracefully, and snorted. "Get up. We still have a ways to go." The amusement in River's eyes softened her tone.

Hawk wagged his tail and jumped to his paws. "I'm up!"

Chapter Seventy-Four

RIVER'S MOOD CONTINUED to improve the farther they got from the Ardgao. By the time it had vanished from view, she was back to her usual self.

Which was slightly less grumpy than before, but at least now Hawk knew there was no bite behind her bark. "Where next, River?" he asked cheerfully, bouncing along beside her.

"To the Fáinéitin, where else would we be going?"

Hawk stopped, the realization slamming into him like a wall of stone. *That… that means we're going to the Scaineadó Desert.* Before River could order him to start moving again, he hurried after her, his mind racing. *I haven't been in the Desert since I escaped…*

A pang of longing filled him. Despite the terrible memories he had experienced there, Hawk missed feeling the hot sand beneath his paws and the desert sun warming his back. They were some of the few things that made life bearable during his enslavement, things that had been a source of encouragement in dark times.

Another source of encouragement had been his mother, who comforted him when he was beaten by their Ice-Fang master, and told him legends of Soluna's history to cheer him up. No matter what happened, Hawk's mother always managed to keep their spirits up.

Until she was brutally killed.

Hawk quickly turned his mind away from those memories. He would never forget seeing his mother's broken body lying at his feet, nor the horrible rage that filled him and nearly cost him his own life.

"If you move any slower, I'm going to leave you behind."

"Ah, coming!" He ran after River, who had already drawn several lengths ahead. *The last thing I want is to get left behind. It's getting a little warmer, which means the feral demons will start waking up from their hibernation. When we get to the Scaineadó Desert, there will be more ferals…because it's hot there year-round…* Hawk paused, a thought hitting him. "Um, River? Do you know where we're going?"

The blue-gray Water-Wolf stumbled slightly, and her shoulders tensed. "Of course I do."

Why do I have the feeling she's already lost? Hawk bit his lip but said nothing. *Does she even know how to get to the desert? She's only visited Gaoibeanna once…and I doubt she's ever set foot in Scaineadó…*

"Do you know where the Fáinéitin is?"

River spun around, snarling, forcing him to fall to the ground in a crouch to avoid her snap. "Of course I know where it is, now stop bugging me!"

"Tha' wasnae a verra nice thing tae do tae yer friend on the noo, she-wolf."

Both wolves jumped at the sound of the strange voice behind them, but while Hawk froze with shock, River didn't waste a moment. In a flash she had leapt over Hawk's head and onto the unknown wolf that had approached them.

Her paws fell on empty air. Startled, the she-wolf scrambled back, her navy-blue eyes scanning her surroundings for any sign of the other wolf.

"Ach, ye'd think Ah was going tae ambush ye, the way ye reacted."

Hawk nearly jumped clear off the path he was so surprised when the wolf suddenly appeared out of the air beside him. He darted away, racing over to hide behind River, who was crouching and watching the stranger through narrowed eyes.

Who is he? Hawk peered at the other male from the safety behind River. The faded black swirl-mark on his right shoulder marked him a Wind-Wolf. He was long-legged, lean-bodied, and even taller than River. Hawk was given the odd impression of looking at a great heron: all legs and very gangly. The wolf's ragged pelt had large clumps of fur missing, and his tattered ears could barely stand upright. His fur was so dirty and streaked with mud that the original color was lost, although Hawk thought it might have been blue at one point. But the strangest things about the wolf were his eyes and tail. He had a piece of hide tied around his eyes, completely obscuring his vision, and a few black feathers tied to the stump of his tail.

"Who are you?" River growled, ready to pounce on the odd wolf.

Despite obviously not being able to see, the wolf pinpointed her exact position and swung his muzzle to face her.

"Ye dinnae need tae be so worried. Ah'm not going tae hurt ye."

Hawk blinked. He could barley understand what the other wolf said through his strange accent.

"Mah cry's Crow, like the black-bird. Ah was passin' by on the noo, an' Ah couldnae help but overhear what ye were sayin'. Ye have tae find the *Scaineadó* Desert? Ah kin help." The muddy wolf gave them an expectant look, somehow seeming to stare at them despite his missing eyes. Hawk was oddly reminded of Fall, although Crow's sightless gaze was much less intense.

River turned slightly back to Hawk. "What is he *saying*? I can't understand a word of it."

"Ah *said*, Ah kin help ye."

"Um, I think he's saying he can help us…" Hawk muttered before adding in a louder voice, "Help us how?"

"Ach, just foller me," Crow growled, and turned to walk away.

Then he vanished.

"Where did he go?" River snarled, rising to her paws. "Great, he offers help, which I don't need, and then disappears on us. I can't even smell the stupid wolf, he smells like the rest of this stupid place."

Hawk couldn't help but agree slightly with her, at least on not being able to smell Crow. He could barely even see the mangy wolf when he was visible.

"Tha' is an insult tae ma mountains, lassie!" came Crow's voice, and suddenly he appeared several lengths away. "An' didnae Ah say tae foller me?"

River's hackles raised and her eyes narrowed dangerously. "How can we follow you if we can't even see you?"

"What? Ye cannae see me?" The scraggly Wind-Wolf sounded genuinely confused. "Ah'm right over here!"

And with that, he vanished once more, his voice echoing across the rocks. "Coom on now, we dinnae have all day!"

"If I get my claws on him…" River took a step forward, but was stopped by Hawk.

"Please don't, River," he said, looking over his shoulder to try and catch a glimpse of Crow. *How is he even moving around like that when he himself can't see? He's just like Fall…although I doubt Fall would be bouncing around the mountains like he's doing.* "We need his help, because we're totally lost in the Mountains. We're going to have to trust him, and we can't do that if you attack him."

Although River growled and muttered something about not needing anyone's help, she nodded in agreement.

"Coom on!"

River groaned, and both wolves raced after the rapidly disappearing form of Crow before he left without them.

CHAPTER SEVENTY-FIVE

RIVER GREW MORE irritated with every passing second as Crow continued to randomly disappear on their journey through the mountains. The mangy wolf managed to stay several paces ahead of them, all the while shouting back at them, "Well, coom on!"

I don't know what's worse, following a half-mad wolf we can barely under-stand on the chance that he might *know where he's going, or trust our own instincts when we have* no *idea where to go.* Hawk scrambled over a small ledge, half dragged by River as the two struggled to keep from losing their guide. *How...and why...is he disappearing like that? He's not dispersing into wind; we'd still be able to* sense *him. But this...this is impossible! He just totally vanishes, with any trace of him.*

Hawk slid away from a dangerous drop-off, so focused on following the strange Wind-Wolf he almost missed the crevice. Crow didn't seem to notice the difficultly his followers had trying to guess where he would appear. He seemed to float across the uneven ground and would miss canyons and cracks entirely with his frequent vanishings. The few times he did stop he would growl irritably at them for falling so far behind.

Finally, as the sun was starting to set and after hours of chasing the elusive Wind-Wolf, Hawk managed to distract Crow before he disappeared, allowing River to ambush him and pin him to the ground. "I want you to stop dancing around, and start *walking* in front where we can see you," she growled, digging her claws into Crow's ragged pelt.

"Ah have been walkin' right in front of ye!"

"We can't *see* you, for Moon-Wolf's sake!"

Seeing that River was quickly losing patience, Hawk stepped forward, but a new voice stopped him.

"Is everything all right here, Crow?"

A young female Earth-Wolf, a little taller than Hawk, stepped out onto the path before them, watching them with dark brown eyes. A nasty scar crossed her chest, marring her pale red pelt.

Suddenly River barked in surprise. When Hawk turned around, she stood alone, and Crow was nowhere to be seen.

"Ah was just helpin' these young paps, an' they attack me far it," Crow grumbled from where he had suddenly reappeared right beside the Earth-Wolf.

The she-wolf didn't even blink. "I'll handle it from here, Crow, you can go now."

The old wolf grumbled a little more before vanishing as the she-wolf padded toward the other two.

"Who are you?" River growled, eying the red wolf suspiciously.

"My name is Deer. How did Crow find you?"

Quickly, Hawk cut in before River could give a sharp retort. "We're sort of lost...and Crow offered to help us. He led us here."

Deer nodded slowly, her dark eyes glancing from one to the other as though trying to determine something. Finally she said, "Are you Hawk and River?"

Both of them froze, shocked. River's eyes narrowed and she tensed, prompting Hawk to take a step forward to stop her from pouncing on Deer.

"How do you know our names?" he asked carefully.

Deer's eyes lit up. "We've been told all about you. The others said you might not come, but you did!"

"Oh no..." River closed her eyes. Hawk looked back at her in confusion, before suddenly realizing what Deer was talking about.

"Come on, the Gathering is waiting for you," she said, turning and darting up the slope behind her.

River groaned. "I didn't want to come here," she muttered. "I don't want to get stuck here. We can't afford waste anymore time."

"We don't know how to get to the Scaineadó Desert. We would have had to stop somewhere for help."

"Yes, but I don't like the fact that we've attracted so much notice in just a few weeks."

"Isn't it better that other wolves hear about us?" Hawk asked, confused. "We've been waiting for over a century for a chance to win this war..."

River's eyes darkened. "It's not the wolves I'm worried about. It's the demons."

"Wh-what...?"

"When...I escaped the Rift, Letorus caught a glimpse of me. I don't know if he saw clearly who I was, but if he starts hearing rumors about a 'Water-Wolf savior,' then he's going to make the connection. He'll hunt the both of us like prey."

Hawk's stomach twisted. He had always known that it would get dangerous if his name were spread as one of the leaders of the rebellion. He knew the stories of the few wolves of the past who had attempted to overthrow the demons. None of them ended well.

But to hear River say that it was very likely Letorus would be searching for them made it seem much more real. The threat of being captured as an escaped slave suddenly didn't seem so terrifying.

"Come on!" Hawk and River looked up to see Deer waiting for them at the top of the slope. River took a deep breath and scrambled up after her, Hawk racing to follow. Deer led them along a winding path that doubled back on itself several times, and Hawk soon lost all sense of direction. They ran past great waterfalls plunging deep into shadowy caverns, down impossibly steep slopes, and through twisting tunnels.

The moons had long-since risen by the time Deer finally stopped. The Earth-Wolf pulled down a wall of stone and ushered the travelers inside. Closing the wall behind them, Deer padded down the dark, narrow tunnel, motioning for Hawk and River to follow. Voices soon reached their ears, and suddenly they found themselves in a large cavern full of Elemental wolves. Hawk stopped to look around in awe, although River was a little less obvious with her surprise.

It was as if an entire mountain had been carved out and made hollow. The ceiling stretched so far up it was lost in shadows. Dozens of wolves were scattered about the cavern, gathered together in groups of various sizes. A few nearest to where Hawk and River had entered looked up with curiosity but quickly went back to what they were doing. Campfires dotted the earthy floor and cast stark shadows on the walls of the cave, while the smoke curled up toward the ceiling. Hawk wondered if there were small holes at the top to allow it to escape.

Deer allowed them a few moments to absorb the sight before continuing on. "I need to take you to the Alphas. They'll be excited to meet you."

Deer led them on a path that wove around the campfires. Wolves looked up as they passed, recognition flashing in their eyes when they saw Hawk and River. Murmurs broke out among the rebels as word was spread about their arrival. Soon the entire cavern was looking their way, and the wolves immediately around them stepped aside to allow them a clear path to the Alphas.

"Ember, Spark, Elm, Bird, Hare, Cliff, the Alphas of this Gathering," Deer said as they drew near a group of six wolves seated within a tall ring of stones, cut off from the rest of the cave. All of them looked up in surprise and curiosity as they approached. "Alphas, I have brought Hawk and River."

The first wolf was a smoky gray female Fire-Wolf with dark red eyes. Her muzzle was almost completely white, but she had a lean, wiry body that belied her age.

Spark was the only other Fire-Wolf in the little group, also female. She was dark yellow with pale blue eyes. Three long scars ran down her shoulder.

Elm, the only Earth-Wolf of the six Alphas, was a burly male with light brown fur flecked with darker green hairs. Half of his left ear was missing, and his pelt was raked with several scars, most of them long and ragged, but his green eyes were bright and mirthful.

Bird was a small, lean Wind-Wolf female with dark yellow eyes and pale gray fur. A long, wicked scar crossed her left eye and curled around her left ear. A similar scar crossed her left cheek.

Hare had unusually big ears, bigger even than a Fire-Wolf's ears, a tan pelt, long legs, and small, nervous dark gray eyes that couldn't seem to keep still. He appeared to be the youngest Alpha.

The last Wind-Wolf, Cliff, was a thick-bodied wolf with dark brown fur and bright blue eyes. To Hawk's surprise, the Alpha had two breed marks. The top one was a light yellow swirl, the Wind-Wolf mark, and the bottom one was an Earth-Wolf's pale green square with a black diamond. *He's a half-breed,* Hawk thought, staring at the dual breed mark. He quickly looked away when Cliff's eyes, bright with amusement, caught him looking. *Half-breeds are rare...especially between opposite primal elements, Sun and Moon...but even more so between polar opposites like Wind and Earth.* Mixtures between the different breeds often resulted in internal conflict between the different elements of a wolf — conflict that greatened when the two mixed elements were opposites.

He must be very, very powerful, despite the internal elemental conflict, or very, very cunning to have gotten to his position.

"River and Hawk?" It was Bird who spoke. The dark yellow Wind-Wolf stood and padded over toward the two. "You're River and Hawk?"

River sniffed. "Yeah, what's it to you?"

Ignoring the irate Water-Wolf, Bird turned to Deer. "Where did you find them?"

"Crow was leading them here. I simply brought them the rest of the way."

"Ah, so that idiot finally decided to appear, did he?" Elm said with amusement. "We haven't seen him for ages, I was starting to think he had finally gone and died on us."

"You may go, Deer. We'll handle this now," Cliff interrupted.

The she-wolf dipped her head and turned to leave.

"So, River and Hawk, eh? I suppose you're the reason we heard the others getting so excited out there," Elm said, joining Bird in inspecting them. River's hackles rose slightly, and a growl started deep in her throat. Hawk pressed his pelt against hers, silently telling her to stay calm. "We've been told lots about you," he added.

"So we've heard," Hawk said smoothly. "Did Lichen tell you?"

Elm barked in laughter. "Lichen? Her entire group, and Cloud's when they arrived, couldn't stop talking about you. Of course, we had already heard rumors from Taladair Forest about how the two of you took down an entire demon fortress, but no one really believed them. At least, not until we heard about your exploits at the Nocte and Algidus Fortresses. Your story is spreading like wildfire. I don't think I've ever seen so many packs on the move."

Hawk felt River tense beside him, but she said nothing. *I wonder if Coal and Sparrow and the others have heard the rumors, and what they think of them if they did...*

Before Elm could continue, Bird interrupted. "Yes, yes, that's fine, but let's get back to business."

The burly Earth-Wolf, Elm, rolled his eyes but returned to his spot.

Bird turned her attention back to River and Hawk. "What are you two doing here? How did Crow come to find you?'

"We're trying to get to the Scaineadó Desert," Hawk answered, when it became apparent that River had no intention of speaking. "We were lost, and Crow found us and said he could help."

"The Scaineadó Desert? What business do you have there?" Spark asked, speaking for the first time. A strange sort of sadness darkened her eyes. "From what we've heard, we thought you would come to lead us."

"We don't have to tell you," River growled, before Hawk could answer.

"Disrespectful whelp, remember who you're talking to." Bird's eyes narrowed dangerously, undaunted by the Water-Wolf's tone.

Hawk quickly intervened. "Please, we mean no disrespect; we just need to find the way to the desert. We did not come here to lead...we have a mission we must complete if any sort of rebellion is supposed to succeed. And…we would rather not reveal our intentions."

The dark yellow she-wolf seemed satisfied with Hawk's apology, as she took a step back and relaxed her stance. "Cloud said something like that. But you're a Fire-Wolf, aren't you? Shouldn't you know the way?"

He hesitated, his eyes sliding away. When he had escaped Ignimor Fortress, Hawk had run blind, seeking only to put as much distance as he could between him and his past. Delirious with hunger and exhaustion, he had barely made it to Taladair alive. There were some parts of his journey that Hawk simply couldn't remember. But having to explain that would mean that Hawk would have to reveal that he was an escaped slave…something that he was wary of doing, even now.

Before he could come up with an answer, Bird closed her eyes briefly and nodded. "Ah…I forgot. You used to be a slave. You've never been to Gaoibeanna before, have you?"

Hawk shook his head. *I guess I can't really hide my past anymore…I'm sure everyone in here knows I'm an escaped slave.*

"We'll help you."

All the Wolves present turned to look at Hare, startled by his sudden input. Despite his frail appearance, he had a strong voice that spoke of wisdom beyond his age. From the reaction of the other wolves, Hawk got the feeling the Hare didn't speak much, and that he held the respect of his fellow Alphas despite his young age.

"But it is getting late," Hare continued after briefly acknowledging Hawk's nod of thanks. "Stay for the night, and rest. We'll send you on your way in the morning."

As that was obviously a dismissal, Hawk thanked the Alphas once more and turned to leave. He felt six pairs of eyes boring into his pelt as he and River walked away.

"Do you think all that we were told is true?"

Hawk paused when he heard Spark's quiet voice. River, too intent on getting somewhere away from prying eyes, didn't notice him stop.

"Of course," Hare replied. "River is swathed in darkness and impossible to read, but Hawk has been marked by his ancestors and given strength by the gods themselves. They are not the ones who will lead us into battle, but they are the ones who will clear the path for us to march. The question is, will they succeed?"

A call from River prompted Hawk to hurry after her, Hare's words echoing in his mind.

We will *succeed. We will not fail Soluna!*

CHAPTER SEVENTY-SIX

LICHEN AND CLOUD were waiting for them the moment Hawk and River appeared.

"You made it!" Lichen said, ushering them away from the Alphas, Cloud silently following her. "Where's Sky?"

"We didn't intend to come here," River muttered under her breath. Hawk laughed a little.

"Sky led us to the Ardgao, but he left to go get Fall and the others," he said, padding after Lichen as she led them to a spot on the edges of the cavern, away from prying eyes. "They're probably on their way now, although I think Sky was going to Taladair to meet with Pine..."

"Who?"

"Ah, the Earth-Wolf who helped us destroy the Obsolium Fortress. She has a small army with her, and I told him she would probably be open to joining forces."

Lichen growled, her eyes glowing. "Excellent. We'll soon have a sizeable force, and with you two leading us, the demons won't know what hit them."

"We're not leading any army," River said with a slight growl.

Lichen looked back at her in confusion. "Then why are you here?"

River sat down and fixed both Lichen and Cloud with a hard glare. "I didn't come to lead an army. I came to fix a mistake made a century ago. I helped you start the rebellion, but it's going to be up to you to see it through. What I'm doing will help your cause, and if I'm prevented from doing it you'll have no chance at winning this war."

"But you can't just leave us!" Lichen exclaimed, before quickly lowering her voice. "Are you going with her, Hawk?"

Hawk nodded silently. Lichen bared her teeth. "After everything you said, you can't expect us to just carry on while you're running around doing Sun-Wolf knows what. You two are the only reasons this rebellion is starting in the first place, you can't just leave it to flounder."

"Yes, we can, and yes, we *will*."

Hawk bit his lip, looking from one she-wolf to the other as the two continued to fight. He was torn between both sides of the argument, and wasn't sure how to step in. *On the one paw, we have to continue our mission. I promised River I would stay with her and help her...but on the other paw, what will happen to the rebellion if we leave?*

A loud, frustrated groan brought him back to the she-wolves. Lichen had leapt to her paws, glaring at River with her fangs bared. "This rebellion will *die* without you." She spun around and brushed by River. "Come on, Cloud. We're going to talk with the Alphas. They *cannot* just let these two go."

Lichen stalked away, Cloud silently padding after her. River just gave a dismissive sniff.

"She is sort of right..."

"Don't you dare suggest we stay here and lead the army."

Hawk flattened his ears against his head and drew away slightly when River snapped at him. "No, I wasn't going to say that. I know we still need to prepare the Song of the Eclipse, and we only have a certain amount of time left...but we can't just run off and leave the rebellion like this."

"Why not? They can figure it out. It'll keep the demons distracted, which will turn some of the focus away from finding us."

"I know, but we have to leave someone in our place who can continue the fight. Sky and Pine could probably step up to do it, but..." He paused. "Did you see the way they reacted when we first entered the Gathering? Everyone was so excited to see us. I'm sure most of them think we're here to lead them. If we just leave without..."

River growled, interrupting him. "What do you want?"

Hawk tilted his head, confused, but then saw that River was looking past him. He turned around and saw a young Fire-Wolf with dark red fur and bright blue eyes stopped mid-step just a few feet away.

"Ah...I wasn't trying to sneak up on you," he said quickly. "I just didn't want to interrupt." The Fire-Wolf gave Hawk a shy look. "Are...are you Hawk?"

"Yes...I am," Hawk said. He glanced over at River, but she had turned away and put her head on her paws, obviously determined to ignore them. "What's your name?"

"Ash, sir." The pup hesitated for a moment before taking a few steps forward. "Is it true, all those stories we've been hearing, that you and River destroyed a demon fortress?'

"Um, yes, it's sort of true. I mean, there were other wolves there too..."

"But you were the ones who started the attack, who led it!" Ash exclaimed, his blue eyes shining with admiration.

"Actually…"

"I'll have you know it was *me* who led that attack," River said irritably, raising her head to fix the young Fire-Wolf with a hard stare. "Hawk was too busy getting himself captured, and the other wolves were too cowardly to do anything until I made them!"

Instead of being abashed, Ash's admiration simply grew. "Wow…that's so amazing…I never thought it would be possible to take on a whole demon fortress like that…much less *destroy* one, *and* a mine, *and* nearly destroy a second fortress…"

The Water-Wolf snorted. "Of course it's possible. The demons wouldn't stand a chance if the wolves of Soluna were to completely unite with each other and ignore their pointless fear of the demons. The only reason you failed before was because you couldn't put your differences aside for *one* moment and fight *together*." Her eyes narrowed, and she suddenly stood and padded over to Ash, who flinched away from her, startled by her inspection. "Who are your parents?"

"Spark, not the Alpha, a different one, and Flash…" he lowered his eyes. "Both of them are dead. Alpha Spark takes care of me now."

"And your grandparents?"

"Uh…Ash and Storm, and Glass and Smoke. I was named for my grandmother."

"Then tell me, is there a Sand and Glass in your lineage?" River asked, leaving both Fire-Wolves very confused. When Ash hesitantly nodded, she sat back with a pleased look on her face. "Then would that not make you of the line of Grianne and a direct descendant of the Fire-Wolf monarchs at the beginning of the war?"

Silence met her statement. Shock flared in Ash's eyes, and he backed away several paces, tail between his legs. "H-how did you know?" he stammered, shooting a few nervous glances behind him. "It's supposed to be a secret…"

Ash is a grand-pup of the Fire-Wolf monarchs? Hawk barely heard the younger Fire-Wolf's worried words. *It's amazing that the line didn't die out over the years…but even more amazing that I'm actually speaking with the wolf who should, by all right, be my leader!*

"It doesn't matter how I know, I just do!"

The young red wolf flinched and looked down. "No one is supposed to know that. Alpha Spark says it's to keep me safe...I'm not even allowed outside the cave...but I think it's more to prevent others from having false hope. Because...because they'd think that I could help lead them to victory, because of my parentage."

"That's a load of rabbit dung," River said harshly. "Just because you're the grandpup of a Queen doesn't mean you actually deserve the title or the position."

Ash's blue eyes filled with hurt, and Hawk sent the she-wolf a sharp look. *She's being too hard on him,* he thought, and almost voiced it, but stopped himself. *But...River herself is the daughter of the Queen who started this war in the first place. She knows what it means to be undeserving of a position.*

"But..." River continued, her eyes glittering. "What if you *could* lead them to victory?" She looked over at Hawk, meeting his shocked look. "You said they needed a leader, someone just as good as us."

"I didn't say that, exactly..."

River ignored him and turned to Ash. "A rebellion is happening. We started it back in Taladair, with our battle at the Obsolium Fortress. But we can't continue leading it. There's something we have to do, something that we have to keep secret. But *you* can lead it."

Ash immediately shook his head. "I couldn't do that! I barely know how to fight."

"Neither did he at first," River said, flicking her ears toward Hawk.

"You...you didn't?" Ash looked over at Hawk, his eyes wide.

Hawk shook his head. "No...I didn't. I was a slave in Ignimor Fortress, in Scaineadó, and I had never set paw outside the fortress walls until I escaped. Even when I joined a resistance group, I couldn't fight to save my own tail." He gave a short laugh. "It's taken some time, and River had to save me a lot at first, but now I can at least hold my own in a fight."

"I had heard the rumors, the ones about you being a slave, but I didn't think they were true. It didn't seem possible that a hero would ever have been so..." Ash trailed off.

"Weak?" Hawk said.

"Not that I think you're weak!" Ash protested.

River snorted. "Of course he was weak at first. Everyone has to start at the bottom."

"Even you?"

River looked like she was going to deny it and say she was always as powerful as she was now, but Hawk silenced her with a look. She nodded stiffly and said, "Yes…even me. Besides, you won't have to lead on your own. If you're still alive, then it's very likely that the lines of Bunchloch and Bréan are alive as well."

"Th-the lines of…what?"

"The Taladite and Gaoibeannan royal families," River elaborated.

"Then…there could be others like me out there?" Ash said, eyes wide. River nodded.

"We could still have our rulers?" Hawk added. *If we could still have our rulers…who better to lead the rebellion?*

"What about the Water-Wolf monarchs? Are there descen—"

River snarled, interrupting the younger Fire-Wolf. "You won't need the assistance of the Water-Wolves. The only ones you need to find are the descendants of King Oak and Queen Dove."

Ash flinched, but nodded.

"How can we find the other descendants? They're probably in hiding as well," Hawk said.

"I know the families of King Oak and Queen Dove," Ash said. "Or part of them, at least…my father had told me it was important to know the family history of the rulers."

Hawk bit his lip, still uncertain. "But will that be enough? It could take months to find the other two…"

"I doubt that," River said. "Rulers have a certain…presence about them; even their direct family has it. Before the war, a wolf could tell the moment a ruler stepped into the room." She turned her attention to Ash. "If you focus hard enough, you should be able to sense when a fellow descendant is near."

Ash nodded. "So…will I have to go look for the other two? Won't news of the rebellion bring them out of hiding?"

"Maybe, but probably not. If *you* heard about a rebellion, would you come racing out of hiding to join?"

The younger Fire-Wolf thought about it for a moment, before slowly shaking his head. "No, probably not…"

"But if Ash is out looking for the other descendants, what about the army?" Hawk asked.

"Pine and Sky, or maybe the Alphas here, will have to lead it," River said. "I'm sure the wolves will be happy with that if they know their rulers will soon return to take charge."

"Then we'll really have an actual army," Ash said excitedly. "Like King Oak did!" The glow in his eyes slowly faded. "But...there's no way Alpha Spark would ever let me leave the Gathering..."

"River and I have to talk to the Alphas tomorrow morning," Hawk said. "We'll tell them about our plan. But...are you sure you want to do this?"

Ash tilted his head slightly. "What do you mean?"

"It's not going to be easy to find the descendants. And if the demons hear that the rulers are returning, they'll hunt you."

"I know...but I can't stay in here," Ash said firmly. "I have a duty to my land. And...my father once told me that one day our family would have to continue what Queen Sand couldn't finish. She died trying to stop the demons from taking over Soluna. We have to win where she failed."

Hawk nodded. "All right...as long as you know the risks." Memories of River telling him of the dangers he would face if he followed her came to mind, and he sighed. *I'll have as much luck turning Ash away as she did with me.* "You might want to go get some sleep. You're coming with us to talk to the Alphas."

Ash's eyes widened, but he straightened and gave Hawk a sharp nod. "Yes, sir!"

The younger Fire-Wolf turned and bounded away, his tail high. Hawk sighed again as he watched Ash leave.

"Remind you of someone?" River said with a little amusement.

"I just...he's so young," Hawk said, ignoring her teasing tone. "I feel like we shouldn't be sending a pup out on such a dangerous mission."

River fixed him with a serious look. "You're not much older than he is. War doesn't care what age the fighters are or whether or not you're on the sidelines watching. It kills regardless. That's the chance we take with it."

CHAPTER SEVENTY-SEVEN

DEEP IN THE Uiscean Marsh, a Shade-Tiger whimpered and cowered in terror as its master stood over it, fury radiating from his body.

"*Are you sure?*" Letorus hissed. His cruel black eyes were narrowed to slits, and he bared his long fangs at the terrified demon crouching at his paws.

Larger than any mortal wolf, Letorus had thick shoulders and solid legs. His claws and upper canines were both unusually long and wickedly sharp. His black pelt was marked only by a long patch of white that masked his face and traced his spine.

"Y-yes, my lord," the Shade-Tiger stammered. "I saw it with my own eyes. Water leapt out of the banks of the river and crashed down onto my brethren, sweeping away all in its path. And controlling it was a blue-gray she-wolf with a navy blue wave mark on her left shoulder. She is the one who caused the destruction of the Obsolium Fortress."

"No!" Roaring with rage, Letorus unleashed a furious attack of black energy that swept over the Shade-Tiger and swallowed it before it could react. The other demons standing guard on the edges of Letorus' throne room didn't even flinch.

"Leave me!" the Overlord cried, releasing another wave of energy. His servants quickly vacated the room, racing to escape the dark magic.

It can't be...not now... Letorus paced the length of his throne room, an unfamiliar feeling of fear twisting his heart.

The Water-Wolves were the only ones who knew the truth of how the demons had come to Soluna, and Letorus feared that they knew how to send him back, or worse...*kill him*. Of course, there were plenty of demons still in the Rift to suppress the wolves still trapped there, but the fear plagued him all the same.

Then, that accursed *Redacta Spiritus* had to appear and tell him that his reign was ending. Letorus had heard of the legends surrounding the creature, called the Winter-Wolf by the lower demons and wolf slaves, but he paid little heed to such unfounded rumors.

Until the spirit itself visited him one snowy night, bringing with it dark tidings and cold threats.

The temperature in the room dropped, dragging Letorus back to the present. Ice formed on the walls and the floor, and snow blew around the room. Within moments the Demon Overlord found himself standing in the middle of a blizzard.

"I warned you this would happen."

Letorus spun around and came face to face with a giant white wolf with bi-colored eyes.

"You gave me riddles and told me my time was coming, Redacta Spiritus," Letorus snarled, using the name the spirit had given him upon its first visit.

"That was all I felt you needed to know," Redacta Spiritus replied in a neutral tone. "Everything must end...*you* are no different."

"I am *Death*! I am *Eternal*! *I cannot die!*" Letorus roared, baring his fangs at Redacta Spiritus. "Even the gods could not defeat me; they were forced to seal me and my brethren in the Rift!"

Redacta Spiritus gave the demon a pitying look. "*You* are not what you say you are. You are simply the pawn of a much greater evil...but one who cowers in the heavens waiting for you to restore his power. And how have you managed while the master is away? He gave you a few simple tasks, and you have yet to complete any of them...I wonder what he would think if he were to know how you have failed..."

Letorus snarled. "You will not breathe a word to Mortaum, Spirit."

"Only if you keep my existence a secret from him, demon."

"It still stands that no matter what you are doing to stop us, you will not succeed. How many wars have been fought against us, and yet we have continued to survive?"

The white wolf tilted its head slightly. "That is only because it is not the destiny of the gods to destroy either you or your master. *That* destiny falls to another."

"The Water-Wolf?" the demon sneered. He thought he had seen something slip out of the Rift among his demons but had dismissed it to be one of his Noxond. Now he knew that this supposed Water-Wolf causing a ruckus in the north was the one he had seen. If she had somehow managed to escape the Rift, then she must have had something to do with Redacta Spiritus's constant warnings about Letorus' looming demise. "She will be dead before she even reaches the borders of this marsh."

Redacta Spiritus said nothing.

"No matter what you say about *destiny*, it holds little power against the one who rules over Death itself," Letorus added, returning the spirit's cool gaze with a smug look.

The wind suddenly picked up as Redacta Spiritus started to laugh. Letorus narrowed his eyes, confused by the reaction. Redacta Spiritus continued to ignore him, the sound of its amusement rising above the roar of the storm. The storm grew in strength until the spirit's form had all but disappeared, and all Letorus could see of the white wolf were its bi-colored eyes.

"If that is true, then why are there still wolves who run free? Why does the land itself elude your grasp? Why do the souls continue to pass on? Why do the Water-Wolves resist you, even as they suffer in the Rift?"

Ice and snow tore through Letorus' fur, and he was forced to hunch his shoulders against the wind and dig his claws into the stone beneath his paws or risk getting blown away.

"The Eclipse is coming, demon, and when it does, everything you know will come to an end."

And with that, the spirit disappeared, taking the ice and snow with it. Slowly, the room's temperature returned to normal levels. Soon, it was as if Redacta Spiritus had never appeared.

Letorus released a breath he hadn't realized he'd been holding and sheathed his claws. He snarled. *I will* not *let some half-baked spirit shake me.*

A knock sounded on the thick doors of the throne room, startling Letorus out of his thoughts. He gave his head a hard shake and ordered the doors to be open. A Darkclaw stumbled through, panting heavily from its journey and swaying on its paws.

"My…my lord, I bring grave news."

The Overlord narrowed his eyes, although his mind was still on Redacta Spiritus's words. "Continue."

The Darkclaw took a deep breath before speaking. "Our mine by the Nocte and Algidus Fortresses has fallen. An army led by a Fire-Wolf and a Water-Wolf destroyed it before attacking the Nocte Fortress. Algidus sent a force to help, but Nocte had already suffered many losses and the army vanished by the time they got there."

"What?" Letorus snarled, baring his long fangs. It seemed he faced nothing but bad news today.

"B-but I also have something I think you will find of great interest," the Darkclaw said quickly, obviously hoping to diffuse its master's anger.

Letorus nodded slowly. "I will be the judge of that."

The Darkclaw swallowed hard but told the Overlord what it had seen during the battle at the mine. When it had finished, Letorus' jaws parted in a feral grin. The Overlord chuckled, his eyes glittering.

This is good, very good... I remember him *mentioning something about his 'family'...but I never expected* this. *It is unfortunate that* he *was killed...but... his brother remains...*

"Bring me Occisor," Letorus ordered. The Darkclaw gave a quick bow before stumbling out of the throne room.

"Let's see if you are still confident when you learn of *this,* Redacta Spiritus," the Overlord sneered, although he knew the spirit wouldn't hear. "That Water-Wolf will never fulfill the *destiny* you think she has."

CHAPTER SEVENTY-EIGHT

A PAIR OF *eyes, silver and red, haunted Hawk's dream. No matter where he ran in the snowy forest, the eyes followed him.*

Suddenly Hawk found himself trapped against a wall of stone, the impassable cliffs behind him preventing any chance of escape. Wind howled in his ears, and the sky darkened as clouds appeared and obscured the blue.

Although he knew who stood behind him, Hawk still whirled around, baring his fangs in a way that would have made River proud.

"There is no need to be so hostile," the Winter-Wolf said, its form barely visible through the snow.

Hawk forced himself to relax, knowing that even if he had to fight he would have no chance against the spirit.

"What do you want?"

The Winter-Wolf cocked its head slightly. "You have grown."

When Hawk said nothing, the spirit continued. "I have only come to ensure certain memories are still in place. Do you remember what I told you the last time we met like this?"

"N-no…" Hawk narrowed his eyes in thought. He vaguely remembered having a dream like this before but could remember nothing that was said in it.

The Winter-Wolf nodded. "Dreams are easy to forget. Listen closely, and take to heart these words. They will aid you."

Before Hawk could say a word, the Winter-Wolf tipped its head back and howled. Hawk immediately cowered, pain splitting his head. And just as before, everything began to fade to black, the voice of the Winter-Wolf echoing off the cliffs around them.

"A demon will turn twice before Sun meets Moon and the King is struck down. Then a sacrifice must be made by the earth-born flame, to banish the Dark and free the land."

CHAPTER SEVENTY-NINE

"HAWK!"

Hawk awoke with a start, but for a few seconds he had no idea where he was. The sight of an irritated River holding a giant bubble of water over his unsuspecting head brought him back to earth. Quickly he scrambled away from her, not wanting to get doused. "Ah! I'm up!"

The she-wolf looked a little disappointed, as though she had looked forward to seeing him fizzle underneath a torrent of liquid. For a second Hawk was afraid she would douse him anyway, but finally she sighed and dissolved the water back into its separate molecules.

"We need to go speak to the Alphas. Ash already ran off to gather them."

She turned and padded away, leaving Hawk to scramble after her, still trying to clear his sleep-fogged mind. He kept thinking back to his dream, although he could only remember wisps of it. The harder he tried to remember, the harder it became to focus. Finally, words started coming back to him, fragments of sentences half-heard. *'A demon will turn...the King is struck down...sacrifice...earth-born flame...'*

The voice of the Winter-Wolf echoed in Hawk's mind, and for a second he thought he saw the ghostly form of the spirit padding beside him. Hawk stumbled, shocked, and the vision vanished.

What was that? Did that come from the dream? Hawk swallowed nervously. *What if...the Winter-Wolf is stalking me in my dreams...?*

A bark from Ash brought his attention back to the cave. The younger Fire-Wolf was already waiting for Hawk and River near the Alpha's meeting spot, practically wriggling with excitement.

I'll worry about that later, Hawk thought. *I have to focus.*

"I told Alpha Spark that you wanted to talk to her and the other Alphas," he said when they approached. "They're waiting for you. Oh, and Lichen is here, too." Ash faltered for a moment. "I, uh, I don't think she's happy with either of you."

River snorted. "That's her problem. Come on, we've got a lot of talking to do."

Hawk sighed, not looking forward to having to explain everything again. The Alphas may have been willing to let him and River go the night before, but if Lichen had spoken to them, then he wasn't sure what they were thinking now. And they still had to try and convince the Alphas to let Ash go and search for the other descendants.

Feeling a pair of eyes watching him anxiously, Hawk straightened and sent Ash a confident look. "Are you ready?" he asked the younger wolf.

Ash wagged his tail and nodded. "Yes, sir!"

"Ah, don't call me *sir*," Hawk said, warming beneath his pelt. "By all rights *I* should be the one calling *you* 'sir.'"

"Both of you, *let's go.*"

Hawk and Ash hurried after River, who turned and padded into the ring of stones surrounding the Alphas. Lichen was already there, but she didn't move when they entered, choosing instead to ignore them.

"Hawk, River…and Ash," Spark said, giving a slight nod to greet them. Her eyes were expressionless, but Hawk had the strangest feeling that she knew why they were here. "You have something you wish to discuss with us?"

To Hawk's surprise, River stepped forward to speak. "I know many are expecting us to lead the resistance, but as we told you last night, we will not," she paused, glancing over at Lichen, "for reasons we can't say. *However,* we will not be leaving the army without a leader…"

"Are you implying that we are not capable of leading an army?" Bird interrupted, her eyes narrowed.

River coolly met the other she-wolf's gaze. "Who do you think is a better choice for leading a rebellion, you or a Wind-Wolf monarch?"

Silence met her question. Even Lichen had turned to look at her, confusion lighting her eyes. Hawk looked around the gathered Alphas, and saw a flash of sadness in Spark's expression.

"The lines of the rulers died out decades ago," Ember said, breaking the silence.

"Are you sure?" River nodded to Ash, who nervously took a step forward to join her. "He is a descendant of Queen Sand. If he has survived, then why not others?"

Ash stiffened when the focus of the Alphas turned to him, but he kept his head held high.

"How do you know that?" Cliff asked, his openly curious look softening his accusing tone. "Over a hundred years has passed since the war began and the families of the rulers were scattered. Anyone can claim to be of royal lineage."

"She tells the truth," Spark said suddenly. "Ash is from the line of Grianne, who have sheltered here since the beginning of the war."

"Why didn't you say anything before?" Ember asked. "You should have told us the descendants of our monarchs were among us!"

"What good would knowing his heritage have done before? You would have done the same as I; keep it secret to avoid giving others false hope." Spark sighed. "Now…things have changed. Wolves are rising up again, and they need someone to lead them. I suppose you want to go in search of the other descendants, correct?" she said, directing the question at Ash.

"Y-yes, ma'am," Ash said, faltering only slightly at the sudden address.

"Very well." Spark turned to her fellow Alphas. "I believe we should allow Ash to seek out the descendants. He was born to become a King, and it is only right he should be the one to find them."

The other Alphas nodded their agreement.

"So…you'll let me go?" Ash asked carefully.

"Yes, you may go, as long as you take Crow with you," Spark said. "He will keep you safe."

"What about the rest of us?" Lichen said, speaking up for the first time. "Who will lead if Hawk and River leave for their *mission*, and Ash is sent on what could very easily be a mouse hunt?"

"Sky, a Wind-Wolf who helped us lead the attack on the Nocte Fortress, went to meet with Pine," Hawk said. "Pine fought at Obsolium, and we have reason to believe that she still leads the forces there. With her and Sky, and you, Alphas, I believe the rebellion will have plenty of capable leaders to guide it."

"Well said, Hawk." Hare stood. "It is the unanimous decision of this Gathering that Ash and Crow be sent to find the other descendants. Hawk and River are free to complete their mission. We will wait here for Sky and Pine to arrive and prepare for battle." He paused, staring straight at Lichen, as though waiting for her to protest. She said nothing and kept her gaze fixed on the ground between her paws.

"You are dismissed. Elm and I will see you out," Spark said, standing as well.

At the last moment, Ash gave the Alphas a bow of respect before whirling around and bouncing out of the ring of stones. Lichen rushed out after him without looking at either River or Hawk.

"She's just disappointed," River said when Hawk moved to call her back. "She'll be all right."

Hawk bit his lip as he watched Lichen vanish into the crowd of wolves beyond, but was prevented from saying any more on the matter when Elm and Spark appeared behind them. "All right, you three, let's go," Elm said, brushing by Hawk and River. "Ash, get back here!"

"Hawk, walk with me for a bit," Spark said, stopping Hawk from following the others out.

He gave her a curious look, but nodded.

"To tell the truth, I knew Ash was going to leave the moment you arrived."

Hawk blinked with surprise. "Wh...what?"

Spark gave a slight sigh. "That wolf has become like a son to me. I once had a litter of my own, but they were killed by demons, along with my mate. When Ash's parents, my good friends, begged me to take their little son in, I couldn't refuse. They were dying, and I missed my own puppies." She paused and raised her gaze to lock eyes with Hawk. "But the night I took Ash in, I had a dream. In it, a large white wolf appeared before me, with bi-colored eyes. The wolf told me to let the 'slumbering ash awaken when the river-hawk flew.' I suppose...this is what it meant."

A cold feeling settled in the pit of Hawk's stomach. "A...a white wolf? Did...did its form seem...indistinct?"

Spark cocked her head in confusion. "Yes, yes it did. How did you know?"

"L-lucky guess..." Hawk swallowed hard and avoided Spark's curious gaze. *It has to be the Winter-Wolf Spark saw in her dream. But why? Why would the Winter-Wolf appear to Spark like that...and warn her about my and River's arrival, and to make sure Ash left to go seek the other descendants?* He shuddered inwardly, remembering his vision. *Everywhere we go, the Winter-Wolf has been there. It found me in the blizzard, then I saw it in Sparrow's eyes, then I saw an image of it here and hear that Spark dreamed of it.*

Maybe I should tell River about the Winter-Wolf... No, River has enough to worry about as it is. She doesn't take well to mentions of it...and I don't even know what its constant appearances mean.

I don't want to add to her burdens.

"We have waited a long time for this," Spark said, interrupting his thoughts. "Whatever you and River are planning, do not let us down. Do not let *Ash* down."

CHAPTER EIGHTY

BY THE TIME Hawk and Spark reached the Gathering's entrance, the others were already there and waiting for them. River looked extremely irritated, Elm looked far too innocent not to be the cause of her annoyance, and Ash was bouncing in his attempt to catch Hawk and Spark's attention. The younger Fire-Wolf quickly settled himself at a stern look from his foster mother, but his glowing eyes betrayed his excitement.

"We're glad you're here," Elm said as they approached. "I don't think Ash could have lasted much longer."

Ash's tail started wagging so hard he shook. "I've never been outside the Gathering before, what's it like? What about the demons? Will I have to watch out for them?" he added, looking a little nervous.

River snorted. "Of course you will. The demons could be anywhere. Never let your guard down for a second!"

The red Fire-Wolf wilted a little, intimidated by River's words. Elm rolled his eyes and gave the small wolf a companionable shove, one that almost sent him sprawling into Hawk.

"Don't worry, Crow will take care of you. Just stick close to him and you'll be fine," Elm said encouragingly. Hawk wasn't so sure, remembering his and River's own adventure trying to follow the old wolf through the mountains.

Then again, Hawk traveled with a Water-Wolf who was liable to bite the head off of anyone who came too close. At least Crow seemed friendly.

"Yes, that's lovely, now open the stupid tunnel so we can get moving," River said irritably. Elm just rolled his eyes again.

"Yes, oh great and wonderful Queen!" he said sarcastically. Hawk winced, watching the shock and horror cross River's face, although Elm had already turned away to move the boulder blocking the tunnel.

The boulder slid aside, and Elm led the way out, Ash close at his tail. Hawk hesitated, looking at River, before following. It was a few more moments before he heard her pad after him.

"Ash, when we leave the tunnel, you must be silent," the Earth-Wolf said, completely serious. "There may be demons nearby, and we do not want to alert them to our presence."

Ash nodded, equally serious, although he still quivered a little from excitement.

"Crow will teach you what you need to know," Elm continued, ignoring a snort from River at that comment, "but here's some advice for you: trust your instincts; often they'll guide you better than logic. If something *feels* wrong, then it most likely is. And don't be afraid to ask others for help, although you may want to keep your quest a secret." Here, Elm's voiced grew quiet. "Other wolves may hear rumors that the descendants of the rulers are still alive, although we will try our best to keep them from spreading, and not all of them have the best intentions. At all costs, you *cannot* let the demons know who you are or what you are trying to do. And if you fail, and I pray to Moon-Wolf that you don't, it would be best to not give others false hope. And the more secret your identity and the goal of your quest are, the safer you will be."

Ash nodded, starting to look very nervous now, but also growing determined.

"If Letorus learns that a descendent lives, he will hunt you mercilessly." This comment came from River. "Wait until you have the descendants gathered and an army beneath you, before you reveal yourself. Take him by surprise."

By now the five had reached the end of the tunnel. Ash recoiled sharply at the sudden change in light, and even Hawk had to stand blinking for a few moments until River roughly shoved both Fire-Wolves in front of her out of the tunnel.

Ash looked around the mountains he had lived in his entire life, but had never actually seen with his own eyes. Hawk couldn't help but wag his tail at the wonder crossing the younger wolf's face. He could imagine what Ash was feeling as he looked around at the great stone monuments rising from the earth around him. Hawk himself had a similar experience when he escaped Ignimor.

"It's...amazing..." Ash said breathlessly.

"Aye, mah mountains are amazin'," Crow said, suddenly appearing in between Ash and Hawk.

Both Fire-Wolves nearly jumped right out of their pelts, and River had to pull up short to avoid running into him. "Would you stop doing that!" she snarled, but only got a confused look in return.

"Stoop doing what?" Then recognition flooded his face. "Ach! Ah remember ye. Yer the rude she-wolf. Ah'm not going tae hae tae travel with ye, am Ah?"

River shook her head and stalked away, but Elm looked rather amused.

"Thank you, Crow, for doing this," Spark said, emerging from the tunnel behind the other four. Hawk jumped; she had been so quiet he had forgotten she was there. Spark turned to Elm. "You may return, Elm. I will take it from here."

The burly Earth-Wolf nodded. "I'll wait to let you in at the entrance, Spark. Don't take too long."

Turning, he padded back into the tunnel and disappeared into its inky depths. The yellow she-wolf walked forward until she stood in front of Ash and Crow. Her dark red eyes were sad as she gazed at the younger Fire-Wolf. "Ash, you have become like a son to me," she began, giving him a lick on his ear. "You are almost out of puppyhood, but I will always see you as a pup, *my* pup. This is a dangerous mission you are embarking on, and if it were up to me, you would not be going. However, this choice is out of my paws." Here she cast Hawk a quick look, and he knew she meant the Winter-Wolf.

"Crow, take care of my son. Keep him safe, and help him find the other descendants."

The old Wind-Wolf nodded, seeming almost sane with the gravity of the situation.

Spark turned to the last two wolves. "Hawk and River, you two have a long road ahead of you. Crow will point you in the right direction to the Scaineadó Desert, but then you must travel on your own." Speaking to all four wolves, Spark raised her voice a little. "I pray to both Sun-Wolf and Moon-Wolf that both your quests will be successful, and that you all will return safely."

River bowed her head in a rare show of respect. "Thank you, Alpha Spark."

The other she-wolf nodded, and then silently turned to pad back into the tunnel. Ash was silent for a moment, finally realizing the importance of his mission. Quickly, before Spark could disappear into the tunnel, he turned and said, "Thank you…Mom. I will return and see you again. I promise."

The dark yellow Fire-Wolf, paused and sent him a soft look, before finally vanishing into the darkness.

"Well ten," Crow said, breaking the silence. "Let's go. We dinnae have all day!"

Chapter Eighty-One

TRAVELING WITH CROW, as Hawk had learned before, was very tiring. Ash, it appeared, was having no trouble following the elusive Wind-Wolf, but that may have been because he was simply following Hawk, who was mostly following River, who was actually the one trying to track Crow. The old Wind-Wolf never seemed to notice he was in danger of losing his followers, and would simply pop up in random places, chatting away with no one in particular, leading them along an irregular path through the mountains.

"Hurry up, ye younglings," Crow would call from time to time. "Ah'm going tae loose ye!"

River would simply grit her teeth and mutter curses under her breath.

Occasionally Crow would appear beside one of them, try to engage them in conversation, which none of them understood very well, only to disappear once more when they finally managed to come up with a response. One time, Hawk took advantage of having the strange Wind-Wolf appear next to him to ask, "Crow, why do you have that strip of hide around your eyes?"

The scruffy wolf gave Hawk a look that Hawk assumed to be one of confusion. "Ye mean ma blindfold? Ah lost ma eyes, an' cannae see. Ah'm told tha' it's a disturbing sight tae see, so Ah cover mah missin' eyes."

That made Hawk even more confused and not just because the Wind-Wolf was hard to understand. "What do you mean, 'lost?'" he asked.

"Ah lost mah eyes, laddie," Crow replied, as if explaining something very simple to a young pup. "An' Ah cannae find them! Ah dinnae ken what happened tae them."

"Ken? What's 'ken' supposed to mean?" Hawk asked, trying to decipher what the old wolf was saying.

"Ach, but dinnae ye worry," Crow said, as though Hawk had never spoken. "Ah kin see with ma ears and ma nose. The wind tells me where tae go, and Ah kin smell ma way around quite fine."

Then Crow disappeared. Hawk groaned when he saw the scruffy wolf reappear right beside River, making her jump. "Did ye hear that, lassie? Ah kin hear every word yer sayin!'"

River shook with barely contained fury, but Crow disappeared before she could do anything.

"Now come on! No more lollygaggin'!"

"I like him, Crow's lots of fun!" Ash exclaimed, padding up beside Hawk.

"That makes one of us," River muttered as the two Fire-Wolves passed.

CHAPTER EIGHTY-TWO

IT WAS NOON by the time Crow called for a halt. Hawk sank gratefully to the ground, exhausted. Ash wasn't very far behind him. River was too proud to show such weakness, although her sides heaved with exertion.

Crow, on the other paw, looked as fresh as if he had just started.

Stupid Wind-Wolf, River thought, glaring at him as she struggled to get her breath back.

They had travelled far, zigzagging across the mountains in a seemingly random pattern, but River had come to notice a method to the Wind-Wolf's travel. As much as he irritated her, she had to admit he knew what he was doing. They had not come into contact with any demons, and Crow had covered their tracks so well even the best Wind-Wolf tracker would find it impossible to locate them.

"This is where we leave ye, Hawk and River," Crow said, and motioned south with a shake of his head. "Just keep headin' south, and ye'll get tae the desert soon enough. Hawk, ye'll start tae feel a pull when ye get close."

River closed her eyes, already feeling a little sick at the mere mention of the desert. She did not look forward to traveling into the heart of fire territory.

Hawk nodded. "Thanks for showing us this far, Crow."

"I wish you could come with us, Hawk," Ash said, looking sad.

"I have my mission, and you have yours," Hawk said kindly. "But we'll meet again, when all this is over."

"That's a promise! Good luck, Hawk!" The dark red Fire-Wolf bounced over to Hawk and gave him a lick on his ear.

Hawk wagged his tail and returned the lick. "Good luck to you too."

River felt a slight tinge of guilt. It was her fault Hawk had been dragged into this mess in the first place. He would be much safer, and probably happier, by accompanying Ash. She quickly shook the feeling away.

I'm going to be selfish and hold on to you for a little longer.

"Come on Hawk, we need to—" River started to say, impatient to get going before she delved too deeply into her thoughts, when she cut herself off in surprise as Ash bounced over to her and gave her a lick too. Crow hacked a bit, in what River assumed was a laugh, at the stupefied look on her face.

"Good luck, River, and be careful in the desert! Water and fire don't mix very well."

"Um…thanks?" River blinked, for once rather slow in recovery.

Ash turned around and ran back to Crow. The young Fire-Wolf gave Hawk and River one last wave of his tail before disappearing around the bend with his mangy companion.

Bubbly Fire-Wolves, River thought, shaking her head.

"Let's go, River!" Hawk said with a wag of his tail. River chuckled a little to herself as she followed her companion in the direction Crow had pointed out.

"We still have a ways to go. I'm not dragging you the rest of the way because you tired yourself out."

Her words made him pause, but River kept walking past him. The sooner they could get to Scaineadó the better, because River didn't want to spend any more time than necessary in the desert.

"River, do you know exactly when the Eclipse is supposed to happen?"

She stopped, but didn't turn around. All she had to go on was the words of Egret, Clan Archeo's Seer. Accuracy was not always a Seer's strong point. Very few were powerful enough to predict anything entirely accurate, and that was when the Seer was in a position to consult the gods. Given that Egret had to divine a way to kill Letorus while still inside the Rift, cut off from any connection to Moon-Wolf, and attempt to keep his activities a secret from the demons, River was lucky that the only thing he had missed was just how much time passed outside the Rift.

"The month before the Eclipse, the two smaller moons will disappear behind the largest one," River said finally. She had to trust that what Egret had told her was true. "All three will turn red, and the sun silver, the night before. We have to make sure that we're ready by then."

River continued down the path, a renewed determination drowning out any discomfort she felt at the prospect of journeying through the desert.

I will not fail in my mission. I will pay for the mistakes my family made.

CHAPTER EIGHTY-THREE

THE NOXOND ONLY had to sniff the ground once to confirm what it already knew. Its prey had been here. It looked up, gazing through the mountains as if it could already see the creature it tracked. With the three moons shining down on its dark red fur, the Noxond growled and took off at a run.

The hunt had begun.

CHAPTER EIGHTY-FOUR

BY THE TIME River finally called for a halt, Hawk was ready to fall over in a dead faint. The sun had set a few hours previous, forcing them to travel by moonlight. River had refused to let them stop to hunt. Hawk was beyond the point of being hungry by now and was simply glad to sink to the ground and rest.

"Stay here," River ordered. "Rather than waste time waiting for you to catch something, I'll just hunt. No lighting fires."

And with that, she vanished into the night, leaving behind a slightly hurt Hawk.

I know, I'll just go and hunt on my own, he thought, *and then when River gets back, I will have already caught something! Then we'll see if she has to 'waste time waiting for me to catch something.'*

He stood, and then hesitated, knowing that River would be mad if he wandered off on his own.

It'll be okay...I won't go far, and I'll just make sure I'm back before she is, Hawk reassured himself and set out.

It didn't take very long to find some prey. Hawk nearly stumbled over a fat hare, which had been so focused on digging out a few seeds from a crack it never saw him coming. The hare and the wolf stared at each other for a few seconds, each looking just as surprised as the other. Then the hare flicked its tail and bounded away. Hawk shook himself out of his surprise and immediately gave chase.

The hare had only run a few feet before Hawk caught up to it, pouncing on it just before it vanished down a hole.

With the hare wedged firmly between his teeth, Hawk practically bounced back to where River had left him. He couldn't wait to see the look on her face when she saw what he had caught.

So maybe it was a really stupid rabbit, and it might have been dumb luck that I caught it, but I still did!

To his surprise, River was already waiting for him, but there was no sign of any prey. The Fire-Wolf paused. *Did she eat without me...?*

"Hawk, where were you? I told you to *stay put*—" She cut herself off, staring at the hare in his jaws.

Eager to earn her approval, Hawk put the hare down and said with a wag of his tail, "Look, I caught a rabbit!"

River shot him a cold glare before turning away. "Humph, so you're not entirely useless. Hurry up and eat then. I'm not hungry."

A little hurt, Hawk lowered his tail and looked down at the hare he had caught. He was so sure he would have been able to make River happy by hunting on his own. But after a quick sniff of the air, Hawk realized what the problem was.

River had not caught anything.

River doesn't want to admit that she couldn't catch anything, Hawk thought with a jolt. He looked back down at the hare. He was very hungry, but he knew that River was probably just as hungry as he was, even if she would never admit it. With a sigh, he picked up the rabbit, padded over to the she-wolf, and dropped it in front of her.

"I…I'm not hungry, so you can have this," he said. River gave him a suspicious glance before hungrily eyeing the hare. Her gaze swung back to him when his stomach growled loudly.

"Erm…I'm going to take first watch!" Hawk said, jumping up to scramble away. "Really, I'm not hungry!"

He quickly settled himself a few lengths from River, pretending as though he wasn't hungry at all and was extremely busy keeping watch. A soft *thump* startled him, and he turned to find River standing next to him, part of the hare at her paws.

"Don't argue, just eat it you idiot," she said, a little amusement in her eyes. "And *I'll* take first watch. I don't think you'd be able to stay awake for more than a few blinks."

Gratefully, Hawk sank his fangs into the hare. He was in no mind to argue anymore. Almost as soon as he had finished burying the remains, Hawk curled up and fell asleep.

CHAPTER EIGHTY-FIVE

THEY SPENT SEVERAL weeks slowly making their way through the mountains and avoiding any demon patrols. River drove them from dawn to dusk, stopping to eat only when it was absolutely necessary. She seemed to have a sixth sense when it came to demons; she could smell them coming from miles away and always shoved Hawk into the nearest hiding spot before dispersing into water.

By the end of the first week, Hawk was completely spent, his paws torn and sore. Most of the time they had to climb halfway up the mountainside before the path straightened out again, which meant a precarious climb back down.

I'd love to be a Wind-Wolf right now, Hawk thought one night, slowly drifting off into an exhausted sleep. *I don't know how River has the energy to keep going like this every day.*

He felt as if he had only slept a few seconds before being prodded awake.

"Get up; demons are coming," River hissed, before dragging him to his paws and shoving him between two boulders before she herself melted into a puddle of water. The minutes ticked by; Hawk grew more and more uncomfortable.

A slim Fire-Wolf with bright pink fur raced by so quickly Hawk thought he imagined it, followed closely by a Fire-Fang and three Hell-Cats. A flash of metal, caused by a stray moonbeam, caught his eye as the Fire-Wolf passed.

A slave collar!

The wolf and her pursuers vanished around the corner, and River remerged from the cracks in the stone. "Let's move; we'll make camp somewhere else"

Hawk squeezed out of his hiding spot. "But River, that Fire-Wolf was an escaped slave! We have to—"

"We don't have time to waste rescuing some idiot Fire-Wolf who was dumb enough to get caught!" River snapped, whirling on him.

"But…"

"No buts!" And with that, River turned sharply and started to stalk away. Hawk took a step after her, and then hesitated. *I can't just leave a fellow Fire-Wolf to the demons, let alone another escaped slave. That could easily be me.*

Coming to a decision, he whirled around and raced after the demons. It wasn't until he had vanished around the bend that he realized he needed some sort of plan for when he caught up with the demons. He couldn't take on all four on his own, and who knew if the other Fire-Wolf was in any condition to fight?

Maybe River's following me...then she could help... He immediately banished the thought. *No, I can't rely on her all the time.*

Before he could lose confidence, he pushed himself to run faster. He quickly came upon the demons and their prey.

The Fire-Wolf was backed against a cliff with the four demons cornering her. She crouched low to the ground, snarling, but Hawk could see the fear in her yellow eyes.

"You thought you could run from us, eh?" the Fire-Fang snarled. "Stupid rat, you belong to *us*. There is no escape."

The Fire-Wolf said nothing, and instead tried to press herself closer against the wall, as though hoping the stone would swallow her and hide her from the demons.

Before any of them could do anything, however, Hawk leaped down onto the Fire-Fang, taking them all by surprise. They rolled dangerously close to the edge before he was able to kick the Fire-Fang away. The Hell-Cats, overcoming their moment of surprise, quickly jumped to attack this new threat.

Suddenly Hawk found himself confronted with all four demons at once, and he realized he was in trouble.

As if his thoughts had summoned her, River appeared and slammed into the nearest Hell-Cat, causing it to knock over its fellows. The Fire-Fang, lithe and agile, jumped away to avoid the tangle of limbs. It snarled when it saw her wave mark. "These are the two who attacked the Nocte Fortress! The Overlord will greatly reward their killers. You three get the Water-Wolf, *I'll* get the Fire-Wolf."

Hawk gulped, and tried not to look too scared. *You got yourself into this mess, there's no backing out now!* He was on his own, as River was occupied with the three Hell-Cats, which, despite their stupidity, were putting up a good fight.

With a snarl, Hawk threw himself onto the Fire-Fang and sank his teeth into the demon's shoulder. It whirled so fast Hawk was knocked flying. He fell to the ground, too stunned to avoid the Fire-Fang's bite to his leg. Hawk yelped and squirmed away from the demon, digging his claws into the Fire-Fang's face to loosen its grip on his limb.

Suddenly both Hawk and the Fire-Fang were swept off their paws in a wide deluge of water. The three Hell-Cats were pushed off the edge of the cliff, taking the Fire-Fang with it. Hawk nearly fell with them, but was saved when River sank her fangs into his scruff and dragged him back to solid land. He looked up to thank her, and stopped. Her brow was furrowed in concentration, and her eyes seemed too dark. Then she shook her head and pulled him the rest of the way. Hawk, suddenly remembering why he had been insane enough to attack the small patrol, turned just in time to see the pink Fire-Wolf barrel into him. His breath rushed out of his lungs as he was knocked to the ground and covered in enthusiastic licks.

"Oh, thankyouthankyouthankyou!" the Fire-Wolf said, her yellow eyes glowing. "I thought I was going to die!"

"Uh…" Hawk said a little stupidly, not quite understanding what was going on. He flicked his eyes over to River and saw her bare her teeth a little.

"I…I didn't do that; it was River…" he started to say, but the she-wolf didn't appear to hear him.

"Great Sun-Wolf, I'm so sorry. Did I surprise you? I was just so happy at being saved, that I acted without thinking," she said, jumping back. "I hope I didn't hurt you…that'd be bad."

Hawk scrambled to his feet and backed away several paces, warily eyeing the strange she-wolf. She was a typical Fire-Wolf: large ears, lean body, short fur, and long legs, but built a little more heavily than Fire-Wolves usually were.

"Um…what's your name?" Hawk asked, for lack of anything better to say. River had yet to say anything, and it looked like she was having some internal battle.

"Oh, I'm Flame. Who are you?"

"Hawk."

"Sun-Wolf, you're Hawk?" Flame's yellow eyes widened. "As in *the* Hawk?"

"Uh…" Hawk blinked, unable to form a coherent sentence. This Fire-Wolf's character had him completely confused. Maybe it was because he had spent the past two months around more introverted wolves, but he had no idea how to react to Flame's exuberance.

"That's so amazing! I've heard *so* much about you!"

Before Flame could continue, River cut in. "Shut up, your voice is annoying," she snapped. "Hawk, we're leaving."

Feeling a little bad that he was relieved to be getting away from the excitable Fire-Wolf, Hawk turned and silently followed River, wagging his tail in farewell. Flame stood, her head cocked a bit, and watched them go.

Chapter Eighty-Six

"Soooo…where are we going?" Flame asked for the umpteenth time.

Hawk tried not to groan and glanced over at River, who tensed. She was obviously trying very, *very* hard not to push Flame over the cliff. It had only taken a few minutes before Flame found them again, and she had immediately glued herself to Hawk's side. No amount of threats from River frightened the pink wolf. Flame acted as though she couldn't hear the Water-Wolf half the time, an action that Hawk could tell was quickly wearing away at River's patience.

"*You* are going to be dropped off with the first creature we see, demon or otherwise," River snarled. "Although at this point I'd pity whoever we encounter. Not even *Letorus* deserves this punishment."

"Are we going to the Scaineadó Desert?" Flame asked, completely ignoring River and directing her question to Hawk. "I can feel the desert pulling us that way."

"Uh…" Hawk said, looking over at River, who was struggling not to send their unwanted companion flying. "Yes we are."

"Why? Why is a *Water-Wolf* going to the home of fire?"

"None of your business!" River snapped before Hawk could say anything. She shot Hawk a look that clearly said '*say one word and I'll tear out your throat.*'

"So, were you a slave?" Hawk asked instead, wanting to avoid River's wrath and distract Flame from the subject of their destination.

"I *was*," Flame said airily, "but then I escaped. My dad was a slave, but he escaped. Oh, I wasn't *born* a slave. The demons caught me a few days ago and put the collar on me. I was a resistance fighter before, but…the group's all dead now."

"As *touching* as that is," River said, her words dripping with sarcasm, "the last thing I need is *another* escaped slave drawing every demon for miles around. Now go away."

Hawk lowered his ears, a little hurt at that, because it sounded like River was implying that he was a burden, but then he noticed something on Flame's collar that made him forget River's barbed statement.

Melded into the smooth metal of the slave collar was an oval silver stone that glowed faintly.

"Flame, is that a slave-stone?"

"Hm? Oh yeah, I had forgotten about that!" Flame exclaimed.

"No wonder her group is all dead," she muttered. "Loud enough?"

"You *forgot*?" Hawk was much more careful in keeping his voice down.

"Huh, I guess that's why I couldn't summon fire before."

She seemed entirely unconcerned about it, leaving Hawk very confused, and continued to chatter about numerous other random things, until finally River snapped. "Shut up!" she roared, spinning around to face Flame, her hackles raised. "Can you stop talking for even a *second*? You have done *nothing* but prattle on and on, and you *refuse* to leave even after I've *threatened* to disembowel you."

Flame drew back slightly, startled by River's outburst. Hawk moved to try and soothe River and stop the argument before it got out of paw, but Flame had already recovered and bared her fangs at River. "*Excuse me* for actually being *cheerful*. Not everyone has to be an emotionless lump *like you*. I can go where I please, and *you* have no say."

With a snarl, River threw herself on Flame, knocking her to the ground. Hawk stared in shock as the two she-wolves rolled, snapping at each other's necks and digging their claws into each other's fur. River had the distinct advantage of being able to use her element, but Flame was lithe and strong and could avoid the water.

"*You're* just jealous!"

"How could I be *jealous* of such an annoying voice? I bet your precious resistance group *deserted* you to spare themselves the torment of being around *you*!"

"Stop!" Hawk shouted, the mountainside shaking a little at the force of his voice. He quickly shot a look up to make sure he didn't start a rockslide before looking back at the two she-wolves, who had both frozen. Flame's eyes were wide with shock.

"River, that was just cruel," he said, a lot more calmly than he felt. He wasn't sure if the she-wolves would appreciate having him interrupt their fight. "Flame—"

Hawk got no further. With a snarl, River pushed Flame away and glared at him. "Fine," she said before turning and racing away.

"River, wait!" Hawk darted after her, but stopped and glanced back at Flame. She had crouched low to the ground, her eyes dim with grief. River's poisoned insult had hurt her deeply. He wavered, torn between wanting to go after River and not wanting to leave Flame alone.

And from the sounds of the hunting calls in the distance, demons had overheard their fight and were heading their way. Flame was in no condition to fight.

With a sigh, Hawk padded over to the other Fire-Wolf and nudged her. "Flame, come on, we need to get moving," he said. "River didn't mean what she said; she's just tired and a little…out of sorts." When she made no move to stand, Hawk gave her another nudge and begged, "Please, demons are coming; we've got to get out of here."

Finally, after what seemed like ages to Hawk, Flame slowly stood. He quickly led her down the path, keeping an ear out for demons, all the while trying to find a place to hide. He didn't know how many demons were coming and had no desire to face them.

Chapter Eighty-Seven

NEARLY TWO HOURS had gone by before the danger had passed and Hawk risked venturing out into the open. Despite Flame's protests, he had to find River. They still had to get to Scaineadó.

River can help me break the slave stone off of Flame's collar, and then she'll be all right on her own, Hawk thought, struggling to follow River's faint scent, Flame following close behind. *Then we can continue on to the desert.*

But either River was very lost or she was trying to keep him from finding her. Her trail was extremely difficult to follow, as it took them on a winding path through the mountains, often doubling back on or crossing over itself.

River, where are you? He sniffed at the ground, trying to decipher the mess of scents his wayward friend had left behind. She had come back to this spot three times, and the trails were beginning to get muddled.

"Hawk!"

Flame's screech startled Hawk out of his intense focus, but before he could react, something large landed on top of him, forcing him to the ground.

"You were foolish to think you could defeat me," the Fire-Fang snarled, diggings its long claws into Hawk's pelt. Hawk whimpered a bit with pain, and struggled to throw the demon from his back. He heard Flame behind him struggling against the demons pinning her to the ground.

"And we can't forget about your Water-Wolf friend, either," it continued, mocking Hawk's helplessness. "We'll find her, too, and tear her limb from limb."

Despite the fear that set Hawk's heart beating faster than a desert hare, Hawk growled in defiance, "You'd have to avoid getting torn apart yourself."

The Fire-Fang laughed. "No matter how strong you think you are, little Fire-Wolf, it will be useless against what we have for you." It looked up at the demons holding Flame behind Hawk. "Take the female, we've got special plans for her."

Before Hawk could try to break free of the demon's grip, the Fire-Fang sank its teeth into Hawk's ruff and slammed him into the rocks. As the world faded around him, Hawk heard the Fire-Fang's taunt. "Sleep while you can, fire-rat, I can't wait to see the despair when you face what we have planned."

And then everything went black.

CHAPTER EIGHTY-EIGHT

WHEN HAWK AWOKE, the first thing he heard was River shouting in his ear.

"If you don't wake up *right now*, I will *throw* you off the edge of this *cliff*, Moon-Wolf help me!"

Hawk blinked, trying to clear his vision, before suddenly remembering what had happened. He jumped to his paws, swaying a little when his head throbbed.

"What h-happened? Where's F-flame? How l-long was I o-out?" Hawk asked in a shaky voice, struggling to stay conscious as the pain in his head increased.

"I don't know, I don't know, and *I don't know*. I was on my way to the desert when…I came across you about five minutes ago." Her eyes narrowed. "What happened to that she-wolf?"

"The demons came back; somehow that Fire-Fang survived," Hawk said, the memories slowly coming back to him. "They took Flame!"

"But they left you? Why would they take her and leave you?"

"I…I don't know." A sickening feeling settled in the pit of his stomach. *Why would they take just her, especially when they know about my involvement with the attack on Nocte?*

"Did the Fire-Fang say anything before taking her?"

Hawk nodded. "It said something about having 'special plans' for Flame… and that it couldn't wait to see my despair when I saw what they were going to do."

River was silent for several moments, before her expression suddenly darkened and she turned away. "Hawk, we're leaving."

Hawk simply stood and stared at the she-wolf in shock. Then he shook his head. "No. I'm going to find Flame and save her."

River stopped but didn't turn around. For several long seconds there was silence.

"I can't leave her to become a slave again," Hawk pleaded. *This might just be a trap for us, but I have to do something to help.* "No one deserves that existence. I know you don't like her, but please help me save her. I can't do it alone."

The silence continued, until Hawk was sure that she was going to refuse. He didn't know what he was going to do if she said no. *I can't do this on my own…*

"Fine. But when we find her, let *me* handle it, all right?"

Hawk blinked, confused and surprised by her answer. She growled a little and shot him an icy glare. "Don't just stand there with your mouth open, get tracking!"

He immediately shut his jaw and started sniffing. When he had caught a whiff of Flame's scent mixed with the scent of the demons that had captured her, he ran after it, River quickly following him.

Sun-Wolf let us find her in time. Hawk hoped the demons hadn't done something terrible. He hoped they weren't about to run straight into a trap. He couldn't shake the uneasy feeling that something wasn't right with the situation.

The grim look on River's face didn't dissuade his feelings at all.

Chapter Eighty-Nine

IT TOOK HAWK ten minutes to track down Flame. Ten minutes of running up and down mountains, narrowly avoiding several patrols, all the while praying to both wolf deities that Flame was still alive and had not yet been taken into a fortress.

What he was not expecting was to see her standing at the base of a cliff, waiting for them.

Shocked, he stopped, blinking for a few seconds, trying to confirm that what he was seeing was actually real. Beside him, River also stopped. Then relief flooded through Hawk, and he raced down the path to meet Flame.

"Hawk, stop!" River roared, and summoned a great wave of water to knock him aside, slamming the Fire-Wolf into the cliff face. Her quick action just barely saved him from Flame's attack.

His breath knocked out of him, Hawk struggled to stand, water dripping from his bright orange fur. Not quite sure of what had just happened, he looked between Flame and River. The she-wolves were already slowly circling each other and snarling.

"What...what's going on?"

"Use your head, Hawk," River growled. "That's not Flame anymore."

"Of course I'm Flame. Who else could I be?" the pink she-wolf answered smoothly, but there was something wrong with her voice. It had a strange quality to it, almost as if she were speaking underwater or there were multiple voices saying the same thing at slightly different times.

Hawk's heart plummeted to his paws.

Dark, sickly yellow in color, with slits for pupils, Flame now had the eyes of a demon.

"What?" he said again in a strangled voice.

"She's a half-demon, Hawk," River answered, keeping her eyes on the other she-wolf, who had yet to make a move. Each combatant watched the other carefully.

"Wh-what?" Hawk said, not wanting to believe it, hoping his eyes were deceiving him. But the cold aura of fear materializing around Flame, and the way her fur slowly darkened, told Hawk they were not.

"Sleep while you can, fire-rat, I can't wait to see the despair when you face what we have planned."

The Fire-Fang's words echoed in Hawk's mind again, and he suddenly knew that this is what it had been talking about.

"This is why I wanted us to leave," River growled. "The only reason they would take her and leave you behind is if they were planning on turning her."

"Too true," Flame said, her jaws parted in a feral grin. "The Fire-Wolf would have only gotten in the way of the blood-awakening ritual, and we didn't want to risk him interrupting it."

River moved to stand in front of Hawk, her head lowered and her fangs bared in a vicious snarl. "Why did you run before, when we first found you? If you were so eager to be awakened you shouldn't have tried escaping."

"My mother sent the Fire-Fang and its patrol to find me, as I was the only one who managed to escape when she turned on us. Of course, I was too stupid at the time to realize it was her, all I knew was that a Darkclaw was attacking and both my parents were gone." Flame chuckled, her fur darkening until it was nearly black. Her eyes lightened into pools of white. Hawk noticed that the slave collar was gone from her neck, and even the small scars that marked her fur had disappeared. "The Fire-Fang collared me to keep me under its claw, but in my ignorance I escaped again. I was very fortunate that they found me, otherwise I would still be a bubble-headed Fire-Wolf."

"You're disgusting," River spat, her eyes narrowed. "You can't even be considered part wolf anymore; you're lower even than the scum of the earth."

Flame snorted. "How are you any different from me, *Water-Wolf*? You, *daughter of the Water Queen*, who spent the past century living under the claws of the demons, trembling in fear. How could anyone who spent so much time in the home of the demons, still be fully wolf herself?"

River threw herself onto Flame the moment the words 'daughter of the Water Queen' passed her fangs. But the former Fire-wolf easily dodged her wild charge.

River suddenly twisted in midair and raked her claws down Flame's side.

I have to do something. I can't let River fight on her own. He crouched, watching for an opening. *Just wait for the right moment to jump in, then I can…do what?* He hesitated for a split second. *River's fighting to kill, but what if there's a way we can turn Flame back to how she was before?*

River kicked Flame into the side of the cliff, winding the other she-wolf for a moment. Hawk saw his chance and went to pounce, but a growl from River stopped him.

"Don't interfere, this is *my* fight."

An icy glare silenced Hawk's protests. When he hesitated, River growled again. "Let me do this alone."

A blast of black fire knocked River off her paws. Flame, taking advantage of River's distraction, lunged for her opponent. River rolled into the snow behind her, dousing her burning coat, and battered Flame with her hindpaws.

"This is my fight, Hawk!" River snarled when Hawk jumped forward to help. She flung a whip of water at Flame, knocking the other she-wolf to the ground, and dove for her throat. Hawk scrambled back to avoid the rolling fighters.

Why won't River let me help her? Why is she so determined to fight Flame on her own?

Hawk could do nothing but stare in shock as the two she-wolves tore at each other. It was much more vicious than their previous fight had been. River fought with a focused, almost desperate determination, much different from her usual reckless rampage.

It's almost as if she's trying to prove something, but what?

Flame howled in pain as River tore her ear from her head and then sank her curved fangs into the smaller wolf's shoulder. River twisted, barely avoiding a deep gash but coming away with several shallow cuts and shoved the other she-wolf away from her. A wave of water rushed past River and crashed into Flame, knocking her off balance. River immediately took advantage of this opening and dragged her claws through Flame's pelt.

Then Flame stepped back into the shadow of the cliff — and vanished.

"Look at you, acting so brave," came Flame's distorted voice from behind River. The Water-Wolf was caught by surprise when Flame dove at her, rising from her own shadow, black flames streaming before the former Fire-Wolf. "Trying to make up for your family's mistake?"

"Shut up," River snarled and launched herself at Flame, aiming to sink her fangs into the other she-wolf's throat. Flame lithely avoided the attack, seeming unhampered by the numerous deep gashes marking her pelt. Both she-wolves were heavily wounded, blood pouring down their sides, eyes alight with bloodlust.

"But it's true, isn't it? As your family spiraled into hell, where were you? Hiding like a puppy, afraid of defying your mother."

"Shut up!" River roared, all of her prior focus lost. She leaped right into Flame's open jaws, water coiled like snakes ready to strike. The two she-wolves clashed again, snapping at each other's necks. River was pushed back, snarling.

Suddenly she stumbled, and Flame, seeing an opening, dove for her throat. Just before her fangs sank into River's flesh, River spun around and sank her *own* fangs into Flame's throat. Taken by surprise, the former Fire-Wolf had no way of avoiding the attack.

With a shake of her head, River flung Flame against the rocks and sent wave after wave of water to keep her pinned to the ground. The deluge prevented the former Fire-Wolf from summoning any fire.

Flame was drowning, unable to reach the air, in the bubble of water surrounding her. For the first time since the battle began, Hawk saw Flame's eyes show fear. They looked, for a second, almost like normal wolf eyes.

"R-river," Hawk said in a shaky voice as River stalked up to Flame, who now lay broken on the ground after the barrage of water had ceased, ready to deliver the final blow. It sickened Hawk to think of what the demons had done to Flame, of what she would have done to him and River, but he didn't want to see her die.

River paused, her teeth bared and poised to strike.

"Don't kill her," Hawk continued, stepping a little closer. "Th-there might be a way to save her."

River looked at Hawk with cold, empty eyes. "Monsters like her do not deserve to live. Death is the only salvation for her." And then she bit into Flame's throat, instantly killing Flame.

Hawk flinched and looked away.

"Once a wolf has turned, there is no turning back," River said quietly, limping past Hawk.

He was still for a moment, unable to look away from Flame's body. Even in death, she resembled the demon she shared blood with more than a Fire-Wolf. Hawk hesitated, before padding toward her. *It's not night, I can't give her a proper burning, and she's been turned into a demon, so it might not work, but it doesn't hurt to try, right?* Hawk thought as he approached Flame's body. If either Sun-Wolf or Moon-Wolf heard, they were silent.

He sat in front of the broken body and tipped his head back in a quiet howl, his voice echoing off the cliffs. "Fallen Flame, may the fires forever burn with your spirit and the sands whisper with your name. May your sins be forgotten, and your spirit made pure, so that you may join your ancestors. Those you leave behind will retain your memory for all time."

It was different than the usual Song of Passing, but Hawk felt it fit the circumstances better. For a few seconds, nothing happened, and Hawk was just about to give up hope when Flame's body began to glow with reddish light. Her fur lightened to its former pink, and her wounds closed. The blood was cleaned from her pelt, until it looked as if she were merely sleeping. Then the light grew brighter, until Hawk had to close his eyes for fear of being blinded.

As the light faded, Hawk heard Flame's voice whisper in his mind. *"Thank you, Hawk. I am returned."*

When he opened his eyes again, Flame's body was gone. Hawk stood for a few seconds in shocked silence, until he realized that the demons that had taken Flame were probably still around, and that they would have heard his howls. Quickly he turned and raced up the path, to find River waiting for him just around the bend.

They travelled in silence until River found a small cave hidden beneath a thick covering of lichen. Hawk was surprised to see that most of her wounds had already been partially healed, although she still limped a little, and he wondered if she had cast Cneasaithe on herself.

"River, how did Flame know that you were the daughter of a Queen?" Hawk asked when they had settled down to sleep.

She hesitated before answering. "I don't know."

Hawk narrowed his eyes slightly and watched her. He had a feeling that River was lying, but she had already curled up and fallen asleep.

CHAPTER NINETY

THREE WEEKS LATER, Hawk, *felt* the desert before he saw it. It pulled on his subconscious, pointing him in the right direction and lending speed to his paws. Pulling ahead of River, Hawk practically flew down the last mountain like the bird that was his namesake, screeching to a stop just before he crossed the border.

Stretching in front of him, starting suddenly where the mountains ended, was the Scaineadó Desert.

River stopped beside him, and they both looked out over the wide expanse of dark-red sand. In the distance, the tips of volcanoes broke the horizon. Intense heat rose from the land of the Fire-Wolves, in stark contrast to the cool mountain climate of Gaoibeanna.

Hawk hesitated in crossing over into the desert. The last time he had been here, he had been fleeing for his life, escaping slavery. He had no idea how close he was to Ignimor Fortress, and had no desire to find out.

Taking a deep breath, Hawk took the first tentative steps onto the hot sand. Immediately a sort of peace descended upon him. He may not have been as affected as other wolves had been, travelling through the different nations, but nothing compared to the feeling of standing in his own territory. The soft, yet burning sand beneath his paws was comforting after the harsh stone of the mountains and the cold snow he had so often fought against. The shimmering heat from the sun warmed his pelt.

Despite the dangers he knew he was going to face, Hawk couldn't help feeling that he had finally returned home.

"We made it, River!" he exclaimed, jumping around in the sand and scattering it all over. "We made it to the Scaineadó Desert!"

"Yes, I can see that. It's a little hard to miss the *sand*," River said, stepping across the border and immediately stumbling. Hawk stopped and sent her a concerned look at the intense discomfort that crossed her face, but her expression quickly cleared and she straightened. "I certainly hope you can lead us around the volcanoes, because I have no intention of getting fried."

"Okay!" Hawk dove into the sand and rolled, relishing in the feel of it running through his fur. He jumped to his paws and bounced after River when she padded past him, obviously having no intention on stopping for long. He took a long breath of the hot desert air, unable to contain his excitement.

I'm home.

HAWK'S EXCITEMENT didn't wear off even after they had been walking under the hot sun for hours. He was so distracted by simply *being* in his homeland, feeling the sand beneath his paws, and seeing the volcanoes belch their fire in the distance, that he didn't notice River's deteriorating condition until she collapsed.

When he heard the *thump* behind him, Hawk spun around, thinking that a demon had somehow managed to sneak up on them. His eyes widened in shock when he saw his companion lying sprawled out on the sand.

"River!" he cried, immediately jumping to her side. He prodded her shoulder with his nose, but she gave no response. Hawk whimpered and tried licking her face to wake her up, but to no avail.

What am I going to do? Why did she collapse? Why won't she wake up? A dozen different questions raced through his mind, making him panic.

"No…calm down," Hawk sat down on the hot sand. "First…let's find some shade…yeah, that sounds good. She's probably just heat sick. I mean, it's cold everywhere else, because it's still early spring…so she's just not used to the heat, and she has really thick fur. That has to be why she collapsed."

He was talking out loud, more to comfort himself than anything. *Maybe I can find an oasis…* Hawk shook his head. *No, an oasis would be bad. Demon fortresses are always built around oases. But I need* something *that will give us a little shade.* His heart soared when he spotted the peak of a small rocky hill on the other side of the dune. Gently taking River's scruff in his mouth, Hawk started to drag her across the sand, intent on reaching the hill.

It took him several minutes, but Hawk finally managed to reach the hill. The sides were made of smooth black glass, but there were enough rough rocks and shards of glass to create a small shelter. It was enough to keep River out of the sun.

This must have been a volcano, or at least part of one, Hawk thought, looking up at the hill after laying River beneath the glassy rocks. *Only volcanoes can create this kind of glass. But I don't sense any fire in it now, so it's probably sleeping. It'll be safe to leave River here. For now, I have to find water.* As a Water-Wolf, even a splash on the muzzle would probably do her a world of good. He couldn't go to an oasis, and he didn't know how to break open a cactus without spiking himself, so Hawk knew that he had to find a small river. Leaving River unconscious and undefended made him a little worried; she would be helpless if demons found her. His only hope was that the stories the slaves of Ignimor had told him were true and demons really did avoid dormant volcanoes because they couldn't sense the fire.

"I'll be back, River," Hawk said, looking down at her and trying to sound brave, even though he knew she couldn't hear him. "I'll find you some water. I promise."

Before he could talk himself out of it, he turned and padded away from the small shelter and out into the bright desert sun.

↶

HAWK HAD NO idea where to look for water.

Despite having spent most of his life in the desert, Hawk had always been contained behind the high stone walls of Ignimor Fortress. He had never been outside before his escape, and didn't know where to find a river or even a small creek. And even though he had come across a few rivers during his flight from Ignimor, he didn't know where he was in relation to the Fortress and therefore would be unable to find them again.

He spent a few hours wandering around, searching in vain for some sort of liquid. He had just about given up and was going to attempt to break open a cactus when he heard the sounds of several demons approaching. Quickly, he looked around for a place to hide, but the only thing he saw was a small pile of rocks.

And with my fur, I'll never— He cut himself off, realizing that his orange pelt, while completely out of place in the forest or the mountains, blended in perfectly with the desert sands. Wagging his tail with triumph, he raced over to the pile of rocks and crouched beside them, carefully stilling his body until he was as motionless as the stones themselves.

A few Fire-Fangs appeared, squabbling with each other and barking in the language of the demons. Hawk forced himself to remain still, not daring to even breathe for fear of being heard. The demons pounced on each other, fighting playfully as they passed, and Hawk was shocked to see that they looked almost normal. They were acting like littermates, not the blood-thirsty monsters he knew them to be.

But that would have changed in an instant had they seen me, Hawk thought with a sigh of relief as the Fire-Fangs continued on their way without noticing him. They would be the demons to watch out for, because, like the Fire-Wolves, they, too, blended in with the sand.

Hawk went over all he could remember of the desert. *Oases mean fortresses, volcanoes are dangerous to be near, and mirages are hard to recognize. The oases and volcanoes are easy enough to avoid… it's the mirages I'll have to watch for. The last time I was here I nearly walked right into a puddle of lava because of them.*

Hawk glanced up at the sky and bit his lip. The sun was setting, and soon it would be dark. He would have to head back to River soon. While travelling at night would be smart to avoid the desert heat, it was also the time when most of the demons in the Scaineadó Desert awoke and patrolled. Travelling during the day was safer, as the only demons they risked encountering were ferals.

Maybe River will feel better when the moons rise and it gets cooler, Hawk thought as he sniffed around, hoping to catch the slight scent of water. Sighing, he continued his search for the precious liquid, deciding that if he didn't find anything over the next dune, he'd go back to where he had left River.

CHAPTER NINETY-ONE

COLD WATER HIT River's face, and she was up in an instant, her head spinning and her vision blurry. Instinctively she bared her fangs and raised her hackles, and although she swayed a little on her paws she still looked ferocious enough to make any would-be attacker pause.

"Easy, Water-Wolf," a voice said. "We're not going to harm you. Can you remember your name?"

River shook her head to clear it before answering, but the action just made her dizzy. "River. Where…am I? Where's Hawk?"

"You may want to lie down again," a bright yellow Fire-Wolf said, slowly coming in to focus. "You've been out at least all night."

"Where's Hawk?" River demanded again, refusing to admit to weakness by lying down.

The yellow wolf gave her a confused look. "Who?"

River's stomach dropped. "There was a Fire-Wolf with me. Where is he?"

"There was no one else when we found you."

River swore. The last thing she remembered was hearing Hawk saying something about the way the eagles were flying in the sky…or other such nonsense… before everything went black. She had no idea what happened after that.

Was Hawk captured…or killed?

She glanced around, trying to get her bearings. She stood in a large cave on the banks of a shallow river. The water flowed into the cave, covering about half of the rocky floor. A few feet from River lay an elderly Wind-Wolf, his black fur so heavily streaked with gray that he appeared almost white. An Earth-Wolf male sat near the edge of the water, apparently to keep watch. Another Earth-Wolf, a female, sat away from the other two, and studied River very closely.

"I'm leaving," River stated simply and started to shakily make her way toward the entrance to the cave, cursing the fact that she couldn't walk in a straight line.

The Earth-Wolf female stopped River only halfway across. She had ragged dark brown fur and a bright green Earth-Wolf mark on her left shoulder. A long, jagged scar split the fur on her head. Her pale green eyes had a strange look to them, as if they couldn't focus properly. It made River uncomfortable to hold her gaze for too long, as the other she-wolf's eyes were far too similar to River's mother's eyes.

"You're not going anywhere, girlie," the Earth-Wolf said, an odd, clipped quality in her voice. Despite her unusually small size, River sensed that the she-wolf was stronger than she looked. "A Water-Wolf wandering around the *fire* desert during the hottest part of the day is just *asking* for death."

"What I do is of no concern to you," River growled, and made to brush by the dark brown Earth-Wolf, when she suddenly found herself unable to move. Her paws had sunk into the stone floor and where held fast by earth.

"Don't get your fur in a bundle. Just listen, will ya?" the Earth-Wolf said when River immediately started to summon the water from the small creek in front of the cave. "I've already got two Fire-Wolves tracking down whoever it was that dragged you to the rock outcropping we found you under."

River let the water flow back to its normal course. The other Earth-Wolf, who had jumped to his paws in case he needed to defend his leader, slowly relaxed as well. River glanced over at the Fire-Wolf, finding it interesting that he hadn't moved even when his leader was threatened. She turned her gaze back to the small Earth-Wolf in front of her. Although River would never admit it, she knew she would have no chance of finding Hawk in the desert. She might as well wander around blind, for all the luck she would have.

"Now then, much better," the she-wolf said with a chuckle. "Sand and Lizard will find your friend…Hawk, you called him? Huh, stupid name for a Fire-Wolf. Now stay put."

Then she turned and marched away, muttering silently to herself. The other Earth-Wolf stepped forward to free River from the ground.

"So now I'm supposed to just sit and wait?" River complained, shooting cold glares at the dark brown she-wolf, who showed no sign of noticing them.

"That would be best," the Earth-Wolf male said. "You are in no condition to go looking for your friend."

"Lizard and Sand should be back soon," the Fire-Wolf added. "They'll find him."

River wanted to argue, but she was still feeling weak from her collapse and decided it wasn't worth the effort. But she couldn't resist throwing one last remark over her shoulder as she curled up in a corner.

"Fine. But if they're not back by the time I wake up, I'm leaving, heat or no heat."

CHAPTER NINETY-TWO

WHEN HAWK FINALLY gave up his search, the three moons were high in the sky. He was exhausted, and desperately hoped that River had woken up while he was gone.

But when he arrived back at the black mountain, River had vanished.

Racing down the dune, Hawk sniffed around the scuffed markings in the rocky sand. He smelled River, demons, and a few unknown wolves, but he couldn't tell how old the scents were. They were too muddled, making it impossible for Hawk even to trace separate trails. Blood was also splattered across the rocks, fortunately none of it River's.

"Okay, calm down. Maybe River woke up while I was gone and went to look for me," Hawk said, trying to stop himself from panicking. His heart beat so hard he was surprised it didn't burst out of his chest. "And then other wolves came here to rest, and were noticed by a patrol…or ferals…River may not have even encountered them."

He dreaded to think of what might have happened if the demons had caught the Water-Wolf while she was unconscious.

Shaking that sickening thought away, Hawk padded back out from under the overhang. *If she wandered off, then River's probably lost. I'll just sniff around for her scent, and track her from out here.*

Satisfied with his plan, Hawk padded around the sands surrounding the dormant volcano. He had just picked up River's scent when the soft noise of shifting sand reached his ears. He spun around to see a Hell-Cat slipping down the slope. For a moment, neither he nor the creature moved.

Then the Hell-Cat tipped its head back and yowled.

Hawk was shocked into action. The moment the hunting call passed the Hell-Cat's fangs, Hawk turned and fled. Five more yowls answered the first, spurring him on to greater speeds. He flicked his ears back, his heart skipping several beats upon hearing the patrol steadily draw closer.

"An orange Fire-Wolf, he might be the rebel leader!" one of them, a Fire-Fang it sounded like, roared. Hawk's heart sank to his paws. *They recognize me.*

"Don't kill him," the smooth voice of a Shade-Tiger said. "Break his legs if you must, but leave them attached."

Hearing that only made Hawk run faster.

He practically flew over the loose sands, his body naturally adapting to the desert environment. But the demons, which had probably been living in the desert for some time and had been doing more running around on the sands than Hawk ever had, were just as fast.

Hawk risked a look back to see how close his pursuers were and instantly regretted it. With his attention elsewhere, he didn't notice the sudden drop in front of him. With a shocked cry, he fell down the slope. Sand poured into his ears and mouth. He landed awkwardly and heard a loud *crack*, followed by searing pain in his right paw.

Ignoring the pain, knowing that he would face much worse if he were caught, Hawk shook himself and tried to stand, only to fall once more. Looking down, he saw that his paw was bent at an unnatural angle, and the sight made him want to vomit.

Several thumps sounded, and Hawk looked up to see that the patrol had jumped down the slope, landing much more gracefully than he had. Within moments he was surrounded, and he crouched down, baring his fangs in what he hoped was a vicious snarl.

"Not looking where you were going, slave?" the Fire-Fang laughed, its dark red eyes alight with hunger as it summoned a Fire-Spirit. Three Hell-Cats, a Shade-Tiger, and a Night-Lynx accompanied it.

It was now seven on one, and Hawk was already wounded.

"Remember, keep him alive," the Shade-Tiger said. "As long as we take him back to Ignimor conscious, it doesn't matter how beat up he is."

Hawk's heart froze in his chest, and his blood ran cold. Time seemed to slow to a stop at the sound of that dreaded name.

Ignimor, the very same Fortress where Hawk had been held captive all his life.

With a yowl of hunger and rage, one of the Hell-Cats leapt onto Hawk. Instinctively he rolled and battered the demon with his hind claws, wincing when his broken paw made contact. Black spots appeared in his vision. As the other two Hell-Cats attacked, Hawk barked and let loose a wide ring of fire that sent the three demons flying into the sands.

But his respite was brief.

The moment the Hell-Cats were blasted back, the Fire-Fang and its summoned spirit jumped into the fray. Hawk's fire was useless against them. On the heels of this realization, an icy cold feeling gripped Hawk, and shook him with terror. The Shade-Tiger had unleashed its aura of fear. The shadows around Hawk, cast by the light of the three moons, came to life and raced toward him.

Bright light! I need a bright light! Hawk grasped onto what he knew to be a Shade-Tiger's only weakness. He lit his coat on fire, focusing all his power on making himself as bright as possible in the hopes that it would keep the demons at bay. Searing heat suddenly surged through him, the flames in his coat roaring as they exploded outward.

With a loud cry, the Shade-Tiger fell back, eyes made for night-vision blinded by the mini sun. The Night-Lynx suffered a similar fate. Both rapidly retreated until they crouched in the shadows of the dunes. The three Hell-Cats panicked as their fur was set aflame, and they yowled with pain and terror before disappearing over the dune behind them.

Only the Fire-Fang and the Fire-Spirit were unharmed. The red-scaled demon barked an order, and the Fire-Spirit jumped forward and latched onto Hawk's leg. He was nearly knocked unconscious when the Fire-Spirit's teeth closed around his broken paw and lost his concentration in his struggle to stay awake.

The two nocturnal demons ran forward once more when the bright light impeding them vanished. The Shade-Tiger spat dark orbs of shadow, which burst into sticky strings of darkness that slowed Hawk's movements. The Night-Lynx was already starting to weave its spell, striving to draw Hawk into its line of vision. The two fire demons intercepted most of Hawk's attacks of fire, protecting the other two. The Hell-Cats were nowhere to be seen.

I can't let them take me; I can't let them take me! He knew what awaited him upon recapture, especially at the very Fortress from which he had escaped. He would rather die a hundred deaths than return there. *I have to fight!*

Hawk fought like a demon himself, with a ferocity that would have made River proud, driven on by a sheer, mind-numbing terror that was increased by the Shade-Tiger's aura. He had no coherent thoughts. He fought on pure instincts, simply reacting when one of the demons attacked.

At first, Hawk started to gain the upper-paw. Surprised by his ferocity, the demons were knocked back by the sheer power of his attacks. Then they regrouped and pushed him back. The tables turned further when the Hell-Cats returned, their fur scorched and smoldering.

Hawk heard a noise behind him, and spun around to avoid whatever attack was coming, only to meet eyes with the Night-Lynx. Everything else faded around him, until all he saw were those wide, hypnotizing white eyes.

"*Sleep,*" the Night-Lynx's voice sounded in his mind.

Chapter Ninety-Three

RAY WATCHED THE strange Water-Wolf out of the corner of his eyes. Although River appeared to be sleeping, the way her ears twitched at every slight sound said otherwise. Ray didn't want to get caught openly staring.

He just couldn't believe he was seeing the very subject of the rumors they heard from both wolves and demons.

I didn't think they were anything more than rumors. The Water-Wolves died out over a century ago. How can she be here?

"Ray, scoot over; you're too close," Storm growled without opening his eyes. "You're radiating heat like a volcano."

"I *am* a Fire-Wolf," Ray said, although he shuffled away from the elder. "You could be a bit more grateful to your caretaker."

"I don't need a damn caretaker."

Ray sighed and rolled his eyes, before turning his thoughts back to the mysterious River.

If she's here, and she's with Hawk…I guess the rumors are true. A Water-Wolf has returned to free the island. But what does it mean for us?

A sickening feeling settled over Ray.

I just hope Spruce doesn't get any ideas to try and join them. It's bad enough that she wants to recreate an old legend by running around and attacking patrols, what if she decides she wants to help 'free the island'? He swallowed hard. *We might even end up attacking a fortress.*

He glanced over at Almond, who was once again keeping watch by the cave's entrance.

I don't think even Almond would be able to talk her out of such a hare-brained scheme. Lizard definitely won't be able to, even though he's her second-in-command. Ray snorted quietly to himself. *Not that that position means anything. Spruce just does what she wants and drags us after her.*

Maybe we should just leave…

For a split second, Ray actually considered escaping. He could take over keeping watch from Almond and sneak out while everyone else was resting. He could find his brother and Sand before they returned and convince them to turn around and run. They could be miles away by the time Spruce discovered them.

He dismissed the idea a moment later.

We could never escape Spruce for long, and I couldn't leave Storm like that. He would never be able to sneak out with me, and none of us would be able to survive on our own for long. How else did we get into this situation in the first place?

Ray sighed and closed his eyes.

One day Spruce is going to get us killed, but there's nothing we can do about it.

CHAPTER NINETY-FOUR

RIVER WAS FULLY awake the moment she heard someone splashing through the cave entrance. Judging by the way the light reflected on the water, it was close to sunrise. Two Fire-Wolves quickly made their way across the river, worry written across both their faces. River leapt to her feet and ran to meet them.

"Spruce!" one of the Fire-Wolves, a she-wolf with pale red fur and pink eyes, called as she approached the rebel leader. "We tracked the Fire-Wolf. He was taken by a patrol."

"What?" River roared, interrupting whatever Spruce was about to say. "*He was captured?*"

The reddish she-wolf looked nervously between Spruce and River, who glared at her, waiting for an explanation.

"Would you *shut up*," Spruce said irritably, "and let me question *my own wolf*? Sand, what happened?"

"When we went back to where we found the Water-Wolf, we ran into a few feral Fire-Fangs. Then we tracked the Fire-Wolf's scent away from the overhang. It appeared that he did a bit of wandering before returning. We found him just as he was being taken away by a patrol from Ignimor—"

"*What?*" River shouted, an unfamiliar feeling of fear gripping her. "We're near *Ignimor* Fortress?" *No, no, no…Ignimor is where he was enslaved…if they recognize him…if his former master is still there…* She refused to finish the thought.

"Yeah, is there a problem?" Spruce asked.

"Of course there's a problem! *Ignimor is where Hawk was enslaved!*"

"An escaped slave? How fun." The she-wolf's pale green eyes lit up. "Let's go rescue him!"

A shocked silence filled the cave, and even River was taken aback.

"Spruce…" the other Fire-Wolf, one with dark blue fur and red eyes, said slowly. River was stricken by his resemblance to Coal. "The Fire-Wolf has probably already been taken into the Fortress. I don't think we're strong enough to fight an entire fortress."

"'Course we are," Spruce replied and waved her tail at River. "Don't you know who *she* is? That's *River*. She and her buddy, Hawk, were the ones who led the attack on that demon fortress back in Taladair. *And they won.* I've also started hearing some rumors about similar exploits in Gaoibeanna."

"Yes, but they had more Earth-Wolves helping them in Taladair. We just have you and Almond. That won't be enough to tear down the walls."

"Are you challenging my authority, Lizard?" Spruce said, her voice suddenly ice-cold. Her eyes narrowed in suspicion. "Last I checked, *I* was leader. Unless you wish to fight me, you *will* obey me."

Lizard immediately crouched low to the floor and flattened his ears.

Spruce swept her cold, pale green gaze over every wolf in the room. "That goes for all of you. You *will* obey me until your dying breath. And even then, the only reason for you to be dying on me should be because *I told you to.* Is that understood?"

Mutely, they nodded. Spruce's jaws parted in a grin. "Good. Prepare for battle."

River watched the entire exchange in silence. The attitude of Spruce was a little disconcerting and eerily similar to how her mother was just before she was killed. She glanced around the cavern as the other wolves prepared to move out. Ray was helping the Wind-Wolf elder into a hidden crevice in the back, while Sand and Lizard busied themselves with erasing any trace of their presence. The Earth-Wolf Almond was arguing quietly with Spruce by the entrance.

For a moment, River wasn't standing in a cave in the middle of the desert. She was surrounded by her clan as they cowered before her mother, forced to do her bidding.

Is it really such a good idea to go along with this Spruce? River watched as the rebel leader snarled at Almond and stalked out of the cave. The other Earth-Wolf shared a quick glance with Lizard and gave a quick shake of his head. Lizard sighed and nodded before leading the others after Spruce. River silently followed.

I don't have much of a choice. I have *to save Hawk.*

CHAPTER NINETY-FIVE

HAWK FELT NOTHING other than an incessant aching throughout his whole body. His head throbbed from the Night-Lynx's nightmares, terrors that had come to life when he had been startled into wakefulness within the walls of the very Fortress he had escaped.

His torment had only continued upon regaining consciousness. Dozens of demons came forth to bully him, biting and clawing and throwing him around until he lay in a pool of his own blood. The slaves, forced to stand by and watch, looked on sadly.

Many of them recognized him.

By the time the demons had finally tired of Hawk, Hawk had given up all hope. Even if River hadn't been attacked by demons while she was unconscious, it was impossible for her to track him here. If she were awake, she was most likely wandering in circles, unable to track even her own scent.

I hope she can still make it into the Fáinéitin, he thought weakly, barely conscious. Even the simple act of breathing hurt. *I hope she doesn't get heat sick again, and that she can make it in time for the Eclipse.*

All semblance of thought fled from Hawk's mind and any little bit of feeling he had left deserted him when an icy voice spoke above his head. "Well, well, what do we have here? Seems you've been wandering a little too much lately, from what I've heard."

Cracking open a single red-orange eye, Hawk looked up in horror to see Lapsus, his former Ice-Fang master, glaring down at him with icy eyes full of hate.

Hawk wanted nothing more than to die right then and there.

CHAPTER NINETY-SIX

RIVER AND SPRUCE stood at the top of a dune, looking out at the imposing form of the Ignimor Fortress sitting in the sands. Its walls enclosed a large oasis, and there were little patches of green poking out from underneath the stone. River eyed the walls, trying to spot any sort of weakness they could exploit.

If we can break the gate open, we can get inside, she thought, eyeing the thick wooden gate. *We'll have to act fast if we want to break in and rouse the slaves before too many demons appear. We can't cast an* Amhríochta; *Spruce is in no state to use such a high-level spell, but even if she was, she and Almond would use up too much power to continue to fight, and I can't afford to lose two fighters.* She snorted to herself. *I almost wish Coal was here. He's the only other wolf I know who's gotten in and out of Ignimor alive.* River paused and glanced over at Lizard. *Unfortunately, physical resemblance is the only thing Lizard has in common with Coal.*

"All right, great Fortress-Breaker," Spruce said, getting River's attention. "What's your plan? You've done this thing before, so you should have something."

She glanced at the rebel leader out of the corner of her eye. "Think you and Almond can crack the gate open?"

"Of course we can."

"Good. If we open the gate the Fortress will have a hole in its defenses. We'll keep the demons off your back and stir the slaves to rebellion. But find a way to *keep* the gate open or we'll be trapped inside."

The three Fire-Wolves looked apprehensive at the idea of charging straight up to the Fortress walls themselves, but said nothing.

"We'll have to get in close in order to do maximum damage," Spruce reminded her.

"With a higher chance to harm the slaves inside."

"So? They will be honored as necessary sacrifices for the downfall of a hated fortress."

"If you kill Hawk, I will personally feed you to the Blood-Frenzies."

"If he's stupid enough to get himself killed, then he's not worth it."

River growled, but Spruce had already turned away. "Almond, come with me. We've got some sand to move."

"You three, let's go," River said. "We have to keep the demons distracted and away from them. Don't get killed, because the *real* battle won't start until we get inside the Fortress."

Then she turned and led the way down the dune, howling a challenge to the fortress, the Fire-Wolves scrambling after her. It took a few moments before the demons, obviously surprised by the sudden charge, raised the alarm. The gates cracked open to allow a patrol to race out, intent on destroying the wolves foolish enough to attack them.

Despite the nausea that had plagued her the moment she left the cave and its soothing water, River pushed her weakness away and threw herself completely into the battle, the four Fire-Wolves close on her heels. Somewhere behind them, Spruce and Almond were howling, and already the earth was shaking.

The dry air made it difficult for River to summon water, but she more than made up for the lack with sheer ferocity. Demons foolish enough to face her immediately turned tail and tried to flee, only to have their escape path blocked by the blood-crazed she-wolf.

A crack split open the sands just paces from River. She threw a demon into the crevice and jumped away to avoid falling in herself, sparing a moment to watch the crack disappear beneath the gate. A moment later the wood groaned as the crack widened, pulling the gate apart. River glanced back at Spruce and Almond, and saw them quickly making their way toward the Fortress, their howls fading away.

"Let's go!" River roared, sinking her fangs into a Hell-Cat's shoulder and tossing it into the crack. Then she ran toward the gates, which the demons were desperately trying to close. The stones above the gate were shifting and tumbling into the open earth below them, taking a few demons as they fell. River continued to howl her challenge to the Fortress, the rush of battle sweeping over her mind. Spruce appeared beside her a moment later, panting heavily.

"Too tired to continue, Spruce?" River challenged, a wild gleam in her eye and her mistrust of Spruce temporarily forgotten in the rush of battle.

The Earth-Wolf raised her head and tail proudly to meet the other she-wolf's gaze. "I'd like to see you try and keep up with me, River." Then she howled and charged for the broken gates, her resistance group racing after her. River snarled and followed as answering howls rose from the Fortress.

They were instantly swept up into the battle. Hundreds of fighters, wolf and demon alike, fought on the edges of the cracks that had torn through the hateful walls. Many lost their footing and fell. A few lucky slaves managed to break off their slave-stones and were battling with the elements as well as with tooth and claw.

Of Hawk there was nothing to be seen, but River was too taken with blood-lust to notice.

"River!"

River looked up to find Spruce standing at the edge of one of the cracks, her eyes wild with the light of battle.

"Bet I kill more demons than you!"

River just snarled. "I already have a head start!"

The Earth-Wolf tipped her head back and howled a battle cry before leaping across the gap. A slab of stone shot out from the wall of the crack, forming a platform halfway across where Spruce landed before she jumped to the other side. She landed right on top of a large Shade-Tiger, cackling madly, and threw it into the chasm behind her.

Pushing away a nagging feeling that she had actually come here to do something besides battle demons, River turned and sank her fangs into a Fire-Fang's throat, wincing a little when its red-hot scales burnt her mouth. She shook her head and tossed it into the crack, its screams echoing off the walls.

More and more demons were being thrown into the deep crevice created by Spruce and Almond. Several wolves also fell into the crevice, shaken off their paws by the tremors that still shook the earth. Slaves all over the Fortress were rising up, realizing that their masters' control was slipping. Powered by the small ray of hope that was shining on their pathetic existence, each slave fought with the power of ten wolves.

Find the leader…13…the Lord Mars of the…18…Fortress, River thought, her eyes raking through the masses for the ruler of the Fortress. *Then Ignimor will fall for good….ha! There goes 20…*

She paused, feeling a slight pull on the edges of her senses. She focused, reaching for the source of the pull.

Then she tipped her head back and howled in triumph.

There's an oasis here! I can feel the water running through the earth. She snarled, casting her power down into the fertile earth and calling up the spring below. She sent wave after wave to come crashing down on demons that fled before her fury. The few demons that managed to survive the deluge met her blood-stained fangs.

Time to find the master cowering within! River threw her last opponent aside, and looked up at the great wooden doors that led into the keep of the Fortress. With a howl and a rush of water, she knocked down the battered wood. Water flowed around her, pooling on the stone floor as she ran through the grand hallways. Most of the demons had been ordered outside to battle the threat facing the Fortress and quell the slave uprising, but River came across a few who were attempting to hide. They soon met their inevitable fate at the Water-Wolf's claws.

Several times she nearly crashed to the floor from the force of the earth shaking. The shakes were growing stronger and more frequent. Some distant part of River's mind wondered why they hadn't stopped, or even slowed. Spruce and Almond hadn't even cast a full Amhríochta.

Cold air hit River's face as she turned the final corner before the main hall of the Fortress. Sensing a demon close by, she slid down the icy hallway before bursting through the doors with a ball of water.

Then she froze in shock.

The main hall of Ignimor Fortress, where most of the day-to-day business was carried out, was covered in sheets of ice. Frozen water coated the walls and created layers of thick glass over the open windows. Cracks patterned the floor like a spider web, as though something had been thrown against the ice repeatedly. Standing only paces in front of her, as though trying to escape the room through the door River had just broken, with chunks of rock falling all around it, was the Ice-Fang Lapsus.

And behind it, encased in ice, was Hawk.

CHAPTER NINETY-SEVEN

BLIND FURY CONSUMED River, and she threw herself at the shocked demon. The ice cracked and melted around them. River sent the resulting wave crashing down on Lapsus, who yowled with pain.

The entire Fortress shook from a large tremor, sending both fighters crashing to the slippery floor.

Quickly recovering from its surprise, the Ice-Fang twisted away from River's next attack and summoned two Ice-Spirits. Then it refroze the water and sent thousands of tiny ice shards flying at her. The she-wolf raised a wave of water in front of her, melting the ice shards as they flew into it, and then dove through. She swerved to avoid getting crushed by a falling lump of stone, but redirected her momentum to tackle Lapsus. She was quickly pulled off by the Ice-Spirits, who froze her paws to the ground. Ice crept up her legs, making her wince as it bit into her skin.

I have to overpower it, she thought, cooling some water into a spear of ice and driving it into one of the Ice-Spirits. It split in half and fell to the ground. *Once I do that, I can take control of Lapsus's ice.*

She turned the spear on the other Ice-Spirit, but it was killed by falling masonry before she could follow through with her attack. All that was left to face River was the terrified Lapsus, its cold blue eyes flicking around for any escape route.

"Attacking me would be foolish," it growled. "My brothers are coming; they sense my distress. You will be overwhelmed."

"Let them come," River snarled, her navy-blue eyes alight with bloodlust. She could practically smell Lapsus' bluff. "I'll cut them down where they stand."

Then she pounced, her teeth bared. Lapsus rolled out of the way and sent daggers of ice flying at River, a mask for its own leap. River hissed in pain as the demon's fangs sank into her shoulder, but she quickly shook it off. She sent her power into the ice around her, struggling to overcome the Ice-Fang's hold over it, but felt the demon pressing back just as strongly on her mind.

The ground shook again. Lapsus's focus slipped for just a moment, but it was all the opening River needed. Her own magic flooded the ice as River knocked the Ice-Fang off its paws and pinned it to the floor with the very ice she had wrested from its control. She didn't loosen her grip even as the room started to crumble around them. Holding several bubbles of water threateningly over the demon, the she-wolf snarled, her eyes darkening and her voice lowering dangerously. "*What did you do to Hawk?*"

"He was an escaped slave," Lapsus babbled, terrified. "I was only punishing him. The other demons were the ones that hurt him and tormented him. I did nothing!"

When River bared her fangs, the demon corrected itself. "I *ordered* the torment! It was a lesson to the other slaves, and punishment for escaping." The Ice-Fang paused, its eyes lighting up with glee. "But you're too late. I froze his inner fire. The stupid Fire-Wolf will die for escaping me!" It started to laugh, but was abruptly cut off when River savagely sank her fangs into its throat and dropped the balls of water, the orbs turning into sharp slivers of ice that sliced through the demon's chest. The Ice-Fang melted before it could even cry out.

"That is *punishment* for angering me," River said coldly, the red mist of battle slowly fading from her sight. She splashed through the puddle left by the Ice-Fang's death and darted over to the block of ice encasing Hawk, ignoring the destruction of the room around her.

"Hawk!" she shouted, although she knew he couldn't possibly hear her. Even River had to wince when she saw the wounds that covered his body. Blood was frozen to his orange fur, his left ear was in tatters, and the left side of his face was a bloody mess. Deep cuts, made by demon claws, marked his sides, and River could tell that more than one limb had been broken.

Sudden fury filled her, and she flew at the ice in a rage, chipping away at it with her attacks. "Stupid Hawk!" she screeched. "Why did you have to go and get captured? Don't you *dare* die before *I* can kill you *myself*! Stupid... stupid...*Fire-Wolf!*"

Chunks of ice fell from the block, knocked aside by her blows. Cracks appeared in the clear ice, webbing across its surface. Several stones, falling from the creaking ceiling above, aided River in her endeavor. Finally the entire thing shattered, leaving her panting in front of its remains.

And still Hawk did not move.

River rushed forward and put her snout by his nose, but felt no breath. She gently touched his side with her paw, only to discover his fur was deathly cold. River gave him a rough shove, hoping to get some kind of reaction.

Hawk's body simply rolled.

"Aaar!" River howled, digging her claws into the slowly melting ice that still covered the floor of the room. A giant chunk of rock, twice as big as River, crashed to the floor beside her, but she didn't even flinch. The rest of the room was falling apart as an urgent voice rang out.

"River!"

Startled, she jumped and spun around, her hackles raised and her teeth bared, ready to rip the throat out of any creature foolish enough to come near.

It was Spruce. Blood ran down her face from a cut just above her eye and was splattered across the rest of her coat. She glanced around the room before her eyes fell to Hawk. Ignoring River's threatening stance, Spruce ran over to his still form and gave him a sniff. "Fire-Wolf, eh? He's had his inner fire put out…"

"I know that, duck brain!" River growled.

"…but he's still alive."

"*What?*"

"Partially."

The Water-Wolf shook her head in irritation. "What do you mean 'partially'? How can he be *partially* alive?"

"I'll explain. Come on," Spruce replied, and turned her attention to smoothing out the large stone beside River into a flat slab of rock. "We need to get out of here, *now*. We've lost the battle, but that's not the worst part. The Scaineadó Desert has always been unstable because of all the volcanoes, but Almond's initial attack and mine did something to send the earth off the deep end. There's nothing we Earth-Wolves can do to stop the ground from tearing itself apart. If we don't hurry, we're going to be the first to experience the fires of a new volcano."

"I'm not leaving him."

"*Tch*, of course not. Get him on the sled; I'm pulling him out with you."

Biting back her resentment at following orders, River allowed the other she-wolf to harness her to the sled with bands of stone. Once Hawk was firmly secured to the sled, they raced out of the room, just before the columns finally gave out under the strain of holding up the room and collapsed. The two she-wolves galloped through the hallways, making several detours as they were stopped by falling rock. River was surprised to see how much destruction the earthquake was causing.

"Move, you stupid Water-Wolf!" Spruce shouted, her pale green eyes bright with an excited gleam. "We have *seconds* before the volcano appears!"

Chapter Ninety-Eight

True to Spruce's words, the ground beneath River's paws was rapidly heating until she was sure her pads would be covered in burns. In places, the earth had already cracked open and was spewing molten rock and hot ash, clouding the air. River was hacking by the time they reached the broken gates of the Fortress's keep, her vision blurry.

Outside, the situation was much worse. The crevice summoned by Spruce and Almond had branched out into several smaller cracks. Lava spilled from them, incinerating anything it touched. The burning bodies of wolves and demons were strewn across the molten landscape. Even the Fire-Fangs could not survive contact with such pure fire.

Only the Fire-Wolves stood any chance at escaping the lava, and most of them still had their powers sealed by slave-stones. River saw Sand, Lizard, and Ray attempting to push back the waves of melted stone to allow the slaves to escape. Almond was nowhere to be seen.

Fighting back the sudden drain of energy she felt from both being out in the desert once more and from her proximity to the lava, River pulled what little moisture she could find from the air and shot a stream of water at the lava before her. Immediately it cooled to solid stone, forming a pathway for her and Spruce to use. Spruce helped by summoning broken chunks of the Fortress to stem the lava's flow.

"Sand, Lizard, Ray, let's *move!*" Spruce barked, directing the path toward her group members. "This place is gonna' blow!"

Ray charged forward, leading the slaves across to join her. Sand and Lizard guided the rest after him, shoving a few who balked at the lava lapping at their paws.

Then just before the last slave crossed, the path cracked. Lizard dove for the slave, a young puppy, grabbed him by the scruff and tossed him across the gap. Ray, who had rushed to the edge, fearing for his brother and Sand, caught the pup and dragged him to safety.

"Lizard, Sand!"

"Go!" Sand shouted, as she and Lizard began backing away from the rising lava. Spruce had already gone on ahead, leading the group of slaves along the path. "We'll catch up!"

River reached Ray just as he crouched to try and make the leap across and shoved him to the side.

"You'll never make it," she growled. "Just move!"

A rock fell from the keep above them, blocking their view of the two trapped Fire-Wolves. Ray tried to squeeze past River, his eyes fixed on the rock between him and his friends.

"I can't leave them!"

"Yes you can, there's nothing you can do for them, now *go!*" River gave him another shove, forcing him to continue down the path. She continued to push him until they caught up with Spruce.

"We've lost Sand and Lizard," River said.

Spruce just sniffed. "They should have been more careful. Keep moving!"

Slowly, Spruce led them across the flowing field of lava, she and River carefully constructing a path to reach the broken gates of the Fortress. Ash filled their lungs and darkened their vision. River continued to weaken from the extreme heat and dryness of the air, but she pushed on, not daring to stop for fear of losing Hawk.

"Help!"

River nearly slipped into the lava, startled by the cry, as the earth still shook like it was possessed by a maddened demon. She recovered and looked up to see an elderly Fire-Wolf male perched precariously on a lump of stone that was rapidly melting from the heat. Naked fear shone in his dark blue eyes.

"Please…help me," he gasped, choking on the toxic air.

"We can't keep stopping," Spruce said coldly, not even sparing the elder a glance. His eyes widened in shock. River looked away as well, and started to follow the other she-wolf, when she stopped.

Hawk would have tried to save him, she thought to herself and sighed. *Stupid Fire-Wolf…rubbing off on me…*

She took a deep breath, focusing intensely on summoning as much water as she could. She sent the pathetically small wave toward the elder, cooling the lava between them. Hope and gratitude shone in his eyes as he shakily leapt to safety just as the stone melted away. Carefully he made his way toward the two she-wolves, struggling to keep his footing as tremors shook the earth, eyeing Hawk's unconscious form with a mixture of shock and pity.

"Idiot! You're gonna cost us our lives!" Spruce snarled.

River growled right back. "Shut up, we'd be no better than the demons themselves if we left him to die."

Spruce's eyes narrowed in anger, but a sudden tremor cut off her next words. Startled, the rebel leader stumbled, her paw slipping on the smooth path. River dove to stop her fall toward the lava, but was held back by the sled.

Suddenly a slab of stone appeared beneath Spruce's paws, catching her before she could slip into the lava. Almond jumped down from a chunk of masonry, his fur singed and one of his forepaws blackened by fire. He grabbed Spruce by the scruff, holding her up as she attempted to regain her balance.

"We will not fall to their level," he said when she pulled away. "We are wolves."

Spruce shook and jumped back to the main path. "I don't need *you* telling me what to do. *Move it!*"

Finally, just as the earth finally cracked completely open and pushed up a mountain of stone and lava, the group reached the safety of the sands beyond the Fortress.

"Run, you idiots! The mountain's going to explode!" Spruce screeched, and raced away, not bothering to look behind her to see if they followed.

Stumbling as the earth shook even harder, cracks webbing out from the rising volcano behind them, the wolves flew over the desert sands. River dragged the Fire-Wolf elder she had saved by the scruff of his neck when he stumbled, cursing with the effort of having to carry two fully grown Fire-Wolves.

The volcano blasted apart, shooting chunks of rock and rapidly cooling lava through the air. Several wolves were hit by the falling projectiles, but they shook off the fire and kept running. Spruce stood on a dune several lengths away, howling for the others to hurry. Lava licked at River's paws as she ran. She dragged both the sled and the elder, who had gone limp in her grip. Suddenly the deadweight was removed as Ray swerved over and took the elder from her. Not bothering to waste breath on thanks, River simply pushed herself to run faster.

The fleeing wolves stopped when they reached Spruce, taking advantage of their moment of safety to catch their breath. The earth still shook, but with less force now that they were away from the source. The lava, spilling into the numerous cracks that continued to break through the ground, had yet to reach them. River was thankful for the rest, although she would never admit it. Her sides heaved with exhaustion and her legs trembled.

Behind her, Hawk still lay unconscious, despite the wild ride.

"Right then, let's see our partially dead Fire-Wolf," Spruce said hoarsely, her throat rubbed raw from the ash of the volcano. Behind her, the fiery mountain still spewed ash and smoke, molten rock gurgling down its sides. The Fortress that was once Ignimor was no more.

Forcing back a growl, River asked again, "How can someone be *partially* dead?"

"Simple, idiot. He's had his inner fire frozen, so his body's dying, but his soul is still tied to it."

"Can he be saved?"

"Poooossibly," Spruce sang, a manic look on her face. River resisted the urge to snap at her, knowing that she might be the only one who could help. "You need to reignite his inner fire, but you don't have a lot of time."

"How?"

The Earth-Wolf laughed. "The only way is to throw him into the Lough Tighrian, and hope he lives. That *might* work. Lough Tighrian *is* the source of all fire magic, after all. But you won't get anywhere *near* the Fáinéitin."

River practically tackled the cackling she-wolf, despite being hindered by the sled. "Take me to the Fáinéitin. *Now.*"

"Fine, we'll take you. It'll be interesting to see the Guardian refuse you entry," Spruce giggled, before suddenly turning very serious. "Now get off me. We're ten days from the Fáinéitin, but we need to get there in eight or Hawk will die. Being out in the sands will give him more time but not much."

Wriggling out from River's grip, Spruce called her group together.

"All right now, who's still here?" She swept her eyes over their little gathering. "It looks like Sand and Lizard didn't make it." Her gaze stopped at Almond, and her eyes narrowed. "I guess this means I have to make *you* my lieutenant again. Do *not* repeat your past mistake."

Almond said nothing as Spruce turned away.

"Almond, Ray, get these slaves free and send them on their way," she ordered. "We gotta move." She pranced off a few paces, continuing in a sing-song voice, "We're headed for the Fáinéitin!"

"I knew it," Ray muttered to himself as he passed, causing River to look up with sympathy. "I said she would get us killed…and now they're gone."

River knew all too well how he felt. "They gave their lives bravely," she said. "They won't be forgotten."

Ray gave no sign of hearing her words.

CHAPTER NINETY-NINE

IMAGES SWAM BEFORE River's eyes, created by her exhaustion and the heat radiating from the desert sand. She dragged her burned paws across the ground, barely able to stay upright. River felt the effects of the desert the moment she came out of her battle-daze, but she had refused to succumb to weakness like she did before. Hawk grew colder with every passing hour, reminding her why she had to keep going. The other Fire-Wolves tried to keep him warm by bathing him in flames, but with his inner fire frozen, his body held no heat.

Ray warned River if they couldn't make it to the Fáinéitin before Hawk froze solid, it would be too late.

Keep moving and don't you dare *stop,* she growled to herself, focusing only on putting one paw in front of the other. She barely even noticed the passing miles.

At some point during their journey, Ray had run back to the cave to retrieve Storm, the Wind-Wolf elder who had stayed behind while the rebels attacked Ignimor. He lagged behind the small group, Ray loping beside him as he struggled. Spruce didn't slacken the pace for an instant, despite Storm's old age, and urged the other wolves on mercilessly, not stopping for anything.

River was too busy concentrating on not passing out to feel irritated about being told what to do. Fortunately they encountered no demons, feral or otherwise.

"Fillothrated skwatam."

River's head snapped up when Spruce's voice filtered through the trance she had fallen into, focused only on moving forward. "What?" she asked stupidly, blinking rapidly as she struggled to register what the Earth-Wolf had said, the heat making her function a little more slowly than usual.

"I said, fillothrated skwatam," the Earth-Wolf replied in complete seriousness, before throwing over her shoulder, "Told you she wasn't paying attention. She probably would have walked right up the mountainside and fried into crunchy bits of Water-Wolf."

"What mountain?" River asked irritably, seeing nothing in front of her. She narrowed her eyes, and slowly the image of an enormous red mountain appeared in front of her. She had forgotten that Ray had mentioned the Fáinéitin was disguised by powerful mirages. The sand around them was tainted black and mixed in with numerous chunks of glassy rocks. More mountains of reddish stone rose up next to the one in front of her, forming the famous ring of fire.

River found it hard to focus on the volcanoes as her attention continued to slide away from them, and she had to fight the strange feeling that she should turn around and leave.

"Well now, River, it's up to you to get inside," Spruce said somberly. "We can't help you anymore. If Hawk isn't plunged into Lough Tighrian…" Her voice trailed off, and she was silent for a moment, shaking her scarred head. "We'll wait for you in the cave." She pointed to a nearby rock outcropping nestled at the foot of a large dune.

With that, she led the other three wolves away from the Fáinéitin. River glared up at the fiery volcanoes, as though she could will them to let her in. "You'd better not try and stop me," River muttered angrily to the rumbling mountains. She took a step forward, only to have the mountains shake in fury.

"*You will not pass,*" a voice echoed down the cliff side, causing River to snarl. "Says who?"

A stream of lava spilled down the volcano, quickly reaching the black sands below and pooling a few paces in front of River. It rose up in the shape of a wolf with red eyes that glared at her. "*I am the Guardian of the Lough Tighrian, and I say you will not pass,*" it answered in a deep voice that shook the ground.

"And why not, oh great spirit?" River asked sarcastically.

The fiery wolf snarled, and a few of the Fáinéitin's volcanoes spewed ash from their tops. "*You would do well to watch your tongue, pup. You have been tainted by demons, and are impure. Even if you were not tainted, I still would not let you pass. You are* Water. *Water would taint my lake just as much as the evil energy from demons would. You would throw the Lough out of balance with the desert.*"

"Save me the speech, *spirit*," the River snarled, baring her teeth. "I *will* enter, no matter *what* you say. I have a Fire-Wolf that needs the fires of Lough Tighrian, and I will do *anything* to get him there. Now get out of my way *before I make you.*"

The spirit snarled right back, causing the volcanoes to erupt with rage. The two stared at each other for a few moments. River desperately hoped it wouldn't come to a fight. Hawk was quickly running out of time, and if she didn't get him to the Lough Tighrian soon…

Finally, just as she was about to pounce on the fiery wolf, no matter how much the world was starting to spin from her exposure to the fire of the volcano, the fire spirit bowed its head. *"Very well…you may pass."*

For a second, River was startled. She had steeled herself for a fight, a fight she wasn't totally certain she could win. Then molten stone started to spill down the rocky cliffs of the volcanoes above her, and she panicked.

"The lava will not hurt you; it will take you where you need to go."

When she heard the voice of the Guardian's spirit echo in her mind, River forced herself to relax. *You're doing it for Hawk…you're doing it for Hawk. Moon-Wolf, does he owe me when he wakes up…if he wakes up…no, he will wake up…or else…or else…I'll kill him for dying on me!*

The lava rose up and enveloped River and the sled carrying Hawk.

She had the vague sensation of movement but saw nothing beyond the bubble of lava. After what seemed to River to be an agonizingly long time, during which she was sure Hawk had died, the bubble finally fell away.

She stumbled to the ground and froze for a moment, looking around her with a little awe.

Before her lay the Sun-Wolf Lough of the Fire-Wolves, shaped like the sun with four rays extending from the near side. It was filled with a fiery liquid that glowed with red light. It roared with the fury of actual fire and cast its angry red light on the volcanic plain around it. Surrounding the lake was the mighty ring of volcanoes, still spilling pools of lava from their tops.

"Spruce, you had better be right about this," River muttered to herself as she slowly made her way toward the lake, ignoring instincts that were screaming at her to turn and flee from the pure Fire waiting before her. A single touch from the lake's magic and she would be incinerated.

Finally, after a slow crawl toward the lake, during which River nearly lost consciousness several times, she stood at the shores of Lough Tighrian.

"Don't you dare die on me, Hawk," River said loudly as she slipped out of the sled, as though the bright orange Fire-Wolf could hear her, before tipping him off and plunging him into the fiery waters of the lake.

River watched anxiously as Hawk sank beneath the surface, before she was knocked to the ground by a viscous shake of the earth. She scrambled to her paws and quickly backed away from the lake, wanting nothing more than to get as far away as possible from it.

The lake exploded.

Almost instinctively River dove behind some large chunks of volcanic glass. All around her the volcanoes of the Fáinéitin shot streams of fire into the sky. Lough Tighrian's water overflowed its banks, rushing past her until it reached the foot of the volcanoes. Realizing that the liquid would soon overtake her, River leapt up onto the glassy rock. The water continued to rise until the lake itself had disappeared, and the entire volcanic plane within the ring of mountains was covered in it like a great basin of water.

If it doesn't stop rising... River shuddered and cut herself off. *No, you* will *survive this...and you'll leave here with Hawk right beside you.*

The reddish light grew brighter and brighter, until River was nearly blinded by the sheer strength of it. The glow shone on the stone of the volcanoes, filling the volcanic plain with red light. Her nausea rising, River dug her claws into the stone, trying to ignore the way it spun before her eyes. She wouldn't last much longer in the presence of Fire.

Don't...give up... she thought, struggling to stay conscious. *No...weakness... you have...to get Hawk...first.*

Despite her best efforts, her body, exhausted from the journey through the desert, couldn't take any more. Her navy blue eyes rolled back into her head, and she collapsed.

CHAPTER ONE HUNDRED

MINUTES PASSED BEFORE the light started to fade and the waters retreated, the glow disappearing quicker than it had appeared. When the fiery liquid of Lough Tighrian had flowed back to its original banks, much more subdued than it originally had been, the only thing left behind was Hawk. He lay on the banks of Lough Tighrian, sleeping peacefully. His wounds had healed, and any poison from the demons had been purified. His fur was unmarked by scars, and even the old ones gained during his enslavement were gone, although his slave collar remained around his neck.

Slowly, Hawk opened his eyes, blinking in confusion when he saw not the cold walls of Ignimor Fortress, but the high cliffs of volcanoes around him and the dimmed waters of a red lake beside him. *I'm in the Fáinéitin... at Lough Tighrian...but how? What happened?*

Hawk stood, shocked to discover he could do so without pain. All of the injuries sustained from his fight with the demons and the torture suffered at their claws were gone.

Where's River?

Tipping his nose up, he sniffed the air for any trace of River. His heart leapt with joy when he caught a whiff of her scent just paces from him, a sign that she stood close by only minutes ago. Sorting through the scents of the environment, he tracked her up the banks.

He stopped at a large chunk of stone and looked up. Above, the tip of a blue-gray tail poked out over the edge of the smooth rock. Tail wagging, Hawk dragged himself up to the top, eager to see River, but he was shocked to find her lying unconscious. He paused, confused.

"What *happened*?"

"*I will show you,*" came a deep voice, not unlike the one at the Ardgao. Hawk spun around, startled, to see the faint form of a wolf made from fire. The wolf touched its nose to the side of Hawk's muzzle, and his vision went black. Images flew across his mind's eye, and he watched with a mixture of horror and fascination as River battled Lapsus, as Ignimor Fortress fell to the jaws of a volcano, as Spruce led her diminished group across the sands, and as River forced her way into the Fáinéitin. When the stream of images ended and Hawk regained his vision, he was left panting slightly.

River did all that...for me? "So I had my inner fire put out...and River brought me here to reignite it?" Hawk asked, shocked. When the fiery wolf nodded, Hawk ventured another question. "You weren't...diminished like this before, were you? What...what happened to the energy of Lough Tighrian?"

"It now resides in you, Hawk," came the answer. *"You contain the pure energy of Fire, although it lies dormant to protect you, otherwise you would be burned from the sheer power of it."*

"But wait...can it still be used?"

"Yes...but only by you. Only you can release the power you have obtained."

Shocked, Hawk fell silent. If he were the only one who could wield Lough Tighrian...then he would *have* to take part in whatever River had planned for the Eclipse.

"Hurry, Hawk," the spirit said, fading as lava appeared around them. *"The Fáinéitin is closing itself off, until its power is returned."*

"Wh-what? What do you mean?"

"All the Elemental Guardians sealed themselves after you released their power. Without the magic of the lakes, we no longer had a way to keep out intruders without closing ourselves off completely."

"Then how are we supposed to return the power? You can't stay sealed off forever," Hawk protested. The sacred lakes were how the wolf monarchs of old were able to communicate directly with the gods. If the Elemental Guardians stayed empty of power and closed to the monarchs, then they would have no way to contact their gods.

"The magic will return on its own. It does not like staying apart from its den for too long," the spirit said with some amusement, before its expression became serious. *"Now go, if you do not leave, you will be trapped."*

The molten rock rose up to form a bubble, and as the fiery wolf disappeared, Hawk managed to shout, "Thank you!"

He thought he saw the spirit smile.

Chapter One Hundred and One

Spruce was very surprised to see *Hawk* dragging *River* out of the Fáinéitin. Truthfully, she hadn't expected to see anyone come out alive. And with the tiny chance that River actually did survive, a chance that had gone down to zero after the volcanoes erupted, then the Earth-Wolf would have expected to see River dragging Hawk's cold dead body.

Naturally, she was intrigued as to what exactly had gone on inside the ring of fire mountains.

Unfortunately, she couldn't pester the Fire-Wolf with questions as he collapsed only a few feet from the base of one of the volcanoes, still weak from his near-death experience. *Sheesh, if you're going to faint, do it on your own time, not when I'm trying to get information from you,* Spruce thought irritably, padding out to meet the unconscious wolves.

"Don't tell me I'm going to have to drag *both* of you back myself." Spruce told Hawk and River.

As they were unconscious, neither one offered a reply.

"Huh. *Knew* I should have made the other three wait out here with me."

She paused and tilted her head slightly, before sighing. "Yeah, yeah, I know *I* was the one who made them wait at the cave, because the pansies were complaining about their petty injuries."

Silently she raised a clump of sand and hardened it into a slab of stone. Then she slid Hawk and River onto the slate, and made it hover beside her as she loped back to the cave where her group waited.

"Water-Wolf owes me an explanation."

CHAPTER ONE HUNDRED AND TWO

WHEN HAWK AWOKE, the first thing he saw was a stone ceiling. He panicked, thinking that he was back in Ignimor Fortress. Then memories flooded back into his mind, including the ones given to him by the spirit of the Fáinéitin. Forcing himself to take a deep breath and calm down, Hawk sat up and looked around at his surroundings.

"Ah, good. You're awake."

Turning, Hawk saw a Fire-Wolf with bright yellow fur and dark blue eyes. Gray peppered his muzzle.

"I'm Ray," the older male said. "How are you feeling?"

Hawk wiggled his ears to test that they were still attached, and then stood and gave himself a good shake. He was glad to find he hadn't simply dreamed he had been healed. "A lot better. Where's River?"

Ray gave him a wry look and gestured with his tail. "Over there."

Standing in the middle of the cave, her hackles raised and her teeth bared, River faced off against a dark brown Earth-Wolf. The Earth-Wolf had a nasty scar on the top of her head, which was devoid of all fur, and an insane gleam in her eyes. The rest of her fur was marked with numerous scars. The Earth-Wolf looked completely at ease, not intimidated in the least by River's threatening stance.

"Can you believe it? The great River, defeated by a little fire."

"I'd like to see *you* last longer against pure Wind," River spat. The Earth-Wolf just shrugged, unconcerned.

"I already have."

Before River could come up with another insult, the Earth-Wolf female turned and fixed Hawk with her pale green gaze.

"Oh, you're up. Finally."

Hawk, sensing she was the leader of this little group, padded forward and dipped his head slightly. "How long was I out?"

The Earth-Wolf thought for a moment, and then shrugged again. "No more than an hour. The rest of you just needed to finish regenerating."

"Regenerating?" He was cut off by the sudden appearance of River, who quickly looked him over.

"I was starting to think you had gone and died anyway," she said coldly, but Hawk thought he saw a gleam of relief hidden in her dark eyes.

Hawk wagged his tail a little. "I seem to remember you shouting at me not to die, or you'd kill me for it."

"Well then, wake up sooner next time."

"So glad to know you care about your little friend," the brown Earth-Wolf said, shouldering River aside. "I'm Spruce, the leader of this pathetic pack. You met Ray." She paused long enough to gesture to an old black Wind-Wolf lying at the back of the cave and said, "The old geezer over there is Storm. Almond's out hunting; he'll be back later. There *were* others...but they had the misfortune of dying..."

Storm? I've heard that name somewhere before... Hawk narrowed his eyes in concentration, and looked over at the afore-named elder, who watched Hawk with curious gray eyes.

Fall's mate! Hawk suddenly remembered, from when Jay had been arguing with his mother over the truth of his father's death. *Can he be the same Storm...? I remember that Jay had said Storm's throat had been bitten...*

When Storm turned to bite at an itch on his back, Hawk saw the scars of a demon's teeth marking his throat.

Why is he here? No, the better question is how did he get here? Hawk padded over to the elder.

"Just a warning, Storm isn't the friendliest wolf," Ray muttered as he followed Hawk.

"Hello, Hawk," the elder said when he approached. "I suppose you're here to prevent me from napping, are you? It's bad enough that Spruce—"

Storm was suddenly cut off when Ray stuffed his tail into the elder's mouth. Shooting Hawk an apologetic look, the older Fire-Wolf said, "Don't mind him, he doesn't mean to be rude, he's just grumpy because Spruce kept us running for a long time."

Hawk chuckled, but bowed his head respectfully to the old wolf. "I just wanted to ask you a question, Elder Storm. Do you...do you know a Fall?"

Storm's head shot up, his eyes wide with surprise. "Fall?" he whispered. He lurched to his paws, ignoring Ray's protests to lie back down. "How do you know that name?"

A little taken aback by the elder's reaction, Hawk hesitated before saying, "I met her in the Gaoibeanna Mountains..."

"She's still alive? What about my pups? Did...did you meet them? Jay, Falcon, and Scrub?"

At Hawk's nod, the black Wind-Wolf's eyes filled with tears. "They're alive...I thought they were killed when I fell. The Shade-Tiger was too much for them, I didn't think it was possible for them to survive the attack."

That must be why he never tried to get word to them, Hawk thought. *He didn't know they were alive.*

"How did you meet them?" Storm asked.

The elder listened silently as Hawk told him about what had transpired in the Gaoibeanna Mountains. He remained silent for a few moments after Hawk finished speaking, his eyes glowing with relief and joy, but soon reverted to being a crotchety old wolf again.

"Humph. I should have known those three would have gotten into all kinds of trouble," he said grumpily. "What kind of Wind-Wolf falls off a cliff?"

Ray sighed, giving Hawk another apologetic look.

"Go away, you pups," Storm growled, flashing his teeth at the two younger wolves. "I want to sleep. I don't care if Spruce wants us to move out, I'm not waking up until I'm done with my nap!"

Both Fire-Wolves hurried to leave the elder in peace.

"I never knew that Storm still had living family," Ray admitted when they had reached a safe distance from the old wolf. "He never mentioned having any, living or dead.

"His family doesn't know that *he's* still alive," Hawk said. "Where did you find him?"

"We found him near the Gaoibeanna-Scaineadó border, washed up on the banks of the Lonradh River. His throat had been slashed, and he had many broken bones, but he was miraculously still alive. We convinced Spruce to take him in, but for a while we weren't sure he was going to make it, much less be able to talk again. But he was stubborn, and he surprised us all by healing rapidly."

The yellow Fire-Wolf turned to look at Storm, who was curled up facing the wall. "And as you can see, he even regained his voice."

The two lapsed into silence. Hawk watched with a little amusement as Spruce tried to needle River into another argument. The Water-Wolf was doing her best to ignore the other she-wolf.

"Ray…" Hawk began slowly. "I, uh…I wanted to thank you for saving me." The memories the spirit of the Fáinéitin had given him flashed through his mind. "I know you lost friends in the attack…"

Ray snorted, interrupting him. "Don't thank me. We didn't have a choice about attacking Ignimor."

"Wh-what?"

"You being captured was all the excuse Spruce needed to take on the Fortress. She didn't care that we stood little chance of making it back out alive." A hollow look came into Ray's eyes. "Liz— my brother and…and Sand…*died*, and I wasn't even given a chance to mourn. I only wish I had died with them."

Hawk winced. He was uncomfortably reminded of the attitudes of Sky and the others toward the Water-Wolves, but Ray's words cut deeper than anything they had said. Sky's group had taken their anger out on Hawk, but it was meant for River.

If it weren't for me, no one would have died. This is just like when we tried to attack the Nocte Fortress. We lost that battle…although we lost far fewer wolves. Hawk started to speak, but Ray had already stood and was padding to the back of the cave. It was obvious he did not want to speak anymore on the matter.

Ray, I'm sorry.

After a few more moments of thought, Hawk stood as well and walked over to River, who was claiming a desert hare from the returning Almond.

"Here," she said as he approached and shoved the hare toward him. "You haven't had anything to eat for some time."

Realizing just how hungry he was, Hawk gave no protest and eagerly sank his fangs into the hare.

"I meant to ask," River began carefully, shooting suspicious looks at Spruce, "what happened after…I…was knocked unconscious? Did you collect the power from Lough Tighrian?"

Hawk hesitated before answering. "Yes…I wasn't sure if we could get a second entry when you could be conscious for it, so I went ahead and released it."

I'll tell what actually happened later, when there aren't others around to hear. River might not want them hearing, he assured himself.

"You can rest for tonight," River said with a nod, causing him to look up in surprise. Usually after visiting an Elemental Guardian, she would mercilessly drive them to the next one, intent on reaching it as soon as possible. "But I don't want to stay here any longer than we have to. Spruce…" She paused for a moment. "She reminds me too much of…my mother."

Her mother? Hawk nodded. "We can leave tomorrow."

"Oh? And where are you going without my permission?" Spruce said slyly, suddenly appearing next to Hawk.

River glared at the brown Earth-Wolf. "None of your business."

Spruce sniffed, not in the least intimidated by the other she-wolf's glare. "I should think it's my business, since it's really because of you two that I lost three of my members."

The Water-Wolf bristled, obviously irritated by Spruce's intrusion. Hawk stood, seeking to appease both she-wolves. *River's dislike of her aside, I don't want them sacrificing any more than they have already.* "We're just traveling west…"

"Why?" Spruce interrupted. "There's nothing of interest west of here, except for the Uiscean Marsh." Her eyes narrowed. "You couldn't be trying to get *there,* could you?"

Hawk hesitated a second too long, and a look of surprise crossed Spruce's scarred face. "You *are.* Why in Moon-Wolf's name are you trying to go to the marsh? Not even *slaves* are sent there. The land is crawling with demons, and word in the trees is the Marsh is crawling with Blood-Frenzies and Noxond. It's nearly impossible to get within howling distance to the border."

"We…can't tell you why," Hawk said carefully. "We appreciate every-thing you've done for us, for freeing me from Ignimor, but we have to get to Uiscean."

Spruce tipped her head back and gave a harsh, maniacal laugh. "If that's all, then we'll lead you there."

"We don't need a guide," River growled, jumping to her paws. Spruce just rolled her eyes.

"We'll be okay on our own," Hawk said before either she-wolf could start an argument. "We don't want you to risk going so close to the border…"

"Are you suggesting that I'm *frightened* of getting captured near the border?" Spruce leered, leaning in close and baring her fangs. "If I was *frightened,* of capture, do you really think I would have attacked Ignimor at all? I don't care why you seem to have a death wish, but a suicidal journey to the border seems like fun."

Quickly realizing they would only waste time trying to convince Spruce to let them go, Hawk silenced River's protest with a look and nodded to Spruce. "Very well. Thank you."

The Earth-Wolf only shrugged and turned to the other wolves. "All right you three, let's move out! We have a lot of ground to cover!"

River snarled and stepped forward to block Spruce's path. "Hawk still needs to rest. I don't want to have all my work wasted when he dies on us because he's exhausted!"

"Meh, he'll live. If having his inner flame put out didn't kill him, nothing will. Oh don't give me that look, River. Being out in the desert will *help* him. If you're going to worry like an old nanny, then worry about yourself. The Moons may be high in the sky, but the Fires still burn in the sand."

Although she growled quietly, River said nothing. Hawk straightened up and tried to look full of energy. "Don't worry about me, River. I'll be fine!"

River gave Hawk a long look before grumbling, "Fine. But I'm not going to drag your half-dead carcass back here if you get hurt again." More quietly, she added. "The sooner we leave Spruce, the better."

"I'm sorry, River," Hawk said as they walked out of the cave after the other four. "But Spruce was going to follow us no matter what. It's better tha– " He cut himself off, his eyes fixed on the sky above.

"Get moving, Hawk!" River growled, side-stepping around him. "We don't have all night!"

Hawk just shook his head. "River, look."

After a slight hesitation, River glanced up. Her eyes widened with shock.

Hanging in the sky was a single moon. The other two moons, which normally hovered close by their larger sister, were nowhere to be seen.

"We have a month," River said grimly before padding away. Almond had noticed their pause and was urging them to hurry up, as Spruce didn't seem to care whether or not she left them behind. "We have a month to get to the Archeo."

Chapter One Hundred and Three

"Are you sure?" the Noxond hissed, digging its claws further into the elderly Fire-Wolf's shoulder. The wolf whimpered and nodded. Pleased, the Noxond purred.

The elder looked up at its captor hopefully. "I...I told you what...what you wanted. Please...let...me go..."

The wolf-like demon leered down at its captive, its black eyes glinting. "Of course," it said soothingly. "You may go."

Then it sank its curved fangs into the Fire-Wolf's neck.

"Go and sink into death's embrace, *slave*," the Noxond growled as the elder's eyes dimmed and his shuddering breaths stopped.

Sneering in contempt, the red demon turned away from the corpse. It had been worth investigating the sudden appearance of a volcano where there should have been a fortress. The elderly Fire-Wolf had been a very good find.

He was the same Fire-Wolf River had saved during the eruption, returning to the place where he had spent his entire life because he did not know where else to go.

It had been a simple matter of exerting an aura of fear over the wolf to get the information the Noxond needed. Its prey had passed through here a few weeks previous and had headed south.

The trail was getting warmer, and the Noxond was closing in.

CHAPTER ONE HUNDRED AND FOUR

RAY RAN IN a daze. The news that they were traveling to the Scaineadó-Uiscean border should have horrified him, but he just didn't have it in him to care.

His brother and the one he had loved in secret were gone, leaving him alone with a crazed leader who didn't even care about their sacrifice. Storm was the only reason Ray still hung on to life, and even that was a thin string threatening to break.

Why did you have to die? Ray saw nothing of the passing red sand dune or piles of blackened stone and heard nothing of Storm's stream of irritated babble. He only dimly noted the sudden drop in temperature and air pressure, and didn't even realize what was happening until Storm's howl jolted him from his thoughts. "Rain is coming; it's going to flood!"

For a split second, utter fear gripped Ray, stopping his breath in his throat and stilling his heart. The night sky above them, previously lit by the moon and stars, had turned as black as a demon's eyes. The air crackled with electricity, setting Ray's fur on end. He had experienced more than one sudden desert storm and knew very well the danger one held.

But what does it matter? Ray numbly followed after Spruce, who was shouting something he couldn't make out. The wind was already picking up, kicking sand into the air. *Either we die in the storm or we die by a demon's claws — it's all the same in the end.*

He dimly heard River shout something about a rock pile, but Ray had eyes only for the sky, waiting for the rain to fall. Storm growled at him, but the words were lost in the wind. The elder shook his head and put on a sudden burst of speed, racing for the rocks just ahead, but Ray made no move to go after him.

Almond, Hawk, or River will make sure he's safe. They don't need me.

He saw Hawk turn around, eyes wide with horror. Hawk opened his jaws to shout Ray's name.

Then the clouds burst open and dumped their contents onto the wolves below. Ray was swept off his paws and sent crashing to the ground. Water filled his eyes and mouth and poured into his lungs. He gasped for air and struggled to stand, but the rain knocked him back down. It only took seconds for the water to rise enough to cover him, and the sweeping current dragged him beneath the surface.

Darkness filled Ray's vision and the roaring of the storm dimmed to a murmur as he let himself go limp.

This is it. Sand, Lizard, I'm on my way.

Teeth dug into the back of his neck, and suddenly Ray was dragged back up to the surface. The sky lit up with lightning, streaking across the clouds and giving Ray a glimpse of dark churning water and sheets of rain. Thunder rang in his eardrums as sound returned with full force.

Ray turned his head slightly, enough to see the one who had snatched him from death's embrace. Hawk's eyes were wide with terror and his legs flailed in an attempt to keep them both afloat, but the sodden Fire-Wolf had his fangs stuck determinedly in Ray's scruff.

Why is he saving me? Why can't he just let me die? Ray wanted to voice the questions aloud, but he could do nothing more than cough as his lungs struggled to take in air.

A wave overtook them both and plunged them beneath the surface. Hawk's teeth slipped for just a moment before sinking back in Ray's scruff, hard enough to send sparks of pain down Ray's back.

Lightning flashed again, even brighter than before, and for a few seconds the stormy night was as bright as the midday sun. A dark shape was streaking toward them through the water, which seemed to part before it.

Then darkness fell over them again.

Now we're both going to die, Ray thought as the current dragged them under again. Hawk yelped, but clung to Ray and struggled to drag them up to the open air.

A body appeared beneath Ray and surged upward, pushing him up with it. Ray spat out a mouthful of water when they broke the surface and shook his head to clear his eyes.

"You stupid Fire-Wolves!" River roared above the rain and thunder. Ray was lying across her back. She ducked her head under the water and came up a moment later with the scruff of a spluttering Hawk in her jaws. When he managed to draw a clear breath of air, she let him go. "Make for the rocks!"

Why are they trying so hard to save me? Ray remained limp as River swam for a tiny island of rocks, struggling to turn the current in their favor and keep the water from shoving them under again. Hawk pressed as close as he could to her side, his eyes narrowed in his determination to keep up. *They're not Sand or Lizard; they have no reason to risk themselves for me.*

Hawk scrambled up onto the rocks, assisted by a shove from River. The she-wolf slid Ray off her back and pushed him toward the rocks. "Get up there before we're fried," she snarled before surging onto a stony ledge just above her head.

Ray made no move to join them. He looked up at them with empty eyes, feeling the water pull on his fur. Horror crossed Hawk's face.

"Ray, come on!" Hawk shouted, leaning down as far as he could. "I'll pull you up!"

"You should have just left me in the water!" Ray paddled his legs just enough to keep his head in the air.

"I wasn't going to just watch you drown!"

"But I *wanted* to," Ray protested. "I didn't want to be saved."

"Do you think Lizard and Sand would want you to die?" Hawk demanded. "They died to save the others, to save *you*. Are you just going to let their sacrifice be in vain?"

A jolt went through Ray, and he froze. A wave washed over his head, obscuring his vision for a split second, but he returned to the surface, spluttering.

"I'm sorry that they're dead, I'm sorry that you were forced into attacking Ignimor. Believe me; I know the pain you're feeling. I…I watched my mother get murdered by demons. I've seen wolves die in my name, die *for* me. It hurts, I know. But it would hurt more if I threw their sacrifice away, if I didn't honor their memory by fighting on for what they died for." Hawk stretched down a little more, his eyes pleading. "If you're not going to remember Lizard and Sand, then who is? Protect the life they gave you and *live*!"

Lightning arced across the sky just as a wave of water rushed toward Ray. He surged toward Hawk, paws scrabbling across the submerged rocks to push himself out of the water. Hawk closed his jaws around Ray's paw and hauled him up the rest of the way. They landed on the rocks as thunder boomed in their ears.

"We're not safe yet," River growled, dragging both Fire-Wolves to their paws. "We have to get to the top and under cover."

She practically threw Hawk to the top of the pile, and did the same to Ray before scrambling up after them.

"Get in," Almond said when Ray managed to regain his footing. He, Spruce, and Storm stood beneath a stone overhang, which the two Earth-Wolves had hastily built from the surrounding rocks. Ray stumbled after Hawk, his limbs suddenly feeling too heavy to move.

"Watch where you're shaking," Storm growled, pressing himself against the wall of the overhang when River shook. The she-wolf only flicked her tail at him, splattering him with drops of water.

Ray sank to the ground in a heap, exhaustion clouding his mind. He coughed, spitting out more water, before lying his head down on his paws. He absentmindedly heated his fur, causing steam to rise as the water evaporated.

I'm alive, he thought, closing his eyes for a brief moment.

"I meant what I said, you know."

Ray opened his eyes again to find Hawk settling himself next to him. The other Fire-Wolf coughed, still trying to rid his lungs of water.

"River and I...we've attacked three demon strongholds," Hawk continued. "One of the battles...we lost. Many have died in those battles, some of them friends. And...I know that many more are going to die before this is all over." He paused, his eyes darkening with sorrow. "If there's one thing I've learned on my journey, it's that when we're at war, there will always be lives lost. It's up to us, the survivors, to make sure that their sacrifices aren't forgotten or made in vain."

That sounds like something Lizard said...long ago, before Spruce found us. Ray allowed his memories to take him back. He saw Lizard saying the same thing to a sobbing Sand as they stood over her dead brother. Ray closed his eyes again. *I had forgotten. They would be ashamed of me if they knew I was going to let myself die like that, after what they did.*

"Thank you, Hawk," he said quietly, without opening his eyes. "For reminding me. I'm not going to let their sacrifice go to waste."

Chapter One Hundred and Five

Hours passed as the storm continued to rage outside the little shelter. Both Hawk and Almond quickly grew weary of keeping Storm, River, and Spruce from starting arguments. Surprisingly, Storm was the instigator of most of them, as River was perfectly content to sit and enjoy the spray of water near the entrance of the cave. Spruce was asleep. Storm wouldn't stop irritating them.

"Ask him to tell you a story," Ray said, after Hawk finally managed to convince River to return to her spot by the rain for the fourth time. Almond had successfully distracted Spruce with a game involving pebbles, and Storm was grumbling to himself at the back of the overhang. "He likes to talk. Just a warning, though, Storm thinks he was born before the war. Sometimes I'll hear him talking to old heroes in his sleep."

Hawk laughed a little weakly. *If he really was born before the war, then he would be* ancient. *Unless he spent the past century in the Rift like River, but I doubt…*

His thoughts trailed off as Sparrow's words, spoken seemingly a lifetime ago, echoed through his mind again.

"Seek out the ancient one, and listen to his story," Hawk said.

Ray gave him a curious look. "What was that?"

"Come on, let's go hear a story," Hawk said, padding over to the Wind-Wolf elder. Ray followed after a brief hesitation.

"Storm?"

"What is it?" The elder gave him a baleful glare. "I already said I'd keep quiet over here and stop bugging them."

"Are you really as old as the war?" Hawk asked, ignoring the look. *Maybe there's another way a wolf could have lived more than a century without being in the Rift, but I just need to know if Storm is the 'ancient one' I'm supposed to listen to.*

"Of course I am. I was born several years before it started, but this damn war has gone on for so long that I'm the only one who has lived long enough to remember."

Ray rolled his eyes. "You can't even remember what you had for breakfast this morning," he teased, obviously feeling a little better since almost dying in the storm.

"Shut up, Alder, I happen to have a *flawless* memory."

"My name isn't Alder."

Blinking, Storm curled his lips and growled. "Don't go changing your name on me, Alder. I know exactly who you are. Now, what did you need, Hawk?"

Hawk tried not to look too amused. "Can you tell me a story?"

Storm sniffed. "Finally, a young one who actually pays heed to the words of his elders. Stories can teach you a lot if only you could deflate your ego a little. Some of these young wolves I meet have enough hot air to make even an Earth-Wolf float."

He paused to shoot both River and Spruce hard glares from across the cave.

"Humph. Anyway, a story…" Storm thought for a moment before continuing. "Ah, I have the perfect one. I haven't told it in a while, so my memory…" Storm trailed off, looking at Ray out of the corner of his eyes. The yellow Fire-Wolf was the picture of innocence. "Just make sure you two don't fall asleep while I'm talking," the elder finished with a growl.

"Many many years ago, before even I was born — Alder don't give me that look — the borders of our lands were not as clear as they are now. The strength of the Elemental Guardians, which gives each land its elemental attributes, waxed and waned in proportion to the strength of the wolves it represented. If the Earth-Wolves were strong, then the spirit within their Crétioll grew strong as well, and the trees of their forest spread to invade the other lands. If the Fire-Wolves were stronger than the others, then the desert sands would spread."

Confused, Hawk said, "But wouldn't Lough Soluna keep them in balance with each other?"

Storm shook his head angrily and snapped. "I was getting to that! Now don't interrupt, unless you think you can tell this story better than I."

When Hawk made no move to comment, the Wind-Wolf continued. "Where was I…oh yes. At this time, Lough Soluna didn't exist. There was no need for it, as each nation had strength equal to the others. But then Rock and Stone upset the balance of power, and even when they were defeated the Island was all kinds of messy. The prey started to die, and the nations started to fight one another. The borders became blurred as the fights became more intense, until Soluna was caught up in a civil war. Sands, mountains, marshes, and forests advanced and retreated as their armies won and lost battles. This is the reason Taladair has mountains and Gaoibeanna has a forest.

"This continued for many years, until many had forgotten exactly what it was they were fighting about. But pride kept any wolf from backing down and seeking a peaceful end.

"One wolf, a female Wind-Wolf by the name of Hawk…yes she is most likely your name-sake, Hawk," Storm added at the Fire-Wolf's look of surprise, "saw the terrible state the island of Soluna was in, and decided to put an end to the fighting. She had lost her entire family to the war and was tired of bloodshed. But she was among the few who felt that the war needed to stop.

"Hawk first tried talking to the generals of the different armies. Some welcomed her but more turned her away. Even her own clan called her a traitor for seeking to end the war without victory to the Wind-Wolves. Finally, Hawk turned to the gods for help.

"Calling on Sun-Wolf and Moon-Wolf, Hawk begged for a way to stop the fighting. She promised that she would do anything, *give* anything, to put an end to this brutal civil war that was tearing her beloved island apart. This is what she was told: No element can stand alone. If even a single element were to disappear, Soluna would fall into chaos. The spirit of each nation is at war with each other, their imbalance causing strife both in the spiritual and the natural realm. You must restore balance to the elements if there is to be peace. When you see our sign, then you will know. Go to the center of the lands, and Sing the four elements together, then bind them with the primal elements.

"You said you would give anything for peace…for peace to come you must give all.

"Despite not knowing what this 'sign' was or how she was supposed to sing the elements together, Hawk travelled to the original center of the four lands. When she had arrived at the place where legends claimed Sun-Wolf and Moon-Wolf had descended from the sky to create the elements, something extraordinary happened.

"At noon, with the great sun high in the sky, the three moons came to rest in front of it, led by the largest moon. Hawk looked up to see a single celestial entity: Moon and Sun together as one. She knew that this was the Sign she was waiting for. She tipped her nose to the sky and began to sing, her voice calling on the untamed powers of the four elements and the primal elements of Sun and Moon. But only the elements of Fire and Wind, which became Sun as they were channeled through the Eclipse, would obey her, as she was a daughter of Sun-Wolf. The moon elements owed her no allegiance, and ignored her call.

"Then another voice sounded. It belonged to a Water-Wolf male whose name has been lost to history, Hawk's companion as she journeyed to find the center of the lands. He sang Water and Earth through the Eclipse, purifying it into Moon, and wove them with the sun elements. Hawk and her Water-Wolf companion sang together, their voices as one, and made the elements heed their call. Through their song, the four elements were tamed and sent back to their Elemental Guardians within each land. The nations regained their former borders, which were made stark and clear. And swirling together at the center of the island of Soluna, around Hawk and the Water-Wolf, were the primal elements. Hawk and the Water-Wolf sang four mountains into existence, one at the corner of each land. These became Mounts Gao, Sca, Uisc, and Tal. Barriers of Wind, Fire, Water, and Earth rose up between the mountains. At their center a lough in the shape of the Sign Hawk had seen in the sky was born. This was Lough Soluna.

"The Song of the Eclipse was ended, and Hawk and the Water-Wolf vanished from our world. They were taken into the sky to dwell with Sun-Wolf and Moon-Wolf. Lough Soluna, created by their song, was declared sacred ground and sealed off. It became the connecting point between the four elements of Soluna, keeping them in balance with each other so that no one element becomes more powerful than the others. And it is said that Lough Soluna is also where Sun-Wolf and Moon-Wolf can enter our world and walk among us," Storm said, then scowled. "Of course, even *after* the creation of Lough Soluna, some wolves will still try to conquer the Island to make *their* nation the strongest. But they can never *truly* conquer another nation, as each element is bound to its native land. At some point the balance will be restored."

That's what River plans on doing with the magic of the Elemental Guardians, Hawk thought, his eyes widening. He barely heard Ray start a debate with Storm over the validity of the story, as the Fire-Wolf had apparently heard a different version. *She's going to sing the Song of the Eclipse…and she's going to try and do it on her own.*

Hawk thought back over the story, and what the spirit had told him at the Fáinéitin.

She can't do it on her own. I have to sing it with her. Even if I didn't possess the Fáinéitin's Fire, the sun magic would kill her if she tried wielding it. She needs a sun element to sing the other half.

"Hawk believes me," Storm said, dragging Hawk out of his thoughts. "And *he* knows how to respect his elders."

"Your memory is less than sharp," Ray said. "I've heard that story three times, but I've never heard of some 'unnamed Water-Wolf'. Why is he even in the story if we don't know his name?"

"How should I know? It happened a thousand years ago. I just know the legends, so unless *you* were alive then shut up and accept my telling."

"If it happened so long ago, some details might have been lost," Hawk said, trying to diffuse the argument. "Things may have been exaggerated as well, depending on who's telling it, so there could be many different versions of the same story."

Storm flattened his ears and growled. "*My* version is the correct one."

"Of course it is," Ray said soothingly. "Why don't you tell us another story?"

"No, you'll just argue with me again. I'm going to take a nap and hope the rain stops soon." Storm shuffled until his back was facing the two Fire-Wolves and swept his tail across his snout in an obvious dismissal.

I wonder if River's ever heard that story, Hawk thought as he and Ray padded away. *She should know that she can't sing the Song of the Eclipse on her own, that it will kill her if she tries.*

When we leave Ray and the others at the border, I'll have to tell her.

Chapter One Hundred and Six

THE STORM LEFT as quickly as it had come, but the floodwaters took several more hours to recede enough for the wolves to continue on their journey. River urged them to go at a blistering pace, slowing only when Hawk and Ray protested on Storm's behalf.

It only took them three weeks to reach the Scaineadó-Uiscean border. Hawk felt a curious mixture of excitement and nervousness as the distant marsh slowly came into view. But all of them, even Spruce, became hesitant as they drew closer to the line dividing the lands. They had been careful to avoid patrols on the journey to the border, but now they were so close to the marsh it would be extremely difficult to avoid notice.

"This is where we leave you," River said after calling them to a halt. "The Lonradh River is just beyond those dunes. Any closer and we risk being seen by the border guards."

Hawk glanced over to the dunes. He could just barely see the dark shapes of trees over the sand. In the near-darkness it was difficult to discern them from the sky above. When he sniffed the air, the faint scent of mud and water reached his nose.

The Uiscean Marsh is right over there, he thought. *We're so close.*

Spruce was surprisingly somber, and nodded without protest. "Well, it was fun. Never attacked a fortress before. If you somehow miraculously survive your adventure in the marsh, come find us. There are plenty more fortresses to go destroy."

"Go north, and look for a Wind-Wolf named Sky," Hawk said, stepping between the two she-wolves. "An army is gathering in the Gaoibeanna Mountains. Storm's family is there, too. I'm sure they'll be happy to see him."

Storm's eyes lit up, and he nudged Ray. "I don't care what Spruce does, but *you're* taking me to see my family, Alder."

"Wonderful, we just might have to pay a visit," Spruce said, interrupting Ray's protests that his name *was not* Alder. "I'd love to—"

River and Spruce stiffened at the same time. River's hackles raised and she bared her teeth. "Demons!"

Not a moment later, eight monsters crested the dunes, yowling their battle cries. Four Hell-Cats led the charge, their white fangs gleaming and their eyes filled with hunger. Three Fire-Fangs and a Darkclaw soon followed them. Spruce immediately launched into action and, without warning Storm, raised four walls of stone from the sands to trap him within them.

"You'd only be a hindrance," Spruce said coldly when he tried to protest. She raised another flat chunk of stone to close off the top. "I don't want to have to worry about you during the fight. You, Fire-Wolves, get the Fire-Fangs. River, the Hell-Cats...*just do it!* Almond, we've got the Darkclaw."

Ignoring any protests from River, the Earth-Wolf howled a challenge and charged the oncoming demons. She and Almond barreled through Hell-Cats and brushed by the Fire-Fangs, knocking them all aside with buffeting sand. Almond threw himself on the Darkclaw, allowing Spruce to duck around them both and blindside the black-furred demon with a blast of sand.

River, although obviously peeved at being told what to do, nonetheless launched herself at the four Hell-Cats, sweeping them off their feet with a whip of water.

"We have to protect Storm," Ray said, drawing Hawk's attention back to the battle. The two Fire-Wolves backed up against the box of stone as the Fire-Fangs approached. "We can't let them break through."

One of the Fire-Fangs snarled and lunged for Hawk, forcing him to duck to avoid a snap that would have taken an ear. He flipped around and raked his claws down the demon's stomach. The scales covering the demon's hide took the brunt of the attack, but Hawk still managed to leave several bloody streaks. Ray grabbed the Fire-Fang and threw it into its companion, knocking it aside as it charged for the two wolves. The two demons scrambled to regain their paws, but Hawk and Ray fell upon them with tooth and claw.

The Fire-Fang twisted and sank its teeth into Hawk's paw, causing him to yelp and jump back. The demon immediately breathed out a stream of fire and hissed, "*Egressus.*"

The flames darkened and convulsed before spitting out the lithe form of a Fire-Spirit. Both demon and spirit lunged for Hawk, who scrambled to avoid the double attack. Ray closed his jaws around the throat of the other Fire-Fang to prevent it from doing the same.

Hawk swept his paw through the sand, scattering the grains and forcing the Fire-Fang to fall back, blinded. The Fire-Spirit, unaffected by the trick, growled and dove through sand. Hawk twisted to the side to dodge, but the Fire-Fang, recovering more quickly than Hawk expected, appeared and clawed Hawk's side.

"Leave him alive!"

The Fire-Spirit threw Hawk to the ground as its summoner glared at the other Fire-Fang, who had knocked Ray back with a well-aimed kick.

"I *know*, I wasn't going to kill him," the first Fire-Fang snarled. "As long as he still breathes, then Occisor cannot claim we ignored orders. Besides, he is more interested in the Water-Wolf."

Who is more interested in River? Who ordered them not to kill me? The cold of fear crept over Hawk's limbs, even as he surged to his paws and lunged for the distracted demon. He closed his fangs around the back of the Fire-Fang's neck and gave a hard shake of his head. The demon's neck broke with a loud *crack*. Behind him the Fire-Spirit burst apart into flames. *I have to get to River. Only high-ranking demons are given names, and if the Darkclaw isn't 'Occisor', then something worse is coming.*

The remaining Fire-Fang snarled, its eyes narrowing in anger, and charged for Hawk. Ray pounced, landing on the demon's back and knocking it to the ground. Blood ran down his face from where he had knocked his head against Storm's stone box, but he had a determined light in his eyes.

"I've got this," Ray shouted, struggling to keep the Fire-Fang pinned. "Go find River!"

Hawk gave a brief nod before turning and racing off in the direction he had last seen River. He practically flew over the sands, his red-orange eyes fixed on the trail of prints before him. Curiously he wondered why River had led them so far away, but realized she must have been trying to lure them to the Lonradh River, where she would have greater strength.

He crested the final dune and paused, uncertain if his assistance was needed. River stood on the banks of the Lonradh, surrounded by pools of water, her eyes bright with the light of victory. Two Hell-Cats already lay broken on the ground, dead, and another was heavily wounded and swaying on its paws. The she-wolf herself was only slightly injured, bearing a few shallow cuts across her back and sides. The last demon was pinned to the ground by River's claws. With a swift bite to the neck it joined its brethren in death's embrace.

Shaking in terror, the final Hell-Cat turned to flee from the battle-crazed she-wolf but ran straight into Hawk's waiting jaws. He tackled the demon as it attempted to escape and bit down hard on the back of its neck. A moment later River appeared beside him and finished the demon by breaking its spine.

"What are you doing here?" River demanded. "I thought you were battling the Fire-Fangs with Ray."

Hawk nodded, wincing when the movement opened up a shallow cut on his neck. "One Fire-Fang is dead, and Ray's handling the other one…" He trailed off, remembering the Fire-Fang's words. "River, I think this is a trap. These demons know who we are. They were ordered by a demon named *Occisor* not to kill us."

Halfway through his warning, River stiffened, lifting her head sharply to stare at something behind him. Naked fear flashed through her eyes.

"Well, I certainly didn't expect to find *both* of my prey at the same time," came a cold, cruel voice. Hawk froze, the cold weight of fear pressing down on him. The very air around him and River dropped several degrees. He whipped around to see who, or what, had snuck up on them, and his eyes widened in horror.

No, it can't be.

A large, wolf-like demon stood on the dune above them, towering over them from its high perch. Its black eyes, almost invisible inside the black fur masking its face, stared at them with hunger and gleamed in the low light of the moon above. The rest of its pelt was colored dark red.

Memories of a demon in a snowy forest rushed back to Hawk's mind, and his breath caught in his chest.

Occisor…is a Noxond.

Chapter One Hundred and Seven

HAWK'S LIMBS FROZE up in fear, but he couldn't drag his eyes away from the nightmarish creature. Even River seemed robbed of both speech and movement, and he thought he saw her shaking a little out of the corner of his eye. The Noxond leered down at them, reveling in their terror.

What's a Noxond doing here? Hawk thought, barely able to think coherently in his fear. *Noxond directly serve Letorus...why is it* here *and hunting us? I had thought that maybe the demons had heard about Ignimor...and were hunting us for that...but* this *means that Letorus himself knows who we are and what we are doing...and wants to make sure we are captured.*

Occisor's next words confirmed Hawk's suspicions. "We've heard many things about you, River and Hawk, but I never would have guessed that the two wolves who are causing the lesser demons so much trouble are nothing more than a couple of trembling whelps."

The insult seemed to galvanize River. Immediately she crouched and snarled. "Yet we have managed to destroy *two* of your fortresses and one of your mines, demon."

"The lesser demons are weak. It is no surprise that they grew lax in their duties," Occisor answered, seemingly unconcerned by River's implied insult. It padded down the dune, its cold eyes latched onto the she-wolf. "They deserved their fate, and would have met with worse at the Overlord's claws had they survived."

"Take another step and I'll rip out your throat," River threatened with a vicious snarl. "Why are you here?"

Laughing, the red-furred demon continued its advance. Its aura of fear grew thicker, weighing down on Hawk like stone. "You are *weak*. I am among the strongest of my kind; it would take the strength of *five* Noxond to defeat me, *petty Water-Wolf.* I was sent by the Overlord himself to kill you and bring him your heads...yours, in particular...because it appears that the Fire-Wolf was simply in the wrong places at the wrong times. But I have a personal grudge against you, Water-Wolf. After all, it was my brother that—"

Have courage, Hawk! The voice echoed in Hawk's mind, drowning out the sound of Occisor's cruel voice. He recognized it a moment later as belonging to the Earth-King as a rush of power flowed through him. With a roar Hawk launched himself at Occisor, taking it by surprise and knocking it off its paws. A blast of fire followed his wild charge, and the earth shook as the two combatants crashed to the ground.

"You just made a fatal error," Occisor hissed, its eyes narrowed with anger. "I would have made your death quick, but now that you dared to attack me, you will suffer long before I kill you."

Fighting the aura of fear threatening to freeze his movements, Hawk snarled into the Noxond's face. "Get away from River!"

"Oh? You actually *care* for the Water-Wolf? How amusing," Occisor leered as it kicked Hawk into the dune. Sand crashed around him and filled his eyes and mouth. The large demon stalked toward him, as he struggled to free himself before the demon reached him. "She hasn't told you, has she? You wouldn't feel so protective over her if you knew who she really is…and what she has done."

Before Occisor could say any more, River broke free of the aura and threw herself at it. Sensing the danger, the demon spun around to meet her attack. The two creatures clashed with fangs bared and claws extended, water crashing down onto them both.

"Shut up!" River growled around a mouthful of fur. "I'm your opponent, don't you dare turn your back on me!"

Contemptuously, Occisor shook the she-wolf off and spat several tongues of fire at her, singeing her fur. Not even a scratch marked where she had been biting.

Noxond have the abilities of all the demons below them, and their skin is so tough it can't be broken by normal attacks, Hawk thought as he dug himself out of the sand, remembering Lichen's words. *We have to attack its weak spot!*

Hawk, seeing Occisor advance on River with its fur alight with fire, leapt out of the sand and closed his fangs around the Noxond's thick tail. He pulled back with all his strength, but only succeeded in making the demon pause. Growling with irritation, Occisor yanked its tail from Hawk's mouth and sent hundreds of ice shards flying at the Fire-Wolf. He yelped as several imbedded themselves in his fur, despite his best efforts to melt them.

"Hawk!" River shouted.

"Where are you looking?" Occisor snarled as it tackled the she-wolf.

Hawk shook the ice from his fur, wincing as he aggravated his side wound from the Fire-Spirit, and ran to where River was struggling to free herself from the Noxond's grip.

"The stomach! Aim for its stomach and its eyes!" he screamed before ramming into Occisor's side. He succeeded in knocking the demon slightly off balance, enough for River to wriggle free. Instantly Occisor turned on Hawk, focusing its aura of fear completely on him. The sudden onslaught of mindless terror gripped him, and he stumbled back.

"You are nothing more than an annoying fly," the Noxond snarled. "Slaves should never raise their claws against their masters."

Sudden movement caught its eyes, and Occisor looked up to see River summoning water from the banks of the Lonradh. The rushing water swept over the sand, crashing into both Hawk and Occisor and driving them to the ground.

"Lay a claw on Hawk and I'll send your broken body to the bottom of the river," the furious Water-Wolf snarled.

The demon struggled to stand, wave after wave of icy water crashing down on it, pinning it to the sand. Hawk, swept away from the demon's aura, scrambled to his paws and raced back over to River, searching for an opening to dive back into the fight.

Forcing itself to its paws, Occisor burst through the waves with a roar and tackled River, sinking its fangs into her throat. With a cry, Hawk started to run forward intent on saving his friend, only to stop in shock when the she-wolf melted away into water. A second later, she reappeared under the surprised Noxond, dragging her claws along its belly. Roaring with pain, the demon batted her aside with a powerful paw. She twisted in midair to land lightly just a few paces from Hawk.

Thinking that they had landed a decisive blow, Hawk flashed River a weary grin. In return, she only growled. "Idiot, take a look."

The demon laughed and bared its teeth threateningly as the skin around its wound closed. Flesh and muscle melded together, until not a trace of the cut remained.

"Do you know why Noxond have no scars, no matter how many battles we fight?" the red-furred demon taunted.

River inched to the side, muttering as she went, "Distract it. I need to get back to the river."

Gloating over a victory it was certain it had already won, Occisor continued, "It's because even if you're lucky enough to land a blow, it doesn't take much to heal. You weak wolves, for all your powers, cannot defeat us!"

Terrified at drawing Occisor's attention but knowing that River needed the water to fight effectively in the Desert, Hawk took a deep breath and retorted with his own taunt. "If we're so weak…then why can't you keep control over us?" he said, crouching as though preparing for a charge. "Even as slaves we still resist."

Occisor snarled. "Do not blame my kind for the mistakes of the lesser demons."

Suddenly shadows leapt up from the ground, urged on by the demon, and transformed into cat-like shapes before launching themselves onto Hawk. Surprised by the sudden onslaught, he barely managed to avoid their blows. He yelped when one shadow-cat raked its claws across his chest, leaving bloody furrows. His mind spun from the pain, and he stumbled.

What's River doing? Hawk attempted to light his fur on fire. He was surprised when the flames appeared immediately, forcing the shadow-cats back. *And why haven't Ray and the others come to help? They couldn't be…* He cut himself off before finishing the thought.

Encouraged by his success in summoning, Hawk dove toward two of the shadow-cats, spitting tongues of flame. Strengthened by the Fáinéitin's magic, the fire roared into existence and tore toward the shadow-cats, shocking Hawk with their size and strength.

A sudden cry from behind him made Hawk spin around, afraid that River had been caught by Occisor. But it was the demon itself that had cried out. The she-wolf, finally making it to the running water, had summoned up a large wave to engulf Occisor before freezing its paws to the ground and its mouth shut. Hawk quickly summoned more blasts of fire to burn away the remaining shadow-cats before racing to her side.

"*This* is how you kill a Noxond," she said coldly, before diving toward the demon's stomach with ice-covered claws and tearing into the tender flesh. Long gashes appeared in Occisor's belly fur, but they didn't repair themselves. Instead, the demon's blood continued to flow onto the drenched sands. Its eyes widened with hate and fear. The ice that had coated River's claws had been transferred to the torn skin and froze the flesh.

"If the wounds can't regenerate, then you can die like any other demon," River hissed as Occisor struggled against the ice, but its struggles quickly grew weak as its life bled out of its stomach. Hawk watched with sick fascination as the Noxond, one of the most powerful demons in existence, slowly stopped struggling.

River immediately turned away from the still body. "We need to go."

"What about the others?" Trying not to wince as each movement he made sent spikes of pains shooting through his body, Hawk looked back toward where he had left Ray and the others struggling. He could still hear the sounds of battle. "They're still fighting."

"There are hundreds of demons patrolling the border between Scaineadó and Uiscean, and Occisor may have brought more demons with it," River said. "The only reason it lost was because it underestimated us. We can't afford to waste any more time. We *have* to get across the border before the entire region knows we're here."

"But…"

"Now, Hawk!" River snarled, whirling back around. "It's almost dawn, and we need to be at the border before then. The others will be fine; they're smart enough to know when to escape. Now *move!*"

Urged on by River, Hawk splashed across the Lonradh and raced off through the sands. He glanced once over his shoulder as they drew farther away from the dunes separating them from the others.

Ray, I'm sorry.

Chapter One Hundred and Eight

RAY STUMBLED BACK from the pile of ash marking where the Fire-Fang had fallen. He weakly shook his head, trying to clear his vision, but blood continued to stream down his face. His shoulder and chest ached from various wounds, and his yellow fur was almost red from the blood of his battle.

He looked up to where he had seen Hawk disappear over the dune in search of River. The younger Fire-Wolf had yet to return, and it had fallen silent from that side.

I hope he's okay. Ray took a deep breath, trying to stop his head from spinning. He froze when the wind turned, bringing with it the scent of more demons.

We can't fight off another patrol! Ray spun around and dove for the bottom of the box of stone. Ignoring the ache and stiffness of his limbs, Ray started digging. Sand flew as he burrowed into the ground. *I have to get Storm out of there.*

Powered by the fear of a second wave of demons, Ray quickly opened up a hole large enough for him to crawl into. He wriggled under the wall and dragged himself into the box.

An irate Storm met him the moment he appeared on the other side.

"Finally. What's going on out there? Why didn't you let me out sooner? I could have helped!"

Ray just shook his head. "There's a second patrol coming, but we're not going to be able to fight it off. We have to escape."

To his immense relief, Storm stopped arguing and allowed Ray to guide him to the hole. Ray crawled through the hole first and scanned their surroundings, not wanting to throw the elder out in the middle of a patrol.

Spruce and Almond were still locked in battle with the Darkclaw, but the second patrol had yet to appear.

"Come on, Storm," Ray said, calling into the hole. "Hurry!"

Although he grumbled under his breath, Storm offered no protest when Ray reached in and dragged him out of the hole by the paw. Ray risked one more glance toward the dunes blocking Hawk's battle from view and hesitated. A moment later he took off, Storm close on his tail.

"What are you doing?" Storm demanded.

"We have to find Hawk and River," Ray said over his shoulder. Then he crested the dune and slid to a stop, his eyes widening in horror. Storm halted right next to him and gasped.

The body of some enormous red-furred demon lay in the shallows of the Lonradh River, blood mixing with the once-clear waters. Chunks of ice bobbed along the surface and lined deep furrows in the sand.

But of Hawk and River there was nothing to be seen.

What happened? Where did they go? Ray slid down the slope, although his instincts were screaming at him to turn around and run far away. He had to find some sort of sign that they survived. Dimly he noted that he had never seen a demon like this one before, but had only heard rumors of one that looked so wolf-like.

The yowls of the approaching patrol reached Ray's ears, barely piercing the fog that had settled over his mind as he sniffed around the demon's corpse, trying to pick up the scent of his missing friends. Storm ran down the slope and attempted to pull Ray away.

"Ray, the patrol is here, we have to go!" His eyes wide with fear, Storm paused long enough to glance back over his shoulder, as though expecting the demons to appear at any moment. Both wolves froze when Almond's pain-filled howl tore through the air.

I have to get Storm out of here. Ray shook himself, bringing his focus back to the matter at paw. "Let's go, Storm."

I hope Hawk's— A low growl cut through Ray's thoughts and sent shivers down his back. Horrified, both he and Storm turned back around to see the supposedly-dead demon stir. A single black eye opened and fixed on the two terrified wolves.

"Run, Ray!" Storm shouted, recovering first and taking off just as the demon snarled and surged to its paws. Ray gaped at the monster towering over him and watched in horror as the deep wounds marking the demon's stomach slowly began to close.

"Where did the Water-Wolf and her little friend go?" the demon growled, taking a shaky step toward the still-frozen Ray. Somewhere behind him, Storm was shouting for him to move, to escape. But with the black-faced demon glowering down at him and fear pressing down on his shoulders like a physical force, Ray was barely even able to breathe. "Tell me and I will kill you quickly."

It's talking about River and Hawk, Ray realized with a jolt. Suddenly he could move his legs again and he was running, away from the blood-stained monster. He rushed past Storm, who scrambled after him, fear granting speed to both. *I have to get away, I have to warn them.*

Ice shot out beneath his paws, sending both him and Storm to the ground in a heap. Ray smacked his head against the frozen sheet and lost precious seconds while his head spun and his vision blurred. Storm was already back on his paws and running again.

Claws dug into his shoulder and rolled him onto his back. Ray yelped with pain, but lost the ability to make any more noise when he was forced to lock eyes with the red-and-black demon.

"Where are they?" it hissed, pressing down on Ray's shoulder. His bones creaked in protest. "*Tell me.*"

Ray opened and closed his jaws several times without saying anything. Even if he did know where Hawk and River had gone, he also knew he would die before telling the demon anything, no matter how scared he was.

His mind went blank, save for one thing. A memory of a spell he and his brother had learned years ago, along with a warning against using it, for the spell tended to take the life of its user.

As it had taken the life of their father shortly after passing the knowledge to his sons, in return for saving them from a patrol.

I'm sorry, Storm, I hope you find your family, he thought, closing his eyes for a brief moment. *Hawk, I entrust our memories to you.*

"Run, Storm!" Ray roared, before surging upward and locking his jaws around the red-furred demon's throat, his sudden movement taking the demon by surprise. Before the demon could recover, Ray snarled, "*Ignire animam meam!*"

"NO!" The demon yowled and tried to shake Ray off, but Ray held on tight. His chest quickly grew hot, the heat spreading to the rest of his body until even his mind felt like it would combust at any moment.

Then he and the demon were lost in an enormous explosion.

Chapter One Hundred and Nine

HAWK STUMBLED FOR what seemed like the hundredth time in only a few minutes. His limbs trembled and his vision swam, but still he pushed himself forward. River ran beside him, seeming to show no sign of exhaustion, despite their recent battle.

He risked another stumble by glancing over his shoulder at the empty sands behind him.

I have a really bad feeling, he thought, swallowing hard, thinking of those they left behind to face the rest of the patrol. Hawk looked up at River. Her eyes were fixed on the land before her, on the dark shapes of Uiscean's trees.

"Do you think the others will be okay?" Hawk asked quietly.

River hesitated before answering. "I don't know. We'll have to hope they can escape."

"Why did we have to leave so fast? Why couldn't we stay to help?" Hawk tried not to sound accusing.

"Because if Letorus sent a Noxond after us, then he wants us dead or captured at any cost," River growled. "I doubt the Noxond came with just one patrol; he probably kept the other one waiting so *he* could have the pleasure of catching us himself. And all our efforts up to this point would be wasted if we were captured before even reaching the marsh. And if we don't make it to the border by dawn, we'll have to wait an entire day before we can cross."

"Why?"

"Dawn and dusk are the only two times when we can sneak by without being seen. The patrols will be changing shifts, and the border itself will only be monitored by a few demons. If we can get past them, we'll be safe. The only fortress in Uiscean itself is Letorus' Fortress." River paused. "But it's also built right next to the Archeo…and the Rift."

Hawk nearly stopped with shock. *We have to walk straight toward Letorus' own Fortress? And the Rift?*

"How will we escape detection?" Hawk asked nervously. Surely the demon Overlord would notice them so close to his Fortress.

"I don't know."

Chapter One Hundred and Ten

SPRUCE WASN'T JOKING *when she said it was almost impossible to get near,* Hawk thought nervously as he crouched behind a clump of cacti, eyeing the lines of demons patrolling the border. Stone outposts lined the division between the red sands of the desert and the water-logged earth of the marsh, each within view of the next. Only the cover of the predawn light had kept Hawk and River's approach hidden.

"There is a period of time, for a few seconds, where the border is unguarded," River whispered so quietly Hawk nearly missed what she was saying. "Only a few lookouts in the outposts will be watching, but the dawn's light will make it hard for them to see clearly. We'll cross then."

Then she glanced at his still-bleeding wounds, and her eyes flashed. "Heal yourself! Now!"

Hawk hastened to obey. Muttering the words of the Cneasaithe, he set to work on healing his many wounds. He focused mainly on the most crippling ones, before moving on to the smaller ones. Just as he was about to pass out from a combination of over-use of his power and blood-loss, River hissed, "We're crossing!"

She was instantly on her paws and sprinting toward the border. She ran low to the ground, trusting in the early dawn light to camouflage her movements. Hawk was hot on her tail, following her closely. The border was empty of demons, but Hawk smelled more approaching. He hoped that the scent of the swamps on the other side would mask their own scents.

Within seconds they had crossed.

Immediately there was a change in climate. The air was so full of moisture Hawk felt as if he were running through snow, but they didn't stop until they were at least a mile from the border. Panting, River called for a rest, eyeing Hawk with an almost suspicious glare. "Why aren't you feeling sick?"

He blinked, a little confused. As a Fire-Wolf, simply *standing* in the territory of his polar-opposite should make him feel weak. But he felt fine, post-battle exhaustion aside.

"I...I don't know. I've never felt sick going into other nations," he finally admitted.

River growled. "We'll rest here for a bit. No hunting," she said shortly before curling up in the roots of a tree and promptly falling asleep.

Hawk wondered if she was irritated he wasn't showing the same kind of weakness she had in the Scaineadó Desert. *I never really thought about it…I mean, I felt stronger in the desert than anywhere else, but even here, in the middle of water territory, I still feel fine.* He couldn't imagine why he was exempt from the effects of being in other lands.

But aside from that, I'm probably the first wolf to stand in the Uiscean Marsh since the beginning of the war, he thought with wonder. *Except for River, of course. Although…if she was here before, why didn't she collect the power from Lough Uisceal?* Then Hawk remembered River saying that Letorus' Fortress was near both the Rift and the Archeo, which hid Uiscean's Elemental Guardian. *She probably had to leave the marsh quickly to avoid detection.*

Hawk turned his attention to the untouched swamps around him. The earth beneath his paws was wet and mushy, and mud coated everything. The trees' thick trunks spread into wide webs of roots that extended far into the many pools of clear water. Large clumps of moss hung from branches full of wide leaves. Water was present almost everywhere Hawk looked, in bodies of all shapes and sizes.

So this is the Uiscean Marsh. He didn't really like all the water, both in the air and on the ground, but it was peaceful here. From what River had said, the only patrols they would need to worry about were from the border. Behind the lines of outposts guarding the way in and out of Uiscean, the land lay free from demon defilement.

Faint yowls reached his ears, and Hawk realized that their brief respite wouldn't last long. Demons had detected their scent, and were on the hunt. River was already on her paws, waking from her light doze the moment she heard the calls. "If they think they can trap a Water-Wolf in her own territory, they're dumber than Hell-Cats," River sneered, her voice sounding stronger than it had in days. She had only slept for a few minutes, but already she looked completely rested and refreshed.

Being back in her home territory, with water all around, must give her strength, Hawk thought. Then River was off and running, leaving him scrambling to follow her. He was soon very glad that she was there to lead, because he immediately lost all sense of direction. River ran through mud pits and pools of water, over rotting logs, and once even under a carpet of tree roots that covered a large stretch of swampy floor. By the time the Bann River came into view, the yowls of the hunting demons had disappeared in the distance. Hawk, despite all his efforts, couldn't even smell his own trail.

Finally, River called for a halt beside a large mangrove tree. Hawk was very dizzy, his sides heaving, and he was very grateful they were able to stop. River didn't even appear winded. She spent a few moments carefully listening for their pursuers, before leading her companion into the roots of the tree. Confused, Hawk slowly followed.

"Tree roots were often used as camps for clans," River said, obviously enjoying his amazement when he passed through the outer curtain of roots.

Beneath the tree was a large cavernous opening that could easily fit twenty wolves. The walls and floor were a little damp and covered by moss and mangrove roots, but it was warm and safe. From the outside, the enclosure would be completely hidden.

Now we can rest for a bit, Hawk thought as he settled on the soft ground. *Probably not for long though…we have to get to the Archeo soon…* "River… how much time do we have?" he asked hesitantly, almost afraid of hearing the answer.

The she-wolf paused. "We have a little more than a week."

Dread filled Hawk. They had about a week to cross the Uiscean Marsh, sneak into the Archeo, and make it to the Rift without getting captured or killed by Letorus.

We have so far to go…and so little time. Hawk thought, with a slight whine. *What will we do if we don't make it?*

He gave his head a firm shake to clear it.

We will *make it, or die trying. This is our only chance to free Soluna. We* can't *fail!*

Chapter One Hundred and Eleven

HAWK FELT AS though he had only slept for a few minutes when River woke him. He was sore from the previous day's fight and the subsequent race through the swamp, and hungry, but he doubted that River would stop to hunt.

"Cover yourself." River splashed mud at his face the moment he emerged from the beneath the tree. Hawk instinctively jumped back to avoid the splash, but only succeeded in slipping on the slick earth.

She snorted with amusement. "If you can manage to stand, cover your fur with mud. The last thing we need is for your pelt to give us away."

At the dismayed and horrified look on his face, River laughed.

He did not look forward to splashing in the muck. It was too close to water for his taste. But grudgingly, he walked over to a puddle of mud and rolled in it, covering every inch of his vibrant fur. It clung to his pelt, making it feel much heavier than it should. He sneezed to clear his nostrils of the soupy dirt and shook mud out of his ears. River looked him over with a critical eye, before nodding her approval. "Good, now you'll blend."

Hawk wagged his tail, glad to have passed her test. He knew that his orange fur, while excellent for hiding in the Scaineadó Desert, stuck out like a wounded antelope in any other nation.

Here in the Uiscean Marsh, they couldn't afford even the slightest notice.

Without another word, River beckoned with her tail and set off. They didn't run nearly as fast as yesterday's chase, but the pace was still faster than usual. Hawk was soon out of breath, still a little weak from hunger and blood loss, but he didn't dare slow.

The excitement of being in an unknown territory, while dampened by the endless sloshing through mud, also helped Hawk to keep going. Every step he saw things he had only heard about in stories.

Great blue herons, startled by their sudden appearance, would spread their great wings and take flight, screeching their outrage. Little horned toads, decorated with vibrant colors, croaked from hidden places. Hawk even caught a glimpse of a great marsh moose, standing alone in the middle of a pond, watching them with calm brown eyes. Tendrils of pale green moss hung from its dark brown antlers, mirroring the pale green of its pelt.

Once, Hawk nearly ran into a giant snake, as thick as he was tall and with fangs as long his foreleg. It was mottled with dark greens and browns, and had bright green eyes that were oddly hypnotic. It was only River's quick reaction and a splash of icy water that saved him from meeting an untimely end at the monster's jaws.

"That was a swamp boa," she said when Hawk recovered enough from his near-death experience to continue running. "My father saved my mother from one, and earned his entrance into our clan." She fell silent after that, her navy-blue eyes unreadable.

Hawk furrowed his brow slightly. *Before, when I asked about her father, she claimed she didn't have one. Why say he doesn't exist? She mentioned him with such hate...* Hawk watched her carefully, although he dared not ask.

They set out again without another word.

For all the beauty and danger of this wild new land, Hawk was a little unsettled by its silence. Except for the slight sound of their pads on the soft swampy floor, there was no noise. Even the birds remained silent. It was as if Hawk and River were the only two wolves in the entire world.

River finally broke the oppressive silence hanging over them, just as he was about to say something for the sake of simply making a little noise. "It's too quiet." She sounded almost sad. "This was always the time that the songbirds would emerge from their slumber and start shedding their winter plumage. We could hear their songs all day long, and sometimes long into the night. The marsh moose would begin their courtship battles, and the swamps would echo with their calls. Even when it was quiet, usually on a hot day or around noon, you could *hear*..." River's voice trailed off, but Hawk was dying to hear more.

Silence fell once again, and he knew she would not continue.

She pushed them to pick up the pace. The miles quickly disappeared as they crossed the wet swampland. Hawk, so focused on keeping up, hardly even noticed the times they were forced to forge a wide river. His concentration, coupled with his exhaustion, gave him no time to think about being afraid of the water.

Finally, after six days of hard travel, they reached the Archeo.

CHAPTER ONE HUNDRED AND TWELVE

IN THE SKY above, a single large moon was rising, its normally silvery surface dyed red as the sun. River spared a single glance at the sky before leading Hawk down a path that twisted through a thick clump of trees. The farther they walked, the more Hawk got the feeling he was in the wrong place and needed to turn back.

We must be getting close, he thought, just as they stepped out into a clearing. He paused, confused at first. The clearing was empty. River must have taken a wrong turn somewhere. Hawk almost said as much, before remembering he had felt similar things standing in front of the other Elemental Guardians. It was all part of the magic protecting the Archeo. He narrowed his eyes, concentrating, and slowly the Archeo came into view.

The clearing filled with a thick mist, a wall of gray that stopped suddenly a few lengths in front of Hawk. It stretched high above the surrounding trees and obscured part of the night sky. Somewhere in the expanse of the mist was Lough Uisceal, but Hawk could see no break in the wall that might denote an entrance.

"We are dangerously close to Letorus' Fortress," River said quietly. "Patrols aren't regular, but we need to stay on our guard and move quickly. He will more than likely sense a disturbance in the mists and send out demons to investigate. Hawk, because you're a Fire-Wolf, it may not allow you in."

Hawk swallowed a little nervously. He had a sneaking suspicion about what River was going to say next.

"If it won't let you in, I don't have time to argue with it. You will have to hide yourself out here. There are no mangrove trees nearby, so find a large mud pit. The water will diffuse your scent."

Nodding, Hawk tried not to show his fear. He fervently hoped that the spirit of the Archeo would allow him entry.

River turned back to the wall of mist and said, "I am River, daughter of Rain and Mist. I seek to use the power that slumbers within this sacred place to defeat the Demon Overlord. Therefore, I beseech you, Mother Moon-Wolf, to grant me safe passage through the Archeo."

The mist started to ripple the moment River opened her jaws to speak. The outermost layer swirled and solidified, until it formed the shape of a gray wolf with silver eyes. Those eyes glared at River with such an expression of hate and anger that Hawk shivered, although the look was not directed at him. Surprise crossed River's face, but she met the wolf's eyes with an equally calm intensity.

"Now you and I both know that's a lie, River," the wolf said in a cold female voice, its teeth bared in a silent snarl. *"I cannot allow you passage."*

The shock in River's navy-blue eyes was evident even from where Hawk stood, surprise on his own face. *I can understand why the Fáinéitin, the Ardgao, and even the Crétioll would refuse her entry...* Hawk flattened his ears. *But for her* own *Elemental Guardian...when she's also the daughter of Uiscean's Queen...to refuse her...*

River quickly covered her expression with a carefully controlled façade. "I need to get to Lough Uisceal. Time is running out for Soluna...and..."

Shaking its head, the spirit wolf cut her off. *"There are rules that must be adhered to. I cannot let you through."*

Then it seemed to notice Hawk for the first time. Its silver eyes softened, and it quietly padded toward him. It circled him a few times, looking him over. The Fire-Wolf held his breath, not daring even to move, although he tried to follow the spirit's movements with his eyes. Finally the misty wolf stopped in front of him.

"He is pure and may pass."

He took a step back, shocked even more than before. Hawk couldn't believe that he, a *Fire*-Wolf, was granted passage through the Archeo when River, a *Water*-Wolf, was refused. For a moment he thought he had misheard the wolf, but the look on River's face said otherwise. Her face closed up and emptied of all emotion, and she pointedly looked away from him. "Go," she said shortly as Hawk continued to gape, looking from her to the spirit wolf. "I will wait out here."

"Come, Hawk, you must hurry," the silvery wolf said urgently. *"You do not have much time."*

Swallowing down his nervousness, Hawk nodded silently and shot River one last look. She had already turned away and padded off to find a hiding spot. Looking back at the spirit, Hawk took a deep breath. "I'm ready."

Then he stepped forward as the spirit wolf lead him into the wall of clouds, and he quickly vanished into the Archeo.

Chapter One Hundred and Thirteen

It was unnerving walking through the thick mists surrounding the lake. Hawk could barely see his snout, much less where he was going. He was very grateful that his guide glowed with a soft silver light, and that the ground was firm and dry. If it weren't for that, he would have most likely lost his way and drowned.

Even so, at the pace the spirit was leading him through the mists, Hawk was forced to focus very intently on where he placed his paws or risk slipping off the path. It afforded him no time to ponder the question he had been silently asking since entering the Archeo.

Why was I allowed in and River refused?

In seemingly no time at all, Hawk broke free of the thick covering of clouds and was presented with the breathtaking sight of Lough Uisceal.

The slim shape of a crescent moon stretched far and wide in the middle of a large, flat clearing, surrounded by the almost-solid wall of fog. The water within the banks of the lake glowed with silver light and rippled as though pushed by a gentle breeze. It was more fluid and graceful than any other body of water he had ever seen.

As the spirit faded away into the mists behind him, Hawk slowly padded forward, forgetting for a moment the urgency of his mission in his awe of the sacred lake before him. He paused for a few moments upon reaching the banks, before looking out across the silvery waters and saying, "I, Hawk, son of Phoenix, stand before you, Mother Moon-Wolf, to beg for your help. The land and your children are enslaved by a monster, and I seek to free them. Only with your help will I be able to do so. If you so will it, grant me the power I need by the Night of Moon-Sun. I swear that I will not use your power for evil deeds, and if I should break my word, my life may be taken as punishment."

Waves crashed on the shore, rising up from the lake, which quickly brightened to blinding levels. Power coursed all around him, but Hawk stood his ground.

Slowly the light faded, leaving the waters dimmer and moving more sluggishly than before. The Lough itself seemed almost empty, as though the divine presence that resided in it was gone.

"Come, Hawk," came the spirit wolf's voice, much quieter, and Hawk turned to see the vague shape of a wolf padding toward him. Quietly he followed it, the light it shed just barely enough for him to see. The journey back through the mists passed much faster, and soon he was back in the open air.

Almost immediately the spirit vanished, leaving Hawk alone once more. He looked around a little nervously for River, not wanting to remain out in the open on his own. A few moments later she rose from a small pool of water, her eyes still dark with a barely contained anger. Hawk watched her warily as she approached.

"Let's go," she said gruffly, brushing by him. "We still have to sneak around Letorus' Fortress."

"Why don't you allow us to escort you there, Water-Wolf?"

All feeling drained away from Hawk's body at the demon's voice, as both he and River whirled around, hackles raised and fangs bared. A Noxond stepped out of the trees, followed by eight demons, which encircled them and cornered them against the impenetrable wall of mist before either wolf could react. The Noxond bared its teeth in a feral grin at their shocked expressions.

How did we not notice all these demons? Hawk thought, struggling to contain his terror. *How did they find us? Where they* waiting *for us?*

"Thought you were clever, didn't you?" the Noxond hissed, slinking toward them. The circle of demons, comprised of a mixture of Ice-Fangs, Fire-Fangs, and Hell-Cats, shifted and watched with hungry eyes, but they didn't break ranks. "Too bad the Overlord Letorus knew where you were headed."

"Take one more step closer and I'll carve your eyes from your skull," River snarled, snapping out of her shock and taking a battle-ready stance. The Noxond cackled with laughter.

"You already tried that once. What, don't recognize me?" the Noxond asked, pausing for a moment. "I'm hurt; I was hoping to see the despair in your eyes as I tormented you to the brink of death. The Overlord wants you alive, but I'm sure he won't mind if you're a *little* roughed up. Unlike you, *I* know when my enemies are dead."

A sick realization filled Hawk, and his heart dropped to his paws.

Occisor...but he should be dead! We killed him!

"I left you alive as a warning to Letorus," River sneered, giving Occisor a haughty look. "But it appears he ignored it. Just try and take us; we beat you once, and we can do it again. *This* time we won't leave the battle unfinished."

The Noxond only snorted. "You *left* me, you say? Lies. You *thought* I was dead, but you failed to kill me. Even your Fire-Wolf friend couldn't finish me off, although even I will admit that his little suicidal spell came very close. But now I will look forward to having my revenge against you. Both of you, now that the little Fire-Wolf whelp has given me reason to target him as well. You, *Water-Wolf*, killed my brother. And you, *Fire-Wolf*, raised a claw against me."

River flinched, and Hawk flattened his ears a little, his slave collar suddenly seeming heavier than it had in months. He froze, the red-furred demon's words slamming into him like a wall.

Fire-Wolf friend...he couldn't be talking about Ray? Hawk shook, the words *'suicidal spell'* echoing in his mind. *What did Ray do?*

"You and your little army?" the she-wolf taunted.

Hawk tried to send her a warning look against baiting the powerful demon, but she paid him no attention.

"Too afraid that we'll defeat you again on your own?"

Snarling, the Noxond took a step forward and unsheathed its claws. "You *dare* to call me a coward? I did not fight at my full strength and did not expect the Fire-Wolf to participate in the battle as well. Without his help, you could not have even come *close* to defeating me!"

"Hawk, make sure its *friends* don't interfere," River ordered, not once taking her eyes off the demon crouching in front of her. Her navy-blue eyes gleamed with bloodlust, and she bared her teeth in a threatening snarl. "I'll show you I can kill you on my own."

"Do not kill the Fire-Wolf, but make sure he cannot escape," the Noxond said coolly to its companions. "You may do what you like with him, so long as we can present him to the Overlord alive."

Dread filled Hawk as the circle of demons snarled and began to approach him. He looked to River, hoping she would have some way to save them, but she was focused completely on the Noxond. He turned back to the quickly approaching enemies, and felt a fear so absolute it was as if thousands of Noxond exerted their aura on him.

Hawk...

Suddenly the Earth-King's voice filled his mind and time seemed to slow as a ghostly images of the first Earth-King and his companions appeared between the demons. Hawk jumped back in surprise, wondering if his terror was making him see things.

We can lend you our strength one last time, the Earth-King said, padding forward until he stood in front of Hawk, looking down with sad eyes. *Save her before it's too late.*

Tipping his head back in a howl that was echoed by his ghostly companions, the spirits raised their voices in a song that made their forms shimmer before turning them into a mist that flowed into Hawk. He gasped as the strength of the Earth-Wolves surged through him, making him feel as though he had the power to challenge Letorus himself.

Time unfroze, and the mass of demons charged Hawk, but he was no longer afraid. He had the power of the first Earth-Wolves on his side. He didn't even have time to wonder about the King's ominous message before plunging into the battle.

The three Hell-Cats reached him first, hissing at him with claws unsheathed and fangs bared. Hawk met them with a roar, summoning a huge blast of fire to knock them off their feet. He pounced on the nearest and breathed out a stream of flames, singeing its fur. The Hell-Cat screeched with pain but was quickly silenced by a bite to the neck. The other two Hell-Cats, enraged by their companion's death, charged Hawk once more. He snarled and darted forward, when a large crack opened up in the earth in front of him, swallowing the charging demons before closing.

Not allowing himself to be distracted, Hawk turned to face the Fire- and Ice-Fangs. They approached more warily, obviously not wanting to run into a blind charge after seeing the demise of the Hell-Cats.

"Why are we cowering like mice?" one Fire-Fang exclaimed, baring its teeth. "We are stronger and more numerous than he! Attack!"

Thus emboldened, the Fire-Fangs charged Hawk. The Ice-Fangs sent shards of ice soaring over the Fire-Fangs' heads toward Hawk. He jumped back to avoid the projectiles, and a wall of earth rose up in front of him. The ice shattered on the unbreakable mass of stone, and one Fire-Fang, unable to check its momentum, crumpled against it. The other Fire-Fang snarled and swerved around it before leaping on Hawk. The two rolled across the muddy ground, coming dangerously close to the Archeo, snapping at each other's throats. With a surge of strength, Hawk raked his hind claws down the Fire-Fang's stomach, before kicking the demon away.

The Fire-Fang stumbled, struggling to keep its balance, before crashing to the ground and falling into the mists. Its screech of horror was suddenly cut off by a yowl of pain, and then there was silence. One of the Ice-Fangs, which had been trying to creep up on Hawk from behind, immediately jumped away from the Archeo. Hawk took advantage of its momentary distraction to shoot a blast of fire at it, an attack that was backed by a crack in the earth splitting through the marshy ground.

Suddenly two cold bodies pressed down on him, cutting off his fire and making the breath leave his lungs with a *whoosh*. He had forgotten to watch the other two Ice-Fangs, who had each summoned an Ice-Spirit to attack. The two Ice-Spirits froze his paws to the ground as the three Ice-Fangs spread a sheet of ice all around him. Hawk would have a hard time keeping his balance if he couldn't melt it.

Wildly he struggled, the cold of the ice creeping through him. He tried to melt the ice trapping his paws, but the Ice-Spirits kept him distracted by raking their claws through his thick fur, drawing bloody furrows in his sides. The earth shook a little, shattering the ice in places, but the Ice-Spirits quickly froze the cracks over.

"We'll teach you for daring to stand against us, slave," one Ice-Fang hissed, and crouched to leap at Hawk, its cold eyes dark with a thirst for blood.

A loud keening split the air.

Hawk and his Ice-Fang attackers froze, shocked, and turned to the source of the cry.

Occisor was panting a little, but relatively unharmed aside from a bloodied eye socket and a few scratches on its stomach. River looked much worse for wear, deep wounds crossing her back and shoulders, and she held one of her hind paws at an awkward angle. She had her head down and was swaying slightly, whining in an eerily high-pitched voice.

With a shock, Hawk realized *she* was the one who made the sound. Even Occisor looked shocked, as it had yet to attack the Water-Wolf in her moment of weakness. Suddenly River looked up, and Hawk's blood ran cold.

River's eyes had turned black and were devoid of any emotion.

They were the eyes of a demon.

The cold aura of fear emanated from her, causing even the Ice-Fangs and Occisor to cower. Almost immediately her wounds started to close, and her paw realigned itself. Soon River stood unmarked and fresh as if she had yet to go into battle.

Breaking out of its moment of shock, the Noxond chuckled, its eyes narrowing. "I knew your blood was strong…but I did not expect you to be able to change without a demon's power."

River curled her lip in a distasteful snarl.

"What change?" she said in a terrible voice. "This is simply an awakening."

She pounced on the Noxond, her pelt quickly turning dark red until it mirrored her opponent's own pelt. The fur around her eyes and down her spine turned black.

"We must warn the Overlord," one Ice-Fang said, and they immediately fled the scene of battle, leaving Hawk standing alone in the face of River's true identity.

Memories of all the times River had shown uncharacteristic violence, demon-like tendencies, the lack of wounds no matter how fierce the battle, the unusual rate of healing of the few wounds she did acquire, and the many times she nearly attacked and killed Hawk in a blind fury flashed through his mind.

She's a demon, he thought with a sickening feeling. He felt as though a bottomless pit had opened up beneath him, and he was falling. *Coal even said she smelt like a demon…and the Elemental Guardians didn't allow her entrance at first because she was 'impure.' She's a demon…but not just any demon…*

…a Noxond…

CHAPTER ONE HUNDRED AND FOURTEEN

THE BATTLE BETWEEN demons unfolding in front of Hawk grew increasingly more violent. Attacks of all sorts, physical or otherwise, were launched by each combatant. Occisor soon realized River was much stronger than it had first thought, and it quickly found itself in a battle for its life. A sadistic grin stretched across her face, and she seemed to take great enjoyment in ripping her claws through the demon's flesh.

With a cry of pain, Occisor fell heavily to the ground, its legs broken. River towered over it triumphantly, her fangs stained with its blood, her eyes glowing with madness.

"Even if you kill me, there are thousands of demons searching for you," Occisor hissed, sensing its approaching death. "The Overlord will send his Blood-Frenzies to track you. You will not escape his wrath."

"Try me," the she-wolf snarled, before sinking her fangs into Occisor's neck, breaking through its iron-hard pelt. The demon jerked once before growing still.

This time there would be no miraculous return from the dead.

The Noxond was no more.

Hawk whimpered, and River's head turned sharply to fix him with a cold, hungry stare. There was no recognition in her eyes as she silently stalked toward her new prey.

Hawk! The Earth-King's voice shouted in his mind. *Our strength is fading; we cannot last much longer in this world. You* must *break free and save River from the darkness that envelops her!*

How can I? Hawk silently wailed, struggling harder against the ice that trapped his paws. Frantically he tried to melt it, but the ice was too thick. *River said herself, once a wolf turns…there's no turning back! She's going to kill me!*

Have courage! She can still be saved; do not give up! The Earth-King's voice thundered in Hawk's mind.

Tipping his head back, the Fire-Wolf howled to the sky, not caring who or what heard him. Large cracks opened up in the earth, breaking the ice, and flames burst into existence all around him. Within seconds he was free and just barely managed to avoid River's wild lunge.

"Why are you running, little wolf?" River crooned, lunging at him again but missing when he jumped to the side. Another crack appeared just as his paws left the earth, but River simply jumped over it. "I only want to play."

"River! Stop, it's me, Hawk!" he shouted, desperate to make her recognize him. "Occisor is dead, you don't have to keep fighting!"

The she-wolf laughed, the sound sending cold chills down Hawk's spine. "Oh, I know *exactly* who you are, Hawk. You're that annoying little Fire-Wolf who's frightened of his own shadow. Moon-Wolf knows how I put up with you these past months."

What? Hawk was so surprised he couldn't dodge River's next attack. He howled with pain when her fang sank into his shoulder. The she-wolf bit down savagely before shaking her head and tossing him aside. He crashed down on the cracked ice with a whimper.

"But...I thought...I thought I was your friend," Hawk said, struggling to get to his paws. A snort met his words.

"Friend? You were a nuisance, but necessary to my plans. Of course, I have no intention of going through with them anymore...so *you* are no longer needed."

Hawk, get up, the Earth-King's voice sounded in Hawk's head, sounding urgent. *We have but seconds left. You* must *save River!*

Gritting his teeth, Hawk lurched to his paws and faced River, who laughed at his pitiful attempt at strength.

"You think you can stop me?" she demanded, her eyes cold. "You are weak, Hawk, and you always have been. I will be glad when I am rid of you."

Her words hurt Hawk deeply, and he flinched as though he had been struck with a physical blow. He looked up at her with broken eyes, wondering if it was even worth trying to stop her anymore.

She was right; he was weak.

The she-wolf froze mid-step, confusion flitting across her face. Her eyes lightened just a little, but she shook her head and they returned to that terrible black.

Hope soared in Hawk's chest.

River, the *real* River, was still in there somewhere.

"River, please, stop this," he begged, hoping his voice would be enough to snap her out of it. The she-wolf only smirked and lunged at him, her blood-stained fangs bared. Hawk scrambled backward to avoid her attack, but fell when pain throbbed in his shoulder and his injured leg gave out.

"RIVER!" he screamed, as his former friend landed and sunk her claws into his sides. She bent her head to bite his throat, when suddenly the cold aura of fear emanating from her disappeared. River's eyes turned navy-blue once more, and her fur lightened to its normal color. Hawk looked up in fear, thinking the change to be a trick of the demon River had become, to see her looking back down in shock and horror.

"H-hawk?" She rushed back several paces. River stared at him for several moments, shock rapidly changing into horror. She slumped slightly and seemed to collapse in on herself. "Hawk…I'm sorry…I didn't…"

Hawk just stared at River in fear. Then, ignoring the fading voice of the Earth-King, ordering him not to run, Hawk jumped to his paws. He didn't even feel the pain in his injured shoulder as he turned and fled, wanting only to get as far away as possible from the half-demon.

River did nothing to stop him. She still did nothing when a large patrol of demons, alerted by the Ice-Fangs, arrived to take her captive.

CHAPTER ONE HUNDRED AND FIFTEEN

HAWK RAN UNTIL his body gave out, and he collapsed in a puddle of mud. He did nothing but shake for a while, not caring if he made easy prey for any demon that happened to walk by. He still didn't move when he heard a voice from somewhere to his right.

"See? Told you he'd be here."

A pair of paws limped into Hawk's line of vision. One of them was badly broken. Shocked, his head shot up.

"Great Sun-Wolf, Hawk, you look like you've been dragged across a field of rocks," Sparrow said, her one good eye glowing with amusement.

Hawk was surprised to see that none of her injuries had healed since he last saw her. "Sparrow?"

"I knew you were bad at smelling out others, but I'd think even *you* would notice the rest of us standing here," came an irritable voice. Hawk looked past the gray she-wolf, and saw to his surprise that Coal, Palm, Eagle — who was still shooting hateful looks at Hawk — Canyon, and Granite stood right behind Sparrow.

"Coal? What are all of you doing here?" Hawk asked, struggling to stand, only to have Sparrow push him back down.

"Don't try to move just yet," she said as the other Fire-Wolf snorted in answer to his question.

"*She* said we need to be *right here* at *this* moment, no matter what. Because she wouldn't shut up about it, we travelled here to make her happy."

Sparrow rolled her eye at his words, and then looked back at Hawk. "We're not the only ones, Hawk. You've been quite busy, and nearly every wolf in Soluna has heard of your exploits."

Hawk's eyes widened. *Not the only ones...could she mean the rebel army?*

Nodding, Coal continued. "Rumor has it you and River are planning to kill Letorus..." his voice trailed off as he looked around for the aforementioned wolf. "Where is that Water-Wolf?"

Sparrow, as though just now noticing River' absence, jerked suddenly and looked around, her eye narrowed. "Yes...where is she?"

Hawk laid his head back down and closed his eyes. Fear flashed through him as the thought of her tracking him down crossed his mind, but he quickly pushed it away. "I...River, she...she's gone," he said in a whisper, not looking up at either wolf.

"What do you mean, *gone*?!" Sparrow exploded. She shook her head and glared down at the ground, muttering to herself as if she was having some kind of internal argument.

Hawk flinched at her anger. He didn't know why she was mad River wasn't here, but he hesitated to tell her exactly why. Opening his eyes, he glanced over at the rest of Coal's pack, who watched the exchange with confusion and interest. Coal, noticing Hawk's hesitation, turned to the wolves standing behind him and ordered, "Fan out, and be alert for demons. Warn me the *moment* a demon shows its ugly head."

Granite nodded, and then vanished into the undergrowth, the other three quickly following him. Then Coal turned back to Hawk and said, "Well? What happened?"

Taking a deep breath, he told them about the battle with Occisor. Sparrow looked shocked, and then her eye narrowed with frustration. She muttered something that sounded like 'stupid spirit keeping information from me,' but Coal remained emotionless.

"I *knew* she felt like a demon," the rebel leader said when Hawk had finished. Hawk winced.

"Shut up, Coal," Sparrow said sharply, earning herself a hard glare, which she ignored. "Why did you leave her, Hawk? She needs you, now more than ever. You need to help her before she is swallowed by darkness."

"But..." Hawk said, looking up again. His voice trailed off when he saw that both her eyes were open now, and once more bi-colored. *The Winter-Wolf?*

"No *buts*. She can't sing the Song of the Eclipse without you, and Soluna will perish if you two fail to sing."

Hawk's eyes widened. "H-how..."

Coal, too, looked confused. "What?"

"You need to go find her. Now. We'll help," Sparrow said, her eyes returning to normal.

"We will?" Coal said skeptically, his eyes narrowed, obviously not sure what was going on.

"Yes, *we will*."

As Coal and Sparrow started arguing about what exactly they would be doing, Hawk thought about what Sparrow had said. It was obvious the Winter-Wolf wanted him to pursue River…but Hawk wasn't sure if *he* wanted to. The sight of his former friend staring at him with hunger as she tried to kill him and hearing her claim he was nothing more than an annoyance kept running through his mind.

Then Hawk remembered all the times he had promised River that he would stay by her, as her friend, no matter what happened. How she came to rescue him, even to the point of demanding entry to the Fáinéitin, despite the dangers the Fire Elemental Guardian posed to a Water-Wolf.

"You're right," he said finally, interrupting Sparrow and Coal's argument. They turned to look at him, surprised at the strength in his voice. *I can't desert River, not when she needs me the most, no matter how scared I am!* "River needs my help. I promised I wouldn't leave her, and I won't."

Sparrow's bright blue eye glowed with pride. "We know, Hawk. If anyone can save her, it's you."

Chapter One Hundred and Sixteen

Letorus was happy.

Happier than he had been in a long time, ever since before Redacta Spiritus had appeared and prophesized his demise.

For standing in front of him, staring at the floor with empty eyes, was the very creature Redacta Spiritus had said would destroy him. Numerous demons circled her, guarding her in case she tried to attack, but the Water-Wolf didn't appear to even realize where she was.

Pathetic. Letorus padded down from his throne, his claws clicking against the stone floor. A thick white stripe covered his face and stretched down his back, with two spikes of white fur extending behind his shoulders. Two large black spots covered his eyes, making them seem much larger and his gaze unblinking. That, combined with his unusually long fangs, gave him an intimidating enough appearance to send some of the demons surrounding River to scurry out of the way when he drew close.

"So…this is the famous River?" Letorus crooned, leering down at his captive. The thick-shouldered demon chuckled. "I have heard much about you, but I have to say, I am…*disappointed.* I would have expected a wolf of your fame to be more…lively."

Still River said nothing, not even acknowledging his presence. He sniffed. "A pity we could not find your Fire-Wolf friend, but from what I heard he's probably dead by now, killed by the wounds *you* inflicted."

This time he got a reaction. River flinched at the mention of Hawk, pain clouding her eyes, but she made no noise. A little irritated by her lack of movement, Letorus tried a different angle.

"I've actually been waiting a long time to meet the whelp of Excursor… better known to you as *Mist.*"

River's head shot up, and she gave Letorus a look full of loathing. "How do you know of my fa—*him*?"

The Overlord laughed and sneered at his captive, who trembled with rage. *Her ignorance is pathetic.* "Because *I* was the one who sent him to this world to make sure some of you *pathetic* wolves found the Rift and freed us!"

River froze, her eyes wide with disbelief. "*What?*"

"Did you *really* believe that your puny clan found the Rift all on its own? No, it's always been there, existing just beneath the skin of this dimension," Letorus said, leaning in close to River and baring his fangs. "All it took was a push in the right spot to open a hole big enough to send a soldier through. He disguised himself as a Wolf, and spent years slowly leading your clan to the Rift. Who do you think it was that drove your leader, *your mother*, insane? Broken wolves are easier to control, after all, and we needed the power she wielded as Queen of the Marsh."

Shocked, River could do nothing but stare. Letorus continued to laugh at her mounting horror as she was forced to face the truth that she and her clan had never been anything more than pawns in the overall plan.

"Restrain her," Letorus said, backing away from River. "It's time she was fully awoken to her true self."

He turned to pad back up to his throne, baring his teeth in a pleased smile when he heard her struggle against her captors. A few demons yowled when she managed to get a blow in, but Letorus knew that even she couldn't fight off all of them.

As a wolf, she is too weak, he thought, stopping just in front of his throne and turning back around. River was pinned beneath two Darkclaws, one of whom had a slight scratch above its eye. She thrashed against them, but they held her tight.

"No!" Her eyes were full of hate and fear as she shouted at Letorus, who only smirked at her struggles. "I won't let you!"

"It's not a question of whether or not you will *let* me, *half-breed*," Letorus said lazily. "Embrace your fate, for there is no escape."

River howled, her voice echoing through the halls of Letorus' personal Fortress, as the demon Overlord approached her, an evil black aura appearing about him before flowing out to envelop her.

Chapter One Hundred and Seventeen

River struggled to resist Letorus' magic, which worked to suppress her own consciousness in favor of the demonic one residing in the deepest parts of her mind. She could *hear* her other self laughing at her wolf self's pathetic attempts to maintain control. *I…will not…give…in…to you again!* She — River, the River that would defeat this demon, the River she was determined to hold onto — snarled.

Her demon self just chuckled. ***Oh, but you already have.***

Memories of her vicious attack on Hawk came back, forcing her to relive every moment. The shock of it caused the she-wolf to withdraw into herself, to escape the reminder that *she* had almost killed the one friend she had ever had since Pebble's death.

No! River shoved the memories away, refusing to let her other self win. *That wasn't me; I wouldn't hurt him!*

Harsh laughter filled her mind. ***Not you? Are you going to claim that it was me? Let's not delude ourselves. I am you. We are one and the same.***

Cold tendrils wrapped themselves around River, ensnaring her and resisting her struggles.

You like to think there are separate pieces of you, the wolf you and the demon me, but that's nothing but a lie you've told yourself for years so you don't have to face the truth.

River snarled at her other consciousness. *The only lies here are what you are telling me. I am a Wolf of Soluna!*

Perhaps on the outside, but appearances can be deceiving. The demonic part of River drew closer, River could feel its presence growing stronger, and she struggled harder to resist the pull of Letorus's power. Her demon self laughed again. The darkness converged in front of River's mind's eye, twisting into a wolf-like shape. Suddenly River was looking at a mirror image of herself, but one with dark fur and a demon's eyes. The other River bared her teeth in a sickening grin.

The only thing that matters is what's in here, in your mind, and I only hear one voice.

Horror filled River. It was her voice coming from the jaws of the demon-River. Her words, her thoughts.

There has only ever been one of us. All this time, you thought there was another sharing your mind, whispering dark things and urging you to give in? The other River stalked closer. *That was never me; it was always* you. *I only exist because you refuse to acknowledge yourself. But you've always known this, it was just easier to push the blame onto something else, otherwise you would break under the weight of it all. And you couldn't have yourself breaking before you were able to throw your life away, now could you?*

No... River strained against the power holding her in place, but her struggles were quickly growing weaker. *It's not true.*

Oh, but it is. And you *know it. You're already accepting it. Know how I know?* The other River snarled and pounced on her wolf self. *Because* I *am* you.

River howled as her demon self sank her fangs into her throat. Darkness washed over her, but this time River did nothing to stop it. She could do nothing against herself.

I'm so sorry, Hawk, River thought as her own consciousness faded.

Chapter One Hundred and Eighteen

100 years before...

RIVER WAS WANDERING again.

She knew it was dangerous to wander the unknown expanses of the Rift on her own. The only light in the Rift came from a few veins of demonic power lining the smooth glassy walls, but they only served to cast a dim, sickly glow over everything. Sometimes, the glow would vanish, casting those in the Rift into darkness. At times like those, even sound was swallowed by the darkness, making each wolf entirely alone and cut off from any sensation. Even when there was enough light to see, demons lurked in the shadows, just waiting for the unwary wolf to stumble into their waiting jaws. With the wolves almost entirely cut off from their magic, they were helpless to protect themselves.

Many had already been driven mad.

River was long past caring about the risks of being on her own. She couldn't stand the pitying and suspicious looks she got from the rest of the clan. They sorrowed for her lost family, but resented her rule because of her connection to the one who brought the demons in the first place.

With her mother gone, River was the acting Queen, unofficially because she had not yet been accepted by Moon-Wolf, but no one challenged her claim.

No one wanted to start a fight in the middle of demon territory, when even the smallest drop of blood would draw the demons like vultures to carrion. They had learned quickly that as long as they didn't attract attention, the demons would leave them be.

Still, the Water-Wolves had lost many during their first few days in the Rift, although no one knew for sure exactly how long it had been since they had been captured. Only the infrequent new arrivals from the outside, thrown in as they were taken by the demons that were silently invading the marsh, marked any passage of time. And even that soon stopped.

The last Water-Wolf to arrive said the demons were invading the rest of the Island, and that it would soon fall.

What really irked River, almost more than the looks, was the way all the Water-Wolves seemed to expect their unofficial Queen to come up with a plan to escape. She didn't even want to be Queen. To her it was a post stained with her family's blood, but no one else would accept the position.

No one else wanted to be targeted by the demons, should they decide to attack.

So River spent most of her time wandering the Rift, sneaking through the numerous narrow canyons of the prison, avoiding contact with any creature, demon or otherwise.

But there was one more reason that had River going farther and farther away from her fellow wolves. Ever since she had been drawn into the Rift, River could feel something…awakening inside her. Something inside called out to the other demons and eyed the wolves with bloodlust. There were times where she found herself stalking another wolf, not even aware of her actions until something broke her trance.

The changes scared River, and at first she tried to talk herself into believing that they were just side-effects of the Rift, but no other wolf appeared to have her problems.

When River had gone so far as to kill another wolf in a blind rage, she ran away. The clan simply thought she and another wolf had been attacked by the demons and gave them both up for dead.

She dared not return to the Water-Wolves, for fear of losing control again.

"Ah, River, I had thought I sensed you nearby."

She spun around at the sound of her father's voice, a voice she had thought she would never hear again. Her eyes widened and her heart froze when she saw him standing a few paces behind her. His dark green eyes were warm and had their usual smile lighting up their depths, and she could even see the scar around his neck where he had nearly lost his life to a swamp boa. River wanted to race forward and bury her muzzle in her father's fur as if she were a puppy with no worries once more.

But something held her back. Something wasn't right with Mist.

"Dad…? What…*happened* to you?" River asked, eyeing the dark furred wolf.

"I was out hunting, and the demons came. I tried to fight, but they had strange powers and took me by surprise. Next thing I knew, I woke up here." He looked around. "Where are Pebble and Creek? And your mother? You're the only non-demon I've seen."

Her eyes narrowed. "You're not my father. The demons couldn't enter our world until the Rift opened, and that was *after* my father disappeared."

The fake-Mist shrugged. "It was worth a try."

His form shimmered and became indistinct. Mist grew, until he was even bigger than River, who was tall for a Water-Wolf. His shoulders broadened and his fur changed to dark red. A mask-like patch of black fur appeared on his face, and within moments a Noxond stood in his place.

"Holding that form was always so tiresome," the Noxond remarked as it rolled its shoulders. "But it was easier in the physical world, where I didn't have to compensate for the extra demonic energy."

The demon was caught by surprise when River tackled it, throwing it to the ground and baring her fangs.

"How do you know my father?"

Laughing, the Noxond kicked her away with its powerful hind-legs. "Know him? Of course I know him, I know him *very* well."

River rolled upon landing and quickly jumped to her paws. "What do you mean?"

"You stupid she-wolf, is it really that hard to figure out? *I'm* Mist, I *am* your father."

Time seemed to freeze for River, with the Noxond's words echoing in her head. Then she shook it and crouched with a snarl. "Liar."

"Is that doubt I hear?" The Noxond tilted its head slightly and its eyes lit up. "Ah, being in the Rift, surrounded by demonic energy, it must be awakening your demonic blood. Of course, it won't be as smooth a transition if the Overlord were to awaken it. This is a more...*barbaric* method."

"Shut up!" River shouted, but she was already shaking.

The Noxond noticed her fear, and continued its taunts. "You can already feel it, can't you?" It stalked closer, a feral gleam in its eyes. "The need to kill, the way the Rift itself seems to press against you...the urge to *destroy*..."

River seemed to collapse in on herself. It was exactly as the Noxond said.

No matter how she had tried to ignore it, she knew she was slowly becoming a demon.

"And I can already smell blood on your fur. Made your first kill? How did it feel to have a wolf's blood run across your claws, to sink your fangs into its throat as its life ebbed away? Exhilarating, *isn't it*?"

"Shut...up..." River muttered, her shakes becoming more violent and her voice getting weaker. She heard something inside her, telling her to just let go and let *it* take over. *No...not again...*

"No, I think I'll keep talking," the Noxond hissed. "To think that I spent all those years among you, and no one ever suspected me. Well, I only say that because the one wolf who found out I wasn't really a Water-Wolf died by my claws. You remember Heron, don't you?"

River froze. She knew Heron. Heron had been her best friend since puppyhood, until he had mysteriously disappeared shortly before the Rift was discovered. His body was never found.

"You...*you killed him?*"

The Noxond snorted at River's look of horror. "He was foolish enough to try and confront me on his own. It was an easy thing to kill him. If he had stayed quiet, I never would have noticed him, but I'm glad he tried to play hero. Playing the *gentle and wise father* was getting tiresome. But the years of acting were worth it in the end. Watching your mother tear her family and clan apart was very entertaining." The demon bared its teeth in a vicious grin, its black eyes glittering. "Almost as entertaining as seeing *you* break when your pathetic little brother fell into the Rift. I was waiting for him, you know. He was quite surprised to see me and couldn't quite bring himself to believe that a demon was his father, even as he watched Mist's fangs tear into him. We needed his blood, the blood of a half-breed to open the Rift, and the blood of a royal to connect it to the mortal world so the rest of the demons could come through."

River's vision turned red, and her blood pounded in her ears. Something inside her roared in triumph when the Noxond turned to give her a startled look, before everything went black.

When River awoke several hours later, the demon's blood was splattered across her fur, and its mangled body lay at her paws. She turned and ran as far as she could, but she could never outrun the knowledge that she was a monster.

When the elders of the clans got together to plot Letorus' downfall, River immediately volunteered for the suicide mission of escaping into Soluna and singing the Song of the Eclipse. She knew she had the best chance of surviving the escape itself because of her demon blood, and this way she could atone for her sins.

She was a child of a demon, a *monster*, and had already killed once.

She had done *nothing* while her mother's madness consumed the clan.

River barely had control of her actions, and she feared the time when she would give in completely to her inner demon and massacre the other wolves.

Sacrificing herself to save Soluna was the only way she could be redeemed.

Chapter One Hundred and Nineteen

Hawk was shocked to see how many wolves had penetrated the line of fortresses and demons along the Uiscean Marsh's borders. Sparrow and Coal led him back to where the main force was gathered. The rest of the invasion army was hidden throughout the swampland, awaiting orders. As he passed wolves, they greeted him respectfully and even bowed.

"Your story's been spread to every corner of Soluna," Sparrow said as they padded toward the center of the gathering. "The wolves are rising up and banding together in answer to the beacon of hope you've lit. Three wolves in particular have been most helpful."

"Hawk!"

A dark red shape barreled toward him, knocking him off balance and making him wince as his many injuries were jostled. Hawk looked down and was surprised to see a familiar face. "Ash?"

"I did what you and River wanted!" the young Fire-Wolf exclaimed, wagging his tail. "I found the other descendants."

"How? What…why are there so many wolves here? How did you get past the borders, how did you escape detection by the demons?"

Coal snorted and interrupted Ash's excited explanation. "We'll explain everything in a moment. First we need to get those wounds seen to and get you some food."

His stomach growled, as if in answer to Coal's words, and Hawk suddenly realized just how exhausted he was. He gave his tail a weak wag.

"Food and rest sounds good."

⌒

When Hawk had eaten and had his wounds packed with herbs, as he didn't dare cast another Cneasaithe so soon after his last one, he sat down and listened to Ash's story. Sitting with him were Coal, Sparrow, Crow, and the other two descendants.

The Wind-Wolf, Kite, was a small dark blue she-wolf with cold gray eyes. She had bowed her head respectfully to Hawk when she had been introduced, but watched him carefully. The Earth-Wolf, Mole, who was light brown with dark green eyes, was more accepting and gave him a cheerful greeting.

"So after Crow and I left you and River..." Ash's voice trailed off as he suddenly realized the absence of the Water-Wolf.

Before he could ask, however, Crow interrupted. "Ach, keep going, we dinnae have time tae waste. Hawk will tell us about River later."

Nodding, Ash continued. Kite shot Hawk a suspicious look. "Well, anyway, after we left you and River, we decided to find the Wind-Wolf descendant first. It wasn't easy, because I didn't know what I was supposed to look for. I met Kite by accident, actually..." Realizing he was getting off topic, Ash shook his head and kept talking. "After finding Kite, we went to the Taladair Forest. That's where we met Coal and Sparrow, and they led us to Sky and Pine, who were planning an assault on the Uiscean Marsh. They needed our help to rally the wolves. We still needed to find the earth monarchs' descendant, but we did what we could. Then Alpha Spark and the others from the Gathering started joining us."

Here Hawk interrupted. "But how could you do that without making the demons suspicious? Even a Hell-Cat would know something's up if suddenly a lot of wolves start appearing around the marsh's borders."

"Ah...well, we had some help. Coal and his resistance group," Ash said, nodding respectfully to the dark blue Fire-Wolf. "He organized the wolves who had already gathered. We also found a whole network of hidden tunnels beneath the Taladair Forest that helped a lot too. And once we found Mole, we were able to send out a call to battle. Then we started our invasion. We had to sneak across the border, but first we had to get rid of the fortresses guarding it. *That* was hard to do, especially when we had to do it secretly, or we'd alert Letorus. We managed to destroy the whole line of fortresses along the Taladair-Uiscean border, without a single demon escaping. Well, we're assuming that because Letorus hasn't summoned his army to destroy us yet..."

Coal snorted. "Assuming that will lead to failure."

"Oh, stop being such a sourpuss," Sparrow complained. "Go on, Ash."

Ash nodded and continued. "We've been making our way toward Letorus' Fortress, trying to remain a secret for as long as possible. With any luck, we'll be at his gates before he realizes we're here, or at least we'll be in a position where we can take him by surprise. We have the army split, with a leader at the head of each group, to make it easier to sneak through the marsh." Ash paused and gave Hawk a questioning look. "So what's your story, Hawk? Where's River?"

Hawk winced slightly. "River's…been captured. I think she's being taken to Letorus' Fortress." He didn't want to go into detail of *how* exactly she got captured, mostly for her own protection, but partly because it would take too long to explain.

Ash's blue eyes widened in surprise. "Captured? We have to go help her!" He immediately jumped to his paws, as though ready to charge off on his own that very minute.

"Calm down, laddie," Crow said, pushing the younger wolf back down with a gust of wind. "Ye cannae help her if ye go off on yer own."

"Oh…right…" Ash looked down in embarrassment.

Kite spoke up for the first time. "We can't risk getting you captured," she said in a cold voice. "You need to remain here with us and lead the army. River has most likely been taken into the Fortress by now. We can save River when we launch our attack on the Fortress."

This time Hawk jumped to his paws. "No! It'll take days to get there; I have to free her *now*." He glanced up at the sky.

A silver sun was just starting to peek above the horizon, its rays shining through the thinning branches of the trees.

It was the day of the Eclipse.

Coal immediately protested, saying that River would survive in the demon fortress, but Sparrow cut him off. "I agree. Hawk has to leave now. Ash, Kite, Mole, you three need to stay here. Continue moving toward the Fortress. Coal and I will lead our pack and escort Hawk to the Fortress. We'll help him break in."

"That's suicide!" Mole exclaimed, his kind eyes dark with worry. "And you could jeopardize the whole army. What if Letorus gets suspicious?"

Sparrow shook her head. "He'll be expecting Hawk to try and rescue her. He won't get suspicious if Hawk is caught."

Hawk swallowed. *I'd rather avoid getting caught at all, but she does have a point.*

"Who's to say that River *can* be saved?" Coal demanded.

Sparrow fixed her leader with a hard, one-eyed stare. "She can. Hawk will save her."

"Then go," Ash interrupted before the argument could continue. "We'll be okay here. Save River, and we'll meet you at Letorus' gates."

Gratefully, Hawk bowed his head. "Thank you, King Ash," he said formally.

CHAPTER ONE HUNDRED AND TWENTY

DISMISSED BY THE leaders, Hawk followed Coal and Sparrow as they went to go round up the others of their group. They found them waiting in a small hollow on the outskirts of the camp. Eagle looked up and wagged his tail as the cloudy gray she-wolf approached, but to Hawk's surprise she ignored him.

"We are going to escort Hawk to Letorus' Fortress," Coal said, getting straight to the point. Palm and Canyon shot each other worried looks, but Granite kept his gaze locked on Coal's. "He needs to get into the Fortress so he can free River. We will not go with him *into* the Fortress, because he stands more of a chance of surviving on his own. We will hide nearby and wait for the army to meet us."

Coal seemed to be watching Sparrow out of the corner of his eye, as though seeking her opinion. Hawk narrowed his eyes in confusion. *Since when did Coal ask for anyone's opinion?* Noticing his eyes upon her, the she-wolf gave an almost imperceptible nod.

"When do we leave?" Canyon asked.

"Immediately."

Canyon nodded and stood, the other three quickly following his example.

"Fan out, but keep within eye shot," Coal said as he led them away from the army's camp, nodding to a few posted sentries they passed. "Stay alert for any demons. If you're seen, howl and run *away* from us. Do not engage in battle, and do not lead the demons back to camp."

Silence met his orders, each wolf aware of the danger they faced by moving toward Letorus' Fortress and of the importance of the army remaining secret. Hawk was almost sick with tension and apprehension. He knew that by now River had to have been taken into Letorus' Fortress, as he didn't see how the Overlord would let a half-demon run free from his control.

What he didn't see, however, was how he was going to sneak into the Fortress and find her. Freeing her from Letorus' control and whatever it was that made her a demon was just as impossible. River's words about Flame continued to echo in his head.

Once a Wolf turns...there is no turning back, Hawk thought as they made their way through the undergrowth, moving as fast as they could without making too much noise. A sickening feeling washed over him. *She knew, she* knew *she could end up like Flame. Was she warning herself about what could happen if she turned?* Hawk swallowed hard, barely noticing the passing foliage. *What if...there isn't a way to turn her back?* Then he shook his head. *No, I'm not going to give up! I* will *save her, even if it kills me.*

A shout of pain and surprise interrupted his thoughts, and Hawk slid to a stop. Eagle's howl echoed through the trees and Hawk turned just in time to see a dozen demons pour out of the undergrowth. Horror filled him.

"Disregard previous orders, stand and fight!" Coal roared, charging past Hawk to tackle the Night-Lynx about to pounce on him "Canyon, Granite, Palm, stay together. Eagle, *protect Sparrow.* Hawk, stay with me."

Hawk immediately ran to the other Fire-Wolf's side.

"I certainly hope you learned a bit on your travels," he said as they faced the charge of three Hell-Cats. Hawk nodded mutely, praying to Sun-Wolf that they could escape this battle safely. "I'm going to need to borrow your fire."

The battle was furious, with each side fighting like wild beasts, ignorant of their own safety. The earth trembled, the wind howled, and flames roared as the wolves fought for their lives. There were too many demons, and even Hawk realized that they would soon face capture.

"Run, Hawk!" Sparrow screeched, and summoned up a gust of wind that opened a small hole in the wall of demons trapping them. Hawk didn't hesitate as he raced through the gap and out into the wild marshland behind him. A Shade-Tiger broke away from the group of demons in pursuit.

Hawk tore away from the bloodbath, the howls and roars of the battle ringing in his ears, but he didn't dare slow. His heart pounded and his paws practically flew over the swampy ground. The Shade-Tiger crashed through the undergrowth behind him, its furious snarls only making Hawk run even faster.

I have to get away; I have to escape. Hawk repeated the words to himself, hating the fact he was leaving Sparrow and the others to die while he ran, but knowing they were sacrificing themselves so he could get to River. He couldn't waste the opportunity they gave him.

He scrambled over a log just as the Shade-Tiger's teeth closed around his hind paw. The world turned over itself before he was slammed into the ground. His head spinning, Hawk struggled to recover enough to escape but was forced to watch as the striped demon turned to pounce.

I'm sorry, River…I failed.

He was thrust into unconsciousness.

Chapter One Hundred and Twenty-One

"**Prepare yourselves!**" Coal shouted the moment he saw Hawk disappear into the undergrowth, his voice rising above the jeers and yowls of the demons. "This will be our last stand, let's give future generations something to howl about!"

Sparrow barely heard his howl. She had seen the Shade-Tiger chase after Hawk and was struggling to slip through the patrol to follow it.

Hawk can't be captured! She stumbled and growled under her breath. *No, no, not now!*

Cold stole over her limbs, slowing her movements. Sparrow wobbled, struggling to remain upright as her body continued to fail. Her breath started coming in ragged gasps, and darkness was already creeping across her vision.

She dimly heard Eagle jump to her side and was barely conscious of his efforts to get her to stand up again.

I warned you. The Winter-Wolf sounded almost apologetic.

Sparrow sent it a mental growl, too busy trying to keep herself awake to make any physical noise. *I have to help Hawk…I just need a few more minutes.*

I cannot. This is only a fraction of myself, and its power is running out. It took a considerable amount of power to bind your soul to the physical realm, and I used just enough to keep you here until I could get Hawk to where he was needed. You knew this would be your fate when you accepted me into your soul.

But River's been captured, and Hawk doesn't stand a chance of escaping that Shade-Tiger without some help. And what about the rebellion? I can't just die now, not after everything I did to get here!

I am truly sorry, Sparrow. The Winter-Wolf's tone held more emotion than Sparrow had ever heard coming from the spirit. It paused for a moment. *Do you want to see the end of the war?*

Her heart was slowing with every beat, and even thinking took far too much effort.

What?

There is nothing more that you can do to help, but you can see what your sacrifice has earned for your friends. I can take your soul with me. The

Winter-Wolf paused again. *It will mean that you will become a part of my spirit. You will not pass on to the next life, and you will not be reincarnated. You will share my fate, and I do not know if I will continue to exist when this is over.*

Sparrow hesitated only long enough to take one more breath.

Do it.

Chapter One Hundred and Twenty-Two

"Sparrow, Sparrow, please get up, *please.*"

No matter what Eagle did, the she-wolf didn't respond. She continued to gasp for breath, her eyes staring blankly ahead. Her entire body was cold to the touch and although Eagle couldn't find any fatal wound, he knew she was dying.

Sparrow took one more shuttering breath, before going limp.

"Sparrow?" Eagle's head spun and his breath stopped in his chest. His blood pounded in his ears. "Sparrow?"

He knew she wouldn't answer.

No! The Wind-Wolf tipped his head back and howled, his voice so full of pain it caused every creature present to wince. Rage coursed through him, blocking out every other thought. He turned a hateful glare to the demons around him as a powerful gust of wind blew through the trees. It quickly grew more powerful and started stripping the bark from the trees and made the branches groan in protest.

Red washed over his vision, and Eagle threw himself onto the nearest two demons.

They will die for killing her!

Chapter One Hundred and Twenty-Three

COAL SWORE UNDER his breath and dug his claws into the ground. The wind tore at his fur like a living creature, threatening to knock him off his paws. He squinted his eyes against the gusts and managed to catch a glimpse of Sparrow's still body on the ground several lengths away.

How was she— no, she said this would happen. Her time ran out.

A large branch, broken by Eagle's winds, caught the Fire-Wolf by surprise and crashed into him. He was knocked off his paws and thrown into the trunk of a tree, pinned in place by the heavy limb. *There go a few ribs,* Coal thought sourly, struggling to move the branch. The action only resulted in sending lances of pain shooting through his sides and black spots across his vision.

The pain stopped just short of his hips. He couldn't feel his hind legs. Growling to himself, Coal reached far into his mind, hoping to come across some trace of power, but found nothing. *Thought as much. Haven't been able to do anything since I escaped Ignimor.*

He took a shaky breath and leaned his head back against the trunk. *But even if I still had my magic, I would not get far. Be a bit hard to crawl with only two legs. Tch, to think that after all I've been through…all I did…this will be how I die.*

The Fire-Wolf curled his lip and looked down to glare at the Night-Lynx slowly stalking toward him. Its eyes glittered at the sight of his immobility. "Take a step closer and I'll burn your eyes from your skull," he snarled, causing the demon to chuckle.

"I doubt that. I can sense your weakness…it's taking all your strength just to keep breathing."

"Granite! Get them out of here!" Coal roared over the Night-Lynx's head. Sparrow was dead, Eagle was out of control, and he was beyond saving, but he had to get the rest of his pack to safety.

"Coal, no!" Palm shouted, shoving aside a demon to try and race to his leader's side. Granite grabbed his nephew by the scruff of his neck and pulled him back before opening up a hole in the ground behind them. Dragging both Palm and Canyon after him, Granite vanished into the depths of the earth, leaving the demons yowling in frustration. They soon turned their attentions to the rampaging Eagle. It would not be long before he was overwhelmed.

"Where are you looking?" A heavily furred paw pulled Coal's muzzle down, forcing him to lock eyes with the Night-Lynx. Immediately a chill settled over Coal's body and he fell limp.

The Night-Lynx's laugh ringing in his ears, Coal struggled to resist the darkness pulling on the edges of his mind. *No, I won't be taken like this!*

Despite his determination, Coal's mind quickly fell to unconsciousness, and he was lost to the nightmares of the Night-Lynx's spell.

Chapter One Hundred and Twenty-Four

Hawk woke to the jeers and taunts of demons. His head throbbed, making him wince when he raised it, and he blinked in confusion. Slowly, the memories returned, and his heart sank as he took in his surroundings.

Please let me be dreaming, please, please, please.

He was surprisingly unhurt, and his fur was clean of mud, but Hawk felt no better because of it. He was lying on a raised platform in the middle of a large courtyard. Slaves from each nation crowded around the base, watching Hawk with eyes full of pity and relief — pity for his dire fate but relief they weren't the ones about to be punished. In all of Hawk's short life, he had never seen wolves so without hope, so broken and lifeless.

Behind the slaves were hundreds of demons of every rank. Hell-cats, Ice-Fangs, Fire-Fangs, Night-Lynxes, Shade-Tigers, Darkclaws, and even Noxond were present, jeering at the Fire-Wolf. They all knew who he was — the supposed savior of Soluna — and laughed at his current position.

I'm in Letorus' Fortress, Hawk thought, all emotion draining from his body.

In front of Hawk, on the platform, was a large pen closed off by shafts of metal. The spaces between the poles of the metal fence were too small for even the smallest Fire-Wolf to squeeze through, but large enough for the waiting mass of wolves and demons to see between the shafts. On the other side of the pen was a tall, wide door leading into a great building of stone. Hawk thought he could see bloodstains at the base of the door, and he shuddered.

Suddenly the horde of demons fell silent, and Hawk raised his head to see what had gotten their attention. The mass of demons parted, as though pulled by some invisible force, and fear filled every particle of Hawk's being.

A massive black demon with a white face and a white stripe extending down his back emerged from the keep. Two large patches of black fur covered the demon's eyes, making it seem as though a pair of enormous eyes stared right into Hawk. Long fangs protruded from the demon's upper lip, which was curled in a satisfied smirk.

Despite never having actually seen him before, Hawk knew the demon to be Letorus, the Demon Overlord. No other demon had the aura of power that clung to Letorus like a physical wrapping, one that Hawk could feel even from the platform.

The demons bowed as Letorus passed, while the slaves cringed and shrank back as though to avoid a blow. He spared none of them a look and kept his eyes trained on Hawk, a smirk playing about his feral features when he saw the stark terror he had inspired in the orange Fire-Wolf. He was accompanied by two Noxonds.

Then Hawk saw a third demon, padding slightly behind Letorus, and his heart caught in his throat.

It was River, her fur dark red and her eyes black and empty. She didn't even look at Hawk as she followed Letorus onto the platform. The two Noxond marched forward, baring their teeth at Hawk.

"Stand, wolf," one of them snarled, "and bow before your Overlord."

Hawk struggled to stand, his head throbbing, but he forced himself to ignore the pain and looked straight at River, who looked back with blank eyes.

"I'm sorry, River. I failed you. Maybe someone else will have the strength to free you."

One of the Noxond hissed and cuffed Hawk around his head, its claws sheathed. "Do not speak without the Overlord's permission!"

"Silence," Letorus ordered, his voice echoing throughout the courtyard. Every demon leaned forward, trembling with excitement. Even the Hell-Cats knew something was about to happen. The Overlord stared at Hawk for several minutes with eyes full of dark intent. Hawk, although he was so scared he wanted to die right then and there, stared back in defiance at the monster that had enslaved his nation.

Finally, Letorus spoke. "So this is the great Hawk, the one who was supposed to have a way to kill me," Letorus taunted. "Of course, *she* was also included in that fanciful rumor, but River has come to her senses. All that's left…is *you.*"

Hawk said nothing, but kept his eyes on River. She didn't appear to notice his gaze, and instead stared blankly ahead. The insults she had flung at him during their battle rang once more in his head, but he pushed those memories aside. He knew she had only said those things because of the demon's blood that ran through her veins.

"You have caused me a lot of trouble, wolf. Two fortresses lie in ruins, and my largest and most important mine is destroyed because of you. These are crimes that are easily punishable by death. But for daring to stand against me and even spreading false rumors that you could actually *kill* me…those crimes can only be repaid with the destruction of your soul, so that you will wander this land for the rest of eternity as a wraith."

Hawk swallowed nervously but said nothing. Several gasps came from the slaves, but they were quickly silenced.

"However, I am willing to lessen your punishment, so that you will only have to serve me for the rest of your life if you do something for me. I will release you, and you will announce to every wolf you meet that my power is absolute and that I can never be killed. Destroy the pathetic hope you gave them, and you will live. Of course, I will have to apply certain…measures to assure your return to me."

Living as a slave under Letorus is worse than death, even worse than becoming a wraith, he narrowed his eyes. *I would have to live with the knowledge that I betrayed my land.* He could never agree to Letorus' conditions.

"No."

Letorus didn't look surprised at Hawk's answer; in fact, he appeared to have expected Hawk to refuse. The watching demons hissed in anger at his outright refusal, and his Noxond guards growled threateningly at him.

"Very well," the Overlord said smoothly, silencing the demonic crowd with a hard glare. "It pains me to hear that answer. However, I believe *this* will be more effective."

The Overlord turned to the crowd and roared, "Slaves! You are about to witness what happens when I am defied! This *Fire-Wolf* has been spreading rumors of my demise, saying that he even possessed the power to defeat me! I tell you now…I cannot be defeated!"

Yowls broke out from the ranks of demons, supporting their leader's claim. Letorus bared his teeth in a feral grin and waited until they had quieted once more before continuing. "My loyal soldiers, I have allowed these pathetic weaklings to live free for too long! There is no more need for slaves, they have proven to be more trouble than they are worth, and for that they will be punished. I condemn every wolf to death, and *demons* the only creatures worthy of life!"

The slaves were in a state of shock, but the demons made the walls of the fortress ring with their cries. Praises for Letorus and battle cries for the promised bloodshed rose from every demonic throat.

Hawk only felt cold. Not only had he failed to save River, but he had failed the whole of Soluna. It wouldn't take long for Letorus' command to spread, and soon the massacre would begin. And with most of the army camped outside the Fortress, very few wolves would be left to defend against the attack.

Please let them get here on time, Hawk prayed. *Forget about secrecy, they just need to be here to stop this madness!*

When the triumphant cries of the demons had finally died down, Letorus turned to Hawk with an evil glint in his eyes.

"River, bite him and throw him in the pen."

There was no hesitation in her answer. "Yes, master."

And then she pounced on Hawk before he could react, and sunk her fangs deep into his shoulder, reopening the wound. He howled in pain and tried to struggle out of her grip. She was too strong and resisted his efforts. Ignoring his protests, she latched onto his neck fur and dragged him toward the pen. With a shake of her neck she threw Hawk into the pen, and the gate was closed behind him.

"Open the doors!" Letorus yowled.

Hawk struggled to stand, whimpering when his injured shoulder throbbed with pain, and turned to face whatever would emerge from the doors. The other Noxond already had its front paws on the top slats of the fence, with a thick rope in its jaws and was pulling the doors open. Hawk gagged when the stench of rotting flesh reached his nose, and he resisted the temptation to vomit.

"*Adgredere ignis lupus! Macta eum!*" Letorus roared and pounded the platform with a heavy paw.

Suddenly the entire Fortress fell silent. Every eye turned to see what would emerge from the open doors.

For a moment, there was nothing.

Then something slowly walked out of the shadows, sniffing the air. Hawk's heart stopped, and the fear that filled him was stronger than anything he had ever felt before, even when he had fought River.

Five more demons padded out to join the first, growling and sniffing the air, until six Blood-Frenzies stood before Hawk, their long tails, each tipped with a vicious barb, whipping the air. Their long narrow bodies were hardly more than skeletons covered in dark gray scales. Empty sockets sat on either side of the skull where eyes should've been, and small slits right behind the eyes served as ears. Their long, thick claws clicked against the stone platform.

Hawk had only heard stories about these creatures. Mindless killing machines that tracked by scent alone, they were driven into an insane frenzy at the first scent of blood, indiscriminately killing everything around them.

Only six of them existed in Soluna, but they were feared almost more than Letorus. It was possible to escape Letorus, but once the Blood-Frenzies were released, there was no chance of survival. These silent and scentless monsters were impossible to sense and never gave up once they locked on to their prey.

Suddenly the lead Blood-Frenzy whipped its head around to face Hawk, its needle-like teeth bared. Immediately, the other five Blood-Frenzies turned as well, their nostrils flaring.

The Blood-Frenzies had scented their prey.

The hunt had begun.

CHAPTER ONE HUNDRED AND TWENTY-FIVE

WITH A SPEED almost impossible of living creatures, the Blood-Frenzies attacked. The Fire-Wolf yelped and scrambled backward to try and avoid their wild charges, but they were upon him in an instant. River stared blankly ahead as five sets of razor-sharp teeth latched onto the Fire-Wolf, making him howl in pain. The sound echoed in River's mind, making her twitch slightly.

The Blood-Frenzies ripped through the Fire-Wolf's bright orange pelt with their claws, dancing away and clacking their teeth when he tried to fight back. River shuddered, the sight of the Fire-Wolf fighting desperately against the scaly demons stirring something deep inside her.

H...awk...?

It was obvious the Blood-Frenzies were toying with the Fire-Wolf, but his efforts to defend himself never slackened. He darted around the pen, struggling to escape their claws, but they were always faster. The Fire-Wolf's screams echoed off the walls of the Fortress.

River blinked.

⌒

SHE COULD SEE nothing, hear nothing. There was only the darkness all around.

River was alone.

She felt a Presence on the edges of her consciousness, a Presence that caused her great fear...but also a Presence that she instinctively knew must be obeyed at all costs.

At first, River had questioned that obedience, but the Presence quickly invaded her mind and choked her life-force.

I am Letorus, your Master, it had said, you WILL obey me!

The pain made River retreat further into her mind, hiding in the blackness. She wanted to fight the Presence but didn't want to leave the darkness. She did not know why, only that something terrible awaited her on the outside if she left the blackness of her mind. A hurt she had caused.

So River hid, leaving the barest instincts to control her body. The Demon within her had been brought forth, but it could not take complete control until

River the Wolf was dead. It slowly drained away at her life, but River didn't resist, all alone with an ache she didn't understand.

Then the Voice came. A familiar Voice, one she knew…yet didn't know. It was faint, but River felt warmth and kindness in the Voice. It wasn't like the voices of the Presence or the Demon that devoured her energy, voices that grated on her ears and caused her pain. It was a Voice she yearned for.

The Voice faded, and River sunk back into the darkness. She mourned its disappearance, but at the same time was glad the Voice was gone. She feared that Voice as much as she yearned for it, because she knew it was a part of the terrible thing she had done, yet couldn't remember.

Then the Scream came. It tore through the darkness, audible even when River crouched and clawed at her ears to hide from the stark pain in the Scream. The Scream hurt her more than the voices of Letorus and her Demon, more than the ache of her unknown crime, more than hearing the Voice.

A Name sprung from the darkness.

Hawk.

Hawk, River said to herself, her throat sore from lack of use. She remembered that Name.

Faint images appeared at the mention of the Name, images of a wolf, a Fire-Wolf. His pelt was orange, and his eyes red-orange.

Hawk.

More Screams came, shattering the darkness. The fog laying over River's mind, muddling her thoughts, was banished. River knew she had to help Hawk. The Voice, the Scream, and the Name all belonged to him. He was in pain, in danger, and the need to help him dragged River out from the darkness. Light shone through the shadows, emanating from the image of Hawk. She could feel the Demon within her yowling with anger at lost prey, and the Presence snarling at her resistance. It tried to beat her down again, but this time River fought back.

She was no longer afraid.

Chapter One Hundred and Twenty-Six

"HAWK!"

The shout startled Letorus, and before he could react River had rushed by him and thrown herself into the pen. She dragged a Blood-Frenzy off of the Fire-Wolf slave with a strangled screech. The other Blood-Frenzies scattered, surprised by the sudden attack. River gave the demon trapped in her jaws a hard shake and broke its neck with a resounding snap. It fell limp in her grasp.

Immediately the other five Blood-Frenzies cringed and started screeching, their voices so high the sound was barely audible, yet it made every creature present cower and cover their ears. Even Letorus had to flinch at their reedy scream. It was as though they had felt the pain of their sibling's death as their own.

How did she break free of my control? Letorus snarled to himself as the Blood-Frenzies recovered and charged River. The Water-Wolf was a blur of movement, spinning and snapping, dodging the Blood-Frenzies' blows and returning them with force. He turned his attention to Hawk, lying in a pool of his own blood and struggling to stand. *Why is she willing to sacrifice herself for a dying wolf? Why do they all resist me so hard?*

"Master, should we pull out the traitor?" one of the Noxond next to Letorus asked.

Letorus was silent for a moment, watching the battle unfold. River had already suffered several wounds, while the five Blood-Frenzies remained relatively unscathed. Hawk had finally managed to drag himself to his paws and was slowly limping toward the fight.

Finally he shook his head. "No. The Water-Wolf was lucky to have killed one Blood-Frenzy," he said finally. "But her luck has run out. Let them die together."

Realizing that some of the slaves had felt a little hope when they had seen that River had broken free of his control, Letorus turned to the crowd. "This Water-Wolf was another who thought she could defy me," Letorus boomed. "She and your kind betrayed you by deserting you when we demons came, yet she dared to come back and give you *hope*. Now look and see where her crimes have brought her! She will die…"

He stopped when he saw that no one in the crowd, not even the demons, was listening to his words. Instead they were staring behind him. Abruptly Letorus spun around, and his eyes widened in shock.

Two more Blood-Frenzies lay dead, and the remaining three were screeching once more, their cries weaker than before. The Fire-Wolf, knowing he would physically be of no help, was summoning blast after blast of fire, using it to heat the Water-Wolf's attacks. The water seared through the Blood-Frenzies' scales upon contact. When the demons cowered in pain, River would pounce on them and tear into their unprotected flesh.

"Stop them!" Letorus roared, not understanding why his most elite demons were failing and furious that the two wolves were actually winning their fight. Before the two Noxond could respond, however, a disjointed voice rang out from the ranks of slaves, echoing across the courtyard.

"Wolves of Soluna! Now is the time to fight back! Hawk and River were pitted against the Blood-Frenzies, Letorus' most powerful servants, and are emerging victorious! Look above you at the sky, and see how Moon-Wolf and Sun-Wolf are joined as one. Take that as a sign that we too must join together as one to drive this demon menace from our island. Letorus' rule has ended, and it is time to FIGHT!"

"Silence!" Letorus roared, his narrow eyes searching the slaves, who were stirring and cautiously looking around them for the source, for the one who dared to speak out against him. He would kill the rebel with his own claws. "Why are you so foolish as to fight us? You are few and *weak*. We will crush you as we have for more than a hundred years!"

The voice laughed. "Few? We are few? Alone and separated as we have been these past one hundred years, we are few. But together as *one*, WE ARE MANY, AND WE ARE STRONG!"

The torches lighting up the courtyard exploded, just as the earth beneath their paws creaked and split open, and a great wind howled over the walls. The three elements converged on the platform before Letorus and solidified to reveal three wolves.

No! Letorus took a step back, his mind spinning as he struggled to understand what was happening.

Three wolves stood before Letorus, staring defiantly up at him without a shred of fear in their eyes. Each wore a collar around their neck, but these collars were much different than the collars Letorus had ordered put on the slaves. The Fire-Wolf's collar was made of woven reeds, the Wind-Wolf's of feathers, and the Earth-Wolf's of smooth polished stone. Letorus recognized those collars; they were the very same collars the rulers of old had worn, before Letorus killed them all. And judging from the way the slaves in the crowd stirred, they too recognized the collars.

"Your reign is over, Letorus," the Fire-Wolf said confidently. "No longer will you defile our land."

As he spoke those words, the earth trembled, the torches flared, and the wind howled once more. Suddenly, wolves from every corner of the island appeared, howling their battle cries. Giant cracks opened in the ground and hundreds of wolves poured out, throwing themselves on their enemies. Within moments the courtyard was buried by a rolling mob of fighters.

Letorus snarled down at the three who dared to defy him so openly. "Kill them," he growled to the two Noxond at his side, and they immediately leapt forward to engage the three leaders of Soluna. The five combatants tumbled off the stage, snarling and snapping at each other's throats.

"Hawk! River! Do what you have to do!" the Fire-Wolf cried before he was enveloped in his own battle.

Letorus whirled around. Hawk and River were facing down the last Blood-Frenzy. Blood poured down its flanks and froth lined its mouth, but it held its ground. Despite its determination to stand, even Letorus had to acknowledge the fact that it would not last much longer.

The Winter-Wolf's warning, spoken so long ago, came to the forefront of Letorus's mind, and for the first time in his life, he felt the cold claws of fear digging into his heart.

No. I will not die at the paws of some mortal wolf. Letorus charged past the pen and took a flying leap off the platform. He shoved his way through the fighters below, intent on only one thing.

I have to get to the Rift.

Chapter One Hundred and Twenty-Seven

HAWK BARELY HEARD Ash's call, so intent was he on fighting the last Blood-Frenzy. Although it had suffered numerous injuries, it continued to fight like a mad beast. River met its attacks with equal ferocity, as her hide was still toughened by demonic power, but Hawk was dizzy from blood-loss.

I can't fall now, not when everyone is here and fighting with me! He gritted his teeth and forced himself to stand his ground.

He saw an opening.

River summoned a barrage of ice shards to fly at the Blood-Frenzy, which twisted and turned to avoid the projectiles. Using her attack as a cover, she leapt through the ice and landed on the Blood-Frenzy. It focused completely on her and sank its fangs into her shoulder.

Its back was to Hawk.

Crouching, he steeled himself to pounce. Ignoring the protests from his pained muscles, he threw himself into the air and landed on the Blood-Frenzy's back. Surprised, the demon jumped and tried to shake Hawk off, but he refused to release his grip. Baring his fangs, Hawk bit down savagely on the Blood-Frenzy's neck, while River attacked from the front, sinking her teeth into its throat.

A jolt went through the Blood-Frenzy's body, and it froze. It bared its teeth weakly in a final silent snarl, before collapsing to the ground, dead.

Hawk scrambled away from the demon's corpse, panting. He could barely believe they had managed to kill all six Blood-Frenzies. Then he sent River a cautious look. "River? Is…is…are you…*you*?"

River wagged her tail slightly, baring her teeth in a weary grin. "Yeah, it's me. I'm sorry…for what I did to you."

She looked nervous. Hawk simply wagged his tail and touched her shoulder with his nose before saying, "I've already forgotten about it." Instead, he directed her attention up to the sky. "River, look."

High in the sky were three red moons, the smallest of which overlapped a silver sun. The dark night sky around the Eclipse was strangely transparent, as though there were another silver light shining from behind it. The other two moons were quickly moving into place, and it wouldn't be long until the eclipse was complete.

"We have to get him near the Rift," River muttered, lowering her head to look at Letorus. Then she swore.

"Where'd he go?" Hawk looked around frantically. The Overlord was nowhere to be seen. *We can't lose him now...if we can't sing the Song of the Eclipse now, we may never get another chance!*

"The coward ran. He saw his power slipping, and he's fleeing. But this will actually work in our favor. I...I can still feel him, in my mind. He's going to the Rift."

Hope soared in Hawk's chest. "Then we just have to follow him."

River nodded, scanning the mob around them. She bared her teeth in a feral grin when she saw the unmistakable shape of Letorus forcing his way through the fighting creatures, making his way back to the keep of his Fortress.

"Let's go," she said, and took a running leap out of the pen. Hawk followed a little more slowly, gritting his teeth against the pain as he scrambled over the tall fence. River blazed a path through the rolling mass of battling wolves and demons, shoving aside enemies and allies alike, although most instinctively recoiled away from her. Hawk barely managed to keep pace with her.

They raced through the doors of the keep just as the fleeing form of the Overlord vanished into the darkness beyond. Immediately the two wolves found themselves in a wide hallway with many doors. River barely paused to sniff the air before running through one of the open doorways. Hawk hurried to keep up, amazed at her ability to track Letorus at such high speeds when for the past several weeks she had been more lost than a blind hare.

Of course, we are in the marsh...

"Hurry, Hawk," the she-wolf growled, apparently unaware of the numerous, slowly healing wounds that marked her pelt, although Hawk was painfully aware of *his* wounds and felt every single one with every stride.

But he didn't dare slow down, lest they lose Letorus.

The walls shook, tripping Hawk and nearly sending him crashing to the ground. He sent a nervous glance over his shoulder when howls reached his ears. *Someone must be casting an* Amhríochta...*we better be careful, or the entire Fortress could collapse around our ears.*

Letorus slowly drew ahead as they chased him through the winding hallways, but River never hesitated even when he vanished around a corner. The demon Overlord never looked back.

Something's not right. Why would he give up so easily or be so distracted he doesn't even realize he's being followed? We're not exactly making any attempt to stay quiet...

They raced down a dark corridor, burst through a broken door, torn off its hinges in Letorus' haste, and ran out into the open. The Fortress loomed behind them, and the cries of battle still echoed over its walls. Letorus was nowhere to be seen.

Hawk felt something stir within him, resonating a little, and looked up at the sky.

Two moons were overlapping the sun. The largest moon was slowly making its way into position.

River swore under her breath, before casting about for the Overlord's scent.

"This way!" she shouted and raced across the swampland, quickly vanishing into the shadowy foliage. Hawk hurried to keep up, not wanting to be left alone in an unknown land. His heart raced with a mixture of fear and excitement as once more Letorus came into view, but he immediately went cold when he saw the demon Overlord had stopped.

"No...no, stop..." River muttered, stumbling and shaking her head. Hawk was disturbed to see that her black eyes were glowing a little.

The she-wolf slowed, leaving Hawk to pull ahead. He hoped River was okay, but he knew he had to go after Letorus.

"*...sanguinem ex creatione, responde mihi vocant. Audi vocem magistri vestri. Surge, et effudit sanguinem de inimicis meis.*" The large demon spun around, his eyes lighting up with glee as he chanted. "*Dele quod habet animam et egressus!*"

With a cry, River crumpled to the ground behind Hawk, who immediately slid to a stop and looked behind him. She had collapsed by the roots of a large mangrove tree, dangerously close to the banks of a fast-moving river, and was convulsing violently. Her black eyes glowed, and Hawk was horrified to see her wounds healing faster.

"Good luck saving your precious friend now," Letorus purred, his eyes glinting with evil amusement. "I have commanded the demon in her soul to destroy her. She will be left as nothing more than a wraith!"

Ignoring the demon Overlord towering over him and laughing at his plight, Hawk raced back to River's side. She shook as though she were possessed, which, in a sense, she was. Small whimpers of pain escaped her jaws. Letorus' laughs faded as he splashed away through the marsh, but Hawk was too focused on River to notice.

"River!" he cried, licking her face in an attempt to calm her. "River! What's happening? Don't let the demon win! You're stronger than it; don't let it defeat you! You're…you're invincible, you can't lose!"

She gave no sign of hearing him, instead she started growling and scrabbling at her ears with her paws, as though to scrape off a bug. Her struggles were getting weaker by the second, and Hawk knew she didn't have much time left.

"No!" he howled. *This can't be happening! What do I do, what do I do?*

The feeling inside him was getting stronger, and it felt as if fire raged through his body. Hawk tipped his head back to the sky and saw that the largest, and last, moon was halfway across the sun.

They only had a few minutes left.

A formation of stars near the near-complete Eclipse caught his eye, and Sparrow's words from so long ago echoed in his mind.

"…and when all is lost, look to the Star Twins, and use their power to bring light to darkness."

"The Star Twins," Hawk whispered, his eyes tracing the faint outline of two Wind-Wolves standing among the stars, gazing down at their beloved land. Desperate for anything that might help River, he howled to the sky.

Please, help me!

Silence met his cry.

His bright orange eyes searched the sky for any sign that his prayer had been heard, and all the while River's struggles were getting weaker. The smell of death was slowly enveloping her body.

Soon she would be a wraith, neither dead nor alive.

Suddenly fire lit up the sky, illuminating each star that made up the Twins' constellation. It outshone even the partial Eclipse. Lines of red star fire raced across the sky, connecting the points of light until the shining image of two Wind-Wolves stood out clearly against the dark sky.

"We have listened, and your prayer has been heard," came two ethereal voices.

Hawk watched with fear and awe as the fiery outlines of the Twins shimmered and moved, before walking down the sky on a path of stars. Their forms grew smaller as they approached, and behind them stretched a wide expanse of black sky, empty of stars. The Twins stopped before him and spared him a glance before looking beyond him at River's deathly still form.

"*She is consumed by evil,*" they said, their voices echoing in Hawk's mind. "*We can banish the darkness in her soul, but it will be up to her to keep the demon at bay.*"

Hawk nodded, not understanding what the Twins meant. He was too worried about River to waste time asking for an explanation. The two Wind-Wolves padded through Hawk, their forms no more substantial than mist, and approached the she-wolf behind him. The stars shining in their coat grew brighter, until they vanished in a burst of light. River, too, was enveloped in the expanding circle of red light, leaving Hawk alone on the outside. He watched nervously, glancing up at the diminishing distance between the final moon and the Eclipse several times, as a dark energy shot through the light. It spun around and grew larger until it threatened to swallow up the star fire from the Twins.

An unearthly song arose from the sphere. The notes gently wove their way through the light, softening the darkness and fading the angry streaks into nothingness. Finally, as the song faded as well, the ball of light exploded outward. Beams of red starlight shot past Hawk (who fought the urge to jump away), filling the small clearing.

When the light faded, River lay alone on the ground. The Twins were gone and had returned to their place in the stars.

Hawk hurried to the she-wolf's side. "Come on, River, wake up," he said, nudging her shoulder. "Wake up!"

To his relief, the she-wolf finally twitched and raised her head. She blinked, struggling to focus her dark gray eyes on him. He was simply glad to see she was still alive.

"Hawk?" she asked a little weakly. Then she whipped her head around, looking for something. "Where is Letorus? His scent is fading...did he escape?" She narrowed her eyes and shook her head. "I can barely see...what happened? I heard his voice in my head, and then suddenly the...the demon took over. It was eating away at my mind..." Her voice trailed off as the memories came back. "I heard you howling, and then smelled two wolves approach me..."

"Is...is the demon gone?" Hawk asked.

River sighed and shook her head. "No. It's still there, at the edges of my mind...I can feel it *taunting* me..." Her voice grew hollow, and Hawk was quick to reassure her.

"The Twins said the demon wouldn't bother you as long as you had the will to keep it away."

She narrowed her eyes in confusion, before shaking her head and lurching to her paws.

"You've got some explaining to do, Hawk," she said. "But now..." she looked up at the sky, only to curse when she couldn't see clearly enough to judge how much time they had left. "We have to get to Letorus before the Eclipse completes. It'll only last for a few minutes."

Hawk nodded, and they immediately set out after Letorus' fading trail. He watched his she-wolf companion out of the corner of his eyes. She seemed weaker than before; her breath came in ragged gasps, and she stumbled as she ran, but River blazed through the marshland, practically flying through the undergrowth. Hawk turned his attention back to running and gritted his teeth, determined to keep up.

Please let us get there in time. He couldn't tell if they were getting closer, or even where to go. His nose was too clogged with the scent of his own blood to smell anything else. *At least we're in River's homeland; otherwise we wouldn't have a chance of finding Letorus.*

He was, however, a little concerned to see River having trouble navigating. She kept to the water, splashing mud all over Hawk's torn coat, and cursed every time she stumbled over the most obvious obstacles.

Just how badly were her eyes damaged? How much can she see?

Can she still fight?

Chapter One Hundred and Twenty-Eight

ANY THOUGHT OF River's potential weakness flew from Hawk's mind when they burst into the final clearing, and he slid to a stop, horrified at the sight before him.

Stretching several lengths high, and standing about shoulder-height above the ground, was a wide crack that tore through the very air. It seemed to draw in what little light the growing Eclipse cast and emanated an evil energy that made Hawk's blood run cold and bile rise in his throat. The ruins of a demon's fortress lay all around. Hawk swallowed, remembering the rumors of a mysterious explosion in the Uiscean Marsh decades ago. Something must have happened with the Rift to have destroyed an entire fortress.

Before the Rift, emanating his own demonic energy, stood Letorus. He chanted something in the demons' language, making the energy grow darker and slowly seep out to cover the clearing.

River snarled and threw herself down the slope, leaping at Letorus with her fangs bared. Hawk shook himself from his frozen state and launched himself after her.

"Letorus!" the she-wolf roared, only to crash down on the marshy floor when Letorus broke off from his chants to dodge. Hawk felt his heart sink when he realized Letorus didn't even have to move, as River would have missed anyway. It sunk even further when he saw that Letorus had noticed River's poor aim.

"I'll admit that seeing you still functioning is a surprise," Letorus purred, dodging the Water-Wolf's wild blows. When she added water to her attacks, he simply froze the liquid and sent the fractured shards back at her. The shards glanced harmlessly off her stone-hard pelt. "But it's obvious you didn't get away completely unharmed, wolf. Having trouble seeing where you're going?"

"Shut up," River snarled and sent a wave of muddy water racing toward the Overlord.

Letorus merely laughed and froze River's water again. But he had forgotten about Hawk, who used the demon's moment of distraction to leap on the Overlord from behind. Before the demon could react, Hawk sank his fangs into the back of his neck.

"Sneaking rat!" Letorus snarled and shattered the looming wave of muddy water, sending the shards right at Hawk. Hawk instinctively lit his fur on fire, which helped to melt some of the shards before they pierced his skin. He grunted with pain as he hit the ground, dangerously close to the Rift. His proximity made his vision swim, and he struggled to remain conscious. The sheer evil from the tear was sickening. A shadow fell over him, cast by the near-complete Eclipse above, and Hawk looked up in fear to find Letorus looming over him.

"Even in this state you are a bigger threat than that half-blind Water-Wolf," he sneered, raising his paw as the deep shadows of the clearing twisted and raced toward him. They leapt up from the ground and formed a ball of darkness that quickly grew twice the size of Hawk's head. Pinned to the ground by the ice shards, the Fire-Wolf could only shut his eyes and wait for the attack to land.

"Don't underestimate me!" River roared and threw herself into Letorus, aiming right for his middle. The demon Overlord stumbled, and his attack went askew, missing Hawk's head by only a few whiskers.

River summoned a massive wave from the swampy water in the small pools surrounding them, an attack Letorus didn't bother freezing. It raced past him and only resulted in flooding the clearing.

"Is your eyesight failing you even more, wolf? If you're not careful, you may go blind."

Hawk struggled to stand and put distance between himself and Letorus, panting as his wounds opened and started bleeding again. He looked up at the sky and saw that the final moon was almost in place. They didn't have much time left. Letorus had to be trapped before the Eclipse completed, so they could sing the Song of the Eclipse and destroy him.

If we don't get killed before then. His vision was already blurry from blood-loss, and he could barely move because of his wounds. River, he knew, was much worse for wear, for although her external injuries had healed, he had no idea the extent of the damage River's inner demon had caused internally. The added impediment of her failing vision lessened their chances for success, especially if River's last attack was anything to go by.

But to Hawk's surprise, the Water-Wolf only bared her teeth at Letorus' words. She shot him a warning look before turning back to Letorus. "I don't need to see."

Realizing what River was about to do, Hawk hurried to get behind her and out of her way.

Confused by River's lack of reaction, Letorus hesitated in initiating an attack. The Overlord was taken completely by surprise when she summoned a great ball of water from the air, holding it in place just long enough for Hawk to heat it with his fire, and blasted it at the demon Overlord.

Her attack slammed into the demon, dead-on, without a trace of her former hesitation.

Letorus yowled with pain as he was thrown into a large mangrove tree. River then summoned more water before freezing it and shooting the sharp slivers of ice at the demon Overlord. She quickly turned to Hawk.

"Listen, Letorus is like a Noxond, he has all the abilities of the demons below him," she said, an ear turned to monitor Letorus. "Aim for his stomach."

Hawk mutely nodded, still curious as to how River had managed to suddenly improve her aim. Her dark eyes were still clouded with blindness.

"Clever, wolf," Letorus growled, picking himself up from the splintered remains of the tree. Blood ran down his thick legs, dripping from a deep gash in his stomach. "You're using the ripples I cause in the water you flooded the clearing with to pinpoint my location."

River grimaced. "I was hoping he wouldn't figure it out," she muttered to Hawk.

"So how well can you see if the water's frozen?"

Before River could react, Letorus stepped back into the water flooding the clearing, freezing it instantly. Try as she might, she couldn't wrest control of the ice from him. Letorus' will was too strong, and the demon within her weakened River's own will in fighting Letorus.

"Hawk! Keep that water melted!" River roared before sliding across the ice toward her opponent.

"I don't think so," Letorus growled as Hawk breathed out large streams of fire to melt down the ice. The flames immediately shrunk as Letorus' power threatened to smother Hawk, tearing them from his control.

Fight back! Hawk snarled and poured more power into the flames. They rose up again, fed by his determination. Shock flared in the Overlord's eyes for a brief moment, before River launched herself at him, leaping blindly through the air, and knocked him off his paws. Hawk raced to get closer and launch a few attacks of his own.

If only we had an Earth-Wolf with us, then we'd have a chance. River and I are at a disadvantage because Letorus can control both our elements, so anything we throw at him is useless. But if I were an Earth-Wolf, I could trap Letorus' paws in the ground...

To his shock, just as he imagined cracks breaking through the soft earth, the ground beneath the Overlord's paws opened. Both River and Letorus were taken by surprise and fell into the shallow cracks. River, however, recovered faster and was quick to jump back to solid land, narrowly avoiding getting trapped when the earth slammed back together.

Letorus reacted too slowly, and the ground closed around his legs, stuck fast. He roared and struggled against the hardened earth holding him, but couldn't break free.

I guess the Earth-King's power didn't leave me completely after all, Hawk thought, glancing down to discover that the cracks had originated from his own paws.

"Hawk! Look at the sky, is the Eclipse full?"

At River's shout, he tipped his head back. His eyes widened with awe and surprise.

The largest red moon had finally slid into place, overshadowing the smaller satellites and carving out a wide portion of the silver sun's center. A strange silver glow emanated from the edges of the sun, gradually fading away into that strange see-through sky. All the stars had disappeared, leaving the full Eclipse hanging in an empty grayish sky.

CHAPTER ONE HUNDRED AND TWENTY-NINE

"RIVER, IT'S TIME!"

Letorus' head snapped up at Hawk's shout. Hawk was shocked to see raw fear fill the Overlord's feral features at the sight of the Eclipse. His struggles increased even more, but the earth held fast.

River's going to try and sing on her own, Hawk thought, racing over to the she-wolf. *I can't let her do that! The song has to be sung by two; she'll burn up if she tries doing it on her own. Plus, I'm the only one who can use the magic of the Fáinéitin.*

"Hawk, keep an eye on him, and don't let him escape," River ordered, stumbling a little closer to the Rift. "If he gets close to the Rift and starts that chant again, he'll unleash every demon in there."

"You can't do this on your own, River."

"I can, and I *will*, there is no need for you to risk yourself in this"

Hawk returned her angry glare, his resolve firm. "The Song of the Eclipse can't be sung alone. You're Moon, but you need Sun. That's *me*. I'm going to help you, River, whether you want it or not. You've gone your whole life alone…but now you have someone by your side."

The she-wolf held his gaze for a few seconds, before nodding stiffly. "Fine. But if you mess up I'll kill you myself before the spell does."

He wagged his tail. "I wouldn't dare."

"You'll have to call on Wind and Fire," River instructed quickly. "Send it to the Eclipse above. The Song will come to you, but make sure you keep pace with me. It's like Amhríochta; we have to stay in sync or it'll fail."

He nodded, nervousness growing in the pit of his stomach. He took a deep breath to calm himself. *This is what I'm supposed to do. I will* not *fail here!*

Closing his eyes, Hawk reached deep into himself for the Fire from the Fáinéitin, at the same time calling for the power he had summoned at the Ardgao. Magic surged through him, feeling hot and cool at once. Images of sand, stone, volcanoes, and mountains raced through his mind, so clear for a moment he thought he actually stood in both the mountains and the desert at the same time. The images vanished, although Hawk still felt the power of wind and fire coursing through his veins. Above, a thick red ring now surrounded the Eclipse. A silver ring soon joined it, and Hawk looked down to see River's cloudy eyes glowing slightly with silver light.

They were ready.

Together, the two wolves tipped their heads back and sang, ignoring the horrified yowls of the trapped Demon Overlord. The rings above them began to glow, until the Eclipse was surrounded by a bubble of silver and red light. The two wolves below, too, began to glow. Hawk's pelt shone with red light, while River's was silver.

It was strange how he knew what to sing. The knowledge just appeared in his mind, although the Song of the Eclipse was more complicated than any Amhríochta. There were a dozen different melodies that had to be howled at the same time. Power surged through his voice, almost as if the Song had a life of its own, and was simply using Hawk to sing itself. His howl rose and fell rapidly, subtly weaving a spell of sound to ensnare the wild sun elements. River, standing a few feet from him, mirrored his song, although her part of it was slightly different to match the gentler moon elements.

Hawk sang of Fire and Wind, and the wild abandon that was characteristic of those two elements. He sang of the hot sands that shifted over an unstable crust, of boiling lava that flowed down red mountains. He sang of the cool oases dotting the unforgiving desert, of cold nights illuminated by fire. He sang of rocky mountains, their snowy tops piercing the sky, of howling storms that stripped the bark from the few trees that dared to grow on the harsh terrain. He sang of the songs the wind sang itself as it danced through the wide canyons of the mountains and of the gentle breezes that lovingly carried the proud mountain birds through the air.

River sang of Water and Earth, and of the calmer and gentler aspects of the moon elements. She sang of the gentle murmurs as creeks ran over the smooth stones, of the thick mists that cloaked the swampy forest. She sang of the roaring waterfalls that crashed down onto broken rocks, and of the ceaseless pounding of ocean waves on sandy shores. She sang of the quiet majesty of the ancient earth, of its life-giving seeds. She sang of the great shakes of the earth when it awoke and of the splitting cracks that separated even the hardest of stone.

They both sang of Sun and Moon. Of how in the beginning, Fire, Wind, Water, and Earth were simply Sun and Moon. How Fire and Wind were *still* Sun, Water and Earth *still* Moon, and how they could become pure once more.

As they sang, the orb of light surrounding the Eclipse grew brighter and brighter, when suddenly a beam of silver and red light shot down and slammed into the Rift. The light from the beam was drawn into the tear in the fabric of space, before exploding outward. Its pure light quickly filled the clearing. Letorus screamed when the light reached him, as though it dealt him a physical blow.

"You cannot hold me like this!" the Overlord roared, still struggling vainly against the earth that held him captive. "I am Death, I am Eternal! *I am Letorus!*"

Hawk! Direct the energy toward him, we have to kill him before the Rift fully opens! River's voice screeched into his mind, nearly startling him into missing a few notes. Fear and resignation colored her words, although Hawk couldn't imagine why she was feeling that.

It took him a few precious seconds to register what she had said. While wielding the power of the primal elements was certainly scary, he was elated at being in control over such ancient magic. He felt like he could do anything, even fly to Sun-Wolf himself.

Focus! He gave himself a mental shake and turned part of his song toward Letorus, feeling River do the same.

Several smaller beams broke off of the larger one and locked onto the demon. His screams grew louder and became fractured, as though hundreds of demons screamed with him. The darkness cloaking his body was banished, seared by the purifying light of the Eclipse. Letorus' evil fought wildly against its destruction, seeking to upset the focus of the howling wolves, but they held firm.

Finally the shadows disappeared, although the demon Overlord himself remained. He yowled and twisted against the pure power of Sun and Moon, his struggles to avoid it hampered by the earth trapping his limbs. Hawk almost pitied the demon for the pain he was going through, but the knowledge of Soluna's century-long suffering at the Overlord's paws hardened his heart.

Letorus' body became illuminated with light until all Hawk could see was a vague outline of the once all-powerful demon. The Overlord screamed in pain, as the light grew brighter, seeking to erase his very existence from the world.

Suddenly Letorus laughed, a hysterical, insane sound that echoed across the clearing and sounded even above Hawk's and River's howls.

"You may have killed me, but I have won!" Letorus screeched as his form started to crack, light shining through the openings. "This night will end in death, and *it will be yours!*"

He continued to cackle until he had burst into an explosion of light and sound.

Letorus, the demon Overlord who had oppressed Soluna for one hundred and thirty-eight years was dead.

Chapter One Hundred and Thirty

WE'RE NOT DONE yet, came River's voice again, this time tinged with weary happiness. *Focus on the Rift, and throw it open!*

Hawk was eager to comply, and threw himself even more into the Song. The light Letorus had become swirled around the beam entering the Rift before joining it once more. The beam grew more intense, forcing Hawk to narrow his eyes against the light, although he didn't dare look away.

The evil of the Rift fought the magic of the Eclipse. It yowled like a demon, straining against the energy pouring into it. River and Hawk howled louder, concentrating all their power on the Song, until finally the Rift broke open. Light burst into the clearing, and with it came hundreds of wolves. Hawk's eyes widened in surprise when he saw who they were.

The Water-Wolves, finally free of their demonic prison, raced into the open clearing, pure joy etched onto their haggard faces at being back in their home once more. Hawk was amazed at the sheer number of wolves pouring forth. They ran past him, hardly pausing for a breathless expression of gratitude for freeing them, before disappearing into the shadowy swampland, no doubt intent on getting as far from their former prison as possible. Other wolves, former slaves fed to the Rift to summon demons, joined the Water-Wolves in escaping.

Finally, when the last wolf disappeared through the mangrove trees, a great wind picked up. Hawk was surprised, and a little disturbed, to see the wind pass right through him without even ruffling his fur. Seconds later, the wind was colored with black energy that tore past him before vanishing into the Rift. Screams of horror and outrage echoed from the energy, rising above even Hawk's and River's howls. They were the screams of demons, dematerialized into streams of evil intent.

The two wolves continued to sing until the Rift stopped fighting their control. River's howl slowly faded away into silence, and Hawk was quick to mimic her. He slumped, feeling very dizzy and glad that the Song of the Eclipse was over. He felt every ache caused by his wounds and was surprised to still be conscious.

"The Song's not quite over, but now the Rift will remain open. It will close on its own when every demon has been drawn into it, and by that time the Eclipse will be over. The Song will have no effect then."

Hawk straightened slightly and wagged his tail.

"Good, because I'm not sure…" he trailed off, eyes widening with horror. The wind from the Rift was slowly pulling River toward its open jaws. "Wait…that…that can't mean…"

The she-wolf gave a sad nod. "Sorry, Hawk, that includes half-demons like me, too."

He took a step back in shock, his entire body shaking. "You *knew?*"

River sighed and nodded again. "That's why I wanted to do it on my own. No one to worry about, no one to hurt…no one to get attached to. Although, now I see I wouldn't have succeeded if I *had* tried it on my own." She paused, wagging her tail slightly, her eyes swimming with more emotion than Hawk had ever seen her show. "Thank you, Hawk…for everything."

The wind pulled harder on River, forcing her to stumble toward the Rift. She was neither able nor willing to fight it.

No, it can't be like this! Hawk took a step forward, Letorus' last words echoing in his mind. *River can't die…I…I won't let that happen!*

Words from a half-forgotten dream suddenly appeared in his mind, and he gasped as the memories returned.

"A demon will turn twice before Sun meets Moon and the King is struck down. Then a sacrifice must be made by the earth-born flame, to banish the Dark and free the land."

A sacrifice…

A strange calm filled him, and before he could talk himself out of it, Hawk tipped his head back and picked up the Song of the Eclipse, singing both Sun and Moon. Sheer terror flashed across River's face when she realized what he was trying to do.

"No! Stop, Hawk! You *can't,* no one was meant to control both powers! *It will kill you!*" she screamed, as though she could shock Hawk to his senses. "Just let me die, I *deserve* it! I deserve to die for everything my family did… for *what* I am!"

I don't care if I die, if it means I can save you, River.

Hawk ignored the she-wolf's shouts, so intent on singing the Song correctly he was barely aware of anything else going on around him. It was even harder than Singing the sun's half of the Song. Now he had to sing all four elements at once, and keep both Sun and Moon under his control. The Song raged under his will, the clash of opposite elements stirring it into a frenzy of wild power. His fur burned with red and silver light, and his eyes became a pair of red-and-silver coals. It took every scrap of his will simply to stay conscious.

Dimly he noticed River struggling to throw herself into the Rift, trying to end the Song before he could do himself too much harm. Hawk started to sing faster, refusing to let River throw her life away. With his continued howling, the process of drawing in the demons inhabiting Soluna had been increased tenfold. Already the wind was clearing of the evil energy that formed the demons.

River was the only one left.

It hurts...I never...realized just how...powerful...both primal elements were. Hawk's vision started to darken, and even the sound of his own howls was lost to the humming in his ears. *It burns.* His mind was fading. He winced, a sharp pain stabbing through his head. *I...just hope...I can...hold on...long...enough...to save...River...*

He put every scrap of power behind keeping her in place, enveloping her with some of the eclipse's light to hold her against the wind. The Rift howled in outrage and its wind increased, trying to claim one more demon before closing, but the force of Hawk's will was too strong.

His strength quickly fading, only Hawk's sheer determination kept him standing.

I guess...this is it...

The beam from the sky vanished, the moons slipping away from in front of the sun, all celestial bodies slowly returning to their natural colors as the sun faded from sight. With nothing to hold it open, the Rift slammed shut, sealing itself with a flash of light and disappearing from sight.

It had closed, and would plague the island of Soluna no longer.

Chapter One Hundred and Thirty-One

HAWK AND RIVER collapsed to the ground a moment after the Rift closed. River was the first to recover and lurched toward Hawk. Her heart froze when she saw his unmoving form. The glow in his pelt was slowly fading. "No, no, don't you *dare* die on me," she muttered as she limped toward him. "Not after all that...*you can't die!*"

After an agonizingly long crawl, slowed by the weakness in her limbs and the sheer exhaustion in her mind and body, River finally reached Hawk's side. She gave a sigh of relief when she saw him barely breathing, but quickly became angry. "Hawk, you idiot!" She hardly had the energy for even that simple action. "You shouldn't have done that!"

Hawk stirred at her voice, and weakly raised his head, his tail thumping the ground a few times before falling limp. "I...I couldn't...bear...to watch... my friend get...pulled into...hell..."

His breathing grew shallower.

"I'm...glad...I could...save you, River," he said softly. Slowly, his eyes closed, and Hawk breathed no more.

For a moment, River did nothing but stare at his still body, her tired mind unable to register what had happened. But even through her clouded vision, she could see that he would not be getting up again.

"Hawk?" River asked quietly, on some stupid hope that her scarred eyes were simply seeing things. When there was no answer, she repeated in a loud voice, "Hawk!" He didn't move.

Then she knew he was really dead.

The cheerful, loyal, brave Fire-Wolf was *dead*.

"*NO!*" River screamed, her howl full of pain and sorrow as it echoed across the silent marsh. She hunched over as her cry faded, shaking. With a strangled sob she buried her muzzle in his fur. The warmth was already leaving his body, and his familiar scent was overpowered by the smell of blood and death. There was almost nothing left of her friend. River choked back another sob as she collapsed on the ground beside him, for once grateful for her damaged vision so she wouldn't have to see the emptiness in his eyes.

Hawk's...gone...

CHAPTER ONE HUNDRED AND THIRTY-TWO

RIVER LAY BY Hawk's cold body for hours, not moving. She didn't know what to do, where to go. Her nation was free again and the demons defeated, yet she did nothing. She had nothing beyond her mission.

She was alone in a dark world she could barely see.

Her ears twitched when she heard someone approaching from behind. The scents of two strange wolves reached her nose, and she jumped to her paws and whirled around to face the soon-to-be-dead idiots who dared to come near. "Get away from here!" she snarled at the two blurry shapes standing before her.

They were both tall wolves, nearly twice the size of Water-Wolves, with faint light glowing from their pelts. The silvery wolf spoke first. "Hush, child, your grief blinds you."

River hesitated at the sound of the wolf's voice. It sounded almost motherly. Kind, loving, but more ancient than anything. Familiar, although River was certain she had never met this wolf before, yet totally foreign and ethereal.

"Who are you?" she asked slowly, cursing the scarred eyes that prevented her from seeing more than a blurred form.

The answer was given by the other wolf. His voice was deep and powerful, one that demanded respect and echoed in her mind as loudly as she heard it with her ears. "The Creators. You know who we are."

River froze, hardly daring to breathe. Suddenly she realized to whom she was talking. These wolves that smelled of stars and all four elements, of Moon and Sun.

"Moon-Wolf and Sun-Wolf?" she asked hesitantly, wondering if she was dreaming. *Or maybe I'm dead, and they're here to punish me for my crimes.*

Moon-Wolf nodded, before glancing over River at Hawk's still form. "He was very foolish to try to harness our power like that. Any other wolf we would have killed on the spot for daring, even before the sheer power of the primal elements killed them."

River's hackles raised. "Don't you dare say that!" she snarled, her voice breaking. "Hawk was…Hawk was trying to save me."

Despite her disrespect in addressing Moon-Wolf like that, the silvery wolf did not appear to be offended, although at this point River hardly cared.

Sun-Wolf, on the other paw, snarled at her tone. "And he had little reason to. You are the child of a demon, an *abomination* that does not deserve to live. How many times have you nearly killed him because you lost control?"

River flinched, remembering all the times she had hurt Hawk, nearly killing him, because she had given into her demonic urges. She remembered the fear in his eyes when she had fully turned and attacked him, and the cruel things she had said to him.

Moon-Wolf's voice was kinder, soothing to River's tired ears. "And yet, he still gave his life for you. In spite of all that you did, in spite of the pain from controlling the power of Sun and Moon, he died so that he could save *you*."

Silence answered the goddess's words. River didn't know what to say. She did not deserve a friend like Hawk, who had willingly sacrificed everything for her, despite all that she had done to him. Even when she had been turned into a demon by Letorus' twisted magic, he still held out hope for her.

"The only reason he lasted as long as he did was because he was both Fire-Wolf and Earth-Wolf, a child of both Sun and Moon."

"What?" River asked, looking up sharply at the two gods standing before her. "But…he has…*had*…no dual breed mark…" She trailed off, remembering their first meeting. She had questioned his unusual name, but he had shown her his single Fire-Wolf mark.

"Look closer, Water-Wolf, and you will see."

River spun around, snarling when she heard the Winter-Wolf's voice. The spirit returned her furious glare with a cool look. Ice stretched across the marshy floor from its paws, and the air around it grew cooler.

"*You!* You sent me after him, *you knew this would happen*!" Only the presence of the gods behind her kept the River from attacking the wolf spirit.

The Winter-Wolf tilted its head slightly. "I warned him a sacrifice had to be made, but I only told him that so he would be prepared to let *you* die. I did not expect *him* to die instead. Now, look, and understand."

It sent a tendril of icy air out to lightly touch Hawk's shoulder. His once-lustrous orange fur frosted over, freezing the dried blood that splattered it, before quickly melting away.

River leaned in closer as something appeared on Hawk's fur, narrowing her eyes in an attempt to see the two shapes. It was blurry, but she could pick out that right beneath the bright yellow flame marking was an Earth-Wolf mark, a dark yellow diamond overlapping a gray square.

"His father was Elk, an Earth-Wolf," the Winter-Wolf said. "I hid his Earth-Wolf mark and locked away his earth powers, and instructed his mother Phoenix to keep Hawk's heritage a secret. This was to protect him until he could fulfill his destiny, so he could avoid the demons' notice."

"He was able to get into all of the Elemental Guardians," River whispered. "Even water. He never felt the effects of being in another territory…and those times when the earth shook from his voice or when it cracked open to trap Letorus…that was *him*."

The Winter-Wolf nodded. "He was chosen by your gods at the beginning of the war to be the one to save Soluna. When the demons came, there was a battle in the heavens. The god of the demons captured the Moon and the Sun, leaving their beloved island alone. I have no power other than foresight, but I was created by the Den-Mother to perform the will of the First Wolves in the natural realm. It was my job to make sure that Hawk was in the right place at the right time."

"What?" River narrowed her eyes, not understanding what it was saying. "Den-Mother? God of demons?"

Moon-Wolf spoke, making River turn back around. "Let me tell you a story, River. There is much you do not know about this world. There are many, many gods that dwell in the heavens, but we are the only ones who have domain over this island."

Sun-Wolf snorted, as though remembering something particularly irritating. "And it is because of us none of *them* can come and meddle," he growled.

River flattened her ears in confusion, but remained silent as Moon-Wolf spoke. Images flashed through her mind, scenes and memories that River had never seen before. Suddenly, she realized that they were coming from the gods before her, as their *own* memories that they were sharing with her.

"Long ago, in the beginning of the world, there was a war between the demons, servants of the god Mortaum, and the angels, servants of the Den-Mother, who gave birth to all the gods. Mortaum was the First Offspring of the Den-Mother, but he wanted to control the world she had created. When the world was split between the twelve eldest offspring, Moon-Wolf and Sun-Wolf were given the island of Soluna. Mortaum, however, was given no part of the world. He became jealous and waged war with the other gods. The war stretched for many hundreds of years until finally Mortaum was defeated and sealed away."

"Who is this *Den-Mother*?" River interrupted, her mind still whirling from the images of great battles fought in the sky. "And *Mortaum*?"

Sun-Wolf growled. "Silence! The Den-Mother is the One who created this entire world and gave the island of Soluna to us, allowing us to create *you*," he said. "Mortaum was the Den-Mother's first born."

Moon-Wolf nodded, and then continued. "The Second War of Angels and Demons began when Mortaum broke free of his prison and attacked the Gate of Heaven. This war lasted even longer than the first and was much more costly to both sides, but Mortaum was vanquished for a second time, his body destroyed and his soul sealed into the Rift, an empty space between the dimensions. His demons were sealed in with him."

River growled at the mention of the Rift, but a glare from Sun-Wolf prevented her from commenting.

"As the millennia passed, mortals and gods alike forgot about Mortaum and his demons. But Mortaum never forgot his defeat. He spent his imprisonment plotting the downfall of the gods, so when he managed to create a small hole in the walls of the Rift, he did not make any immediate attacks. Instead, Mortaum ordered his loyal general, Letorus, to invade the island of Soluna. Letorus, in turn, sent a Noxond to infiltrate the wolves and lead them to open the Rift fully from the outside, so that Mortaum could release his demons. When the Rift was opened, Mortaum struck, attacking the two Wolf deities, favorites of the Den-Mother."

The images faded from River's mind, and she blinked to clear her vision, a little disoriented by seeing the story play before her.

"We were taken by surprise," Moon-Wolf growled, her eyes glowing faintly with anger. "Mortaum sealed us away and forced us to watch as our land was invaded. Soluna was sealed as well, preventing any of the other gods from sending assistance."

"So that's why you did nothing while we suffered for more than a century."

"Insolent…" Sun-Wolf took a step forward, but Moon-Wolf interrupted.

"Yes, we could do nothing. We were trapped in our own territory," she said sadly as images reappeared in River's mind. "However, Mortaum did not foresee one thing. How it pained the Den-Mother to see Her children fighting and the wolves suffering under the demons. She sorrowed even for Mortaum, evil as he was, for She loves all Her creations. But even the Den-Mother was unable to break through the barrier Mortaum had placed around the Island, an evil barrier of dark magic that repelled the pure creating magic of the Den-Mother.

"So She devised a plan to save the island and the Wolf gods. The Den-Mother took the twisted powers of Mortaum and mixed it with the power of Sun-Wolf and Moon-Wolf, and bound the three powers together with her own. The creature that was born had the cold of Mortaum's evil, the storms of Sun-Wolf, the fluidity of Moon-Wolf, and the knowing of the Den-Mother.

"This was the Winter-Wolf, of icy form unknown."

River looked back at the Winter-Wolf, who listened impassively.

"The Winter-Wolf opened its eyes and saw. The whole of the world was laid out before it, and it saw everything that was, that is, that will be, and that could be. The Winter-Wolf saw what needed to be done to drive the demons from Soluna, and defeat Mortaum.

"It left the Den-Mother's presence, and entered Soluna, bypassing the barrier that only barred full children of the Den-Mother. The winds howled in its presence, and great storms of ice and snow were summoned wherever it tread, and it set out to cause the death of Letorus, the source of Mortaum's power."

River looked up at the spirit in shock. "Then...you *manipulated* everything so Letorus would fall? All the plans we made...the struggles we went through in the Rift...trying to sneak out...*guessing* when the time was right...*none of that mattered?*"

The spirit shook its head. "The sacrifices you made were necessary. You were the one who gave Hawk the strength to continue, in spite of your treatment of him. You were the one who brought him to where he needed to be."

"So you *did* know he was going to die!"

"We did not expect him to give up his life for yours, Water-Wolf," Sun-Wolf boomed, his fury barely contained. "We only needed him to close the Rift and kill Letorus, the avatar of the god of demons, so that we might be free. And yet, he went beyond our expectations and sacrificed himself to save you."

Before River could give the Sun deity a sharp retort, Moon-Wolf's cool voice cut across her thoughts. "It is because of that selfless act that we have decided to give Hawk his life."

River froze, not believing what she had heard. "W-what?" She didn't move as the two First Wolves padded by her to approach Hawk. Then she spun around and backed away a few paces, not wanting to get in the way of whatever they were about to do.

A red and silver glow emanated from the two deities' pelts, surrounding them like a protective bubble. The glow increased until it included Hawk as well and expanded to cover the entire clearing. River was forced to look away, her weakened eyes unable to take the bright light. Howls rose from the glow weaving a Song of Life from the gods.

Slowly, the Song faded, and with it the glow. River opened her clouded eyes to find the clearing was empty, save for Hawk's still body. She quickly limped over to him, sniffing for any signs of life. *Please wake up, Hawk, please…* She paused, narrowing her eyes in an attempt to sharpen her vision. She could just barely see the changes the Song of Life had made in the Fire-Wolf.

His bright orange coat, now free of any wound or scar, was streaked with silver. The slave collar still encircled his neck, a memento of his past, but was etched with strange markings, blessings from the Wolf gods. His left shoulder now bore a new mark: a red sun partially circled by a silver crescent moon, the symbol of Sun-Wolf and Moon-Wolf.

He stirred, and River's breath caught in her chest. His ears twitched, and Hawk let out a groan. River sighed with relief when his red-orange eyes, now flecked with silver, fluttered open. Slowly, Hawk raised his head and looked around, catching sight of River's worried face.

"River?" he asked slowly, as though unsure of what he was seeing. "Where… what happened? I…I saw the Rift close…and you…you were getting sucked in…but then everything went black." He paused and shuddered. "It was so cold…but then…I heard your voice…and I saw these two brilliant wolves… they…they told me to go back…" His voice trailed off, and he looked up at River for an explanation.

She looked down at him, relieved. "You saved me, Hawk, that's what happened."

Epilogue

Year 20 of the Age of Healing

ALTHOUGH THE RIFT had been closed and Letorus defeated, many demons still wandered the land. But through the hard work of many brave wolves, the nations slowly returned to their former glory. It would be many more years before the scars of the war were erased, and the earth reclaimed the land taken by the fortresses, but the wolves stood strong in their resolve.

It was a time of reconstruction, but it was also a time of peace. Soluna howled her joy to the skies, free of the demon plague, and her wolves eagerly threw themselves into the task of rebuilding their lands.

After the Demon's Purge, Hawk and River vanished. Their great deeds, however, were not forgotten. Hawk's story and River's quest were howled throughout the lands, and told to every pup. Many wolves, regardless of breed, were named for these two heroes. King Ash even created a special day to celebrate Hawk and River and their part in the fall of the demons.

What happened to the two heroes? We may never know. Many believe they were killed by the Rift itself, martyrs to their cause. Others believe they still wander the island, hunting demons from the shadows.

A few believe they no longer live in our world, but instead dwell in the spirit realms, silently watching. In a time of great need, those wolves say, they will return to save Soluna, as the Last Guardians of our land.

You would do well to remember this story, of when demons ruled the Island. It serves as a reminder of the great things that can be done when the Wolves of Soluna band together.

For in the words of King Ash, alone and separated we are weak, but together we are many and strong.

⌐

THE THREE YOUNG wolf pups sitting before the stranger stared at him with wide eyes. Seeing their rapt attention, he chuckled. "Did you enjoy the story?"

One Earth-Wolf pup nodded eagerly. "Yes sir! It was really neat!"

The other two puppies were quick to agree with him.

"Can you tell us another one?" a young Water-Wolf asked, her eyes pleading.

Laughing, the stranger shook his head. "I think you three have had enough sneaking around for one night. It's time to go back to your parents."

As if on cue, all three puppies let out a groan.

"Aw, do we have to?" the Water-Wolf pup asked.

The Wind-Wolf pup stuck out his tongue. "They're just going to shout at us and put us to bed. We want to explore!"

The stranger chuckled again. "You have to be careful out here, especially at night, because demons still roam the land. Your parents wouldn't want you to get hurt, would they?"

Silence met his question as the puppies looked away a little shamefully.

"Hawk!"

Startled, the three pups looked up behind the stranger to see a large wolf-like form silhouetted against the rising moons.

The Water-Wolf pup took a closer look at the stranger, and her eyes widened when she saw his silver-streaked orange pelt, metal collar, and the Mark of Soluna on his shoulder. "You're Hawk!" she exclaimed, causing her two companions to look more closely at the stranger as well. "*The* Hawk!"

The Fire-Wolf laughed a little. "Yes, I'm Hawk."

Before he could say more, the wolf standing behind him padded closer and snapped in an irritated voice, "We have to go, *now*. I don't want to hang around babysitting some puppies."

"I know, River. I'm coming," he said and stood. Then he gave the three puppies a stern look. "Make sure you get back home quickly, and no more wandering around at night. I might not be around to save you if you get caught by a demon."

Mutely, they nodded, obviously awed at being in the presence of the two legendary heroes.

Giving the puppies one last toothy grin, Hawk turned and padded after River, who had already vanished into the trees. Soon even his gently glowing coat was swallowed up by the shadows. It was several moments before the Water-Wolf pup stood and tried to sound commanding, like she imagined River and Hawk would.

"All right, come on, we have to go back," she said firmly. "We don't want to worry our parents."

"No one's *ever* going to believe us," the Wind-Wolf said incredulously as the pups stumbled through the bushes.

The two heroes waited in the shadows long enough to see the parents, guided secretly by River, discover their pups. The puppies fell upon their parents with excitement, their chatter faint in Hawk's and River's ears, trying to escape the relieved licks of the older wolves. The she-wolf snorted. "Foolish pups. There might not be any demons left to snap them up, but there's plenty of dangerous creatures in the forest that wouldn't think twice about eating them."

"Oh, so you didn't do anything *foolish* as a pup?"

River sent him an icy glare. Hawk just gave her a companionable shove before turning away from the small group of wolves below.

"Come on, Sun-Wolf and Moon-Wolf are waiting for us."

"So what? They can wait however long we want them to," River muttered, turning as well.

"We already kept them waiting for twenty years while we cleared out the remaining demons," Hawk said. "It's only polite that we answer their summons promptly."

"As if we were going to leave our work unfinished."

Hawk chuckled quietly to himself. Then he stopped, glancing back over his shoulder. River sent him a curious look, pausing as well.

"What?"

"They said we had a choice," Hawk said softly. "We don't have to join them in heaven. We could stay here. I know we chose to stay hidden, so we could hunt down the rest of the demons in secret…but we finished our mission. We could find our friends."

River's eyes softened slightly. "We both died that day by the Rift, in one way or another. We don't belong in this world anymore. Besides, if I were to return, my people would want me to lead them. You know I can't be a Queen, not after how my mother used her power to destroy our nation, not when I'm half-demon. There are wolves better suited to leading."

"I know." Hawk looked away. He might be able to return, but he knew he could never leave River.

"Let's go," she said, before silently padding away. Soon they came upon a cloud of stardust, glowing softly in the darkness. A line of stars rose from the cloud, rising up through a gap in the branches above to form a pathway up to the sky. It was their path to the heavens.

"Ready?" River asked.

Hawk silently nodded, and together they stepped into the cloud. The stardust shimmered slightly, floating out to encase them with light. The stars ran through their fur, burning away the last bonds tying them to the mortal world. Hawk and River continued walking up the starlit path without a glance backward, their earthly mission complete. In the island below, the night seemed to darken even more, as though the land itself mourned the loss of her heroes, but a silent voice whispered,

They will come again.

ACKNOWLEDGEMENTS

WOW. I CAN'T believe I actually wrote an entire book. Thinking back to the birth of this story, around 2009, it amazes me how much effort I've put into this. Originally, River and Hawk were really just a couple of random wolves with no sort of back-story starring in some random bunch of paragraphs strung together because I was bored. But they both sunk their fangs into my imagination and refused to let go until I actually had a story developed for them. That was the birth of Soluna, the Wolves, and later the birth of an entire mythical world full of stories and fantastic lands.

It makes me a little sad that I've finished, because now Hawk and River have grown up and are on their own now, their story complete. I probably won't write another book about them, and if I do, they won't be starring as the main characters. Future stories about them will most likely be short stories of the different legends that have grown up about them as the years pass in Soluna. For even when you finish reading the book, time is still passing in Soluna, stories are still being created, and new heroes are being born.

But you never know. Inspiration can strike me at any time.

So on to my actual thanks.

First and foremost, thank you to my brother Kevin, for being my first editor. For all that you may claim you don't like L.A., you're pretty good at it. You were invaluable in keeping me sane and motivated. And keeping me slightly more focused on the project at hand. I will eventually get you that bag of M&M's I owe you.

Thank you to my other siblings, John and Caitie, and to my parents, Peggy and John. You guys were what kept me writing, and kept that horrible disease known as "writer's block" at bay. Having to stick to a strict schedule of bi-weekly updates made sure I didn't slack off, and "end up on the streets", as Kevin would say. I apologize that you had to read the WIP first, with all my inconsistencies and horrid mistakes, but you also helped me fix those mistakes.

A huge thank you to Mr. Fricke, who went over my story with a fine-toothed comb and helped me see things that I, as the author, never would have seen on my own. You prepared me for putting my story out into the world.

I could write a book as long as this one filled with words of thanks for the awesome folks over at Lucky Bat Books, with extra copies for Cindie and Jeff. A year ago I never would have imagined that I'd be standing here with an actual published book. You guys taught me a lot and helped me accomplish my dream. Thank you, thank you, thank you.

Well, I think that's all. I won't waste any more time with my drabble. I hope you enjoyed my story, and maybe even inspired you to create your own.

ABOUT THE AUTHOR

M.B. SCULLY has been writing epic stories since the third grade, according to a rather embarrassing folder her parents have saved over the years. A native of Lubbock, Texas, she spent her childhood and teen years as a military brat, moving all over the U.S. Amazingly, the file of embarrassing stories survived every move.

When not writing, Scully enjoys riding horses, teaching riding lessons, and doing barn work (the stalls end up much cleaner than her home, which is covered in books and precarious stacks of paper). Any spare time spent indoors involves way too many fandoms and very deep discussions about said fandom with family and friends.

Find out more here: www.mbscully.com